T0361611

HEMLOCK

MASCOT
BOOKS
an imprint of Amplify Publishing Group

www.mascotbooks.com

Hemlock

For more information, please contact:
Mascot Books, an imprint of Amplify Publishing Group
620 Herndon Parkway, Suite 220
Herndon, VA 20170
info@mascotbooks.com

Library of Congress Control Number: 2024918907
CPSIA Code: PRV1224A
ISBN-13: 979-8-89138-310-4

Printed in the United States

To Jessica, this writer's writer.

HEMLOCK

PHILIP HOLLAND

MASCOT®
BOOKS
an imprint of Amplify Publishing Group

CHAPTER 1

When all this began, I remember thinking, *My father is going to kill me.* Of course I did not mean that literally. But in the end, he did seek to have another man condemned to death—and not just any man but a man I esteemed most highly, one whose life I considered to be an example to myself and even to our nation. A man, therefore, who became the victim—at my father's hand—of a grave injustice.

That is my belief. However, as with all things, you must judge for yourself.

My name is Palleias. If that sounds Greek, it's meant to. Many of us were named that way, once. It started back in colonial times, here in Philadelphia, the city people fondly referred to as the "Athens of America." Then, after the Revolution, when we became a nation more than fifty years ago, the practice spread to most of our major cities. You could still find the English, German, French, Scot, and Irish names, of course, but more and more you also found children, especially boys, named after the Ancients—Socrates, Plato, Aristotle, Xenophon, Alcibiades, Anytus—or with semi-Greek, invented, Americanized names, such as mine, Palleias, or my father's, Antonyn. Or the victim I mentioned, Teacher Scotes, whose father had attached an *S* before the family name, preferring the old Greek to the Old English.

For a time, I thought what happened had been solely my fault. I say "thought," though I cannot fairly say that I did much of what constitutes thinking back then, and that, too, was my fault. If I'm being truthful, I must allow that I did have a hand in Teacher Scotes's arrest, in his conviction, in his imprisonment, and in what ultimately came to pass. Some part was mine—though one I consider, nearly two years later as I write this, to have been marginal. My guilt, it turns out, ran much deeper.

It was April 19, 1831, and a bright morning, and I do remember thinking that my father was going to kill me, because when I saw them on the road ahead, turning to descend the short road to Gray's Ferry, I knew that I would follow, despite having promised Father I would not. The Darby Road, on which my mare Betsy pulled me and my wagon, was dry but not dusty. The Schuylkill flowed visibly below and through the trees, with glimpses of the city beyond.

I had spent the night in an inn beside the turnpike, having been two days before in Lancaster, making stops along the way to visit farmers, millwrights, shopkeepers, and sometimes those who waited by the road just to talk to anyone from the city—to hear what was happening, what was planned, what was up for vote. When your father is one of the most prominent representatives in the nation, and certainly in the state, people want to talk to you, whether to learn or plead, and this my father knew. So I traveled for him, since he had not time to do it himself, making myself available in his stead. And in turn I learned what troubles lay upon the people, what they needed, wanted, liked, and disliked. Other representatives sent agents to the taverns to silently observe, listen, and try to glean what people were saying, but Father never stooped to that. Besides, we heard their agents' reports in committee.

Sometimes my journeys took me not far from our home in the city, and sometimes I spent a week traversing the state. Formally our address was High Street, in the great Doctor Franklin's old house, but the people had taken to calling it Market Street because on Wednesdays and Saturdays the farmers and artisans would travel east, south, and north to sell their produce and wares, so Father insisted I refer to it as Market Street too.

This time, even though it was four days' journey to Lancaster and back, my father had wanted me to take the dray; I had wanted the coach. He did not like to remind people of our wealth; I prioritized comfort and giving brief transport to those on foot if I could. We settled on the wagon. Sometimes you have to defy your father.

Which is similar to what I was thinking when I saw them in the distance—Xephon, Alcidia, and Teacher Scotes—about to disappear over the rise. The three of them moved slowly and on foot, as Teacher Scotes always did, barefoot even, while the others were not, because though many a young person might have followed him, some practices even they found too arduous. Xephon was in riding boots, though he was not riding. Alcidia I didn't know. I knew *of* him—he was a trained soldier, often dressing in uniform despite there being no current cause, considered the most able and handsome man of our generation, certainly in our city and by the ladies, whom he frequented. He was also said to be ambitious and, now that he was thirty and of age, soon to seek election to the Assembly. During my time with Teacher Scotes the year before, Alcidia had not been with him. But then Teacher Scotes always welcomed new acquaintances.

Because my father had mentioned nothing for many months, I vaguely hoped that he had cooled, giving me leave to try again, though I understood this to be fantasy. Really I had come to see my promise to stay away from Teacher Scotes as shameful—because of something Teacher Scotes himself had said the very day we met, something that made me question much of how I had been living.

Do others find it as difficult to contemplate their own weaknesses and faults? I imagine so, or else Teacher Scotes would not have urged himself and others to think so critically, to examine issues of justice and goodness, what it means to live well, and whether one is living up to one's conclusions about such things. To that point in my life, I had done little: a few attempts at lawyering, clerking, printing. I don't know if my failures came from lack of skill or of desire; I seemed to possess little of either. If I *wanted* anything, it was to write poetry, and I spent many hours while traveling for my father composing poems in my head. I observed the trees, the farms, the rivers, and tried to capture how I felt in words, images, and rhymes.

But none of it mattered: I was to be an elected representative. For as long as I could remember, Father had wanted it desperately on my behalf, had tolerated my excursions principally because he had anticipated their futility, and I complied, even taking comfort in his having set my life for me.

Father had also made it clear, whenever the topic came up—when a profile had been written or if we saw him walking in the city with a group or should I comment that his associates were mostly young—that Teacher Scotes, while to be respected for his youthful contributions, was now someone to be avoided. So when Father learned last year that I had ignored his advice and spent several weeks in Teacher Scotes's company—several weeks that I loved—he became extremely upset with me, quite agitated really, and outright forbade any further contact. His alarm was so at odds with my own experience that I found it difficult to comprehend, but when I asked him to elaborate, he just got angrier. So I abided by his wishes, as I always did.

Shortly after, he sponsored an act that made it a capital offense not to believe in the ideals of our nation and to corrupt the young, defined as anyone under thirty. I was twenty-seven then. Even now I cannot accuse my father of passing a law with the intention of targeting one citizen, but I also cannot dismiss the possibility, knowing how deeply he cared about my future. I took solace in the fact that such laws were rarely intended to be enforced but only to encourage good behavior and discourage bad.

Before I could lose sight of them, I set Betsy to the light clopping that she liked, understanding that they might no more want to see me than my father wanted me to see them. At this time of morning and on this road, they could be heading for the amphitheater itself, though I doubted it because Teacher Scotes never attended Assembly. Just then a rumble and a cry came from behind, and a frantic driver and team of four pulling a

Conestoga thundered past, almost clipping us and swaying ahead and vanishing past the turnoff. Ever since the recent votes—first to grant a team of four to every farmer more than three miles from any city, no matter how large the farm, and second to eliminate all tolls—the roads had become hazardous with the teams. After I'd calmed myself (nothing seemed to shake my mare), I scanned ahead to find the three, afraid that in the commotion they might have seen me, but they were gone.

I flicked Betsy into a trot. She had worked hard these past four days, and I was mindful of not exhausting her. When we reached the fork that descended to the bridge, I eased her to the edge, and there we held. The muffled sound from the amphitheater, now just visible across the river and above the trees, met our ears.

To me, this was one of the most beautiful spots anywhere. Not a quarter mile below stood the tavern on the left, just before the floating bridge. On both sides of the road, the land sloped up, like a trough, and rose again, without the trough, across the river. This side was thick with trees and shrubs and flowers; the other was fields and grazing cows. I rarely had occasion to come this way—a way General Washington himself had traveled to the city, until he retired to Virginia when our first national constitution did not include the position of president—for usually I crossed the Market Street Bridge or perhaps the Upper Ferry Bridge, if headed for more northern parts. But neither shared this beauty, and the tidal flows of the river, at different times of day and in different lights, could give gentle movement to the solemn and peaceful scene.

I sighted Teacher Scotes and Xephon milling by the tavern, near the entrance to the bridge. Not yet ready to encounter them, I had begun to back up my confused mare when I was yanked from my seat and hit the dirt, though not hard because whoever had grabbed me also supported me. With thumbs pressing into my shoulders, he held me down. I heard the sound of Betsy's startled steps, and I looked up into the bright light. It was Alcidia.

"Why were you trotting?" he said. "Were you following us?"

Today he was not in uniform, but I felt his strength—having already experienced his stealth—and did not try to rise. Instead I squinted and could see his blond curls better than the expression on his face. He released me. I sat. He squatted and eyed me. He was just two years older than I, but something in his demeanor made me feel much younger.

"Are you *trying* to get him arrested?" he asked.

I could tell that he neither expected me to answer nor cared if I did. He stood and helped me up. I wanted to dust myself off but somehow thought I had better not without permission. He continued to glare. I almost admired the way he faced me, knowing who I was. Betsy craned her neck, eyeing him, and again shifted in place.

"I see you have met Palleias, Alcidia." It was Teacher Scotes calling from below. He and Xephon were climbing, Xephon bounding ahead, Teacher Scotes striding into the hill. I wondered how much they had witnessed.

I had not spoken to Teacher Scotes since last summer, having never explained my sudden disappearance, though I was sure he had surmised the reason, and I had seen him only from a distance, in the shops or at a mill or farm—you could not help seeing him around—and if I came upon a location where he was, I left to escape his notice.

Xephon reached us first. "Palleias," he said and went directly over to Betsy. Xephon was about three years my senior—larger, bearded, and where I was reticent by nature, he was a bellows, amiable and loud. He considered himself a budding historian and had been accompanying Teacher Scotes for years. I had liked him very much those weeks last summer when I joined them.

"She is beautiful," he said, holding Betsy's reins lightly in one hand and rubbing her nose. "But I don't recognize the breed. The shape of her head is extraordinary."

"Percheron," I said. "The first of her kind in our country."

"The benefits of power, no?" He winked.

"A gift to my father from France."

He squatted before the horse and stroked her front legs. He lifted one. "A high hoof. And a thick horn. She'll keep her frog." His hand glided upward. "Good bones up to the fetlock, not too straight. They won't jar you when riding, but strong. And thick and muscular thighs." He reached up, then stood. "Her broad chest gives her beauty and strength."

Betsy stood for it all. I was uneasy and wished Xephon would stop touching my horse. I might have spoken, but under the watchful eye of Teacher Scotes, I refrained.

Had you never met Teacher Scotes, you nonetheless would have known him by sight, just from his reputation. He was widely known—sometimes admired as wise, if odd, though more often criticized as perverse and to be shunned. Everyone considered him brave, however, because at fifteen years of age, he had fought under General Washington at Trenton and Princeton that Christmas when the war turned, was wounded, and returned at Yorktown. Most considered him ugly, too, partly from his looks and partly his dress. He was tall, almost as tall as I, with a rather oversized head and curly gray hair, an eagle's beak–like nose, smallish upper body, and the largest calves of any man I've seen—the size of the posts in our English-style houses. Though thin, he gave the appearance of being top- and bottom-heavy at the same time, and at seventy, he seemed to have lost no strength. This, I assumed, came from his walking most everywhere, in virtually all weather. He always wore a plain white linen shirt, never a waistcoat; a pair of dark breeches in the old style, which appeared to have been mended and turned and mended again; and never any stockings. When still, his feet gripped the earth like talons.

Alcidia, Teacher Scotes, and I stood on one side of my wagon, Xephon on the other, tending to my horse.

"I believe he was trying to track us," Alcidia said. "Probably spying for his father."

"Why do you think that, Alcidia?" Teacher Scotes asked.

"He began cantering just as we reached the rise."

"And does the one necessarily follow from the other?"

"Well, no." Alcidia seemed sternly averse to a lesson at this moment. "But we must be careful."

Teacher Scotes turned to me. "Are you hurt, Palleias? Can we assist you in any way?"

"I am not hurt."

Betsy snorted. Xephon had walked off, but I knew that she would stay, though untethered. By now it was midmorning, and the sun warmed the spot on which we stood, even as much around was wooded and in shade.

"I did not see what happened, but your trousers are soiled and your hat is off," Teacher Scotes said.

"I was not wearing my hat, and I slept in these clothes last night."

Teacher Scotes regarded Alcidia, who was regarding me. Then he turned to me again. "Alcidia is known for his zeal and for other qualities. He recently asked to travel with me and to learn. In this last, you two have much in common." I did not know what to say to that, so I just stood, tepid, as was my usual. "It is good to see you again, Palleias," Teacher Scotes said. "So . . . were you?"

I knew he meant, Were you following me? and if I lied, he'd be able to detect it. I suppose my unresponsiveness betrayed the truth, because he said, "We are heading to Assembly. Alcidia is interested in studying the proceedings. Would you care to join us?"

The invitation thrilled, but I hesitated. Assembly was where my father would likely be, and though prepared at last to break my promise, I was still fearful of doing so. The fear touched something more than just his disapproval, though exactly what I could not tell. It would take events this very day to illuminate it.

"But you never attend Assembly," I said.

"Teacher Scotes!" Alcidia said. "Surely that is unwise." He turned angrily to me. "Don't you have somewhere to be? Must you be so irresponsible?"

I had no need to answer that one either, because just then came Xephon, high-stepping out of the woods and brush, carrying a clump of vegetation in his outstretched hands.

"Palleias," he said excitedly, "I have found some wild carrots for your mare. They must have jumped Doctor Say's fence." He had reached the horse, and we could see that he held some roots with long reddish-green stems.

Teacher Scotes yelled, "Xephon, fling that back into the woods! Do not hesitate—fling it!" Stunned, Xephon, who was an accustomed protégé, flung the plant back toward where he had come, with great strength and without question. "Now touch nothing!" Teacher Scotes said. "Nothing on yourself or anyone. And proceed to the river and wash your hands thoroughly. When done, ask at the tavern for a slab of their soap, which you should then discard in the river. Do it now!"

"What is it? What have I touched?"

"Poison hemlock," Teacher Scotes answered.

Though I had not gotten a good look, that Xephon had found hemlock was likely true. From Europe it had arrived not many years before and now was growing wild. Xephon was not yet in danger; he would have had to ingest the plant, especially the root. But likely the poison was on his fingers. It was so toxic that trace amounts could kill man, cattle, horse—so toxic that we had begun using it as a humane alternative in capital crimes.

For a moment Xephon appeared frozen, a state reflected in his subdued murmuring voice. "I have heard that it favors riversides," he said. This was the naturalist in him speaking, seemingly by rote, even though he was under threat. "I have also heard that it is spreading uncontrollably throughout our nation." Then a little sparkle hit his eyes, and he looked up in the direction of his teacher. He grinned. "Much like democracy," he said.

"Xephon!"

At Teacher Scotes's booming voice, Xephon sprinted down the hill, his hands raised ahead of him.

Looking back on that moment, as I have many times, I cannot say whether Teacher Scotes even then foresaw how such varied elements— himself, Xephon, Alcidia, the hemlock, the idea of democracy, and me—for a point in time came together on a simple road and in a young nation, elements that in a just world might have been disparate but in ours were suddenly and forever linked, like earth and sky and water. I expect he might have, because he had that skill in greater abundance than anyone I knew—the skill of projecting the consequences of that which he thought, saw, encountered—and it occurred to me that perhaps his outburst at Xephon came from fear not only for his protégé's life but for his own.

Myself, I thought nothing of Xephon's comment at the time. But if Teacher Scotes *had* seen what could come from this improbable encounter of people, things, and words, he did not say. In fact, by his actions you would have thought otherwise, for he proceeded not to drop his invitation but to reissue it.

He motioned for me to sit with him on two large rocks beside the road. We had been following Xephon's distant movements, and Teacher Scotes reassured us of his safety. Then he said to me, "You may join us if you want. Or, if you prefer, walk with us till we reach Assembly, and we will say goodbye. As soon as Xephon is ready, we'll cross the bridge. There is much we wish to observe at today's session."

With a sullen look, Alcidia enticed Betsy with some greenery to the side of the road. At first she resisted, then her shoulders relaxed, her front knee bent, and she allowed herself the steps being asked of her.

"I would like to go with you," I said.

"Splendid. Then it is settled." He placed his hands on his thighs as if to rise. When he saw that I did not, he remained seated. "Yes?"

They were eyeing me, and though Teacher Scotes likely understood what I was thinking, he would entertain my problems only if I raised them and not complain of them for me, as was his way. Then it occurred to me that Alcidia's protestations offered me a respite, an excuse to join them on a less conspicuous day, so I said, "What if my father sees you with me, as he likely would? Might that not cause you difficulty?"

"That is the reason you hesitate?"

I nodded.

"Then, Palleias, you wound me, for I would not have expected such an insult from one I consider to be a friend."

Our sitting together in the sun had warmed me with feelings reminiscent of being in his presence last spring and early summer. And it was a joy to hear him call me friend, especially given what had happened.

"My intention was in no way to insult," I said.

"And if the outcome of our action contradicts our intention, which should matter most?"

His manner was kind, as ever, such that I did not mind the apparent rebuke and easily replied, "The outcome."

"So your reason for not attending is concern for me?"

"Yes."

"And that concern is based on knowledge that I myself do not have?"

"No," I admitted.

"Then the risks to me that you consider are risks that I myself can judge?"

"Yes."

"And yet you would decide for me on my behalf?"

Beside us on the road was fresh activity—riders, a wagon, a family on foot. Alcidia watched us with restrained displeasure. Beside him, Betsy grazed. "You're right," I said to Teacher Scotes. "I am sorry."

"So you will join us?"

Weakly, I nodded.

He smiled and said, "Last we discussed, your plans were to pursue a career as a representative. Is that still the case?"

"Yes."

"Have you been to Assembly recently?"

This question I could answer more comfortably. "I have not attended open debate for years."

"Well then. How better to prepare for your career than by reexamining its procedures? I have promised to comment for Alcidia as we watch. Might not this be useful to you as well?"

"Teacher Scotes," Alcidia interrupted, "I fear that we may miss the morning's proceedings. I am eager to witness the scheduled votes." He guided Betsy back onto the road.

Teacher Scotes stood. "As usual you are right, Alcidia. Let us not delay any longer." Far below, sitting on the steps of Gray's Tavern, the diminutive Xephon watched us.

"Since you are driving and we are on foot," Alcidia said to me, "you may go ahead of us, so that we do not bar your way."

"Tut, Alcidia," Teacher Scotes said. "Where are your manners? You are welcome to cross the bridge with us, Palleias, and if you change your mind and prefer to join us another day, I will welcome you then also."

So I mounted the wagon and clucked Betsy to a walk, with Alcidia and Teacher Scotes leading. The bridge I had to cross anyway. I also knew that when we reached the amphitheater, with the Assembly already in session, I would do what I had long determined to do, if presented with the chance, and would follow them inside.

CHAPTER 2

The National Amphitheater is the most revered building in our nation. Not ten years after we achieved independence from Britain, it was completed on the Schuylkill's eastern shore, on the grounds of the old naval arsenal. Carpenters and stonemasons from every state came together in an act of solidarity, led by Teacher Scotes's father, one of the best-known stonemasons of his time. It was built in the tradition of the amphitheaters of antiquity, with limestone from quarries that bordered the turnpike to Lancaster, hauled by cart and oxen and assembled with remarkable speed by hundreds of laborers using cranes of massive ropes and pulleys. That it would reside in Philadelphia was a given, Philadelphia being our capital and located at our nation's heart.

Though we were proud to be one nation and a single political entity, the amphitheater's design honored our roots as independent states. Thirteen sections, each a thousand seats, looked down upon a wooden stage. They were arranged geographically: the most northerly, for Massachusetts; the most southerly, for Georgia; the rest in between, as on our map. The limestone benches on which our citizens sat faced west, as if we had turned our back on Britain. From the upper rows, you could see the winding river and the vast country beyond. On the stage the representatives' chairs, 169 in all, faced east, arranged in thirteen groups of thirteen, mirroring the amphitheater's sections. In front of the stage was a grassy open area—the Pit—where the herald presided and citizens could speak.

The uphill stretch of Gray's Ferry Road that linked the bridge and the amphitheater was still not paved, and Teacher Scotes's feet were muddy from our crossing, the weight of travelers upon the bridge having caused it to submerge just so. His breeches and shirt required drying too because Alcidia had been mischievously splashing him. We climbed through a peaceful meadow, then tall cedars, and could hear the sound before we saw the building, and the building appeared before us soon enough.

Cheers arose distantly. The crowd would likely be an ample one, it being sunny and not too hot, and ever since the passing of the act that provided ten demos pay for any citizen who attended, the crowds had gotten larger. If you arrived by eight o'clock, you were handed a tin disc, and if you departed at adjournment—often well into the afternoon, for there were always many bills to discuss—you could exchange it for a note. On this day the northern sections, which were the only ones visible as we approached, were nearly filled.

Alcidia and Teacher Scotes walked ahead. Xephon guided Betsy. I joggled on the bench, holding her reins. At the open, western end, we turned and hugged the towering stone. Along the high wall were arched openings. Through them you could enter or leave your section without disrupting the debate; the front was roped off, anyway. The Pennsylvania section was at the back, which at last we reached. Through the arch were the dark narrow stone steps. From inside came a cheer and then the herald's muffled call: "Who wishes to speak?" Xephon released Betsy and went inside. Alcidia hung behind, still defensive in my presence.

"What shall we, gents?" Teacher Scotes asked, giving me leave should I require it, for he was loath to press an action upon anyone.

"Allow me just one minute," I said, for I preferred to enter separately.

Teacher Scotes placed a hand on mine. "If we do not see you, have safe travels, and perhaps we will be fortunate to meet again soon."

Then they headed in. I watched them rise till they disappeared. Presumably at the opening they would reverse direction, ascend with Xephon, and find some open seats. Father would surely see them.

I jumped off the bench and guided Betsy to a post in the stippled shade of a thick elm, where she could nibble peaceably. Then I, too, entered and climbed in dimness till I reached the warmer opening and there beheld the sight.

People who visited from foreign countries often wrote of their experience of entering our Assembly. There was nothing like it in all of Europe, and likely not in history. For ours was a pure, representative democracy—at its core, an elected, unchecked, unicameral legislature—the most advanced the world had known. Today, having learned from Teacher Scotes and since read works that were then prohibited, I know that it was not the system envisioned by the leaders of our Revolution, men like Lawyers Jefferson and Adams, Scholar Madison, and General Hamilton, all of whom had been early captured by the British and had not survived the war. Later, when we ratified the Constitution of '83, any voices similar to theirs were too feeble to be heard. So instead we chose to perfect the past. We felt we had the greatest venue, sophisticated procedures, and symbols that made our politics our own. We especially excelled at the symbols, such as the Democracy Bell, which sat atop the old Statehouse and chimed yearly at the celebration of the Fourth. But the greatest of our symbols was VOP.

VOP was the reason so many master carpenters had been called upon back then and had been needed ever since to effect its nearly constant repairs. Forty feet above the representatives he stood, as high as the highest row of seats. Or I should say the *face* of VOP stood there, for he was head only, an intricate, latticed assembly of smoothly planed boards. I faced him, as he faced every citizen in attendance, ready to pronounce his resonant "Aye" or "Nay" upon the final vote for each legislative act. When he was made to sound, the votes had already been taken, and those assembled knew the results by a show of the representatives' hands. But his pronouncement was the symbol of that vote—Voice of the People.

I looked across the Pit toward my father's seat upon the stage, saw him in it, and remained where I was, a step down in the stairwell. He had not yet seen me. I had hoped he might be absent; he would often wait at home for my return from being away, because the people's mood these days was bad, and he worried for my safety. That he was here meant a momentous vote was scheduled. All around him on the stage sat the representatives in their greatcoats. Even today I cannot see that style of coat without thinking of him. To merely see one is to feel its coarseness and inhale its woolen smell. Having been elected to thirteen terms, he had many times patched or mended his and just once reluctantly replaced it.

It is difficult to describe what it was to be the son of such a father. To others, he was the famous Antonyn, known the nation over, the only man who had been elected the year he came of age at twenty-five (only later was that age deemed too immature and revised to thirty) and then reelected to every term since, for twenty-five years. To the citizens of our state, he was esteemed, at least by most, because as he himself would say, no representative can be esteemed by all. "To represent the people is to meet the greatest needs of the greatest number." In this, he was tireless. When not in Assembly, he was in committee or with those who had made formal requests or proposed acts, and of me he inquired regularly about my travels. Given his influence, both in the state and the nation, he could sponsor and pass most any act with the least support. Add to this his appearance, which was tall and lean and handsome. Such things, he said, could never hurt a representative, and he teased that my "even better looks" would serve me well when the time came.

That was how the people knew him. To me, he was much more. I know that I am prone to exaggeration, but here I do not think so. What *is* a father? Though others might answer differently, for me the answer was, Everything. For all my life and because of him, I had never wanted for anything, material or spiritual. When I was uncertain, his words were like the turnpike that led me home. He was the map for me to open; his advice, the route I knew to follow.

Teacher Scotes, of course, would have questioned such thinking because if he exhorted anything, it was to define one's terms. My saying that my father was "everything" would for him have been a challenge. He would have asked for additional examples of fathers, to see beyond the one, then assessed their similarities and differences. Whatever I might answer, he would question further, until I proposed a definition that well subsumed the examples I had given. When he engaged me in this way, as he had on several topics the year before, as he did anyone who asked him, we might talk for hours until we both were satisfied or I requested that the dialogue end. The first such conversation we ever had was in fact what bade me break my promise to my father and rejoin Teacher Scotes this morning.

Between the representatives and me, a lone citizen stood in the middle of the Pit. It was difficult to determine his profession. The bedecked herald stood at his shoulder. To my left and right, people yelled, laughed, whistled, nearly filling every section. Before the promise of pay, this level of attendance would have indicated interest in the scheduled votes. Now we could not even count on familiarity with the issues.

"Fellow citizens!" the speaker yelled with outstretched arms. "What is being considered is a faster and safer way of travel!"

"By way of an iron carriage propelled by steam!" someone yelled, mockingly. There was laughter.

"You have seen it work on the rivers!" the speaker yelled. "I tell you that the men whose venture we consider have also seen it work on land, in England, where just such vehicles transport coal from mine to mill!"

"Cursed England!" someone yelled.

"On magical iron rails!" someone else yelled.

I stepped onto the landing and turned to face the seats. I had to shield my eyes to find Xephon, Alcidia, and Teacher Scotes, near the aisle about halfway up. Toward them I climbed. Perhaps the sun would shield me from my father too. Then I thought, Don't be a coward.

"Does anyone wish to speak?" the herald said.

"Vote!" someone yelled. "Yes, vote!" someone else yelled.

"Does anyone wish to speak?" the herald said again.

They watched me come: Xephon, nervously, from his seat closest to the aisle; next, Teacher Scotes, serenely; and Alcidia, his face as rigid as the stone. I sat on the end, next to Xephon, and looked down upon the stage. From his seat, my father stared up at me without expression. The previous speaker left the Pit to return to the Delaware section.

"If no one else wishes to speak," the herald said, just as loudly as before because sound carried in this place extraordinarily, "then a vote will be taken."

"Huzzah!" Often the crowd cheered the close of any business: the sooner the proceedings finished, the sooner they received their pay. Only so many votes were scheduled for a given day.

The herald turned to face the representatives, which dampened his voice. "Those in *favor* of granting a charter to a so-called railroad company in these United States, raise your hands." The representatives stood, as was the practice, and a modicum of hands went up and, with them, some answering boos. At that, the three counting clerks began to peck with their fingers; when done, each would tally his number and report it to the recording clerk.

How the votes would fall was rarely a product of the day's debate. But in Assembly the people gathered to hear the representatives, who spoke first, and then, if they so desired, to augment what the representatives had said. In a way, what happened in Assembly was but another symbol because the people had elected the representatives, and the representatives had already solicited the views of the people and were expected to vote as they saw fit. But to give the people voice and grant a final chance to express their wishes was still seen as a proud moment, one that preserved and honored the greatness of the ancient world.

"Those *against* granting charter," the herald said, once the recording clerk had nodded, "raise your hands."

More hands went up, to resounding cheers. Again the counting clerks began their pecking. When all was completed, the recording clerk presented his tally to the herald, who received the book with both hands. He faced the people.

"The vote is 50 aye and 112 nay. The act is defeated, in the name of the people."

"Huzzah!" An overwhelming cheer went up, followed by lingering murmurs.

"A great day for the stagecoach!" someone yelled.

"A great day for the canals and hardworking shippers!" someone else yelled, from the New York section.

There was another cheer. A few began to exit by their aisles, but most remained.

As was the custom at this point, the representatives, who were still standing, all turned to face VOP. As was also the custom, the representative who had sponsored the act walked to the back of the stage, where a long fixed speaking horn of cochleate design curved from its cradle, about chin high, all the way to where its bell lay wedged inside VOP's large, opened mouth. What happened at this point was solemn, though it served little practical purpose and would be heard in only half the city and, of course, nowhere in the country, where people would read of the results in their newspapers.

The representative behind the cradle held the metal in one hand, leaned forward in his heavy coat, put his lips to the mouthpiece, and uttered the loud deep "Nay" that filled the amphitheater and spread behind us, the vibrations no doubt chilling even the most frequent Assembly visitors. This ritual—more than any other—was what my father said captured the spirit of our nation.

As the representatives all took their seats, and the herald conferred with the clerks and prepared to convene the next debate, Teacher Scotes leaned across Xephon and said to me, "I am glad you could join us, Palleias. Will you stay for this next vote? It is one that Alcidia especially wants to witness."

On the stage, Father was staring up again, as likely he would, on and off, for the duration, so I decided not to look at him. Nor did I want to give Teacher Scotes, Xephon, or Alcidia the least hint of what I was feeling. "I would like to see the next vote as well," I said, a touch too formally.

Teacher Scotes nodded and straightened. I felt awkward in his presence. Alcidia leaned forward and glared at me. I had never asked Teacher Scotes about his reasons for staying away from Assembly, and though Father once had mentioned it disparagingly, he hadn't explained it either. That he would attend today at Alcidia's request showed his love for Alcidia and for Alcidia's promise.

Then Alcidia dropped concern with me and asked, "Can the defeated act be raised again?"

"As soon as any rep wishes to raise it, if he can pass it through committee and schedule it for Assembly," Teacher Scotes answered.

I knew that for every question Alcidia could ask, Teacher Scotes would have an answer. From my time with him, I had observed his method, which was thorough study, close observation, extensive questioning, and persistence—sometimes even long bouts of thought wherever he happened to be, if a problem particularly vexed him. In such moments, you could not distract him even if you wished to. It was a behavior that gave some qualms, thinking him, if not a threat, then someone to be suspected. One of the worst things to be accused of then was being learned—a "Pen-and-Ink man" was the epithet—which would have been ironic if applied to Teacher Scotes, for he never wrote a word.

From below, the herald said, "Fellow citizens, we are ready to commence with the next act." He had returned to the center of the Pit. The post-VOP commotion subsided. "Fellow citizens," he said, "are you ready?"

"Ready!" came the shouts, before they settled to a murmur.

"I will now recite the preamble to Act 1831-4-67." He lifted a page, one hand on top, one on the bottom. "Whereas the recent difficulties have caused a decline in commerce and left many families without work or with reduced income, and whereas many of the nation's farmers, artisans, and manufactories have borrowed significant sums in order to meet the demands of the recent boom years, and whereas such debt now burdens their homes and businesses to a degree that further depresses our commerce overall, be it therefore enacted by the democratic people of these United States, and by the authority of this elected Assembly in their name, and it is enacted, that all debts deemed to be unpayable by a special committee to be convened are forgiven and are hereby deemed legally uncollectable by their creditors, this act to remain in force until the special committee has determined that all pertinent cases have been reviewed."

A large cheer arose, and many people stood, clapping. When this had nearly subsided, someone yelled "Huzzah!" and a new swell rose. Here and there, in various sections, a few people remained stiffly seated, their neighbors prodding them to stand as well. Out of the corner of my eye, I observed Teacher Scotes, who remained seated and impassive. This, I thought, must be the act that brought my father here, rather than await my arrival home. Along with every other representative, he had stood to clap too. Though, unlike them, he was eyeing us.

CHAPTER 3

"Citizens—respect!" the herald yelled. He gestured for the crowd to quiet. Many began to sit, as did the representatives.

"Pass it!" someone yelled.

"Citizens!" the herald yelled.

"Pass it!" two or three more yelled. More of the crowd sat.

"Citizens!" the herald yelled. "Let debate begin!"

"Citizens!" A lone representative yelled and stood. It was Representative Lycon, from our state. I knew him from his visits to our home; he was both colleague and friend to my father. As sponsor of the act, he would be first to address the Assembly. "Citizens, thank you for attending today to join in this important debate and this great cause."

"We're with you, Lycon!" someone yelled.

"Pass it!" someone else yelled.

Representative Lycon raised his hands. "Thank you, citizens, for your support. As you know, these are difficult times. People like yourselves, all across our nation, are suffering, unable to pay their bills, unable to find work."

"Help us!" someone yelled.

Representative Lycon acknowledged the general direction of the comment. "Such acts as these we do not take lightly. It has been some years since we've had need of such a one. But this body, convened in your name and constituted to serve you, cannot be idle when your needs are clear.

This is why I sponsored this act and why I call upon my colleagues here today to pass it!"

Another large cheer rose, and some people stood to clap, though they did not remain standing long, as Representative Lycon pressed his hands before him. "Which of my colleagues would also like to speak?" he said.

To his right on the stage, a short man stood. He was from Virginia. "I wish to speak!" he said. Representative Lycon sat.

The newly standing representative yelled out, "I wish also to express my sympathy to those here and, by extension, to those not here for the struggles you face today. The people of my state know the concern I bear them, and those who are visiting from Virginia, I salute you." A cheer arose from the Virginia section, not far from ours. "And to all I say that I support the act sponsored by my colleague from Pennsylvania!"

From his own seat, Representative Lycon again looked to either side. "Which other of my colleagues would like to address this esteemed Assembly?"

"I wish to speak!" This time, a long-haired, muscular man, whose greatcoat seemed too small by several sizes, stood at his seat in the North Carolina section. He looked as though he might once have carried masts for a shipwright. "I, too, know many citizens from my state who cannot repay their debts. Debts—as my fellow citizens have written me and as you have told me in the taverns of our great capital—they were tricked into accepting by ruthless merchants who shamelessly lent them money they could not repay!"

"Shame!" came several cries.

"Forgive the debts!" cried several more.

Seated in the amphitheater like this, among the cheers and cries and pronouncements of the representatives and crowd, I recalled my dislike of being here. It was an old uneasiness, and I could not tell its source. When I expressed this feeling to Father once, he chastised me. Most people who attended, he said, revered what they had witnessed. To witness what happened in this building was to witness an act of birth, every day and anew. My father, who said he felt privileged to have played so central a role for so long, insisted that one day I, too, would feel the same. I, too, would delight in assisting the people in birthing the acts that they required.

The representatives continued to trade statements. Dozens spoke, across the span of about an hour. Most seemed supportive of the act; a few tentatively questioned a detail here and there, usually to boos; some, you could not tell their sentiment, though they spoke at length.

During the debate, the crowd grew increasingly boisterous. The few who remained seated were dressed mostly in the sharp vests or white linen trousers common to the upper sort. And they appeared relatively young, as if inexperienced enough to consider attending such a vote.

Now that most everyone surrounding us was standing, Alcidia leaned forward again and whispered angrily at me, "Isn't it time for you to leave?"

Teacher Scotes answered, still looking forward, "Come now, Alcidia, we don't want to be rude, do we? Besides, has it occurred to you that Palleias may have more cause for concern than I?"

This struck me, and it confirmed that Teacher Scotes likely understood why I had stopped following last year.

"The difference is," Alcidia said, "that I have scant interest in his concerns. I care for yours."

"You are a loyal and devoted friend," Teacher Scotes said.

"I am not concerned," I said, a bit shakily.

The debate among the representatives ended. Representative Lycon, calling for further comments from his peers, received no reply. It was time to solicit comments from the citizens.

The herald approached from where he had been standing near the stage and again retook the center of the Pit, raised his chin, and spread his arms. "Fellow citizens," he said, "does anyone wish to speak?" In unison, the crowd began to sit.

"I wish to speak!" someone yelled from far away, in the Georgia section. At last they were in sun, and the light was white upon them.

A man in heavy boots, plain shirt, and broad hat proceeded down the aisle. He was tall but bent and slow moving, like a farmer.

"I wish to speak!" someone yelled.

"I wish to speak!" someone else yelled.

The herald raised his hands again. "You may all speak in your turn. This gentleman is recognized," he said to the Georgian, who by now had reached the grass and was approaching the herald and the spot where sound traveled best. The herald stepped aside and extended his hand, directing the man to turn and face the crowd. Some people laughed.

"Fellow citizens," the man began in a gravelly voice. "I am a cotton grower from the state of Georgia. One of my reps invited me to come. I have never traveled from my state. I am staying in a fancy inn in the city. It is strange to me. The mattress I am accustomed to at home is still of straw."

"So is ours, friend!" someone yelled.

"No shame in that!" someone else yelled.

"I told my rep I would speak to you, though I have never spoken to a group outside my family." There were shouts of encouragement. "You may ask how it is that I have time to make this journey, when I should be tending to my crops. It is because I am desperate. Soon I may have no crops to tend to."

I glanced at Teacher Scotes. The speaker was the kind of man he regarded highly. During my time with him, we had visited every farmer, artisan, builder, and shopkeeper that our travels took us near. He loved to watch them working. In observing work, he grew especially keen. He paid particular attention to their methods and their rationales. Watching him now, as he listened intently, I could tell he took an interest in this man's difficulties.

The man removed his hat to wipe his brow, then replaced it. He scratched the back of his neck, just above his rounded shoulders.

"Soon I may have no crops to grow," he repeated, "because the prices I can sell them for are far lower than when I bought my acres. For all my life, I had been a modest tobacco farmer, but with the rush to grow cotton, and the money that could be made in it, I borrowed greatly to purchase the land on which I now grow it too. I had never borrowed before, believing that debt was to be feared. But how could I pass up the opportunity to make a better life for my family? Our local bank and some of our merchants were keen to give us loans, so I took them. I have always been an honest man, and I believe in repaying debts, but without relief I may lose more than the additional acreage that I purchased. I may lose everything." He turned to regard the representatives behind him, and I could see my father nodding. Then he turned back to face the crowd. "I ask the reps to pass this act so that I may return home once again a free and upright man."

"Hear, hear!" came shouts all around, and the man began his slow ascent back to his seat.

The herald stepped forward. "Does anyone else wish to speak?"

What followed was a procession of farmers, coopers, bricklayers, blacksmiths, merchants, shipbuilders—men and women of nearly every occupation—to tell of how they had borrowed to expand their businesses and improve their lives and now were unable to repay their debts, since the pullback had come and some prices, which had risen to extremes, had fallen so precipitously. It seemed as if this happened every several years or so, and each time the consequences grew worse.

Men and women filled the aisles, waiting to be called by the herald to stand before the crowd.

"I used to sell my wheat at a half demos a bushel. Now I'm lucky to get a quarter," a farmer from Maryland said.

"I owe for the goods I bought on credit," a merchant from Connecticut said, "but those I owe I cannot pay."

"My ships are half-finished," a shipbuilder from New York said, "but I have not the funds to finish them."

"Forgive the debts!" was the unending cry. From across the amphitheater, people started calling out their predicaments, no longer waiting for a turn. Soon nearly everyone was standing and shouting. The herald had backed up and did not attempt to control the proceedings, even turning to the representatives as if seeking guidance on what to do. I had to lean to see between the bodies of those who had risen in front of us, and I caught the subtle shake of my father's head, indicating to the herald not to interfere with the raging of the crowd. From discussing the nature of such moments with him, from overhearing other representatives seek his counsel, from watching him interact with countless citizens across the years, I knew that my father understood the people best and that the herald would do as he advised.

I wondered whether I should stand up also, so as not to antagonize those around us, but next to me Xephon, Teacher Scotes, and Alcidia remained seated. We were like four mushrooms in a forest, positioned quietly at the foot of the swaying trees. At least we were shielded from the stage.

Alcidia turned to Teacher Scotes. "If you were a rep," he said, loud enough to be heard over the shouting, "what would you do now?"

"Since you are interested in being one, let me ask you," Teacher Scotes replied, as loudly.

"I am not afraid," Alcidia said.

"Then you are braver than I."

Gradually the tumult lessened. Finally the herald called, "Does anyone else wish to speak?" He was obliged to inquire until no one answered. "Does anyone wish to speak?" he called, and people in great chunks began to sit, as if a scythe were cutting through a field. When the sound was down to murmurs only, the herald called one more time, "Does anyone wish to speak?" Scanning the amphitheater, one arm extended theatrically in front of him, he made his final sweep.

"Vote!" came the new cries.

"If no one wishes to speak, then the vote will be taken." He turned to face the representatives behind him.

"I wish to speak." A deep, measured, heavily accented voice came from below us, in our section. The herald sought the voice.

Almost directly between us and the herald, a man stood. "I wish to speak," he said again. Like the representatives, he wore a black greatcoat, and like theirs, it was worn, though of a finer wool. He was slightly hunched and bald, but for hair around his ears and in the back, which he wore *en queue*. I knew him: this was Merchant Girard, and at more than eighty years old, he was older even than Teacher Scotes. Everyone would know him, not just Pennsylvanians, and certainly all the representatives. He was one of the richest and most famous men in the nation, one of the wealthy few whose reputation had remained untarnished. More than once he had loaned great funds to the National Bank and had twice volunteered to run our city's hospital when the yellow fever hit and the middle and upper sort were fleeing. At a time when it was risky to be perceived as rich, he was among those who did not hide their wealth.

Often had I seen Father confer with him, claiming him to be above reproach. On occasion Mother would prepare a special meal when inviting him to be our guest, and Father seemed a different man when he accepted and agreed to come. We called him "Merchant" because our custom was to refer to people by their professions, to honor honest labor as against the old, hated British aristocracy. Work was the great leveler; no one was better than another who worked. Even those who did not work we referred to by their former labors or, if they had never worked, by their desired ones.

Merchant Girard shuffled through his row, down the aisle, and into the Pit. The calls for a vote quieted. The herald stepped aside, and Merchant Girard nodded to the representatives before facing the crowd.

"Ladies and gentlemen," he began in the accent of his native France, not straining but speaking in a normal voice, which we could hear as if seated just before him. He stood stolidly, his expression made grave by the sustained closure of his right eye due to a childhood affliction.

For all of Father's talk about my inevitable rise to be a great representative, there was much about the role I did not understand, though I would never have admitted so. But one thing I did understand—not only from his statements but also from his sometimes anxious countenance and those of his colleagues when not in the public eye—was the fence that every representative needed to straddle in order to govern and be reelected every two years.

People's needs often clashed with those of others, Father often noted, such that he could rarely satisfy everyone, often disappointed many, and was therefore obliged to consider how his vote affected not just the country but his own political fortunes. After all, to serve the people at all, you must remain in office. This he called Survival Rule Number One.

Of course, most difficult to balance were the needs of the lower sort with those of the upper sort. People of the upper sort, like Merchant Girard, funded businesses, employed people, initiated trade among the states and with other nations. Their needs were important and had to be acknowledged. But the people of the lower sort, far more numerous, had even greater needs, which Father especially sought to meet. Even questionable needs could not be ignored, because to serve at all, you must remain in office.

On the stage below, Father listened to Merchant Girard with interest, and I was thankful to at least temporarily be out of his attention. Every so often, Alcidia looked over as if desirous of strangling me. Next to him, Teacher Scotes sat upright, calmly fixed on the spot where Merchant Girard stood.

"I wish to address you," Merchant Girard said, not raising his voice; the effect was to further dampen the murmuring. "Some of you," he said, "have borrowed money from me. Others have borrowed from people like me. Still others have come to make your views known. I myself have come to speak to all of you, though I do not attend this meeting often. I address you—you directly, not your representatives on this stage—because it is your bidding that they do. What they do they do because you ask it. I know that when times burden us, when policies fail or seem to do more harm than good, we blame them, I included. But this can be an error. I have lived many years and have witnessed much. Like a few of you, I even remember the days before the war."

"What is the point of this?" Alcidia whispered. "He is taking a risk even being here. His is the very skin being denounced."

Teacher Scotes did not answer.

Someone shouted, "Sit down, sir!"

Another shouted, "Vote!"

A third shouted, "Someone help the usurer back to his seat!"

A few boos responded to that. Behind Merchant Girard, the herald raised his arms. People knew that the crowd could sometimes turn against its own disruptive members, so the calls progressed no further. If the Assembly had to stop because of a riot, no one would be paid.

Merchant Girard continued as if he had not been interrupted. "I wish to say only this, as my sole contribution, and then I will sit down. I ask: What is the meaning of abolishing debts, except that you purchase something with my money, and then you have what you purchased, and I have not my money?"

"Boo!" came shouts from all around, though not, it seemed, from everyone; at least some in the crowd wished to grant the elderly man his moment. After all, the most cherished value we learned since school days was political participation, the sacred right of hearing from our representatives and being heard in turn, here in this sanctum and in the streets.

"I have said what I wanted," Merchant Girard continued, "and I will say no more. But there is one man here today we should hear from also. A man whom I observed arriving, though I understand that he, too, rarely attends."

It wasn't until Xephon snapped his neck sharply left that I understood who Merchant Girard was referring to. Alcidia turned crimson.

Merchant Girard raised his arm and indicated our direction. "I ask Teacher Scotes to address us on this matter." People from all around looked our way. "Many of you know him to be wise," Merchant Girard went on. "Perhaps he would be gracious enough to stand before us and tell us what he thinks about these matters. I ask him respectfully." He bowed.

My father's eyes were again upon me, and I sensed, as only I could, the roiling within him. I flushed and warmed.

"Teacher Scotes!" came shouts from around the amphitheater. "Let us hear from Teacher Scotes!" Those nearest to us smiled and clapped boisterously in encouragement.

Merchant Girard shuffled back toward his seat. Stepping into the vacated space, the herald called out, as was required, "Does anyone wish to speak?"

"Teacher Scotes!" came more shouts.

Teacher Scotes leaned toward Alcidia, though still facing forward, and said, "It seems as though I am to speak at Assembly." There was humor in his manner, though I saw nothing funny.

"Decline," Alcidia said.

"You wished to learn about the process," Teacher Scotes said. "Imagine how much more we'll have to discuss later if I participate."

"Decline," Alcidia said again. "Please."

From below, the herald said, looking up at us, "Does anyone wish to speak?"

"Teacher Scotes!" came more shouts.

Teacher Scotes stood. "Do not fear, my young friend." A cheer followed, not a wholly respectful one but interspersed with laughter, as if at a spectacle or circus. Addressing Alcidia, though looking down at me as he walked past, he said, "At least in this building we are safe."

CHAPTER 4

He descended. I watched him, as most everyone did. Truly he was odd looking, especially from behind, with those melon calves and bare feet, stepping silently down the limestone, as if on wool. And though I knew that his dress, indeed much of what he did, was motivated by economy, allowing him to wander and discuss ideas with people in and out of state, and though I knew that many people knew this too, still some laughed at him, laughed despite his vitality, which exceeded that of younger men. It made me uneasy, their laughter. Did they laugh because they knew him not and were ignorant of his virtues? Or did they laugh because they knew him well, and my desire to learn from him simply betrayed my foolishness? I knew my father's answer and, thinking this, looked down upon him again, watched him watch Teacher Scotes, then turn to me. I caught his eye and looked away.

The crowd was still both clapping and laughing when Teacher Scotes reached the Pit and turned to face them, unlike Merchant Girard not acknowledging the representatives. The effect of his turning was only to complete the comic picture: the oversize head with curly gray hair, beaked nose, and undersized torso above those legs. Smaller now and directly below us, he seemed to accept his own disparagement, steady in the smiling expression of his eyes, unmistakable even at this distance. He raised both hands to shoulder height. The crowd quieted.

"I thank good Merchant Girard for his invitation to speak," he said, nodding toward Merchant Girard before scanning the crowd, at ease, I thought, though his preference was always to converse with individuals or small groups; never, to my knowledge, had he addressed so large an audience. "I know that he would not ask me unless he considered it of some importance, because he knows, as do many of you, how unusual it is for me to be here." Some people laughed in recognition of this truth; a few booed. "He also knows of my propensity to question rather than pronounce"—people laughed at this, too, less benevolently—"and how awkward it therefore is for me to stand in such a place. Even now my inclination is to talk to you as I do my friends and those who seek my conversation, to question you your thoughts and invite you to question mine. And together arrive at a better understanding than we had before." Here he paused and jutted his chin, as if to accentuate the comical atmosphere he had stepped into. "I suppose I could question you now, beginning with this fine gentleman here"—he pointed to his right—"and that fine lady there"—he pointed to his left—"but there are thousands of you, a vote is imminent, and I do not wish to delay it. Not to mention that our New England friends are unused to our April sun and have been baking in it for some hours now."

A general and friendly laughter went up. Someone from a southern section yelled across, "You forgot your parasols!" to even further laughter.

Xephon hissed at Alcidia, "What are we going to do?"

But Alcidia only watched and whispered, more to himself, "What is he doing?"

Below, many representatives also whispered among themselves, most with disagreeable expressions.

"It is doubly odd that I speak to you," Teacher Scotes continued, "for I normally deem it a failure to spend more time speaking than listening and questioning. In that, I consider myself not a teacher, though somehow the appellation has stuck. Rather, I am a midwife, as some of you have heard me say, perhaps more often than you cared to." Again came brief laughter. "My mother was a midwife, and I studied her profession. But where she was a midwife of the body, I am one of the soul. I assist in the birth of ideas, assessing their readiness and, upon their emergence, their prospects for long lives and well-being. And just as my mother never gave birth for anyone, so I never think for anyone." You could tell from the diminishing joviality and increasing murmurs of the crowd that many were becoming impatient, though I liked his analogy and had not heard it before. Then he called out with greater energy, "What is the matter before us? That there should be a forgiveness of debts."

"Forgive our debts!" someone shouted.

"Help us!" someone else shouted.

"Very well," Teacher Scotes said. "Let us proceed to examine the issue."

There was a smattering of groans. The crowd began chanting, soon thunderously, "Vote—vote—vote!"

Something disorienting struck me about this spectacle. I had spent months thinking about my time with Teacher Scotes, wondering if we'd ever meet again, yet here I was, sitting on the hard stone next to two of his best students, with Teacher Scotes himself below and in front of a great crowd, my father witnessing it all. When I awoke this morning, I could not have envisioned such an occurrence, yet here it was. The pressure of the seat, the noise of the crowd, the dampness on my forehead, the sensation of colossal Xephon sitting close and VOP ahead—none of it seemed real. Teacher Scotes continued talking, though the crowd was bent on shouting him down, as they famously could do. The herald cried out but did not control them. Still, even over their shouts, we could hear Teacher Scotes's words. My impression was that to him, it did not matter. That it was not they whom he was addressing at all.

"How do we resolve the question?" he was saying. "Is it a question of right or justice? Is right or justice on one side of the issue or on the other?"

"Yes! It is right and just to forgive our debts!" someone yelled. There was general laughter.

"Perhaps so," Teacher Scotes said. "Who among us can explain what is right and just, generally? I mean the category of things and how we know when something is so?"

"Vote!" came the general cry. "Herald, call for the vote!"

Teacher Scotes did not acknowledge the cries but paused, as if awaiting an answer. Receiving none, he said, "Perhaps this line of questioning is unproductive. Perhaps the issue is not of right or justice. Perhaps instead"—and here he paused at length, which seemed to quiet the crowd somewhat—"it is an issue of economy and of plans and ventures and employments."

"Perhaps you can take your seat!" a man shouted, half standing and angrily shaking a fist, again to general laughter. At the laughter, the man looked around, smiled, and sat.

"Very good, then, let's investigate whether the question can be resolved as an issue of commercial and national health," Teacher Scotes said. There were greater moans and gestures of exasperation. "Who can say in general what makes a nation prosperous?" At this he showed his palms, as if inviting answers.

"Oh, come on!" someone yelled.

"Free us from this inquisition!" someone yelled, to muted laughter.

"A nation is prosperous when the people are not laden with debt!" someone yelled.

"Should there be no debt, then?" Teacher Scotes addressed his question in the general direction of the speaker.

People started stamping their feet. But the sound of Teacher Scotes's voice, projected strongly from that mysterious spot, could almost overwhelm whatever noise opposed it.

"I need my debt," someone yelled. "I could not have started my business without it."

"What is this endless talk?" someone else yelled. "Call for the vote!"

"The vote, the vote!" came the chant.

"One last thing, and I will sit down," Teacher Scotes said.

"Huzzah!" came the even louder cheer.

Teacher Scotes indicated someone in the crowd. "As the gentleman said, let us set aside these inquiries into justice and prosperity. I have another matter to put to you, if you will permit me."

"Do we have a choice?" someone yelled.

"I have heard it said," Teacher Scotes continued, "that two routes are navigable in crossing the Atlantic, one northerly, one southerly. By show of hands, which is the more efficient one?"

This question caused an irritated and mystified murmur to spread until eruptions occurred. I myself was puzzled by this line of questioning.

"He's mad!" someone shouted.

"Or perhaps this question you prefer instead. This past winter there was an illness that caused much distress in many of our largest cities. To what should we attribute its cause? To insects? To refuse? By show of hands."

At this the herald stepped forward, gently placed his hand on Teacher Scotes's shoulder, and whispered to him. Teacher Scotes inclined his neck to listen, then straightened, and the herald took a step back, clasping both hands behind him.

"The good herald has asked that I complete my thoughts and accede to the vote, which is due." A large cheer went up. Teacher Scotes raised a hand. "And of course I will abide. I leave you with this one thought. You have asked the reps to forgive your debts. If your response today is any indication of the support of your fellow citizens generally, then the reps will do just that." A lesser cheer went up. "Like Merchant Girard, I have followed such matters for nearly fifty years, albeit from afar, and feel confident in claiming that your will is their command." A greater cheer went up, and many people stood to clap.

"Vote!" came the cry.

Teacher Scotes climbed out of the Pit, but instead of returning to our row, he disappeared into the stairwell, the one we had entered by, without so much as a glance in our direction. Immediately, Alcidia and Xephon rose, squeezed in front of me, and scampered down.

For one last time, I looked down upon my father, who was following their exit. Quickly I rose and made my descent, eyeing only the steps before me, until into the dark and cooler stairwell I turned, followed by the herald's diminished voice: "If no one else wishes to speak, then a vote will be taken."

"Huzzah!" followed the dampened cheer.

Betsy bobbed at my approach. By the time I had untied her, the three were turning onto Cedar Street, headed toward the city. I followed.

For many blocks ahead, the road was nearly vacant, the wide straight line of broad gray stones bordered by the two narrow raised brick sidewalks. This far west, Cedar was still in places lined by woods and irregularly by homes and farms, though it had been paved years before at the people's expense because it was a main route to the amphitheater. Soon after, every road west of Broad had been paved because the Pennsylvania representatives did not want visitors from other states or nations to see a mud-gridded capital at any point between its major rivers. The expense was great, and other representatives resisted, but eventually they went along because each state had its own expenses that also required the cooperation of representatives from around the country. Betsy and I preferred the dirt that still existed west of the river and north of Broad; it was more even and softer.

In the distance was a carriage or two, and between them and me and facing away were Teacher Scotes, Alcidia, and Xephon, on the flatter sidewalk, which Teacher Scotes preferred for being easier on his feet and freer of animal waste. From the manner in which Alcidia gestured, I gathered that he was exhorting them to walk faster. Then he turned, saw me, and spun away abruptly. At this both Teacher Scotes and Xephon stopped and turned and waited. Alcidia kept his back to all of us. Bearded Xephon's expression was direct and bland.

I reached them.

"Palleias," Teacher Scotes said, "were you seeking us?" Something in his manner suggested that he was almost impressed by my appearance.

"Yes," I said.

"Very good. We are en route to Simon's. Would you like to come?"

This was precisely what I wanted, for Simon's was his favorite place to engage in dialogues—he went there almost every day—and I had avoided visiting it with him last year, for being too conspicuous a gathering. Then, before I could respond and from behind, where the rumblings of the amphitheater had dimmed, there was a sudden and much louder cheer, followed by the deep and muted voice of VOP drawing out its long "Aye," followed by a second cheer. I grinned at the timing.

Teacher Scotes laughed.

CHAPTER 5

The first day I ever spoke with Teacher Scotes was in the spring of 1830, also a beautiful day, also one in which I was returning by the Darby Road, a perfect day for stopping at the Botanical Society, within sight of the same bridge and tavern where we were to meet again almost exactly one year later.

On a hill overlooking the river with its great sloped lawn and gardens and famous ginkgo tree, the National Botanical Society occupied the old Woodlands, once the country seat of Botanist Hamilton and his family. After the first Distribution, it had been opened to all to visit freely, to walk and rest among the abundant flora that the Hamiltons had imported from around the world. Not only was the property stunning, but so were its surrounds, with the winding Schuylkill bordering it and visible far into the southern distance; other former estates, up and down the shorelines; three bridges within sight; and the shot tower, on the opposite, more northern bank. It was acre upon acre of peaceful beauty, where hundreds came to walk or picnic. It was an excellent spot for me to frequent, and Father encouraged me to do so.

That day, I had told Father I intended to visit and, upon entering the drive, saw that a large group had assembled just in front of the great white-pillared house, at the crest of the open lawn before it inclined to the river. Teacher Scotes was among them. He and a few others were standing, while the rest were sitting.

What I knew of Teacher Scotes was mostly from what I had read and heard and from Father's intermittent expressions of dismissive and contemptuous disapproval. But I knew that he knew of me because not long before, when I happened to be walking in the city, I passed him on the sidewalk, coming the other way. I think I had been gaping because when we were nearly side by side, he looked over and said, "Young Palleias" and continued on.

So when I came upon him at the gardens, I was intrigued and edged the wagon closer. Though I could hear little of what was being said, his manner struck me as falsely demure, a veneer that covered a supreme confidence. He was conversing with a well-attired man, who also stood but seemed less confident. After a time, another man, standing at the back, wearing a hat and trousers that ended above his ankles, saw me, walked over, and spit on my wagon as he passed. This sometimes happened. Then others turned, rose, and approached. I retrieved my memo book. I can't say that their attention didn't give me pride; to have people seek you out and need you is exhilarating.

At some point Teacher Scotes noticed me too, I who was the cause of his group's disintegration. Our eyes met. I suppose to counteract the effect I was having on his following, he called over, "Perhaps our young friend would like to join in our discussion?" He had a friendly manner, but I wasn't fooled, being aware of his reputation. By now the crowd was larger around me than him.

I called back, "Thank you, no." When the man to whom he was speaking walked away, the rest of his audience dissipated, and he wandered off alone, down the hill and toward the river.

For the next little while, I talked with those who pressed against my wagon, then excused myself. I hitched my horse and made as if to enter the building—it was imperative to limit the time groups held you, otherwise they could hold you all day—but instead descended the lawn toward Teacher Scotes, who stood in the shade of a thick willow, next to the narrow path that ran at water's edge. I thought that if I interrogated—even challenged—him, my report of the exchange later would be pleasing to Father. He was looking out across the river, hands behind his back. Just the other side of him was a stand of birches. Tiny creepers and nuthatches hopped up and down the trunks. A breeze rose and rustled the willow.

When I reached him, he looked over and smiled. He seemed genuinely pleased to see me. Given that I had ruined his gathering up the hill, I was surprised by his reaction and somewhat irritated by it. With a haughty tone, I said, "So you know who I am?"

Reacting with none of the defensiveness I expected, he answered, "Of course. I knew your father before you were born." I wondered if this was true or why he might be saying so. Certainly Father had never mentioned it. He kept his hands behind his back and did not turn to face me fully, as if I were just anyone he had encountered, and his not using my name gave his reply a jarring sense of intimacy. I felt intimidated, in a way I never did. Most of the notable people I met intimidated me, though differently.

"My father does not think highly of you" was what I said.

"And you? Do you also not think highly of me?"

I had heard that he would lure you into unwanted debates, so I tried to keep control. "My opinion is irrelevant," I said and immediately regretted it.

"Oh?"

He waited for me to elaborate, which I resisted. Then I said, "My opinion is irrelevant because I know only what he has told me."

"Then how much can you know?" Though his words seemed a challenge and an insult to Father, his tone was light and amiable.

"Since you claim to have known my father," I said, "you know that he is a great man and an excellent judge of character."

"I believe he is," he said. "I gather, then, that you pursued me here in order to chastise me? It's not often I have such a prominent person as yourself helping to correct my character. Would you believe me if I told you that I welcome it?"

Something about this question again put me on the defensive, and I wondered who might be in earshot. On the main drive, high above on the hill, two carriages crossed, one entering, one departing. On the water, a low barge pulsed by. A hundred feet behind me, three people sat upon a blanket near the shoreline.

"In my travels," I said, "I sometimes see crowds around you. What do you discuss with them?"

"If you come upon us again, consider yourself welcome to join. Everyone is."

"What do you discuss?"

He shrugged. "Whatever is of interest. Usually the great issues—what is right, what is good, what is just. What it means to live well."

"Is that for you to say? Is that not the people's business, to be legislated?"

At last I had succeeded in shaking him somewhat. He turned to face me directly and more slowly said, "Fortunately, Young Palleias, I myself know very little." He showed his palms. "Were you to join us, you would see that I mainly ask questions. What few claims I make are always trussed by an understanding of how little I do in fact know."

"Some people say you are dangerous," I said.

"Dangerous—to whom?"

"To those who speak with you."

"How so?"

I did not answer.

He made as if to ponder a moment, though I knew that he had heard the charge before. "I can't imagine that many consider me dangerous," he said. "But those who do, I trust, simply ignore me and avoid my company. Surely no one claims that I force myself upon them?" He waited, but I did not answer. He continued, "If they judge me in that way, there are countless spaces where they will not find me. And since I don't write books or pamphlets or articles for our newspapers, they needn't fear encountering me there, either."

"People cannot always judge for themselves," I said.

"You mean they cannot judge whether I am dangerous to them?"

"Yes."

He feigned another reflection. "If that is so, would you permit me another question?"

I gave the slightest nod.

"If people cannot always judge for themselves," he said, "on what basis do our representatives pass laws to fulfill their desires and expectations—representatives who are chosen by the people, whose every act is made legitimate by the people's will? This would seem to put the people in a risky predicament, asking them to approve and oversee any and all issues when they cannot always judge for themselves."

"Careful, Teacher Scotes, lest you blaspheme."

"I only ask a question," he said demurely, fanning his fingers.

I decided then to lessen the pressure and encourage him to talk further, thinking he might disclose something that would be significant to Father. "I mean," I said, "*some* people cannot judge for themselves."

"I see. And you?"

"Me?"

"Can you judge for yourself?"

Only later, after spending time with him, did I appreciate his capacity to stop you with a question like that—one that, if you let it in, held it fast, and actually tried to answer it, could upturn you. I saw him do it many times. Somehow he knew the question you needed most to hear, and in my case, despite all my bravado, he had unearthed my greatest weakness and probed it—but also my greatest strength, I like to think, in that he may have predicted that I would not dismiss the question. Or at least consider it eventually, for under the pressure of it then, I could focus only on the face of the man who was observing me so closely.

When nothing finally came, I looked away. Then I addressed him squarely. "In the future," I said, "please consider that this venue may not be the appropriate place to carry on your conversations," and I walked off.

That night at supper, I did not report the encounter to my parents. All day it had preoccupied me, and something in me resisted telling them. When they asked about my visit to the gardens, I produced my notes on both the crowd that had assembled when I entered and the one that assembled later, when I untethered my horse to leave.

The next time I spoke to Teacher Scotes was at a sawmill, well north and west of the Upper Ferry Bridge, during the first leg of a two-day loop I intended to make in a stretch of fine weather. An innkeeper along the way happened to mention that Teacher Scotes and a few others had visited earlier. He indicated the direction they had gone.

Ever since our encounter, I had hoped to come upon him again, though this time not to confront him. In active search I stopped at a few sites before happening upon the mill, which sat at the end of a long, leafy path, a hundred yards downstream from a small falls, where the river rolled over an outcrop, churned, and rushed southward. It was an opportune site because the large wheel consumed a strong flow year-round, which was not the case for most mills. The mill itself was a long, squat wooden building. The noise of the rushing river, the grinding wheel, and the heavy rhythmic thumping of the saw frame all intensified with my approach and were louder still at the open doorway, through which Teacher Scotes was visible inside. The noise deafened when I entered.

He stood at a railing—he and five young men and women—looking away at the giant jagged saw, which rose and fell. On the other side of the railing, two mill hands stood next to the blade, observing it closely. The first to catch sight of me was Xephon, whom I had met but never really spoken to. Teacher Scotes then turned and gave a big smile and, not attempting to shout above the din, motioned me into their circle, where I was acknowledged with nods from everyone.

When the cut was done, one of the men pulled a lever to close the gate valve, and the blade stilled. Then he pulled a different lever to a second wheel, and the carriage returned. This left only the sound of the river underneath and sufficient quiet for Teacher Scotes to begin asking questions, having said not a word to me. Apparently he had volunteered to assist in the mill work because once everything was secured, the operators assigned us—Teacher Scotes included—simple tasks such as sweeping, carrying, plucking stuck chips from a few mechanical crevices.

Teacher Scotes had chosen this mill for precisely the reason I had noted: its unusual positioning along the rocky river. Yet what I had not noticed was the millpond they had built at an elevated point, allowing them a controlled yet accelerated flow whatever the level of the river. The speed of the blade and the consistency of its motion explained the nearly fifteen hundred linear feet a day the mill achieved. Its arrangement, construction, and results clearly impressed Teacher Scotes.

When the group disbanded, I told him I had found the demonstration interesting and asked if I could join him at a future time. Given my behavior at the gardens, I expected suspicion or refusal, but he only welcomed my request, though I admit that people were not accustomed to refusing me anything. He named the sites they planned to visit in the coming weeks, and avoiding stops in the city where family friends or acquaintances might see us, I met up with them as often as I could.

One site I especially recall was an ironworks, which sat at the head of a wide and slow-moving stream that fed a larger river in the distance, framed by woods. Where once I might have considered the details of its setup and operation to be mundane, hardly worth a notice, after this visit I saw them as remarkable.

Three buildings fronted the wide mouth of the stream. Ore deposits formed naturally in the silt, making supplies plentiful and easily acquired, and the water itself was calm and shallow but deep enough for flat-bottomed boats to take the finished product away and return with fresh supplies. Also nearby was calcium-rich gabbro aplenty. Behind the buildings the land rose to a high plateau where there was another stream, which fed a large holding pond. It was the perfect site for the work: a single placid spot that was both the source of the raw material and the finished products' link to the wider world.

The holding pond above had four gates that each fed a canal. Each gate when opened released a small waterfall into a large overshot wheel, one beside the first building, one beside the second, and two beside the third. The second building was a forge; the third, a rolling and slitting mill. But the first was most impressive. It was half wood and half stone, the stone being a massive conical tower that rose from the river basin to the plateau and was topped by a wooden walkway that ended at its opening. The tower was the blast furnace, and the workmen transported the ore and gabbro from below to the opening at the top and carted from the vast woods the charcoal they produced continuously. They fed the furnace day and night. It was lined with sandstone and, we were told, could withstand three thousand degrees.

Inside the wooden house, massive leather bellows inhaled and exhaled and stoked the flame, driven by the wheel and by long rods with hooks. Ingeniously, a cam opened the bellows, and a rock-filled box counterbalanced to close them again. By some miraculous process, molten iron flowed from the small mouth at the base of the furnace into troughs of sand. This they called pig iron, which they transferred to the second building, where workmen pounded it into bars, first by hand, then with a large mechanical hammer. Those bars in turn went to the rolling and slitting mill. By the river there was also a secluded shack, a blacksmith shop, where one man made a thousand nails a day from the stock that was not sold as bars or rods.

And so it went—from site to site, from countryside to village and back again, from the smallest shops or smiths to the largest farms and mills. We visited printers, shipbuilders, coopers, stevedores, farmers, dry goods shops, grist mills, looms, carriage makers, tinners, blacksmiths, lawyers, weavers, teachers—sometimes briefly, sometimes for half a working day, depending on how helpful or intrusive we seemed to be. Teacher Scotes questioned much, though others of us did too, and Xephon wrote voluminously in his books. I was amazed by how engrossing could be the simplest demonstrations, especially amazed by how fixed Teacher Scotes could become and, with every passing day, less comprehending of my father's disapproval of him.

Often he stood upright and unmoving, his eyes unblinking, absorbing what he witnessed. When once I found myself more entranced by him than by the work, he caught my glance and said, "Goodness, Palleias, there's little to be learned from watching me."

How strange it was, experiencing those weeks as pure excitement—I, who had lived at the very head of state. It was a period like no other in my life. I don't know which was more embarrassing, the enjoyment I felt or the fact that I had never wondered about the simple act of producing something. To see person after person and group after group transform materials, often the rawest substances of the earth but also those already shaped by others, into something else entirely, something useful, even indispensable to our well-being, moved me, filled me with a kind of hopefulness, a sense of discovery, as if it were not occurring all around me all the time and had been all my life. Perhaps there was a kind of blindness to how I had lived, though I doubt that many others saw what we were seeing, at least not in the way we were seeing it.

As exciting as this witnessing was, something else inspired me even more.

One day, while resting in shade beside the turnpike to Chester County and during one of our longer journeys, we were recounting what we had been observing—the diverse activities, large and small. About an hour into it, Teacher Scotes began commenting at length himself, which he rarely did. Case by case he described how the people we witnessed had developed plans, using knowledge they acquired, then acted on those plans: they took first the mental then the physical steps to achieve what they envisioned. This was as true, he said, for those who originated a process, hired crews, and purchased materials and tools to carry it out as it was for lone men and women who clipped nails or pulled levers. After he had talked a while, he asked us to test this proposition against examples of what *we* had observed. It was the first of several such sessions he was to lead in my presence. And it was thrilling; here we were exploring a topic—the process by which people made things—but what struck me most was not so much our answers as our method. For weeks we had amassed examples and now were seeking what they had in common and how they could be classified, something we could do only by examining them minutely.

Sometimes he gave us assignments, usually involving abstract questions such as What is justice? What is property? What is love? What is generosity? He would charge us to consider how people used such terms, seek examples (and examples and examples) that were relevant, and suggest better definitions, if we could. He guided us, but we did the venturing; he pointed out the road, but we walked it and, having walked it, began to feel that all roads could be walked and that all destinations were attainable. It was liberating. For Teacher Scotes, this approach was the best of what the ancients had bequeathed us; to master it was to make adulthood possible, to raise yourself from four legs to two, as in the riddle of the Sphinx, and face the world around you with the power to apprehend it.

Right away I tried applying our method to everything I observed: people, their habits, actions, dress, and speech; animals, roaming freely or in pens; buildings, old and new; the weather, in calm and storm. The world became my laboratory, everything a source of learning.

One day when I found myself alone with Teacher Scotes, I described what I'd been doing and how his method made me feel. I was so enthusiastic that I must have missed his reaction, because I cannot recall it, and I was eager to ask a question. If organizing observations into definitions and general propositions—induction, he called it—was so essential to knowing, did not deduction also play a role? Sometimes, I told him, having reached some understanding by his method, I then used deductions to suggest further ideas still, ideas that, given what I thought I knew, might also be true and that could be tested by new inductions—a kind of "if this, then that," where the "that," though requiring corroboration, functioned as a pointer toward even greater knowledge. I asked him, "Might this be a valid way to proceed?" I admit to being proud of the idea. And judging by the way he looked at me, I believe he was impressed by my thinking of it too.

Though part of me wanted to describe my experiences to my parents, I could not; after years of Father's reproving comments—comments that now made little sense—I knew how he would react. Instead I invented stories of what the people I was supposed to have been visiting had told me. It wasn't difficult to do; what I heard on the road was mostly repetition, anyway. I was somewhat worried that Father might want to follow up particular cases, but not overly so because what mattered to him most was not so much the cases as my ability to listen. In that way, my journeys were part tribunal, with me upon the stand, for he always said that even when we cannot listen anymore, we have at least to try and as deeply to the person at day's end as we did to the first that morning.

In my room at night, I mulled my days with Teacher Scotes, mimicking how closely he examined things. They were nights of pleasure and of wonder, and for the first time in a life spent in the company of people, I experienced the joy of being alone. The joy of thought.

It all ended not six weeks after it began, as of course it had to.

Unbeknownst to me, one morning on his way to Assembly, Father happened upon someone I was scheduled to meet with later that day, the leader of a group of loom operators. Father was in a hurry and had no time to attend to the woman, who was agitated by something the representatives had or had not done. To assuage her, he mentioned my impending visit, a visit he said he had encouraged (this was only somewhat true; I had proposed it weeks before) and that he would hear the report of our encounter when he saw me that evening. Of course I knew nothing of his promise and spent the day instead with Teacher Scotes, rather than with anyone I was scheduled to meet. That night she appeared at our door, and Father, after confronting me in her presence and hearing my excuse that I had been detained by other visits, was forced to invite her in. After she left, he interrogated me further—having clearly not believed my account—and I revealed the truth about my whereabouts. I hadn't really wanted to continue lying. Disobeying him was, to me, a grave sin.

Though until that moment I had understood the fact of my father's opposition to Teacher Scotes, I had not appreciated its intensity. As I described to him the places we had visited, he went from sitting and vacuously staring to pacing the second-floor study in which he had me trapped. He pressed me on what we had discussed; I told him, only people's methods of working. He asked if we had discussed politics; I assured him no, we had just examined how we know things, which I had found helpful, really. This only agitated him further. Then he extracted my promise never again to come within a quarter mile of Teacher Scotes. For a long time that night, I lay awake, overhearing Mother and Father downstairs in a seemingly urgent discussion, though I could not make out what they were saying.

Less than a month later, Father sponsored and led the passage of the act (1830-6-40) that enforced a belief in our national ideals and prohibited corruption of the young, in a process more accelerated than even he was typically capable of. It was one of several dozen acts that summer and hundreds that year, and it joined our voluminous statutes with hardly a notice. I doubt anyone even understood its genesis—anyone, that is, other than three people: Father, me, and Teacher Scotes.

At times that autumn, I would sit alone within the bricked-walled boundaries of our courtyard, amid the peaceful lawn and gravel walks, connected only by sound and smell to the city outside, wondering whether Teacher Scotes was angry at me for having approached him that day at the Botanical Gardens and later at the sawmill. I did feel guilty about the part I played in making his life more difficult. I did not worry because I knew that Father wanted me to stay away from Teacher Scotes more than he wanted to enforce the law. So I stayed away, but what I could not drop, what would not leave me no matter how much I deflected it, was the meaning of our time together, everything I had learned, and the question he had put to me: Can you judge for yourself?

CHAPTER 6

W‍e had turned up Broad and onto Market, where Simon's shoe shop
was. Tomorrow was a market day, so on Market Street were lines
of two- and four-horsed wagons clopping slowly in both directions and
hitched on either side. At a hundred feet wide from river to river, the street
allowed for travel even when crowded. And crowded it always was on
Market Day.

Four groups of people came out: those to sell, those to buy, those to
beg, and those to protest the rising prices and lack of work; these last
congregated on the sidewalks and read aloud from newspapers or yelled
atop crates, over the heads of listeners. The rest would be headed either
to or from the sheds, which covered three blocks, starting at Front Street,
interrupted only by the cross streets of First through Fourth. Many of
them watched us pass. I am certain they recognized Teacher Scotes. Some
would recognize me. Though he was surely of greater note, I avoided
catching eyes with anyone for fear of being accosted.

I thought it funny that a famously barefoot man frequented a shoe
shop, and perhaps Teacher Scotes enjoyed the irony too. He liked the visits
mainly, I think, because Simon welcomed anyone to converse with
Teacher Scotes, shoemaking needs or no, while he himself worked and
listened. Perhaps this policy improved his business, though judging by his
perennially dusty inventory, not so much. In addition to toppings, he
made custom shoes, and this attracted some representatives, who liked

that Simon's custom shoes did not appear so. In general, the demand for custom anything had fallen for a generation, along with our general fortunes. In turn the representatives attracted Teacher Scotes, being a fond target of his, should any be willing to talk.

Teacher Scotes admired Simon for being one of the first to bring back right- and left-footed shoes, as he admired many for their innovations. He once said of Simon that Simon was a good shoemaker because he possessed the knowledge of what a shoe was and what it was meant for. I thought, Doesn't everyone? For his part, Simon admired Teacher Scotes, and it was known that in the evenings, upstairs in his residence, he recorded the conversations he had overheard that day. Because Simon was getting on in years, these small books filled many shelves. His wife threatened to burn them every winter for fuel. In this she could not have known how prescient she was.

Though it was a modest shop, there was room for an ample gathering. Simon worked at the back, behind a railing, sitting on his low bench, leather-aproned, cradling his lapboard, surrounded by piles of pegs and nails, rows of lasts, a water bucket, and assorted tools at hand. Two apprentices worked beside him. Outside, the buildings either side of his and across the street were of brick, but Simon's was of blond wood and was unadorned. To me it seemed a bright and active workshop. Having so long plied his craft, he had little difficulty pegging and stitching while listening and from time to time observing his visitors.

On the way to the shop, Teacher Scotes never mentioned the fact of my father's seeing us and, because he had not, Xephon and Alcidia had not either, though I could sense such thoughts in their awareness. For his part, Alcidia just ignored me, as if angrily resigned to my presence. This disheartened more than angered me, for I was prone to criticizing myself too. Reactions like Alcidia's simply reinforced my uncertainties and confirmed my self-appraisal.

On the street in front of Simon's, people bustled. While I secured Betsy, the others went in, and by the time I entered, they were conversing with

Simon, who was seated on his bench. Only one other person was in the shop, a plainly dressed gentleman who was perusing a shelf of boots. Wearing a simple vest, worn trousers, and a flopped hat, he could have been almost anything. He was as young as in his thirties or as old as in his forties.

As I approached, Simon observed me with a sharp expression. He had short gray hair, a narrow face, and noticeably oversize hands, which pressed a piece of leather to his lap. When I reached the railing, Teacher Scotes said, "I imagine you two have met. Palleias, say hello to Simon. Simon, this is Palleias, Antonyn's son."

There are two reactions I get when people learn that I'm my father's son. One is to describe some difficulty they are having and what they want or need. When this happens, I am obliged to listen and note what they say. The other is what Simon did when I had first met him several years before, which is to darken somewhat, though this time he did not, because this day I was Teacher Scotes's companion.

"Welcome once again, Young Palleias," Simon said to me, rather formally.

"Business is good?" Teacher Scotes asked him.

This question, thankfully, directed Simon's attention away from me. "No better than the last time you asked or any time you've asked for years now." His manner was more sanguine than his words, as if this were a running joke between them. The room smelled of sawdust and was warming from the midday sun. Outside came the metronomic clopping of horses and the intermittent shouts from passersby.

The other man, the one who had been inspecting the boots, approached Simon and took a position next to me. He regarded us. To my left were Teacher Scotes, Xephon, and Alcidia. A sense of pride hit me, standing with them.

Simon acknowledged the man. "Founder Haydock, meet Teacher Scotes. And this is Palleias, Xephon, and Alcidia." He indicated each of us with the point of his awl. "I am doing some repair work for Founder Haydock," he said to us.

"How do you do?" Teacher Scotes said.

The man's face animated, though wryly. "Teacher Scotes," he said, talking past me at the railing. "I have heard of you. You're the one who goes around trying to prove to people that they are wrong about everything."

Teacher Scotes chuckled, and the man seemed taken aback by the reaction. "Founder Haydock, I assure you. I myself know too little to be going around disproving people of anything, let alone everything."

In the short time I had spent with him, I had witnessed this happen frequently. People who had heard of Teacher Scotes would strike up conversations, usually with the intention of combatting him on some point that they believed he believed. That was not why Teacher Scotes sought conversation, but I never saw him refuse anyone, though I did often see him disappointed by how some conversation had gone. Afterward, he would reflect at length on what he himself had done to contribute to the difficulties.

Founder Haydock wanted to know what we had been discussing. Teacher Scotes explained that we had visited Assembly, where an act to approve one company's plan to build the first rail line had been defeated. Founder Haydock wanted to know what a rail line was: being a country man who operated a small ironworks out on the Susquehanna, he wasn't privy to all that was happening and had missed yesterday's *Peep Hole's Daily*. The *Peep Hole's Daily* ("Your Eye on the Nation") was the Philadelphia newspaper that described the acts scheduled for vote.

As they spoke, I stepped back to facilitate their exchange. Xephon and Alcidia drew closer, and a man and two women who had entered the shop, seeing us and, I think, recognizing Teacher Scotes, took up positions just behind us as well. Then someone else came in and joined too, making for an audience of sorts. Throughout, Simon looked up and down from his work.

"Of course the people's will is the arbiter of the right and the good," Founder Haydock said, somewhat out of the blue, I thought, but seemingly in response to Teacher Scotes's account of the vote we had heard.

Still a few more people entered and came over to investigate. Most of them had likely not come in for shoes but had noticed something happening from the street.

"The right and the good," Teacher Scotes said. "Now *there* is a worthy topic." Despite the newly formed gathering, Teacher Scotes directed his attention only at Founder Haydock. For him, conversations were best one-on-one. He would neither play to the others nor request their participation. "What do you say, Founder Haydock? Shall we explore it together? I myself value any chance to better understand this topic and always appreciate meeting others who share my interest. I find it helpful to discuss ideas, rather than just ponder them alone."

With one hand on the railing, Founder Haydock, still floppy-hatted, sidled into the space I had vacated between him and Teacher Scotes. Surrounding them were the three of us, and surrounding us were the others, who now stood a few rows deep. It occurred to me that we had formed a mini amphitheater of our own.

"Everyone knows what is right and good," Founder Haydock said, a touch aggressively for my taste. I knew from experience that even people who said they wished to discuss such subjects often did not really wish to.

"Tell me then what they are so that I may benefit from your understanding," Teacher Scotes said.

"When the people voted to limit the importing of iron, that was right and good."

"Ah, but that is not what I asked you," Teacher Scotes said and waited. Founder Haydock looked puzzled. "What I believe we claim to be seeking," Teacher Scotes said, "is the *meaning* of right and good, what they are in themselves, what is their definition, their essence. What you offer is an *example* of the right and good."

"What do you mean?"

"Well, if you were to ask me to define 'work,' let us say, and I pointed to Simon here and said, 'Shoemaking, that is work,' would you find that to be a satisfactory answer?"

"No."

"Or if I said 'shipbuilding' or 'tinning' or 'milling'?"

"I understand your point. Those are examples but not the definition of 'work.'"

"Exactly. And how might we state such a definition?"

From Founder Haydock's thoughtful expression, it appeared that his belligerence had been diverted or softened. "I would say: to work is to produce something useful to yourself or for exchange with someone else, whether as an employee, farmer, artisan, or independent proprietor."

Teacher Scotes raised his hands. "Excellent! That seems a fine definition, as good as any I've heard. I can see that you and I make fruitful discussion partners. So, given that distinction, shall we return to our original question?"

Without hesitation, Founder Haydock offered, "The right and good are that which the people want."

"Very good. Let us then proceed to examine that proposition and see if together we can corroborate or improve upon it."

Founder Haydock looked down and up several times. "There is nothing to examine," he said. "Everyone knows that it is true." He appeared a touch ill at ease.

I attempted to assess the group behind us, but those adjacent had pressed close, and it was difficult to turn. Over their heads I could see that the room had mostly filled. People might even have been amassing outside the door. I peeked at Xephon, who gave a little wink. Next to him, Alcidia watched intently.

"Then I am still to catch up," Teacher Scotes said. "For while I do not disagree with what you said, neither do I know enough yet to agree. That is why I appreciate our investigation."

"You just want to prove it wrong, as people say you always do." Founder Haydock's manner appeared now more as at the outset.

"People do me an injustice if that is what they say. But perhaps this is not a conversation we need have now. Perhaps we should part amicably, with my appreciation for having made your acquaintance, and agree that if we encounter each other again, we can resume our discussion then." Teacher Scotes extended his hand, but Founder Haydock did not take it.

"Go ahead and disprove it, if you can," he said.

How Simon was getting any work done I don't know, but he continued stitching and, in his manner, taking us in.

Teacher Scotes hesitated, pressing his lips together, though his eyes stayed bright and directly attentive to Founder Haydock. He stood hip against railing, straight, not propping himself. There was nothing that energized him more than just this kind of discussion with a willing partner. I had sometimes wished that even when partners were unwilling, he would press ahead for our collective benefit, but I had witnessed enough exchanges to know that he would not. At the same time, he tended to take people at their word, and this man had expressed a desire to continue.

"Let's do this, then," Teacher Scotes said. "You formulated the proposition thus: 'The right and good are that which the people want.'" Founder Haydock's eyes went up and down. "So it would seem to follow," Teacher Scotes said, "that it is right and good to *do* what the people want."

Founder Haydock eventually gave the slightest nod.

"Now, when we say 'the people,'" Teacher Scotes continued, "to whom are we referring? To all the people? To every American citizen?"

"Certainly not. You are playing some kind of trick already. Everybody knows that when we say 'the people,' we mean the majority of people as expressed through their representatives in Assembly."

Teacher Scotes raised his eyebrows but in a friendly way. "My dear Founder Haydock, I can see that you have a very bad impression of me. For myself, I am only trying to do my part to ensure precision in our discourse. Perhaps you've found, as I have, that sometimes it's the smallest assumption, hidden and implicit in the way we use language, that trips us in the end and blocks our understanding. At any rate, while I wish you didn't suspect me so, I do appreciate your holding us to account in how we approach our subject."

"That may be," Founder Haydock said. "But it seems to me that we move too slowly, that my point was the next logical step."

"And here we are: the right and good are what the people want as expressed through the votes of their representatives in Assembly."

"Yes, and I have seen many occasions where reps who did not vote as the people wanted were thrown out in the very next election," Founder Haydock said.

"As have I. So our reps do vote then according to what the people want, more or less?"

"Yes, which is the very virtue of our system, would you not agree?" Here, Founder Haydock scanned the crowd, at first as if seeking approval for what he had said, then as if gauging who was listening.

"Perhaps," Teacher Scotes said, directing his attention only at Founder Haydock. "But you may be a step ahead of me, because I still think we are investigating the meaning of what is right and good. And it would seem difficult to assess the virtue of our system, as you say, before knowing what *is* the right and good. We might send ourselves in circles."

At this some people laughed. Teacher Scotes did not acknowledge the laughter, but Founder Haydock jerked to look again into the crowd; in doing so he gazed directly past me.

"If you say so," he said, looking back.

"Let me take your lead on one point of method, Founder Haydock. Let's do begin our examination with examples, for that is the best means by which to understand the essence of a thing. Would you agree?"

"Better that than to stick our heads into the clouds and talk only about hoity-toity, airy-fairy, loosey-goosey nonsense." Saying this, Founder Haydock fluttered his hands above his head and widened his eyes. At this the crowd gave a big laugh—some also fluttered their hands—which seemed to please Founder Haydock, who for the first time showed his crooked teeth. People of course knew that he was making reference to the production some years ago of *The Clouds* by Playwright Stephens at the Chestnut Street Theater, which poked fun at some prominent intellectuals, most of all Teacher Scotes, and in which Teacher Scotes was portrayed as ridiculing our traditions and insulting the people in general. Looking back, I see this accusation as being flatly unjust; if anyone had his head in the clouds, it was not Teacher Scotes but people like me.

"Quite so," Teacher Scotes said, with a small smile. "Now, taking account of actual votes in recent years, have we not seen occasions where in one year the reps passed one act only to pass another a few years later that legislated the opposite of the first?"

"What do you mean?"

"Take, for instance, the case of steamboats. First they were permitted, then they were prohibited, now they are permitted again. Three separate acts, one reversing the prior and then again."

"So? That was because the people changed their opinion of them." Upon speaking, Founder Haydock gave a worried look.

"No doubt," Teacher Scotes said. "Yet this would seem to contradict our proposition that the right and good are that which the people want."

"What do you mean?"

"Well, by judging one act better than another, we seem to be referring to a different standard of right and good than just that the people wanted it. There must be something other than the people's desire that we consider. For example, the consequences of the act."

"And?" Founder Haydock seemed wary.

"Consider this. A few moments ago, you mentioned the act that limited the importing of iron as being an example of the right and good."

Founder Haydock stood taller and with an edge of defiance. "It was," he said. "Before that, merchants from every state bought the cheaper imports, instead of our bars, rods, and nails, and I almost had to shut down and release my ten men. Without that law we all might have been out of work, and work is not easy to find these days."

"Yes, and that would have been tragic, I can see. But it also seems to me that you have changed your argument, for in stipulating that the act was right and good, you first did so by saying it was right and good because the people wanted it, but just now you did so by referencing its consequences, specifically its consequences to you and your men."

"I still don't follow."

"To consider the point from a different angle, let's ask ourselves how others might have been affected by the act. For example, what of the farmers or carpenters who bought the rods and nails to repair their implements or to construct buildings and houses? It would seem that prior to the act's passing, they could purchase their iron more cheaply by importing it, making life a little easier for them and making their food and houses less expensive for the rest of us."

"But that is not what the people wanted."

"Just so. In fact, is it not true that whatever the people want can be brought up for a vote? That any act may be proposed and voted on without restriction?"

"Of course. Ours would not be a true democracy if that were not so."

"Now let us say that some rep was to sponsor an act to repeal the import blockage and allow citizens to again buy iron from foreign markets, iron cheaper than that which you can produce in your foundry. Is it not possible that such an act might be passed by a majority?"

"Well . . . I suppose anything is possible."

"And were that to happen, being an expression of what the people wanted, would such an act not also be an example of the right and good?"

"You are just posing hypotheticals."

"While we are posing hypotheticals, shall we consider another? Not long after our founding, a law was passed abolishing slavery and the slave trade, much to the chagrin of our southern neighbors. It was a close vote, but it passed nonetheless, and now slavery exists nowhere in our thirteen states and has not for some decades. Now all citizens, no matter their race, are considered just that: full citizens. So that law, too, was an expression of the people and, I assume, therefore also an example of the right and good."

"That is absolutely true and a good example of what I have been saying. Slavery was an abomination, and it was a glorious day when that act passed. It happened not long before I was born, by the way."

"You and I agree most definitely in our estimation of that act. It may indeed have been the best vote we have ever taken. Now here's the hypothetical. We agree that any act may come before Assembly to be voted on?"

"As I said, that is the essence of our system, to use your word."

Teacher Scotes smiled gently. "True. So what if an act proposing the reinstatement of slavery were passed? Would that not too be a reflection of what the people wanted and thus an example of the right and good?"

One could see that Founder Haydock had had just about enough and was probably regretting having instigated this exchange in the first place. At this point, he seemed to be looking for a way to exit gracefully without having to proceed another step. With a stern expression, he said, "You are twisting things again. My point was not that a majority vote in Assembly *determines* the right and good. Clearly, slavery or a lifting of the import ban would be bad. My point was simply that the vote is the best way to *implement* the right and good."

"Wonderful, Founder Haydock!" Teacher Scotes said. "Now we truly are advancing our cause, it seems to me. For we are now distinguishing between the *standard* of the right and good, which is where we started and which we now suggest is something independent of what the people want—and the best political system to *achieve* the right and good. Perhaps that should be our next examination."

"Bravo, gentlemen," someone in the back shouted, to some applause.

The feeling in the room seemed genuinely benevolent toward both men. I was glad to see it, especially given the reception Teacher Scotes had just received in Assembly. It was like that for him: he could be both beloved and reviled at once—by the same individual, the same crowd, the same nation.

But Founder Haydock did not project the same benevolence. You could tell that he was irritated—probably in part by having been unable to sustain his position but also, it seemed, by something more. Hunched, he shot a glance at me, Xephon, and Alcidia, accidentally poking me when trying to indicate us in the cramped space. He snapped at Teacher Scotes, "How old are these men here?" He appeared to be faintly shaking.

"Not all are over thirty, Founder Haydock," Teacher Scotes said, with an odd calm, in contrast to Founder Haydock. "For example, Young Palleias here."

"Then I am leaving. You may be indifferent, sir, but I for one do not intend to be arrested for committing a crime." And he bumped my shoulder and squeezed past and into the crowd, calling out, "I bid you good day, sir."

I watched him reach the door and push it open; it resisted because of the crowd outside. No sooner had he exited than people backfilled the path he'd made, like molten iron into his foundry's sandy pig, though the door remained ajar longer than needed. I thought someone on the outside might be propping it open to ascertain what was happening inside till I noticed another man wresting his way in, plowing the reverse path that Founder Haydock had just vacated. He didn't have to get far for me to see that it was Father.

CHAPTER 7

He should have been in Assembly for at least a few more hours. Obviously he had sought us out, having guessed where Teacher Scotes might be.

The crowd murmured in recognition of the tall black-coated man who was politely but firmly wading toward us, excusing himself. With a kind of aggrieved awe, which results from accepting a man as your superior when you've been told that you are his, they pushed back to give him passage. He reached me and said, "Follow me," raised his chin and said, "Pardon the interruption, Simon, but I need to borrow him," then turned and exited by way of the same human gully. He acknowledged no one else. I tailed him through the parted crowd.

The light was sharply white beyond the awning, then shaded again under the next awning, and like that—alternately bright and dim along the sidewalk—all the way to Tenth Street. I kept pace and avoided colliding with some hogs and then a farmer who was shoveling waste into a wagon, none of which Father seemed to notice. At Eleventh, before we reached a group of protesters, he turned the corner, continued several steps, and stopped. I reached him.

It is uncomfortable to recall what being alone with him was sometimes like back then. When the object of his full attention, I could feel emotions from a much younger version of myself. He stood with one hand resting on a post; his presence was commanding. I knew that he expected me to speak, and when I didn't, he calmly said, "I'm listening."

"Yes, sir."

"Tell me this hasn't been going on for weeks."

"What, Father?"

"Palleias."

"No, just today." This seemed to relax him some, but only some. "I was returning to the city when I encountered them crossing the river. Since we were following the same road, we walked together. Then, when we got to Assembly, I decided to go in because my time was free and because I hadn't attended for a while."

Not tolerating the diversion, he said, "You are free to attend Assembly any time you want."

"Yes, sir."

"And what did you discuss?"

"Very little. Just about how Alcidia wanted to witness Assembly and Teacher Scotes agreed to take him." He waited. "Alcidia asked a question or two about procedure, and Teacher Scotes explained."

His look was searching. "And that speech he gave? What did you make of that?"

"To be honest, I didn't know what to make of it."

"And Simon's?"

"A customer started asking him questions."

He stared. Then he inhaled slowly and seemed to relax. "I don't know what to think, Palleias. . . . Did you not promise me? Did the words 'I promise' not leave your lips?"

Eventually I answered, "Yes."

"So you break your promise but do it in a way that I will discover it. I suppose you are to be commended for your lack of stealth. Was this an act of defiance of some kind?"

"No, sir."

"What, then?" I could not answer. "Palleias." He seemed genuinely at a loss, and I could tell he did not appreciate my reticence. "It pains me to say this, but sometimes you act just like a child. You say you understand, you lead me to believe that you do, until you do something that makes me think you never understood."

"Don't say that, Father."

His eyes widened. "I shouldn't say it because it's false or because it's true?" He waited. Then he looked away and back again and said, "Perhaps you no longer trust what I tell you."

"No, that is not it."

"Perhaps you question my wisdom in such matters."

"No."

"On this particular issue, might I not know better?" Eventually he said, more gently, "It's the advantage of having a father who's a reasonably well-known representative, wouldn't you say?"

Some people squeezed past on the sidewalk. A carriage jangled by. I made as if to observe them all. When I looked back, he had reestablished the firmness of his gaze. "I don't think you fully appreciate the damage that being seen with him can cause, if you are to join me in two short years. He has made himself a bellwether. Do you want the public to see you as just another of his sheep?"

His words startled me. He had never claimed that associating with Teacher Scotes could threaten my career. This better explained his original prohibition. Momentarily I, too, worried over what I might have done. But his description of Teacher Scotes as the head of a mob-like herd seemed the opposite of the man I knew.

"Palleias?"

"Yes, I understand."

"*Do* you trust me?"

"Of course."

"Good." Then he added, with greater calm, "Let's hope little damage was done."

It might have ended there, but being anxious now myself, I said, "It was only a few hours."

"Even so, how many people saw you? They know who you are, Palleias. You are not a private citizen. You are almost as well known as I.

Why else do I have you travel the state to meet with people? I don't need you to do that." He tapped the post. Then he made a shooing motion. "So long as it doesn't end up in the *Peep Hole's Daily.*"

I hadn't thought of that either and wondered how worried I should be.

"Palleias!" The voice came from behind me. At the nearby corner stood Teacher Scotes, Alcidia, and Xephon. It was Teacher Scotes who had called out and now approached, the others following.

I glanced at Father; his face had already assumed that nondescript unreadability he excelled at. Without a glance at me, he said, "We'll discuss this more at home."

Upon reaching us, Teacher Scotes addressed me. "I didn't have an opportunity to say goodbye, Palleias. I wanted to let you know that we'll be making excursions over the next few weeks and that you are welcome to join us."

The five of us made a small circle, a concerned-looking Xephon and Alcidia at each of Teacher Scotes's shoulders, my father just off mine. That the two older men stood together in my presence was another of the day's unrealities, and I felt a mild disorienting sway. To me they were like two commanders meeting on the battlefield—my father, the tall, handsome, groomed pillar of health; Teacher Scotes, the unkempt, scraggly, disproportionately bodied go-about, the unlikely paragon of virtue.

So far as I knew, they hadn't spoken for decades. I was somewhat shocked that Teacher Scotes had extended the invitation in his presence, and I waited for Father to answer for me now. When he did not, I understood the bind I was in. Of course I had to decline Teacher Scotes's offer; he would know why, and for this I again felt shame. I said, "Thank you for your company today." My formal tone jarred even me, and I was careful to avoid the appellation "Teacher" because Father despised it. "And thank you for your invitation. But I am much occupied with the people's business and cannot fairly abandon it to attend your sessions."

Teacher Scotes eyed me pleasantly for longer than was comfortable. Then he turned to my father. "Representative Antonyn, please forgive my manners. Allow me to introduce Xephon, and here is Alcidia, whom you may have heard of." He twisted once in each direction as he introduced them.

"Xephon," my father said, extending a hand to one and then the other. "And Alcidia, yes. I believe this young man is known widely and deservedly so. How is your family, Alcidia?"

"Very well, sir," Alcidia said. "At present they are enjoying time abroad. Thank you kindly." He bowed slightly, and his proud bearing, athletic build, golden curly hair—and my father's nod in return—pricked me with jealousy.

Upon further thought, my father said to Alcidia, "I have heard that you have ambitions to be a representative. From what I surmise, you have a promising career ahead."

"Thank you very much, sir."

Father may have also been thinking, Then why are you associating with this man? but gave no indication, not even one that I could detect. On the street beside us, the traffic built—now of strollers, carriages, and a few men on horseback. Preparations for Market Day would soon end, and I suspected that Father would prefer we not remain at this spot much longer.

He placed one hand on my shoulder as if to initiate the process of leaving. "We bid you gentlemen good day," he said. But before we took a stride, he addressed Teacher Scotes one last time. Not impolitely, he said, "We all know this to be a country with generous laws, tolerant in sentiment. But you of course are also aware that such liberality does not imply license and that the people's generosity is not without limits. As well as anyone, you understand the law and what we are free to do—and not." His tone was no stronger than if he had been commenting on the weather.

Just as cordially, Teacher Scotes responded, "You do me a service in reminding me of that. My age, and the fact that we have so many laws, sometimes distracts me from the knowledge of what I may and may not do."

In a tone of supportive counsel, my father added, "You are aware that it takes but one citizen whom you may have aggrieved for any reason to accuse you, however fairly or not."

"I am well advised," Teacher Scotes said.

The two regarded each other till Father said, "Good day" and guided me away.

After we separated, Father returned to Assembly. I retrieved Betsy, and we wandered—to places of no great import, other than that we loved them. We visited the fountains at the old City Centre waterworks and drifted northward through the undeveloped district of Spring Garden, then east to the Kensington docks. There, on my favorite spot, we rested under the elm that had replaced Colonist Penn's, which, sadly, had fallen when I was a boy. Nearby, a lad in tattered trousers fished with a stick from the grassy slope and a large gold-banded ship at pier swallowed and disgorged barrels, which were raised on many arms and passed to and from the shipside drays, accompanied by the cries of men and jingling of harnesses, and against the pier the water lapped, and the wood creaked and knocked. For the first time that day, I felt hungry, having eaten nothing since morning.

I recognized the ship. It was the *Good Friends*, one of Merchant Girard's. His own wharf was a few blocks south, across from his home and office. When I was a boy, this port received a hundred ships a day from other states and countries, some traveling thousands of miles to exchange their cargo. These days we were fortunate to see a third as many.

I sat there some good time. By late afternoon, the activity had calmed. The loaded ship had sailed. A last few ships passed in the orange light, their white squares and triangles floating in each direction.

Watching others work had for me become a means of grieving, I think; it was what I took to when feeling most unhappy. Father was holding to his proscription with as great an intensity as before, for reasons clearer to me now than then. He feared that associating with Teacher Scotes would taint me ruinously, and as always, my instinct was to accede. No doubt he had good cause for worry—certainly I did not doubt his acumen—and the risk he cited was grave. Just hours before, I had felt the promise of a new beginning. Now I felt worse than on the day I had stopped seeing Teacher Scotes a year ago.

But I was also long past deeming acquiescing to be proper. I thought, Should I not convince myself of what my father claimed? Should I not judge also? Alcidia, for one, had chosen just the opposite: to learn from Teacher Scotes precisely to bolster his ambitions, ambitions that were similar to mine. Likely he was wrong and Father right, but I also knew that long experience, like Father's, could sometimes fossilize your assumptions. Perhaps people valued Teacher Scotes more today than years ago, when Father knew him best. Perhaps they would be more magnanimous in appraising me than others. And it was not as though I planned to see him every day. Good conscience bade me test the proposition further. Yet I also knew that I could loll with Betsy for endless days and still be in a muddle. Father, on the other hand, was certain.

Perhaps to question more acutely was precisely what Father wanted from me; perhaps my customary unquestioning acceptance was why he saw me as a child who required his direction. But if I were to draw him out, I'd have to do it now, when next I saw him, when he would assume that I was only raising what I would have raised had we not been interrupted. As he himself had said, we would discuss this more at home. I had but one chance to try, before things hardened, though I was anything but confident in the outcome.

CHAPTER 8

I had lingered at the pier so long that by the time I reached home, turning from Market into our brick archway, the light was dim. In our courtyard the sound of Betsy's hoofs no longer echoed, and Father and Mother appeared at a front window. Probably they were holding supper. I stabled Betsy and rolled the wagon into place between the carriage and gig.

"Are you hungry?" Father asked upon my entering. He seemed more sanguine now. "Your mother has spent much trouble in preparing your favorite meal."

I could tell this from the smell alone. Though we raised chickens on our small farm, we rarely ate them, because Mother had to turn them many hours to sufficiently soften the meat.

We ate at one end of the long table in the east room, the large dining room where Father entertained up to forty at a time, just as Doctor Franklin had once done. When his ship was lost during his return from France, after he had signed the treaty that ended our war, his family, too, was drowned—in turmoil. His grandchildren possessed the house for many years, finally relinquishing it in disrepair. It was then that Father bought it, for a price generous by more than double what anyone else was offering.

The north and south windows were open, and a breeze floated about our necks. Instead of the pewter, Mother had set the porcelain, which she normally kept for guests. She was clothed simply, in a white cotton print dress. Being thin and tall, especially with her hair up, she could make even modest attire appear elegant. Father was in vest and open collar. The candles on the table and the fireplace flickered both in the room and on the windows, which were darkening.

Despite my transgression, the mood was pleasurably cordial. Even so I decided not to reengage my father right away, to let them both relax from the day's efforts. Mother's day would have been especially long. She had not only prepared a difficult meal but had attended three or four societies because Father knew that she could be a better ambassador than he. She was well read and able to converse on many subjects and had a kindness that was widely known. But even had I planned to raise my questions then, I could not have because no sooner had we started than we were interrupted by slow footsteps at the front.

People often came at mealtime, hoping Father to be at home. He did not discourage them, would even invite them in for tea or to dine. I awaited the knock, then rose to greet whoever had come. There upon our steps was Merchant Girard and a young woman on his elbow, a grand-niece, I presumed. I pulled the door and bade them enter.

"I am very sorry to trouble you at home," Merchant Girard said in his accented voice, his open eye directed right at me. I felt privileged that he had apologized to me and had not waited for my parents. "I was hoping to speak to your father and am somewhat pressed to visit."

As at Assembly that morning, he wore his dark broadcloth and white cravat, and his thin hair was combed neatly from his temples. I led him to the dining room with effusive salutations, as I knew my parents would expect. Father especially afforded him respect, more than he did most citizens. The young woman remained behind.

Father and Mother had already risen. "Merchant Girard," Mother said. "Please do come in and join us at supper." They approached, one from each side of the table.

"To what do we owe this honor?" Father said.

Merchant Girard took Mother's hands. "Madam, pray, forgive my intrusion, and thank you for your kind offer. But I wish to be brief with your husband's time. Would you allow me just a minute of your evening?"

"Of course, sir," my mother said. "Palleias and I will take our leave. You are welcome to stay as long as you like."

Father had not signaled me to stay, as often he would, for the benefit of my training. We passed into the adjacent room, Mother continuing back into the kitchen. I sat upon the sofa at the shared wall, where I could overhear the conversation.

In a kind of strained politeness, Merchant Girard again apologized for his unannounced visit, but he was, he said, traveling the next day and felt the matter could not wait for his return. He admitted to much regret at the outcome of the day's vote on debt relief and some measure of betrayal, he was pained to say, at how it had transpired.

"I was most especially surprised by your vote, sir," he said.

Father acknowledged the offense but quietly suggested that he had not in fact promised to vote a certain way—that he never could do so—or to deliver the votes of others but only to consider with utmost seriousness Merchant Girard's position, alongside the concerns of Father's many constituents and the nation's will. While acknowledging the burdensome consequences of the new act to Merchant Girard, he said he also knew well the long history of proven ability and patriotism "of such a great man as yourself." Father was referring to Merchant Girard's outsized loan to the National Bank many years back, before the issue of paper currency, when our national funds were all but depleted.

"It would seem that my patriotism affords me little," Merchant Girard said. "My financial situation aside, I experienced again today my scant influence upon our citizenry. It would seem in my old age I have become an object of disapprobation." He proceeded to recount the many costs he had borne across the years. We all knew his story. With each Distribution he had lost some land, which he had once farmed for the purpose of stocking his fleet, and thereupon had to reduce the number of ships he built and sailed. While he still lived and worked in his ample home on Water Street, he had given up his others. He had built schools and hospitals in a Philadelphia that returned him nothing. "And at your request," he reminded my father, "I did not prosecute those brick and lumber thieves who tunneled onto my property, accounting for their lack of employment at the time." For these and other actions he had come to expect a certain regard from his political representatives and his fellow citizens. Not to mention for his generous donations to their recurring election campaigns.

"I regret how today's events must appear to you," my father said. "And I assure you that you have my allegiance. I know that you appreciate the delicate balance I must keep, that sometimes I must say or do things publicly that appear to be against you, even though I am well aware of your worth to us all and am duty-bound to defend you in the end. If I am combative in my speech sometimes, it is only because combat is inherent to my profession. Perhaps you would appreciate my position more if you heard the desperate stories that Palleias and I daily hear. But leaving that aside—and here is my most important request—please tell me if there is something I might do to mitigate today's effects."

"You may sponsor the repeal of the act," Merchant Girard said. "That is why I came without delay. As we both know, once the act is in effect, there will be little remedy."

At this there was a pause.

"It is a legitimate request," my father said. "Are you sure you cannot join us at table? We can discuss the matter at length."

"Thank you, no. If I stayed, I could only press upon you the effect that the act will have upon my family and my business. But I have done that already, when it was first proposed. Permit me to remind you that I have numerous loans outstanding, some of which date to our last time of difficulty, and which many of your colleagues asked me to extend, against my better judgment. Not to recover my principal would seriously undermine me."

"Of course I will do everything in my power not to let that happen," Father said. "As your long experience tells you, what one piece of legislation takes away another can give."

"I regret to say that my long experience also tells me that the nation of my youth, the one before our revolution, when we lived under what was then termed the tyranny of the British king, was not so meddlesome as this."

It was then that Mother returned to discover me sitting against the wall and beckoned me to follow her upstairs, where I could no longer overhear. But I could not have missed much, because by the time we reached the second floor, the front door had opened and closed, and I went to the window to dimly see the old man and young woman navigate our steps and then our courtyard. I immediately went back down to find Father.

He had returned to the dining room and taken his seat, one arm extended on the table before him, the other over the back of his chair. He appeared subdued, the stamp of penitence upon him, till at last he acknowledged my presence.

"Go and find your mother," he said, "and tell her that if she wishes, we may resume our meal."

By the time we had resettled, my father had set three glasses and poured wine from the cooler we kept on the sideboard. He sipped absentmindedly while Mother served more meat and greens. We ate quietly, both Mother and I surreptitiously regarding Father.

He looked drained. I did not often see him like this. Rarely did he lose his energy, though the people's business could be fatiguing. Now he appeared dejected, as if by something more than Merchant Girard's visit. There was nothing to do for the moment but eat, and we became a voiceless triangle—he seated at the head; I, at his right; Mother, at his left, across from me. Their faces pulsed in the candlelight.

Earlier in the day, at water's edge, it had occurred to me that you could know a person for a long time—your entire life even—and still not really know him. Until just the summer before, I had never known of Father's association with Teacher Scotes, a youthful relationship that perhaps had influenced him in ways I did not understand. This was not the first time this had happened. Some years ago, on a night like this when Father's spirits seemed as low, Mother had taken me aside and shared another fact I had not known.

When he was a boy, not long after the war had ended and the National Constitution was ratified, his father had owned one of the largest farms in the state, west of the city, on a prime spot that gave him access to fertile soil, much timber, and river transportation to markets outside of Philadelphia. He had built it up across years, purchasing lots from others who moved westward still, cleared them slowly, chopping what he could and girdling what he could not. He established mills and other artisanal operations across his holdings, and he hired a substantial crew to farm his lands and man his ventures. Gradually, he achieved wealth and fame, becoming known as one of the "thousand-acre" men, though his holdings were in fact much larger. He was very proud of what he'd done and was especially pleased to have helped retire our war debts and assisted those who fled the British occupation of '77. He was also a champion of the Greek democratic ideal that had overspread the country by then, so much so that he named his only son Antonyn.

Then came the first Distribution, passed by the first Assembly. Virtually that entire Assembly had been elected on the promise of it, and it passed easily in an early session. The act limited the holding of large estates by single families and required the passing of what were deemed excessive lands and properties to others who had less. By the time it was fully implemented, much of my grandparents' property had been taken, and they settled after that on about a hundred acres of wheat, barley, some vegetables, and livestock.

Some of the lower sort from southern and northern sections of the city moved west onto plots carved from the newly distributed lands, and under the act, the plots were never to be increased from those original demarcations. This rule changed somewhat in later Distributions, after my grandfather had passed. To hear Mother tell it, my grandfather accepted the act and did not complain, but she suggested, without quite saying so, that Father was affected deeply, that it touched his young life in a way that seldom abates in anyone.

The outlines of the story of course I knew but not the part about Father. It was, she said, his first experience of the forces endemic to his homeland, and he had learned to both respect and fear them as, sooner or later, I would too. Father had once said to me that Merchant Girard reminded him of my grandfather. I wondered whether he was thinking of that now.

We continued to eat in silence, leaving Father to his thoughts. Only after some time did he revive, though now more agitated, more as he had been at Simon's.

"So did you learn your lesson today?" he said.

His manner was so altered that I felt I could but nod.

Mother rose to clear the table. We had never hired servants, though we could easily have afforded them. People appraised this policy differently. To some, there was virtue in providing the unemployed with income. To others, there was vice in rending society into classes, more so than it already was. To still others, there remained a whiff of the old slavery in the policy, for they equated wages with bondage. All told, because more people seemed to oppose the idea, Father felt it better to do without, and Mother was supportive. Only when Mother was about to leave the room did Father express his appreciation for the meal, which I seconded, and she acknowledged sweetly. All I could think was, Please return. But she did not.

"Why the long face?" he said. I watched him finger the stem of his glass without raising it.

"You look tired, sir."

He had pushed his wrist against his temple but removed it at my observation. "I am all right."

It wasn't often that I sat this close to him and for this long. Either I was traveling, or he was otherwise engaged. Even his meals he took quickly, when he took them at home at all. As exhausted as he was, he still cut a great appearance. His vest was unbuttoned, his chest broad. He had a jawline that people called square and hair that was graying only at the temples.

"Can I get you anything?" I asked.

"No, thank you."

It was hardly the moment to challenge him, which is how he would interpret any questions. But whatever his mood, to delay would be worse: it would only prove me inconstant in his eyes.

"Father, may I ask you something?"

"Of course." His voice was testy, so I did not continue right away. Then he said, without the heat, "If you are concerned about the damage of your action, worry not. I am certain nothing will come of it."

"I am relieved at that. I hadn't realized what could happen."

This he should have chastised, but he instead nodded, as if lacking sufficient energy to think about my words. "Don't worry about *him*, either," he said. "He will not pursue you. If you keep your distance, he'll keep his." Then he gave a look, to ensure, I gathered, that he had correctly surmised my concern.

I mentioned then that Teacher Scotes had claimed last year to know him before I was born, and I asked whether this was true. He admitted freely that before his first election, he had spent a little time with Teacher Scotes, thinking he could learn; instead he discovered that Teacher Scotes had nothing good to teach, that his students were perceived as having questionable judgment, and that having questionable judgment was the worst reputation a representative could have.

I said, "I imagine that when you left him, you worried that you might have hurt your election chances. Did you understand immediately that he was a liability?"

"Not fully," he said. "That came later."

"So you left him for a different reason?"

"As I said, I found what he taught to be of little worth, even odious."

I knew of nothing odious in what Teacher Scotes taught. "Looking back, do you think that being with him did in fact hurt your candidacy?"

"You know well that I won that election handily." He regarded me. I nodded. Then he said, "I left before it could hurt me. Why the questions, suddenly?"

"I wonder if people's perceptions of Teacher Scotes may have changed."

"He is as disparaged as always. He comports himself no differently today from then."

"Some people seem to like him."

"You are speaking of a few young men and women who have no better occupation than to walk the streets and chat idly?"

"Alcidia likes him."

"Alcidia is a dangler and a fox."

To this I could respond nothing since Father had complimented Alcidia to his face that very morning. Eyeing me, he then said, "Palleias, what is all this? Twenty-five years tells me that I know whereof I speak. Do you really feel the need to question me? Thankfully, you have the benefit of my experience."

"It's just that I thought—"

"Well *don't* think. Not about this."

That silenced me. Though I had fantasized otherwise, my questions were the last thing he wanted. All he sought was a firmer commitment this time that I be true, to impress on me the gravity of my error, and to ensure that I would not sin again. But I was not quite ready to relent, so I ventured, "Recently I have been thinking that last year, when we first discussed it, I never told you what it was like being with him. What it was like for me. I never described my experience to you."

"Because you knew it was irrelevant. At any rate, I know what it was like."

"You do?"

"Of course. He asked questions, provoked you, got you thinking, stirred you up." He waited, then gestured as if to say, And? "Anyone can question, Palleias. Anyone can tear down. He is not so innocent as you might think." Then he seemed to switch the subject. "This morning, for the hours that you followed him around, were you not concerned that you might be putting *him* at risk?"

This answer I delayed giving. "He does not approve of others judging on his behalf."

"Is that so?" Our large house creaked. The breeze through the windows smelled of charcoal. Given Father's remarks about Teacher Scotes's lack of innocence, I decided that sharing my experience would only inflame him.

Then he inhaled dramatically. "What I described to you of Scotes is all you need know. As I said, you seem to doubt the truth of it."

"I don't. . . . I hardly know him. And you know the people better than anyone. But . . . he does not seem to be *only* reviled."

"He does not have to be *only* reviled to undermine you." He squinted. "Is this of any consequence? Of what possible bearing does it have on what you did?" He showed his palms, just as Teacher Scotes sometimes did. Then fatigue overtook him again, and he closed his eyes, touching them with thumb and finger. Holding that position, he added, "I am very tired and disappointed enough not to trust what I might say. May we discuss this another time?"

He did not rise at once. I could have detained him further, but I did not, and the moment was lost. But before leaving, he revived himself to make one last pronouncement. Standing beside the table and looking down, he said, "Having chosen to break your promise and to question me rather than renew it, you leave me no choice but to tell you this. If I catch you again in Scotes's presence, I will take it as your decision to reject my counsel, and I will have to withdraw my support for your career. Palleias, you are my son, you will always be my son, and you know that I act only in your interest. But you have demonstrated that you cannot be trusted to do the same, so I must press upon you even harder the consequences of your thoughtlessness. I will withdraw my support, and if you think you can get elected without me, you are free to try. But I assure you that the first question will be why I am not backing you, and that question alone will sink you." He awaited my response, then took my silence as license to leave me all alone.

Part of me did not believe that he would so blithely shatter my career. He had only wanted one profession for me, was even more committed to it than I. But if I'm honest, what I really feared was something different: the possibility of ending up entirely on my own. That if I disobeyed again, he might release me to the winds and leave me unguided in total, leave me to navigate the world alone. This, I understood, was what I'd felt earlier that morning, on the Darby Road, when Teacher Scotes invited me to Assembly.

For just a moment, I almost wished I'd never met Teacher Scotes, for up till then, I'd been content: I had a future and a father. Now I faced an impossibility. My mind said, Learn from Teacher Scotes. My fear said, Remain your father's son. Neither provided a strategy for doing both.

This is not a justification for what I subsequently did, but it is my explanation.

CHAPTER 9

In Philadelphia our inns and taverns teemed, not only with our national representatives but also with the multitudes who sought them out. Thus our lodging and transport establishments prospered, and we received more than our share of funded projects. These of course were advantages but disadvantages too, for there was no escaping the crowds, who made their voices heard in light of day and dark of night.

They could run the streets like rivers through brick canyons, rush the threshold of some office or official's home, then dissipate, like a fog. Sometimes they arose as if by magic; sometimes they were summoned by the partisan dailies and broadsides. To them, voting for their representatives was not enough, and they supplemented their ballots with the streets. Whatever brought them out, we tried to gauge the durability of their arousal and on what occasions we could leave them be and when we need respond. As my father always said, if a capital is the nation's soul, then its crowds convey the nation's moods.

Had their energy instead been channeled into productive work, such as I had examined with Teacher Scotes, who can estimate what they might have done? But with little left to do, they felt the need to sometimes rise, as if against some counterfort they could not see but knew they had to break. Yet they also seemed to hold their fight as futile, could even laugh when transforming themselves from balloters to banshees. Did something more than lack of work explain what overcame them and left the strain upon their faces?

On their behalf, the representatives had been granted the authority to satisfy every need. In Philadelphia you saw it in our waterworks, where massive wheels pumped water to the highest banks of the Schuylkill and wooden pipes like veins carried it to the Delaware. You saw it elsewhere in the subsidies to replace wooden houses with brick, especially where congestion risked fire. There were National Hospitals in every city; newly paved roads, especially in the north, where dirt was impassable half the year; and new canals—the most astonishing things—man-made rivers through which passed even large, round-bottom boats. We compensated the out-of-work and increased the income of the lower sort. There were even funds for "birthing and burying"—as my father would say—a cradle-to-grave foundation upon which every citizen could build a life.

There were the national regulatory agencies, too, committees established legislatively and based in Philadelphia, with branches in every state, whose purpose was to protect us all. One obliged people to save for austere times by compelling deposits in branches of the National Bank. Others set professional and artisanal standards to ensure quality in our wares. Still others decreed certain foods and activities to be wholesome or unwholesome.

At our founding, when all power was vested in the Assembly by the Constitution of '83 and the representatives were given authority to legislate at will, spending had been small. Most of it was funded by voluntary liturgies, on the Greek model (not the compulsory late Roman one), in which people like Merchant Girard and Merchant Astor from New York gave freely of their wealth. When this proved insufficient, the National Bank provided loans to the Assembly, to be repaid from future coffers. When this debt became concerning and the people rejected representatives who tried to raise their taxes to retire it, the Bank sought new funds.

First it took the coins it collected each year in taxes, melted and reminted them with a lower silver content, though at the same denominations. In this way more coins were available to spend on new projects that the representatives might offer. But when the merchants and shopkeepers caught on and stopped appraising the new coins at their face values, prices began to rise.

Nor did the double-demos, which was created by the Bank soon after, fool them. At twice the size of the former demos, it was supposed to represent twice the value, but wary of what had happened with the demos, people took to weighing them and discovered that the double-demos had not twice but only half more silver than the demos, and prices rose further.

Finally the Assembly empowered the Bank to issue a paper demos, untied to silver, and required that people surrender their coins and stop using them in exchange. In response, coins were hoarded; there were many thefts; and for a time, we had to root out the illegal trade with foreign merchants. Further laws strengthened the penalties of the prior ones, and the galena mine in Phoenixville was idled. From there, the Bank issued as many notes as needed, to fund our many offerings. In fact, it was the unlimited nature of our notes, untethered from the metal, that freed the representatives to pass most of what they did.

But then prices began to really rise, alarmingly so. What once cost a demi-deci-demos later cost a demos; what once cost one, cost twenty. Eventually came the Price-Relief Acts, which mandated maximum prices for the worst-offending goods, but this only seemed to make scarce the products they addressed and did nothing to quell the larger trend. Proprietors who obeyed the legal maximums had their stockrooms overrun because their shelves were always empty, and those who priced above the maximum to match demand were reported to the authorities and sometimes assaulted by the public, who accused them of gouging the people.

We also began to see accelerated expansions in some commercial activities, followed by general panics when work would stop, leaving half-built homes and mills and quarries. It was a phenomenon that puzzled even the representatives, who privately expressed alarm at the subsequent distress. I myself attended committee meetings where the figures were reviewed.

Gradually, through it all, began the protests and sometimes riots. Less were people working, less could they afford, and it seemed that the more the representatives did, the less secure the people felt. At some point I think they started losing confidence in us completely, that we, their supposed benefactors, no matter whom they elected to Assembly, could not help them after all. In response, we hired more watchmen to patrol at night and constables and marshals for the day, paying them extra to mitigate the violence.

Though my father understood the nation's moods, could speak to people as if certain of their minds, it was an ability I had none of. At least until the evening he abandoned me, when I was overtaken by a mood that seemed akin to theirs because like them I, too, now suffered from pledges made yet unfulfilled, perhaps never to be met. I was not a little angry at my father. I had not allowed that he could threaten me in that way, I who had always done his bidding and who now only sought persuasion—but he refused me even that.

When eventually I encountered Teacher Scotes, Xephon, and Alcidia again, it was on a Market Wednesday in May, a few weeks later. By then I was ready to come upon them somewhere and undertake my own assessment of what was right to do, apart from my father's direction. I was walking south on Third, headed for the National Bank and toward the early sun, and the people were already in the streets, flowing against me, presumably advancing toward their twice-weekly protest at the sheds. For the moment they seemed intent upon their purpose, and their sound was only a buzz. I waded slowly. Even after I squeezed over to the sidewalk, it was difficult.

Because of the encounter with my father outside Simon's, Teacher Scotes might have since decided to withdraw his invitation, but I doubted so, because he had twice that day invited me: once before my father intervened and once after. There was some risk that I would be discovered, but only slight. For one, Father had not discovered me the year before; I myself had confessed. Two, I would see them but infrequently. And three, anyone who did happen upon us was not likely to betray me: people were too much struggling with their own difficulties to be concerned with mine. Nor did I see how those who did disapprove of my association could undermine my future electability, contrary to what my father said. There would be too few of them (I would keep to the countryside and avoid encounters in the city), and Father had always assured me that when the time came, a comfortable majority of Pennsylvanians would naturally vote my way. In all, the more I considered implementing this plan, the less concerned I was.

I saw the three of them in the distance at the entrance to the bank before they saw me. They were looking down upon the crowd. The bank itself had two tall floors and was in the ancient style, with six large Corinthian columns atop the marble steps and matching pilasters and white marble across the façade, but for the windows and front door. It dominated every building on the street. Incongruously, its sides were brick because during its construction the cost of marble had risen so rapidly. This alteration had always troubled Father because the nation's bank, he felt, should inspire confidence in the people.

Xephon stood against a column, which dwarfed him, and Alcidia and Teacher Scotes sat shoulder to shoulder. Alcidia saw me first, stood, and eyed me for the duration of my approach. Then Xephon saw me too. Teacher Scotes rubbed his feet and continued watching people pass with a look of melancholy all his own, as if what he witnessed saddened him. He was so preoccupied that I reached the steps before he finally turned.

"Greetings, Palleias," he said, as if no time had passed and nothing had occurred. He did not get up.

Normally, it was easy to forget that he was seventy, given how much he walked and that he never tired of conversing with strangers or with us. This day, however, he seemed fatigued. His plain linen shirt hung loosely, and his breeches looked faded. His face held a pallor.

Alcidia's face, by contrast, was rigid. "Are you headed inside on business?" he asked.

"I am." They waited upon my next words. "I am sorry not to have found you sooner," I said. "But as I mentioned when I saw you last, I have been extraordinarily busy."

Though likely understanding the true reason for my absence, they spared me my account. It was not difficult to read them. Alcidia was suspicious and would be no matter what. Xephon would assume my virtue, that either I had convinced my father of the value of joining them or had simply openly asserted my intention. This last might worry Xephon, but he knew enough—we all knew—not to raise such worries on behalf of Teacher Scotes.

If Teacher Scotes was concerned at all for his own safety, he gave no indication. He only said, "We were just observing the crowd before we went in. The operation of the bank is of special interest to Xephon."

"I, too, have been observing them," I said.

"It is not a joyful sight," Teacher Scotes said.

I climbed the steps and looked down upon the passing people, wondering what he saw. Then, perhaps displeased by how cordially our conversation had begun, Alcidia said, "How *is* your father?" Obviously he was probing for information.

"He is well, thank you."

By now the street was full. The crowd flowed like cooling lava; only a few here and there raised their heads to glance up in our direction. Amid such an unperturbed procession, you could stand among them safely until you couldn't, and you had to sense when things might turn.

"Allow me to leave you for a moment to conduct my business," I said. "Then we can talk more." In truth I had but one account to review, but I went in.

In contrast with the sunlit marble outside, the bank inside was in near darkness, and a moment passed before my eyes adjusted and the light that angled through the high windows took effect. High above was the barrel-vaulted ceiling. A center aisle led directly to a smaller entrance at the back. On the right, behind four columns, cave-like, was a long counter, behind which stood several clerks; on the left, also behind four columns and an ornate wooden barrier, were four large desks, manned by men of proper dress. There I found an assistant cashier, who jumped to attend to me.

Upon my business being completed, I turned to face the entrance and held in place a moment because just then the noise of the crowd outside grew markedly louder, even though no door had opened. Those around me noted it too. Such sounds always made one uneasy. Then a tall panel of the heavy door swung out, revealing a silhouetted Teacher Scotes, Alcidia, and Xephon. The surge of sound that coincided collapsed when the panel closed behind them.

I walked over. I could, I thought, restrict today's visit to the confines of the bank and take up again outside the city when our schedules matched. And if my rejoining was problematical for them, they could always disinvite me. When I reached them, Teacher Scotes asked Xephon, "Where should we begin?" And with that, questions about what had happened to me after Simon's were no more.

Immediately a man approached. He was heavy, with sparse gray hair entwining a balding top, and was dressed in tails, though with no cravat; instead, his shirt was buttoned to his throat.

He offered his hand. "Do I have the pleasure of meeting Teacher Scotes?" Teacher Scotes accepted the hand. "I am Potts, cashier of this branch. I am aware that you are an admirer of productive men and women. If it pleases you, I am the man who oversees this operation."

"Indeed I do admire them," Teacher Scotes answered, managing a smile, though still subdued. Then he introduced me, Alcidia, and Xephon. At my name the cashier gave a look, but I do not think he recognized me. Mainly he took an interest in Alcidia, who, as always, was well dressed, with a trim waistcoat, and hatless. Xephon, in rougher attire and of country mien, got only a cursory acknowledgment till Teacher Scotes remarked, "My friend Xephon here is writing a book on household and business management," a fact I did not know. I did not think Xephon capable of such an achievement, and I felt envy and a searching examination of my own activities. It was a prick that lasted but a moment.

Cashier Potts regarded Xephon with a bit more interest than before. "Permit me to show you gentlemen around," he said to Teacher Scotes. "After all, this is the people's bank."

As if on cue, the crowd outside roared—why, we could not know— then the noise subsided, though settled at an even louder level than before. Cashier Potts smiled nervously.

He introduced us to a few colleagues in the main room, then took us to a locked case that contained on one shelf a few gray coins of the now defunct specie, one coin showing the image of two heads facing each other in conversation, and on its reverse, an image of the amphitheater and VOP. Other shelves displayed notes of various size that were then in circulation. Xephon questioned him briefly, and Cashier Potts cheerfully answered.

Teacher Scotes addressed Cashier Potts. "I imagine, if you don't mind my observing, that holding such a responsible position among all this currency, you must be quite wealthy. I congratulate you." The intention of the comment, I knew, was to aid Xephon in his investigation.

Cashier Potts stiffened and pulled both lapels. "I can assure you, Teacher Scotes, that I am far from wealthy."

"Forgive my presumption," Teacher Scotes said. "What is wealth, anyway? I sometimes find that question to be more vexing than it first appears. Isn't that so, Xephon?"

"The people are wealthy, not me," Cashier Potts said. "I am but a steward of their wealth. And but one steward, at that. As you may know, there are dozens of branches like this in the nation."

Here again the noise outside surged. I wondered what might be happening. As if eager to provide some remove, Cashier Potts led us to the second floor. As we climbed, Xephon, who registered nothing but what bore upon his investigation, inquired as to the uses of the bank's holdings, whether much was loaned to farmers, artisans, or manufacturers. The cashier replied that no, in present times, few people could afford such loans. Much of the bank's holdings went to fund the national expenditures. Without the bank, most of what the people needed could not, in fact, be funded.

We reached a private office with dark wood and three large ornate desks. A plate on one announced the cashier's name. The walls were high and thickly shelved with green and red bank books. One tall window gave sufficient light to obviate the need for the lamp on the desk. Cashier Potts had taken his seat, having positioned three chairs for us across from him.

"I gather," Teacher Scotes said, reviving our conversation, "that those notes you showed us, and those stored in your vaults and at other branches, represent the wealth of the people that you were referring to."

"Indeed they do," Cashier Potts said.

"And yet even now," Xephon said, scribbling, "we observe how the people clamor for work and how they claim to be unable to afford their lodgings or food or other necessaries. Judging by what we hear in Assembly and in the newspapers, most people do not consider themselves wealthy. Perhaps the repeated printing of additional notes has still not been sufficient."

The cashier tugged gently at his coat again, this time in a self-satisfied way. He smiled at Xephon, seemingly happy to instruct the younger man. He even glanced at Teacher Scotes, as if acknowledging their allied roles in educating the next generation. "Of course we hope it *is* sufficient," he answered. "But—and this is the art—we are also wary of supplying too much. You seem a hearty fellow, so perhaps this will not apply to you, but cannot even healthful food in excess quantities become unhealthy?" Teacher Scotes seemed to enjoy this analogy or that one was being made at all. "We fear we might actually be approaching that level now," the cashier continued. "You are aware of the rise in prices in recent years? Well, that is the other side of the scale, so to speak. Too many notes, too high a tipping of prices." Upon making his point, he leaned back.

"Indeed that makes sense," Teacher Scotes said. "For were it otherwise, then some notes being good, more notes would be better. Thus, if notes themselves were wealth, it would follow that the national printing should be unlimited. For it is not often that we speak of suffering from too much wealth but rather from too little."

"I see the point," Xephon said. "For it would also seem that if everyone had new notes and simultaneously brought them to the same shop, the sudden abundance of notes in hand would not of itself produce an increase in what was on the proprietor's shelves. His inventory of dry goods and such would be the same. In fact, confronted by this sudden and increased ability to pay on the part of his patrons, would he not simply charge more for his existing stock?"

"Clearly we all agree on the basic point," Cashier Potts said, though of a sudden, he seemed less enthusiastic about the topic. "This is what necessitates the need for balance."

"In a sense," Xephon added, "does this not also imply that the wealth we speak of is in fact the goods on the proprietor's shelves more than the notes brought to exchange for them? After all, when people speak of lack, they mean lack of food, shelter, clothing, animals, transport, and the like. They do not really mean that they lack notes, per se. Or, if they feel the lack of notes, it is because they envision what the notes will buy. Given the option to choose, they would take the goods."

"Perhaps we have pushed the example too far," Cashier Potts said. He shifted in his chair, evidently taking less pleasure in our company. Knowing Xephon, I knew that he intended no offense but was simply warming to his subject. I had noticed that he had this propensity to become enamored of the tasks he set himself, a quality that I both admired and envied. Teacher Scotes often counseled us in our questioning: Seek answers from those who know but desist the moment they express a desire to withhold. People must feel themselves free to speak, else you are pressing them to do what they believe will cause them harm. At the same time, don't presume to know their wishes until they express them; rather, freely question until their words and actions stop you.

But I had to wonder whether he was contradicting his own advice, because he cut off Xephon's interrogation. "Perhaps we have taken too much of your time," he said to Cashier Potts. "You have been generous in giving us so much of your day."

"I do have a question or two more," Xephon said.

A large commotion arose from within the bank. Though one floor up and behind closed doors, we heard it unmistakably. Cashier Potts startled. Teacher Scotes waited upon him, as if nothing had happened. Cashier Potts rose and said, "Please excuse me." He left the office and shortly returned to stand in the open doorway. Behind him we could hear the now unencumbered rumbling from the first floor till someone shouted, "Let's cast our sheep's eyes at some of our money!" followed by boisterous laughter.

"Regrettably I must return to my duties," Cashier Potts said, holding the door as invitation for us to leave. Mustering friendliness to deflect his apparent anxiety, he said, "You are always welcome in my branch. Now, please allow me to escort you out the back door."

We followed him downstairs. At the bottom I could see that the floor had filled. Both front door panels were open, and the shifting crowd was penned loudly between the railings on each side. More were pressing in. They were in a romping mood, however. Not riotous.

Cashier Potts exited to lead us. Xephon and Alcidia each took an arm and did not let Teacher Scotes pause to observe the crowd. Last on the threshold, I was forcibly grabbed and turned. The stranger who held me yelled in my face, "We're in the money!" Then he laughed, released me, and pressed his way back in.

In the shade outside, we exchanged a hasty "Good day" with Cashier Potts.

After we had walked a block or so, during which I said I was due elsewhere but would look forward to seeing them again, Teacher Scotes asked Xephon, "Was it worth seeing?"

Xephon flipped his notebook and slid it into his pocket. "Yes!" he said. "There are other sites I must visit immediately."

Not wanting them to think me eager to depart, I asked, "Will your book be a polemical treatment?" At this both Teacher Scotes and Alcidia smiled, as if anticipating the response.

"Oh no," he said. "I would rather emphasize the positive."

Observing him, I felt my own enthusiasm swell, chasing his.

CHAPTER 10

Accommodating both my schedule and my preference for meeting the three outside the city, Teacher Scotes attempted to blend his travel plans with mine. Xephon, preoccupied with his own endeavors and gentler in nature, seemed unbothered by my presence. Alcidia remained on guard. I was delighted to be back among them.

One day, when I mentioned that a trip of mine would take me to the Upper Darby, Teacher Scotes suggested we all spend an afternoon at his home, which was on the way. I knew his house to be secluded, which made it all the more enticing.

We agreed that I would rendezvous with Xephon and Alcidia at the Market Street Bridge and that they could ride with me by wagon the nearly three miles to Teacher Scotes's house. It being May, western roads had become more passable and crowded, with farmers transporting more by wagon than by river. I had some concern of accidents and the ensuing publicity, but we tended to travel slowly and carefully, looking out for runaways or jams that might put us at risk. Betsy was steady; she would not bolt or panic and seemed to enjoy our easy pace. In truth, I could have left her at home sometimes, not always needing her to reach the group, and I would have enjoyed the walks, but not to take her might have raised suspicion.

It was a simple journey: across the bridge and southwest on the Darby Road almost to Cobs Creek. There a short road veered due south. I was a little uncomfortable being with them without Teacher Scotes, but my fears turned out to be unfounded. Xephon talked cheerfully and virtually without end, and Alcidia, ever watchful of our surroundings—of trees and rocks and those who passed us by—seemed nevertheless tranquil and more accepting of my company. For much of the trip, Xephon sat with legs to his chest, teething on a long piece of straw. Both he and I wore floppy hats, mine mainly for disguise. Next to Xephon and behind me, Alcidia squatted athletically, hatless, his blond hair rustling. He had worn a pair of purple velvet pantaloons, no doubt to annoy Teacher Scotes, who disapproved of such ostentation and who considered his efforts to correct Alcidia something of a minor career. I found myself glancing back to regard Alcidia, his intense, military bearing making him as always a figure attractive to behold. By virtue of his looks alone, he could be elected representative, his many further qualities aside.

He sought always to compete with everyone at everything, and at one point, he and Xephon broke out in a wrestling match, once we were off the main road. Even Betsy, keeping stride, craned to study the commotion. Xephon, the larger of the two, eventually got Alcidia fast by his golden neck, exclaiming things like, "Quick, don't soil your dress!" until Alcidia bit him. Xephon yelped and shook his hand out. "You bite like a girl!" he yelled.

"No, a lion," Alcidia said.

Alcidia's reputation was prodigious, a fact that pleased him greatly; indeed, he seemed to relish ways to boost it. For example, some years ago a group of river pirates began commandeering flat-bottoms that transferred goods well west of the city, where our meager Navy couldn't reach them. Though often armed with pistols or muskets, the crews seemed unable to defend themselves, because none could afford to hire men skilled in warfare, given the remoteness of the action. The problem grew and began to bankrupt some millers. Then one day Alcidia traveled west, tracked the pirates, and volunteered to join a crew. After several voyages back and forth, there was an ambush, and Alcidia almost single-handedly killed several marauders, found their hideaway, and burned it. For a time, piracy in that part of the country stopped. Alcidia never accepted pay for his role, and I don't know whether it was his fighting prowess or his magnanimity that secured his renown. Nor was it the last time he engaged in such an act. Had we gone to war, I think we would have appointed him general.

Not far from Teacher Scotes's house, we passed a clearing. "Stop the wagon," Alcidia yelled.

He leaped off. Part of someone's farm had been set up as a baseball field, and a group of men were playing. Alcidia ran over. Xephon looked at me, rolled his eyes, and we watched.

Alcidia stood among the players and apparently talked his way into hitting. I hadn't even known he played, and Xephon himself doubted that he had. But after letting one toss pass, he swung and sent the next one high and far—how far we couldn't see because the opening in the trees was not that wide. But Alcidia kept running till, like the sweep of a clock's second hand and in less time, he had come full circle. He shook hands with some of the players, who must have asked him to stay, because he gestured in our direction as if to say he couldn't. Then, grinning, he sprinted back to us and leaped into the wagon. "Onward, Palleias," he said and pointed. Xephon rolled his eyes again.

Teacher Scotes's house sat singly in an opening of woods off a lightly traveled path, backed by the sound of a rushing springtime river, across which was a fenced-in field where cows grazed. His house was a log cabin in the old German style. Its one unusual feature was an addition at the back, which extended from the halfway point to an equal distance beyond the original footprint, making two overlapping rectangles out of what had been one. It had two windows and a door facing front and two chimneys at opposite corners. He had moved there long before becoming a husband and a father, leaving his father's large brick house in the city. Selling that house dearly and buying this much cheaper one was how he had since been able to travel the country and walk the land as a philosopher, taking a little money here and there for tutoring or relying on the generosity of friends.

We three had become more attentive, I noticed, as we passed through a clearing and approached the house from the wobbly path off the road. I became aware of the noise we were making, even though it was not excessive: Betsy's slow clopping, the tinkling of metal from her bridle, and a few rattles from our lolling wagon. I was aware of the noise because sitting cross-legged on the grass beside the front door was Teacher Scotes himself, his eyes shut and his hands resting on his ankles. Faint smoke rose from both chimneys. We stopped, disembarked, and hitched to a post out front, but Teacher Scotes neither moved nor opened his eyes. We knew not to disturb him, not that we likely could. So we each took a seat in the grass, on the other side of the dirt strip that led to the front steps.

It was Ansea, his wife, and Sophia, his daughter, who greeted us instead. Sophia, tall for her twelve years, with long braided hair, leaped from the front door to the grass, forgoing the steps and seemingly without fear of interrupting her father. Her legs were spindly, quite the opposite of her father's, and powered by a surprising colt-like spring. She smiled brightly but resisted speaking, waiting upon her mother, who soon appeared in the doorway.

Ansea was much younger than her husband, by about twenty-five years. Her wispy red hair was pulled up, and she, too, was thin. Both mother and daughter were aproned and had soot spots on their arms and clothes. It was Ansea who, in a most welcoming fashion, invited us in. Since I was the stranger, I felt her hospitable attention especially directed at me, and we passed through the small doorframe into the first room, which struck me as darker than it would have been had it not been so bright outside.

Xephon and I pegged our hats, and then he and Alcidia positioned themselves next to a few chairs that were arranged around the main table by the hearth at one end of the room. Apparently the chairs were new and of a different make from those they had seen on their last visit, judging by their remarks. Leaving them, Ansea offered to show me the rest of the house and some of their modest collectibles. When we passed into the addition, Sophia followed, eyeing me happily. More than once her mother admonished her not to follow so closely, and she obeyed but still fairly skipped as we walked.

I noticed her eyes, which seemed just like Teacher Scotes's: gray, bright, and sharply alert. I am not sure whether it is more correct to say that her eyes were like his or his were like hers, because in truth, though aged, he tended to gaze upon the world more in the manner of a child than that of most adults. I had noticed this quality before, but it was exemplified by the face of his daughter. Fortunately for her, the rest of her appearance was more like her mother's, both in proportion and regularity.

The small brick oven next to the fireplace was fired in this room also, matching the one in the other. On a small table before it were assembled a number of covered pies and plates of various foods, protected from the flies that had found their way in. Where the other room contained a small bed, presumably Sophia's, this one had a larger one, four-posted, with a mattress that appeared to be of feathers. I was pleased that Teacher Scotes would allow his family this luxury.

Ansea wanted to show me what was special about the addition. "Are you interested in construction?" she asked me. "As you may know, Scotes's father was a builder, and Scotes has always followed the advances in that trade." She pointed out the framing, which, though for a modest cabin, was of a cut of wood I hadn't seen before. "It's from New England," she explained. "A builder there took to producing what they call two-by-fours. And though we had this section built some years ago, the method hasn't yet been imported to our state. Scotes brought some home after a visit. He often brings back examples of what he admires elsewhere. On his last trip to New England, he returned with a few barrels stuffed with cod, a delicious fish. It will be our pleasure to serve you some later."

"Luckily we do not eat it often," Sophia said, making a face.

"Why hasn't this cut of wood yet arrived here?" I asked, fingering it.

"In their correspondence with Scotes," Ansea said, "they claim to be struggling to make a go of it."

I was impressed by Ansea. She projected the intelligence of my mother and the similarly allied support of her husband's business.

We returned to the first room to find Teacher Scotes standing with Xephon and Alcidia. Apparently he had been chiding Alcidia for his clothing, because he looked over at me and said, "Alcidia continues to revel in the spring." Alcidia, in response, raised his arms and chin, as if imitating a blossom. Then Teacher Scotes approached and held me by my shoulders. "Welcome to our home," he said.

"Palleias takes an interest in construction," Ansea said.

"Then you must show him the view out the back door, so that he can examine how the two buildings have been joined."

At this Ansea paused and regarded her husband. Something passed between them before she eventually nodded just so and invited me to follow.

We stood in the doorway, looking out upon a grassy corner where the extension jutted from the original outline of the house. Not far from the house, the grass became brush, trees, and stream—by itself, a bland sight. Ansea pointed out nothing special about this setting or how the buildings joined, and I noticed nothing more than a single two-by-four, nailed from ground to roofline, from which the normal slats extended— certainly not the arrangement Teacher Scotes meant for me to note. When Ansea did not comment, I did not inquire. I sensed that she had nothing to tell me, and there seemed little for me to see. But then I noticed what likely had caused the moment between them and Ansea's hesitation. Below us and to our left, not far from the step and in the corner, was a small mound of recently disturbed ground. Grass was not yet reasserting itself, indicating that little time had passed since the earth had been churned.

This was not an uncommon sight, especially among the large farmers and more wealthy merchants who owned land outside the city. It was an open secret: citizens buried money on their property. You could tell what kind by the nature of the ground. A hole that had been dug some time ago and since was overgrown likely contained coin. All the representatives and magistrates knew that people did this, and Father always said that there was no reason to harass otherwise good citizens for such an offense. A more freshly dug spot, by contrast, likely contained notes, and such plots could only be found on the property of the richest citizens. Many had taken to stashing funds in this way after the more recent Distributions, as a way of appearing less wealthy; to stash notes inside the house or store them in a bank was to risk their discovery. Accessing such piles was perilous and had to be done in the dimmest light, without lantern, accompanied by an armed family member or trusted hand, for there were always trespassers lurking, mindful that a lucky discovery could pay off handsomely. The richest families sometimes hired men to dig and refill hundreds of empty plots across many acres, just to deceive would-be robbers.

We sat for dinner, around a table filled not only with the fish but with apple pudding and pie, turnips, corn, and bread, all in warm tins. As each changed hands, its smell stood out from the others. Only the small oven remained heated, and the room was cool and well shaded by the trees behind the house. I did not mind the absence of forks; we ate instead with knives, as I remember doing as a boy.

On my side of the table were Xephon and Alcidia. Across from me was Sophia, then Ansea and Teacher Scotes. The conversation was light—not without a few remarks about Alcidia's pantaloons and not of intellectual matters that had been inspired by our investigations. Alcidia talked of his desire to travel south. Xephon told a humorous story of a large hog he had witnessed racing in and out of homes in the city, where it had been loosed to scavenge waste but instead had taken upon itself to explore block after block before being captured and returned to its owner. Teacher Scotes and Ansea seemed content to enjoy their guests' stories, as I was content to listen quietly, myself not being much of a storyteller or conversationalist.

I was somewhat unnerved by Sophia's directing much of her attention at me, eyeing me studiously. Though she was a child, I found myself

wondering what she was seeing: I often judged myself deficient at understanding what I was conveying to others; I even lacked awareness of the
subtle motives behind my own behavior. In these ways I had the unset-
tling feeling that I did not know myself and that others were more
attuned to my propensities and proclivities than was I. Though Sophia
stared, hardly relenting to lift a morsel from her plate or follow the
conversation, I did not stare back. I did, however, wonder what had
been said to her about me or whether nothing had been said and she
herself was in the process of unabashedly forming her own opinion. I
at that age would have been incapable of forming my own opinion of a
stranger, but this child gave the impression of being very different on
this score.

After dinner, Teacher Scotes, Alcidia, Xephon, and I returned to the
front and sat again in the grass by the steps. Sophia soon followed.
Xephon rose to escort her to Betsy, who was nibbling grass, and proceeded to describe some of the features of the breed. It was late afternoon,
the light had colored, and the crickets were quieting. When they were
done with Betsy, Xephon and Sophia came to where we sat, he next to
me and she falling against her father to wrap her arms around his neck
before sitting restfully beside him while retaining an embrace. Teacher
Scotes leaned into her affectionately and kissed her hair.

"Sophia," Teacher Scotes said, "did you know that our friend Palleias
here is a poet?"

"No!" she said, flinging her arms off her father. "Recite us a poem!"

"I am not really a poet," I said.

"Do you make up poems?" she asked.

"Sometimes."

"Then you are a poet!" Her triumphant conclusion had all of the
logic-induced enthusiasm I associated with her father.

"He also plans to run for representative," he said.

"Alcidia! Like you!" She turned to Alcidia, who was leaning on an
elbow in the grass. "Perhaps you both will be representatives at the same

time!" That Alcidia's expression did not change suggested that he had already considered this possibility, though I, for some reason, had not. He was old enough to run this year, elections being in the autumn, and likely we would stand side by side in some future Assembly.

Because he had been addressed, Alcidia swiveled into a sitting position and crossed his legs. "And you," he said to Sophia, teasingly, "will you be joining us in the Assembly when you are older?"

"Oh no," she said. "When I am of age, I will be a physician."

How, I thought, could she have more conviction about her plans at twelve than I had about mine at twenty-eight?

"And where will you practice?" Xephon asked her. "Rome? Paris? London? New Jersey?"

"I haven't decided." She jutted her chin in exaggerated theatrics. "Perhaps China."

I caught that she was likely joking but could not stop my exclamation. "China!" Everyone laughed. Sophia gave a big smile.

How peaceful our surroundings were, how different from the city! The secluded path that connected house and road through abundant trees was protective, though the road carried little traffic anyway. Out here, west of the city and far from VOP, you never heard its eastward intermittent "Ayes" and "Nays." In a short while, we would leave. I had promised to drop Alcidia and Xephon at the inn where I would lodge, not far from here, and they could catch a coach back to the city.

"Sophia," Teacher Scotes said, "be sure your mother does not require help, and tell her I will be in shortly."

Sophia sprang up and leaped toward the house but then as quickly swung around and approached me, extending her hand. "If I don't see you later," she said, "it was a pleasure to have made your acquaintance." I took her hand, bade her the same, and she sprinted through the door.

When she was gone, Alcidia turned to me, as if he had been waiting to do so. "And you, Palleias, is it still your intention to stand for election someday? I ask because I have observed your keen interest in our investigations and discussions—in ideas, in the *idea* of ideas—and you rarely speak now of legislating or governing."

This is what I mean about how much is visible to others. What you yourself regard as internal only they in fact can see. Or worse: what you yourself are blind to, they are not. We are sometimes plainer to others than we are to ourselves. Or perhaps this fact describes only me and cannot be generalized. Spending time with Teacher Scotes had alerted me to what are and are not proper inferences.

We sat in a close circle. It was an intimate gathering, and in their presence, I felt more comfortable than I ever had in anyone's. But, aware of their intelligence, I had nevertheless remained embarrassed about my inner confusions and weaknesses. So in a moment of self-pity, caught off guard by the attention suddenly turned on me, I answered Alcidia's question. "If I have the opportunity."

"If you have the opportunity," Xephon said. "Why would you not have the opportunity?"

"What I mean is," I said, regaining my defenses, "one never knows what might happen." I looked at Teacher Scotes, who was listening but not at all reacting to my words.

Alcidia regarded me for a moment, then released his pose to pluck a tall squeaky blade of grass. Fingering it, he asked the next question in a manner so offhand that it masked the vigor of his probing.

"Why did you say 'If I have the opportunity'?" he said.

Before I could answer, Teacher Scotes said, "Alcidia is still wary of your presence. He considers it a threat to my safety that you are with us."

"Is it not?" Alcidia responded quickly. "Can you really doubt that his father disapproves of his associating with you?"

Teacher Scotes directed his attention to Alcidia. "Should you not also be concerned?" he said. "After all, while I am sometimes admired, I am also hated, it would seem. That, too, is not in doubt. When the day comes, might not those who observe you so regularly in my presence deem it prudent to oppose you, and might they not also proclaim loudly why they do? After all, your youth, beauty, and accomplishments will not necessarily be evaluated as positives among all voters. Not everyone reveres such qualities. Have you considered this?"

Subdued by the scolding, Alcidia answered, "It is more important that I learn from you than take such considerations into account."

"More important to whom?" Teacher Scotes asked.

"More important to me," Alcidia answered. "At any rate, I do not believe that associating with you will hurt me in any way. The people will know I've learned from you, and their main concern will be whether they trust me to serve their interests. All other considerations will be second to that."

I knew Alcidia would not back down, even from a challenge issued by Teacher Scotes. It was one of the qualities Teacher Scotes admired in him. Still, I had to wonder whether this questioning was directed only at Alcidia.

"And that is what you intend to do—serve their interests?" Teacher Scotes said. When Alcidia didn't respond, he turned to me. "We have been discussing the importance of examining one's ambitions fully." I absorbed the point. "Alcidia believes that he will be able to lead from the inside," Teacher Scotes added. "It is a proposition we have been considering at length."

"Why couldn't he?" I asked. I had always assumed that the job of a representative was to lead the nation, to effect change in ways that would benefit people. "What else is needed if not leadership by our reps?"

"A new constitution," Xephon said.

I was stunned. "What is wrong with our constitution?"

Xephon did not answer and appeared chagrined at having spoken. Nor did Teacher Scotes respond directly. Instead he asked me, "Might this also not explain your father's concern with your presence here? I imagine that he, too, fears the effects my company could have on your political popularity. If you are to seek election, might you not be undermining your chances now?"

Xephon asked me, "Does your father still disapprove of your being here?"

But I was back to mulling Alcidia's answer. Would spending time with Teacher Scotes truly hurt my chances? Did my father really believe that my being here would hurt me? I doubt that even Teacher Scotes believed it. I knew him to pose such questions not to express his own opinion but to prompt you to examine yours.

Distracted, I answered Xephon, "He has threatened not to help me if I returned here against his wishes" and knew immediately I had said too much.

Xephon regarded me. "So that is why you say you might not have the opportunity. When you told him you were meeting with us, he threatened to withdraw his support."

I did not answer right away.

Alcidia, absentmindedly fingering the grass and looking down and to the side, spoke up again. "Your father does not know you are with us."

Still I did not answer.

"You have come without telling him," Teacher Scotes said, studying me. "Because if he knew, he would withdraw his support for your ambition."

Though I searched for ways to deny it, I had no choice but to nod my admission.

Xephon looked stunned. Alcidia appeared unmoved.

"Do you still want his support?" Teacher Scotes asked.

"I need it," I blurted. Which I felt was true: to be elected, there were positions to obtain, people to become known to, newspapers to appear in, funds to be raised.

"But he will only give it on the understanding that you not visit with me?"

"I cannot be elected without his support."

"Yet you seek that support in violation of the terms upon which he agreed to give it?"

His question hit me bodily. He spoke without compassion, addressing not my wants or feelings but my words. He was prompting me to do what he had just advised: examine my ambition. I felt alone, no longer among friends. They awaited my reply, attempting no rescue.

I attended to the cooling grass under my hands and the expanse of quiet sky above the smokehouse and converging treetops. When I took the others in again, I realized that my diversion had not caused a corresponding one in them and that they still hung upon me.

"What should I do?" I said. "Without his help, I have no prospects."

"That was not my question," Teacher Scotes said, gently.

"He's my father. He *should* help me," I said.

"*That* is your problem," Alcidia shot back, now completely animated. His tone alarmed me.

"Alcidia," Teacher Scotes said.

"You want him to take care of you as much as the rest of them do," Alcidia said.

Probably because of my stricken hesitation, Teacher Scotes relented. His tone was kind. "Do you wish to pursue this discussion further?"

"I don't know."

"Then I will ask you only this. Is it your judgment that your needs and desires justify whatever action you take to obtain them?"

Of course not, I responded mentally—that is not what I meant. But in truth I was not certain what I had meant or what I had been doing. That was my perennial problem: I was never certain of anything.

There it was: in but weeks I had found a way to displease both my father and Teacher Scotes, and by the same action. Alcidia dropped his inquiry. I felt additionally embarrassed to have undermined my character in Xephon's eyes.

We stood to leave before dark. I was happy to go. Something had changed, and I was no longer certain I would be welcomed the next time I appeared. *If* I appeared. Perhaps I would only be welcomed if they were certain that my father had agreed to my choice. Ansea and Sophia came out to embrace us and return our hats. Under the pretext of preparing Betsy, I separated myself from their final exchanges. Away from them I remained with her and stroked her coarse neck. She stepped lightly in place under my touch.

The three of us were quiet on our slow, swaying ride to the inn. Mercifully, the trip was short.

A sign painted with a red lion greeted us; Alcidia eyed it as we approached. The inn was a wooden house with a slanted roof of great reach. Behind distant trees the reddened sun was setting. A few people congregated on the porch, whether relaxing or awaiting the coach. I dreaded having to encounter them, hoping that no one that evening or at breakfast would recognize me.

When I halted at the front, Xephon climbed down and, standing alongside me, wished me well, as he would, but conspicuously did not express the desire to see me again soon. Behind me Alcidia lingered in the bed. Of course I wanted to see them again, though I was feeling bitter. I assumed that the idea of my departure from their company would have pleased Alcidia, but he was only pensive. This softened me because for all his contentiousness about my presence, I imagined that we were becoming friends after all.

Before climbing down, he said, "You are his favored son, you know."

As usual, I went silent from not knowing what to make of a remark. Clearly neither Xephon nor Alcidia anticipated much of a reply because they patted Betsy once each before settling on a bench to await their coach. I supposed I could have waited with them, could have questioned Alcidia his last statement, but I was weary of talk and of examination and of the constant self-reflection about all that was wrong with who I was.

The next evening, when I saw my father for the first time in days, I of course did not inform him of where I'd been.

What happened next I never saw coming.

CHAPTER 11

June arrived. A thunderstorm cooled the air and washed the brick; the south-facing walls of our buildings looked orange in the sun after the rain. Though construction had all but stalled, we still took pride in our structures, built from bricks baked from our own clay, dug between our streams from pits, like so many small red-gray ponds, like wounds.

The city was transforming, being dressed in fresh attire for the fifty-fifth anniversary of the Declaration, now just weeks away. New canvas replaced old on the awnings of the storefronts that stretched from the corner where I stood all the way to the masted river nearly a half mile away, past the divided line of sheds. Street-bridging banners were already up. Cracked crosswalks were being repaired.

Since my visit to Teacher Scotes's house, I had kept away and would do so till I could reckon a way to discuss it with my father. My friends had justly chastised me. Then, one day when I was walking home, I heard a commotion across the street and saw them in conversation with an older man I did not know. The conversation seemed animated. I crossed discreetly and concealed myself in the doorway of an empty shop some ways away. Many shops were empty then, and fewer people lived in the city. More had taken up farming, far west of the river. They farmed sufficiently for their families, without a surplus with which to trade.

I observed the conversations surreptitiously. This much I had come to understand: that the people I loved most were the people I most hid from.

My relationships with family and friends were based on stealth, on a kind of fraud, as when the cooper sells a barrel made of pine that he claims to be oak. The material I was made of, what I truly thought and felt, others could not see, lest they treat me differently from how I sought to be treated. Or perhaps what I hid from others was what I was hiding from myself.

To better hear what they were saying, I stepped into the street, passed behind a row of bonneted wagons, and casually took up behind the last one, such that an observer might think me preparing to cross or waiting upon someone's arrival. I made eye contact with no one, took care on the uneven stone, and appreciated how wide the street was. The four men stood on the opposite side of the same wagon, at the horses' noses, at the corner of Market and Fourth. Though I could not see them and they could not see me, I heard them well.

The older man was bemoaning his still young but grown son, who had taken up as captain of a merchant vessel despite his father's prohibition and threat of disinheritance. The father considered shipping to be an unsafe and unsavory profession; the son had gone anyway and was still away at sea. Having received no letter from him, the father was distraught and had sought Teacher Scotes's advice. Seemingly of some means, he was considering chartering a vessel to trace the son's route.

Teacher Scotes was assuaging him that the son was not so late in returning, that shipping routes were often irregular, and that merchants maintained a fleet equipped for policing the routes and defending against troubles. These points seemed to mollify the man. Then discussion turned to what the father planned to do upon the son's return. He had already approached a few representatives and was drafting a bill with the aid of his attorney that would stipulate more stringent requirements for becoming a ship's captain. Without money, he reasoned, his son could not, under the drafted bills, afford the cost and time to attain his captain's license and would have to give up his commission.

Of course Teacher Scotes questioned him this strategy, and of course the man became agitated, though it was difficult to discern the source of his agitation. As usual, Teacher Scotes offered few arguments. But I never heard the resolution of the conversation because at about the peak of the father's exasperation, the winded voice of another man, whose steps had come clicking down the sidewalk, announced itself firmly.

"Excuse me. Are you Teacher Scotes?"

"I am."

The man asked for a word.

"Of course, sir," Teacher Scotes said. "Perhaps you would like to join our conversation? The good Doctor Worthen here and my friends Xephon and Alcidia and I were just discussing the role and challenges of fatherhood."

But before the man could answer, the voice of Doctor Worthen said, "I will take my leave of you and thank you for your time." I peeked around the canvas and saw him stride across Fourth and pass under an awning and into the milling crowds.

"Then what can I do for you, sir?" I heard Teacher Scotes say. I withdrew and again stood directly behind the wagon and out of sight.

There was the rustling and snap of a sheet of paper. The man cleared his throat and raised his voice, as if making an announcement. "I, Mathias, have sworn to this indictment and affidavit. Teacher Scotes is accused of not believing in the ideals that the nation believes in. He is also accused of corrupting the young. The penalty proposed is death."

There was a gasp, which came either from Xephon or me.

I leaped from behind the wagon. It was an impulse, and I was awkwardly aware of being suddenly visible. "What is going on here?" I demanded. The four stood in a circle at the corner. Xephon, whose back I had approached, turned with a start. Others nearby stopped to witness what was happening.

"Palleias!" Teacher Scotes exclaimed with a big smile. "You do have a way of popping up when least expected."

Alcidia recoiled and pointed an arm at me like a musket. "Again he was following us!"

There are times when I most value being my father's son; this was one of them. The man who had accosted Teacher Scotes was thin, with a tall hat, plain black trousers, and boots. His expression of wide eyes and open mouth suggested a stunned distraction at my appearance, but as the moment lengthened, I detected relaxation and even mirth on his stubbled face.

"Who are you?" I asked him in a deliberately uncivil tone.

"Humbly, I am Mathias, Young Palleias," he said calmly, irritatingly so. "I am a poet, of no import, but am a great admirer of you and your family."

I was accustomed to strangers saying my name, followed by complimenting me and my family. I had long ago learned not to trust them. "So you know who I am."

For many years, whenever I encountered someone who claimed to be a poet or who had written a poem, I felt a jolt of envy: they were doing what I wanted to be doing, while I was destined to be elsewhere. But of late I seemed to be reacting less in this way.

Alcidia had backed away a step or two and broke the dam of our circle. It gave me the feeling that, at this moment, I had greater power to protect Teacher Scotes than he did. Then I realized that Teacher Scotes likely needed no protection, that though under our system any citizen could initiate an accusation against any other, many cases never reached a preliminary hearing, let alone a trial. This man Mathias was for some reason angry at Teacher Scotes and had misdirected his anger into a frivolous suit. Probably all my appearance had really accomplished was to reveal that I had been concealing myself behind a wagon. Realizing this, I lost my bluster.

Teacher Scotes remained calm, even sympathetic. "Tell me, Poet Mathias," he said, addressing the man formally (though I doubted he really was a poet). Being addressed in this way caused the man to unlink eyes with me and face Teacher Scotes. "What have I done to make you so dramatically cite such violations, before me and my friends and now this gathering public?" Teacher Scotes indicated the small group that had assembled, including a few mounted riders spinning slowly on their horses.

I closed ranks, stepping between Xephon and Mathias. (I refrain from appending "Poet" to his name.) Taking advantage of the space vacated by Alcidia, Mathias separated himself from me; Alcidia receded further. Xephon eyed me from his towering benevolence, and I could tell that he did not know what to make of the situation—of the accusation or my presence.

"It pertains to my son, sir," Mathias said to Teacher Scotes, with a slight quaver.

"And who is your son?" Teacher Scotes asked.

"I could name him, but I take it to be unnecessary since he is unlikely to be recalled by you as a unique boy, with unique thoughts and needs and wants, but rather as just one of the many indiscriminate youths that you seek to influence, without regard to their well-being or future happiness." Obviously these words had been rehearsed.

At this characterization of himself, Teacher Scotes suddenly seemed more earnest. "I assure you, Poet Mathias, if that is your impression of me, it must arise from someone who knows me not at all and has been poisoning my reputation for your consumption. For myself I would say that the opposite is true, that to me, every man and woman, boy or girl, is unique—indeed, is only an individual, with only individual thoughts, needs, and wants."

The onlookers pressed in, and I found myself wondering whether this particular congregation was for or against Teacher Scotes.

Mathias seemed to take note of the gathering, and this restrained him somewhat. "My son has related to me a certain conversation he had with you recently."

"Absent knowing who he is, I have no way to address your concerns."

"He is a playwright, apprenticing under Playwright Stephens. He is the proud recipient of the national funds deployed for the creation of his work. I might add that I, too, have proudly received such funds, for my poetry."

Teacher Scotes thought for a moment. "I remember the conversation," he said.

"He did not appreciate the implication of your questioning."

I did not need to hear what the conversation had been about. Having heard similar exchanges before, I could replicate how the back-and-forth had likely gone.

Teacher Scotes would have "implied" nothing but would have asked something akin to whether people would pay to see Mathias's son's plays voluntarily. If so, what was the need of the national funds? If not, the funds having been obtained from those same theatregoers involuntarily, by taxing people who would not choose to attend, what was their justification? Likely he had raised that single question before the son had stormed off, as artists often do when questioned so.

"Had I known that he was so uncomfortable, I would have proposed a different topic," Teacher Scotes said. This would also have been true, but Mathias was beyond mollification. He had arrived solely to complete his errand, and he did so by formally reminding Teacher Scotes that he was required to appear before the chief magistrate in one week to answer this charge.

I could tell that the surrounding murmurs were unnerving him.

On Market to our left, wagons and horses were now crawling through the thickening street. Around us, the sidewalk was also full. Mathias took neither route, instead pushing into the crowd and departing via Fourth itself.

In following his movements, I noticed that Alcidia, too, was gone.

CHAPTER 12

"I promise you," I said to Teacher Scotes, "that I will seek to get this dismissed and make that blackguard regret that he ever attempted such effrontery."

Teacher Scotes stood quietly, blinking now and then. I could not tell what he was thinking.

The crowd began to dissolve. No one addressed us, but those pressing by did not shy from taking our measure.

"Where is Alcidia?" Xephon said. I had wondered the same thing.

In the same quiet mood and not looking at us, Teacher Scotes said, "I fear he might attempt something rash."

"Alcidia? Why? What could he attempt?" I asked.

"Against Mathias?" Xephon asked.

"No," Teacher Scotes said.

"Then against whom?" I asked.

Now Teacher Scotes did look at me, but he did not speak.

"I will pursue Alcidia," Xephon said, abruptly passing between us, bumping several passersby, then heading south along the sidewalk on Fourth.

We regarded each other. "You were following us?" Teacher Scotes said.

"I am deeply sorry."

"Why did you not just rejoin us?"

"I was ashamed."

He thought a moment. "Did you never tell your father of your wishes?"

Quietly I answered, "No."

He thought a moment more. "Was this the first time you followed us since we last saw you?"

"Yes."

He became pensive.

"Whom might Alcidia be pursuing?" I asked.

He ended his ruminations to answer. "I would not have expected someone like Poet Mathias to act alone. Perhaps I am wrong." This thought seemed to relax him.

"As you know, charges like this are usually dropped," I said.

"That is true." He seemed less in need of reassurance than I.

"My father will help."

To this he did not respond, except to say, after a pause, that he was expected home and should begin the walk.

I offered to drive him if he could wait upon my fetching Betsy—an act of some bravery, I felt—but he declined. "I will see you again soon," he said, "and we will resume the many enjoyable conversations we began these past months."

Home for me was only blocks away, so I proceeded there expeditiously. When I arrived, Mother was tending the courtyard garden. Father was not yet home. Instead of going out to her, I went in. I loved my mother; she was gentle and caring to people from city and country alike and revered by all who knew her. But I was never inclined to consult her on matters of consequence. Since I was very young, she had rarely counteracted Father's advice, as if she preferred they be united. I loved her but just the same refrained from approaching her with concerns.

At dusk he finally appeared, emerging from the archway. I had been watching from the window. The moment he entered and raised his head, I took up my cause. I told him of Mathias's accusation. I admitted that I had been following them but had not been with them and so had witnessed what had happened. Father may have disagreed with Teacher Scotes, may have been willing to champion this law to shape his and others' behavior, but he was also just, and he revered our laws too much to brook their misapplication.

"Come with me," he said. We climbed the stairs to his study and seated ourselves in soft leather and low light.

"Mathias didn't do this," he said.

"Do you know who did?" I recalled Teacher Scotes's observation that Mathias likely hadn't acted alone.

"I do."

"Then who?"

"You," he said.

I blinked; he was calm, as if expecting my nonreaction, and he did not wait for me to speak. "Did you think me unaware of your return to their company?" I feigned reflection. "Your visit to Scotes's house, for instance?"

"How did you know about that?"

He compressed his lips but did not show his usual exasperation, as if resigned to its futility, and when he spoke, it was firm but without rancor. He claimed that this had been his point all along and it was why associating with Teacher Scotes was dangerous. Given who I was, there was no escaping notice. There were no secret congregations, not for me. Nothing I did was purely private. I still did not understand how he knew. Had some stranger seen us in the wagon and sought out Father to inform him? Who would do that?

And when I remained mute, still imagining scenarios, he added, "Since you seem so bent on destroying your career and your life, you leave me no choice but to intervene."

The "intervene" hit me. "I still do not understand," I said. I was beginning to, but he would not help me. "But Mathias . . . "

"You are indebted to Mathias," he said. "We both are. Mathias volunteered. He was present during a moment of great agitation for me, found me wearing out the floorboards over your fate and was willing to help."

Father was observing me with such composure I realized that the creaking of leather was from my own chair. The unrelenting press of his bearing only unnerved me further. Unlike me, when confronted with a difficult situation, he decided in a flash. Then his meaning sank in, and I was blank. He seemed to wait upon me, to see if I would exclaim. When I didn't, he seemed almost disappointed.

"But it's a capital crime," I said.

He did not speak until I held his gaze. Almost reassuringly, he said, "That is an unlikely outcome. Do you think I would pursue it if it weren't?" Although the law specified death, convicted felons could propose alternative punishments, which our juries often granted.

"At the least, they'll ostracize him," I said. "What will become of him and his family? Across our border is undefended wilderness."

"There is also the possibility of a fine," he said, though less convincingly.

I wanted to be reassured. I wanted to believe that nothing could happen. Father's being behind this meant he thought the people would support him, that more would side with him than Teacher Scotes, that his was the popular position. It had to be, for in the nature of his profession, he could not act otherwise.

"Is this really necessary?" I said. "You have convinced me. I will stay away."

"You've said that twice before."

"I give my word."

"That, too, you've given twice before."

This boded ill for Teacher Scotes, but Father was saying that a conviction might be of little consequence. This happier thought allowed me to consider my own situation.

"So this means that you will be withdrawing your support for my candidacy?" Though hesitant to raise it, I saw no way not to.

"You know I would not do that. Is that not why you returned to him?"

That night I slept not at all and at first light dressed, intent on finding Xephon to inquire how Teacher Scotes was faring. Then I decided that further contact with me would only worsen matters, as would confronting Father and begging him to end the case. If I stayed away, manifestly so, Father might relent and have Mathias drop the charges before the date with the chief magistrate; he must know that his point was made with both me and Teacher Scotes. But if I continued my defiance and sought out any one of them again, he might drive us all the way to trial, where, in the hands of citizen-jurors, anything could happen. He was my father and only sought the best for me, but the more I deliberated, the angrier I got. I knew to guard against rash action, so I kept to my scheduled route for that day, guiding Betsy through the poorer neighborhoods of Southwark on the Passyunk Road.

There it was Xephon who found me.

Apparently, he had trailed me from a distance through the denser blocks, waiting till I had reached more rural parts. He came upon me quickly, galloping his horse from behind and, without a word, crowded me off the dirt and into some brush. Our horses came to rest, shoulder to shoulder. When I saw who it was, I held my protest.

He nosed his horse skyward, circled around, and came up beside me in the opposite direction. He sat tall, leaning forward, and seemed less amiable than usual. For the moment, the road, shack-walled behind me and tree-lined far ahead, was sparsely traveled.

"For once it is I who stalk you," he said sternly, though teasing. "I am glad to have found you at such a location." As if amplifying our anxieties, his horse jerked uneasily. Xephon's leg bumped my wagon, but he didn't flinch.

"I am not glad," I said. "For Teacher Scotes's sake." He understood my meaning but ignored it.

"I cannot bring myself to believe that you conspired with your father in this." I thought it astute that he had surmised my father's involvement when not even I had.

"This is agony to me," I said. "And punishment. This is my father's way of separating me from the three of you forever." He regarded me as if pleased to have his suspicions about my father confirmed. "And Teacher Scotes?" I said. "Does he suspect my involvement?"

"Teacher Scotes finds it difficult to think ill of anyone."

"Does he know you are here?"

"No."

"And you? Do you harbor any doubts?"

"With me you will have the opportunity to prove otherwise." Then he asked, "Have you seen Alcidia?"

Approaching from ahead, a line of carriages reached us and passed dustily. The gray sky, which had been sitting coolly on us, brightened and warmed.

I told him no, I hadn't seen him. "We can't remain here," I added.

Xephon made as if preparing to leave. Before he left, he tried to press me into service with exaggerated claims that only I could get the charges dismissed. I tried to persuade him of the opposite: that my pleadings might *ensure* a hearing and a trial, that the more I defended Teacher Scotes, the more I would force Father's hand. I was relieved to have arrived at this justification for not acting. Overemotionally, I insisted that the best thing I could do was convince my father by my acquiescence that I intended never to see them again, convince not by words but actions. As I spoke thus, my voice sounded alien and abstract.

"I hope you are right," Xephon said in a manner conveying doubt that I was. He rode off explosively.

Teacher Scotes had been charged by Mathias on a Monday. This meant that he, Mathias, and any other witnesses would have to appear next Monday, June 13, before the chief magistrate. Having heard both sides, the chief magistrate would determine whether the case should proceed to trial. All that was required was the least evidence of guilt for the case to be deemed worthy of full investigation in open court.

On Thursday, I began checking the Postings of Proceedings at the old Statehouse on Chestnut Street. Mathias had filed the charge, which was then displayed on an outside wall for all to see, secured against the brick and under glass. The posted charges, written as Mathias had spoken them, would remain there until they were either dismissed or the hearing was completed. The wall was at the east end of the complex, where the hearing would take place, in the room that two generations ago housed our highest court. The building at the west end, where the Continental Congress once met, had since been extended and now housed our major trials. Chances were if you found yourself one day in the east end of the building, you would find yourself soon after in the west.

When on Friday the notice was still there, I became anxious. I stood atop my wagon to see above the crowd, formed by those who liked to stop and peruse what was on the wall. Their murmurs, more energetic than usual, likely came from seeing Teacher Scotes's name. When on Saturday it was still there, I sweated coldly, knowing that the office was closed and that any dismissal of the charges would have to wait till Monday morning, before the scheduled time of the hearing, which was ten o'clock.

In other words, it would not happen.

CHAPTER 13

Are the reasons for our actions always genuine, or may they be pretenses, decoys, self-blinding ploys? I refer not to the reasons we describe to others, but to those we tell ourselves, privately, in the raucous silence of our own minds.

I have learned not to generalize too easily about human behavior, not to believe that what is true of one person is necessarily true of another. Teacher Scotes, for instance, seemed unable to be anything but honest with himself. Many times had I witnessed him challenge his own thinking and cite the evidence for his conclusions so that others might correct him if they could. And if they could, he would freely explore his own errors. It was the very manner we sought to emulate. Yet in the week before the hearing, I had hesitated to plead his case before Father, waiting instead till the time was gone for action. Was it for the reason I imagined, that keeping silent would best help Teacher Scotes's cause? Truly, I cannot say. Such uncertainty I now believe to be a consequence of not thinking carefully about every issue in my life, large and small, making it difficult to trust myself when I most needed to.

Father was scheduled to take the Saturday evening ferry to New Jersey for Sunday meetings with some Delaware and New Jersey representatives. When I arrived home around midday, he was upstairs filling a portmanteau, according to Mother, who was downstairs setting for dinner. I assisted her, which Father observed when he came down soon after, lightly cupping the back of my head upon approaching. The dining room was comfortably bright, without the heat of direct sunlight, and cooler than the outside air. When we sat, he leaned back and commented to Mother that I appeared to still be growing, that he thought it had to be illusory, and that my height and handsomeness made not only them proud but soon would be a source of pride to all the nation. Mother smiled but did not answer.

We dined, making small talk. Father recounted his plans and bid me to assist Mother in his absence. If strangers were to call, I was not required to meet with them but could invite them to return the next week. I had accompanied him on trips before and wondered whether he'd invite me now, but he preferred not leaving Mother alone these days, and I imagined he was conveying trust that, on the eve of the proceedings, I would not abuse his absence and would honor my promise not to visit Teacher Scotes. I took this supposition and his general calm as an opening to engage him as I had otherwise avoided doing.

"Having not seen Teacher Scotes since Monday," I said, "I wonder how he fares under the pressure of his approaching hearing. I have wondered how any man might."

Father answered tenderly. "I know you have kept true," he said, referring to my staying away. "And your concern for him becomes a lawmaker. No representative relishes the meting out of penalties, even under laws he himself has championed. Do not worry about Teacher Scotes," he added, and I was struck by the appellation "Teacher." "As well as any man, he can prepare himself for what awaits him."

I asked Mother if I might speak with Father privately. "Your mother may hear whatever you'd like to say," he said. But she expressed contentment that the two statesmen of the family, as she put it, wished to confer on important matters, adding that she had her own to attend to anyway. Father liked that she had addressed us in this manner.

When she was gone, I rose from my chair and walked to the window. Within our courtyard walls, we were secluded, though we lived at one of the busiest locations in the city. The walls seemed ever to shield us from the faint and faraway sounds of VOP.

My back was still to Father when he said, "I don't say you're fully wrong in your admiration of Scotes. He is not without his qualities. He fought in the War. He is learned, in many ways. And whether you agree with him or not, he is a man of beliefs, as I'm sure you sensed, as much as he likes to suggest otherwise." I turned but remained at the window. "I admired him once too," he said. "When I was tender of years, like you."

"But your opinion changed."

"Time passes. One matures. I came to realize that while some of what he suggests might sound reasonable in theory, most of it is wrong and ultimately dangerous. Trust me, someday you will see it that way also."

Nothing I had learned from Teacher Scotes gave credence to Father's estimate. But I did not want to question him because Father sometimes construed questions as challenges, and I needed to preserve his calm.

"I am the one at fault," I said. "Because of my disobedience, he now faces trial. My guilt weighs on me."

Father's face was pleasant. "No. I was wrong to give you that impression. Fear not, you are not to blame. Son, I would not have initiated proceedings had I considered Scotes to be innocent." Then he regarded me closely. "You understand that much about me, do you not?"

"Do you think it will go to trial?" I adopted the tone of a novice lawmaker eager to learn his craft.

"It is likely," he said. "Especially since I myself will be there." I sensed that he had been waiting to inform me of these blunt truths.

This was the worst news yet. Unlike Mathias, Father was the most formidable of opponents. Yet I masked my reaction and calculated my response.

"Why do you think it likely?"

"The legal threshold is low."

I held a moment, as if searching for a question. "May I ask you about the law?"

"Of course."

"The law has two parts," I said, slowly. "Which part do you think the magistrate will find applicable?"

"Both."

Again I projected a dispassionate consideration. "The second part," I said, "asserts corruption of the young. When the law was passed, what did you and the Assembly mean by 'corruption'?"

He placed his palms onto the arms of his chair and leaned back. "We thought it more appropriate to leave it undefined and for the jury—for the people—to decide."

"For the people to decide."

"The most democratic approach, no?"

I nodded. I thought of the precision Teacher Scotes always sought in definitions. I said, "The first part of the law—it asserts lack of belief in the ideals of the nation. Which beliefs will be cited as lacking, do you think?"

Father smiled, as if he knew what I was doing and was not bothered. Our even having this conversation conveyed his trust in me. Shortly he would depart and yet was arming me with information that could be valuable to Teacher Scotes were I to breach my promise, though he knew I would not.

"Will you be standing by that window for our entire discussion?" he said good-naturedly. "Come, sit . . . and cease towering over me like VOP, which daily I am in the shadow of already." I took my usual seat to his right. Upon my sitting, he said, "Perhaps you can answer your own question. What ideas have you heard from him yourself, in your meetings?"

Thankfully, I had a response. "In my experience, he rarely expounds any ideas at all, as you have said. Virtually everything he utters is a question."

"Clever man he is," my father said. This time, I waited for him. Eventually he folded his hands and fixed upon me earnestly. "You ask which beliefs of his will be cited?"

I nodded.

"He does not believe in democracy," he said.

"*He does not believe in democracy?*" I could not suppress the force of my reaction, a reaction and force that seemed to please my father.

"He does not," he said. "Now do you see why you are not to blame for his arrest and that he is not entirely innocent?"

I was speechless. This was truly an ominous accusation. Under the law, such a belief could easily be deemed both an affront to our highest ideals and, if it was proven that Teacher Scotes had expressed such beliefs to anyone under thirty, an egregious corruption of the young.

I knew not what to think. I had never heard Teacher Scotes argue any such thing. The only political comments I could recall had come from Xephon, who had likened our system to hemlock and remarked about our needing a new constitution. But even those didn't necessarily imply antidemocratic reform, and most importantly, they hadn't come from Teacher Scotes. Of course there was the dialogue at Simon's, but that topic was the right and the good and was proposed by Founder Haydock, who also provided all the answers.

When Father's gaze became unendurable, I offered, "I did not know that to be the case. I have never heard such views from him myself."

He watched me a moment longer, and I understood that my fervor had persuaded him that I was telling the truth. "I can understand his reticence in your presence, given who you are." He paused. "Do you still question how I have comported myself?"

"I was not questioning it."

Softly, he smiled. Some sort of blow had stunned me, but still I wondered, If I myself had not heard such comments from Teacher Scotes, how had Father? Teacher Scotes wrote nothing and had spoken in Assembly just once in years, an appearance I had witnessed (and what was said in Assembly was protected, anyway), and as well I knew, Father had had no discussions with him either, not for a generation. But the moment passed and, as always, I allowed such riddles to bolt rather than corral them.

Could Father's charge be true? No one questioned this our greatest value and achievement, the very basis of our almost fifty-year-old founding. Not a single voice. On Monday Teacher Scotes would stand in court and be made to answer to the official force of law. But I could not let the conversation end without hearing more.

I asked, knowing this could never be the case, "Does he advocate monarchy then?"

Perhaps seeing the opportunity to at last sever any further interest I might have in Teacher Scotes, Father's answers came steadily and intensely to this my final line of inquiry. "I do not think he advocates much of anything, any longer," he said, "but only seeks to undercut what we believe in."

"Why?"

"There are such people."

"Is that what he told you back then, that he did not believe in our system?"

"Oh yes. He was quite explicit back then."

"Why? What reasons did he give?"

"Put simply, he does not believe in the people." When I was too dumbfounded to respond, Father gave a single nod, as if to say, Believe it.

"But from what I've seen, he has great admiration for people."

"Not people," Father said. "*The people.*"

I sat, dumbly. Father said, "Now you see why I broke relations with him all those years ago and why he is a threat, not just to you but everyone."

A few hours later, Father left. The next afternoon we received word that he had changed his plans and would sup at the home of a Delaware representative, remain there overnight, and return in time for the Monday morning hearing.

I spent that Sunday evening by myself in our second-floor library. Usually I went straight to my third-floor bedroom. But for some reason I wanted to be among books.

Our collection was considerable and a source of pride. It had come with the house when we bought it. Some volumes had been gifts to Doctor Franklin from men like Lawyer Jefferson, Lawyer Adams, Doctor Rush, and others, whose libraries had mostly been acquired by the National Library. The books spanned the ages, from the Greeks and Romans to Pufendorf and Locke. Most were now illegal to teach or obtain—long ago the Assembly had prohibited works that could be considered anti-democratic or simply cast aspersions on our system—and not even we had read them. Besides, books were for the upper sort: only people of means could afford more than a few. Even Teacher Scotes had to borrow from wealthier friends, sometimes in exchange for lessons for their children. But in our family, we did not fear appearances because people knew we had not purchased the books we owned.

I wondered what Teacher Scotes, Xephon, and Alcidia were doing at that moment—how they were preparing to answer the charges. Father always said that one must think beyond the present moment to the potential consequences of one's actions, that not to do so was to invite calamity. How the truth of such maxims becomes clearest when you violate them!

In hindsight it was evident that all the ingredients of this moment had been present in that one—that day, just weeks ago, when I pursued them, was jumped by Alcidia, and ended up accompanying them to Assembly. Likely Teacher Scotes had seen the ingredients and had invited me anyway, knowing what might happen. Had he wanted to support my desire to learn, despite the risks to his person, or had he rather used me for some purpose of his own? Was his a benevolent or malevolent influence? I was no longer sure. What Father had said about him colored all and was horrible to contemplate. To believe as Father alleged Teacher Scotes did was to put a finger in our collective eye and become an "other," an alien, an outsider, with no desire to belong. It was akin to professing atheism. On this point even I, back then, could agree that to attack a people's ideals was to speak as if to destroy.

If ever a moment called for me to think things through and take sides, this was it. Instead, I gave up at the start, as I typically did—gave up any chance of understanding and of action. Never would I be able to make sense of it. So I slouched in sticky leather, surrounded by shelves of unread books, fixed upon the stolid panes of tall black glass on our southern wall. When at last the glass lightened and the time approached to leave for the courthouse, I rose with just this hope: that these late troubles would somehow go away and I could think of them no longer.

CHAPTER 14

It being a Monday and not a market day, the crowds on Market and adjacent streets would at least be passable. The day was overcast, such that our city's colors were three: gray, green, and red-orange. The air was still; the freshly leaved branches and newly sprouted flags, in anticipation of the Fourth, hung limply. After a breakfast just of coffee, I dressed formally, in greatcoat, and began the short walk to the courthouse.

There being one case scheduled before ours, I strolled, in no rush to meet the day's events. When at last I cut over from Market to Chestnut and approached the old Statehouse, I was confronted by an astonishing sight.

On the broad sidewalk before the steps that fronted the court was a small farming band, including a plainly dressed farmer who stood tall and less bent over than most, and four muscular farmhands. With them were a tall, dark horse and two giant, shiny black oxen with white horns, yoked, their necks shoulder-high to their master. Dragging by chain on the ground behind them was a large stone boat stacked with farm implements and a gleaming plow, the plow's arms raised as mutely as the legs of the animals. Man and beast alike held quiet and were gaped at by small assemblies on either side. They must have been waiting upon the courthouse to open, for they stood directly in front of it.

At just before nine o'clock, Mathias arrived, veering in my direction and extending his hand when spying me. He wore that same tall hat from a week ago, of an outdated style that had been abandoned for its being associated with the upper sort. I shook his hand. Then, at nine, the large doors swung on their hinges and a court official pinned them ajar. Even though we were scheduled second, anyone who had business before the court was allowed to witness earlier proceedings, so Mathias and I ascended the wide stone steps, entered, and seated ourselves on wooden chairs against the wall on the right side of the room.

It was not a large room, perhaps forty feet square, with a rail just inside the entrance that extended all the way across, corralling off a space for spectators to stand at the back. At the front was a high stage, also behind a railing, supporting a long table with five leather chairs, just before a bay with three tall windows. Four of the chairs were low and empty; the center chair was high-backed, almost royal, and was occupied by the robed chief magistrate. In front of the stage was a modest table, at which sat two officials working their quills, and a seat for the third, who still manned the front door. To the side, opposite us, was a small white jury box—structured like a simple child's maze—which would not be used today. There was a cold fireplace on the wall behind the jury box and one on the wall near us. Most everything in the room was painted white, including the walls, with dark wood trim. The room's most outstanding feature was in its center: the small defendant's dock. It, too, was painted white.

At first we puzzled over why no one followed us in, then we heard the official who was still standing in the open doorway speak to someone outside. "I don't understand, sir. You wish to bring the oxen and the horse inside the courtroom?"

As he listened to the inaudible reply, an unkempt farmer in a straw hat entered and was followed by six other like men. They passed through the railing at the back and approached the front desk, where the two officials took their names. They must have been the prosecuting accusers, because the officials allowed them to remain where they were, whereupon each took up seats in the old jury box. All the while, the official at the entrance had been listening to whatever was being said to him outside. When done listening, he appeared perplexed and, in his confusion, turned in the direction of the chief magistrate, who sat serenely atop his judicial perch.

Chief Magistrate Rhoads was well known to Father, well known in general for his wisdom, erudition, and just sensibilities. I was glad that he would hear Teacher Scotes's case. He was white-haired, red-faced, stocky, and of like age to Teacher Scotes. I had heard from Father that he tended to clasp his hands before him and that this gesture alone somehow complemented his studied thoughtfulness and gave one confidence in his deliberations. He sat so now and, having witnessed the exchange at the entrance from afar, said not loudly but clearly all the way to the administrator there, "I gather the defendant wishes to bring in evidence for his defense."

"Yes, sir," the administrator said. "He has three large animals and many implements."

"Tell him that won't be necessary," the chief magistrate said. "Ask that he leave someone behind to tend them and say that when the time comes, I will step outside to view his evidence."

The administrator did so, then we heard their steps before the tall farmer and three of the hands appeared, passed through the railing, the farmer taking his position in the defendant's dock.

Apparently he was a successful farmer who was being accused by his neighbors, the seven men who had been waiting in the old jury box and now approached the front table. Though in possession of far greater plots of contiguous land, these farmers, so they argued, produced lower yields, year after year, than did the accused, and they attributed his success to magic or sorcery. Because older laws existed against such practices, the prosecuting farmers did have standing to make the accusation and obtain this hearing. Apparently they all sowed the same crops—wheat, barley, Indian corn—yet for some reason, the defendant reaped many more bushels per acre. In describing the situation, they became agitated, every now and then jabbing in the direction of the defendant. The scene was painful to watch: being chronically hunched, the farmers strained both to address the chief magistrate above them and to jab behind them. The chief magistrate listened calmly, his hands clasped atop the long table. More than one accuser spoke, and the chief magistrate regarded each in turn. When they were finished, he asked if they wished to call any further witnesses, and they answered no.

"Very well," he said, in that same calm manner. "How does the defendant answer?"

"Chief Magistrate," the man said, "I request to show you the evidence of my innocence that I have assembled outside the doors of this court."

The chief magistrate stepped down from the stage and walked out the front door. He was strikingly short, appearing more so because of the height he had descended from. The administrators followed, inviting the defendant to follow them, followed by his hands, followed by the accusers and several onlookers, who had lined the back railing. Mathias and I looked at each other and quickly fell in behind the others.

We all gathered at the base of the steps, on the sidewalk, in the still gray morning, with a larger group of onlookers surrounding the official audience, the chief magistrate himself almost nose to nose with the giant oxen. The oxen were unguarded but tranquil, and one muscular gent held the reins of the horse. The accused farmer proceeded quietly to describe his operations, the implements he had brought, why they looked as they did, why his animals looked as they did, and how he had come to own his farm, which for years he managed for another man but a few years ago had purchased. Again the chief magistrate listened mutely, though seemingly struck by the massive load that the oxen had apparently been dragging.

When the defendant rested, the chief magistrate asked him only, "How far was your journey this morning to reach this court?" to which the farmer answered, "Three miles, sir." "Please take up your position again in the dock," the chief magistrate said, then reentered the building. The rest followed, including an even bigger group of onlookers.

The same official that had manned the doors before remained and barred further onlookers from entering, and just before I, too, reentered, I glanced eastward and saw Father at some distance, approaching on foot. The enjoyment of the moment left me. Then I happened to glance westward. There, also at some distance, were Teacher Scotes, Alcidia, and Xephon, and this fact only quashed my spirits further.

Back inside, the accused farmer was speaking, though still softly. "So you have seen, Chief Magistrate," he said, "my implements of husbandry and my farmhands, robust, well-conditioned, and well-clad people. My iron tools are of first-rate quality, my plough massive and unyielding, and my animals stout and strong. These, in truth, are my implements of magic."

"Is there anything else?" the chief magistrate asked.

"Yes, sir. But it is impossible for me to exhibit to your view or bring into this hearing those late-night toils of mine, my early morning watchings, our strains, and our fatigues. These, too, explain the prodigiousness of our output."

For a farmer, his language was extraordinary. Apparently the chief magistrate thought so too, for at this statement, he uncharacteristically raised his eyebrows.

There followed a stillness, matching the day outside. Then the chief magistrate rapped his gavel. "The case against Farmer Plinney is closed," he said, "and will not proceed to trial."

CHAPTER 15

The courtroom cleared, including the onlookers at the back, who were allowed to stand for one case only. In flowed a fresh group in their stead and took up the full space, three rows deep. Following them was Father, whose bearing and vigor always drew the eye when he entered a room, and this made Mathias jump up next to me, hat in hand, and join Father at the front to confer with the administrators. When done, they took chairs next to the jury box.

I was not sure why Father wanted to be here. Ensuring that the case went to trial was part of it, but legally the hurdle was modest, and Mathias's coaching would have been completed. There were risks to his attending. Though Teacher Scotes was unpopular, he did have his supporters, and Father generally avoided offending anyone, if possible.

Not a minute later, Teacher Scotes, Alcidia, and Xephon entered too, and the door was closed behind them.

Theirs was a formidable three-man team. Teacher Scotes proceeded to the defendant's dock and enclosed himself. He had not changed clothes for the occasion—same shabby white shirt, same dark breeches—risking, I thought, a show of disrespect or indifference, which affected even how *I* appraised him, especially having learned of his beliefs. Judging by their expressions, some in the audience likely felt this too. Inside the box he stood erect and faced front, toward the chief magistrate, in full beaked profile to me.

Xephon and Alcidia could have taken two loose chairs anywhere but chose to stand behind Teacher Scotes in the space between him and the back railing. Xephon stood tall, his hair and beard wet and combed. Alcidia seemed tense, his blond hair out of place, his expression morose. Teacher Scotes's love for him was great, which must have intensified the pain of anticipating what his teacher was about to endure.

One of the administrators stood and read the charge, and this commenced the hearing. The chief magistrate then invited the prosecution to present its argument for why this case should go to trial. At this Mathias nearly hopped into the center of the room, to a spot between the chief magistrate on his platform and Teacher Scotes in his box.

I had disliked Mathias from the moment I'd seen him. Had I been practicing what Teacher Scotes taught me, I would have named the details that produced that opinion, but this would need await another time.

Mathias gestured back and forth, now at the chief magistrate, now at Teacher Scotes, as if passing buckets down a line or giving a bad (I am certain) poetry recital. Theatrics likely intended to compensate for the thinness of his arguments. He told the story—one I knew was coming—of what Teacher Scotes had questioned his son and how the son had been offended. The chief magistrate listened politely, though with a line of skepticism on his lips. When the chief magistrate said nothing in response to his first story, Mathias uneasily began his second.

He had attended Assembly, he said, back in April, as he often did, being, as he was, a responsible, engaged, and participative citizen. Often he sat for the entire session. This would have earned him many demos, of course, which caused me to wonder how much poetry he was writing, despite having received, as he claimed, national funds for that purpose. This past week I had sought his works but found no books under his name, and no publisher had heard of him. Only the editor at the *Peep Hole's Daily* admitted to having published one poem but could recollect no details.

Apparently Mathias had been in attendance the same day I had joined Teacher Scotes, Alcidia, and Xephon—the day that Teacher Scotes had spoken. But no sooner had he begun describing Teacher Scotes's speech than the chief magistrate held up a hand and addressed not Mathias but Father, who was still seated to the side.

He said, rather seriously, "Surely this court does not have to remind the esteemed representative that citizens are free to speak their minds without constraint in Assembly and that the law that governs this case does not apply within that building." Of course not only my father but everyone knew that people had full freedom of speech in Assembly, on the premise that the best laws would arise if representatives and citizens could speak without fear of legal consequences. This is what freedom meant to us: the freedom to vote.

Father bowed slightly. "Of course, Chief Magistrate, forgive me. The error was mine and not Poet Mathias's." Because Father certainly knew the rules of Assembly, a fact not lost on anyone, it was likely that he had expected Mathias to take this tack. So despite the law, those at the back of the room got to hear what Mathias had said.

Mathias, however, seemed not to understand that he had just been banned from proceeding with the story, because he tentatively resumed. The chief magistrate raised his hand again.

"Have you any further evidence?" he asked, this time directly of Mathias.

Mathias had to think about this. "No, sir," he said.

"Then I have a question," the chief magistrate said. He meticulously restated Mathias's story about the exchange between Teacher Scotes and Mathias's son, then asked if he had the facts substantially correct.

"Yes, sir."

"Then would you be good enough to elaborate, Prosecutor Mathias, on how that conversation is evidence that Teacher Scotes does not believe in the ideals of the nation and corrupts the young?"

I almost felt sorry for Mathias, his being so unskilled. I myself knew well how the heat and shame of such moments could be sickening. I wondered if Father understood when Mathias first volunteered that he would be partnering with such incompetence. Most of all, I felt vindicated: given their case so far, Teacher Scotes hardly seemed the ideological vagabond that Father had portrayed, and my respect for and desire to learn from him might still be legitimate.

Mathias simply repeated what he had said. "I submit, Chief Magistrate, that Teacher Scotes questioned my son the wisdom and value of the national funds for playwrights and, by extension, for all artists."

"Continue" was all the chief magistrate said; he waited patiently. Mathias looked at Father.

From time to time throughout this testimony, I took the measure of Teacher Scotes. His bearing never changed. He looked steadfastly upon the chief magistrate and evinced neither pleasure nor pain at Mathias's strained attempt to make his case. Xephon matched his look, also stoic and immutable. It was Alcidia who appeared preoccupied. His intelligence was great; perhaps he sensed that dire events were imminent, despite Mathias's ineptness.

Finally Mathias said, "My son depends on those funds. Not to receive them would be a corrupting influence. And the act that created them was duly voted for in Assembly."

"Like you, Prosecutor Mathias," the chief magistrate said, "I infer from Teacher Scotes's questions to your son that he may have disapproved of the funds and the act that authorized them. What I ask is how his disapproval of this act, or any particular act, equates with the serious charges you bring against him."

"Chief Magistrate?"

"When the act was voted for originally, did not some citizens and representatives oppose it, perhaps even many citizens and representatives, though eventually it passed?"

"Chief Magistrate?"

"And despite the act's becoming law, might those same citizens and representatives who originally opposed it still think it ill-advised?"

"Well . . . they might," Mathias said.

The group at the back chuckled, for the first time calling the officials' attention to their presence. The chief magistrate calmly scolded them. I credited Mathias for admitting this much, but then I don't believe he saw where the exchange was going.

"This is where your argument eludes me," the chief magistrate said. "That Teacher Scotes disapproves of an act need not prove that he rejects the ideals of our system, which in fact asks citizens and representatives for their views on myriad concerns. Does it not? That is, it asks for their opinion and obedience but not their agreement with individual pieces of legislation."

Again Mathias looked at Father, who remained passive. For the first time, I noticed the slightest brightening of Teacher Scotes's mien. I imagined that he was pleased to hear a conversation based on his beloved method of questioning.

From what I knew, Teacher Scotes had never been accused of anything, had never accused anyone of anything, had never observed a preliminary hearing or been a member of a jury at trial. Knowing his propensity to be intrigued by whatever was new to him, I suspected that despite his being the one in jeopardy and possibly guilty, he was studying the players, the procedures, and the process.

All Mathias could say then was "Chief Magistrate" again—it would have been comical, how many times he said it, had the situation not been so tragic—and the chief magistrate took the initiative to advance the proceedings. "Have you anything further?" he asked. Father faintly shook his head, and Mathias reported that he had nothing further.

"Very well, thank you for your testimony." The chief magistrate waited for him to sit. Then he addressed Father. "Prosecutor Antonyn, have you any testimony to add?"

"I have," my father said and rose.

I don't know why I was surprised to see him standing before the administrators' table and the high stage, because it explained the reason he had come at all. Yet what could be his testimony? Other than to relate what Teacher Scotes had said years ago—a desperate strategy, for those words certainly would be deemed outdated. Testimony had to be first-hand, and the only recent contact I knew of had occurred outside Simon's shop, that fateful day, when nothing of any import had been said.

To me, the room darkened slightly, as rooms sometimes do when clouds pass, though the sky was already overcast when we entered. Father looked up at the chief magistrate, who sat royally but diminu-tively in his tall chair, there being sufficient space on its backrest for another head above him. As august a personage as the chief magistrate was, the presence of Father overshadowed him. Out of nowhere I remembered the day when, riverside, I had observed the loading of Merchant Girard's ship—an odd association, but it came because there appeared now another kind of ramp before me: Teacher Scotes in his box; then Father, somewhat taller; then the chief magistrate, taller still upon his perch. Months later I might have enjoyed the symbolism: the judicial overseeing the legislative. But these were not the relationships that existed in our system.

"Chief Magistrate," Father began, "I will be brief, but I do not want to begin my testimony without first a word of respect for Teacher Scotes. I don't exaggerate when I say that I stand here with a heavy heart. Teacher Scotes is an elder citizen, a man who fought bravely and was wounded in our great war, and a man who engages with his fellow citizens and is sometimes loved in return." At this he briefly nodded in Teacher Scotes's direction but without making eye contact.

"Your word of respect is noted," the chief magistrate said.

"We are not before this court to question his sincerity but rather to challenge, regrettably, his unlawfulness. We are one people, united in our values, and it is never easy to amplify discord among us. However"—and here he paused—"I myself am in possession of evidence proving that Teacher Scotes, tragically, does not in fact believe in the ideals that our nation believes in and, because he disputes our ideals in the presence of the underaged, is also in fact guilty of corrupting the young."

Murmurs rose at the back. I have heard it said that in the European courts, judges rap their gavels at the least noise from observers, but here the people are supreme, and official bodies hesitate to restrain them. The chief magistrate did nothing.

Probably knowing that the chief magistrate would await his next words, Father delayed, as if to intensify the drama. Despite all I had reflected on the day before, I thought, frantically, Father *has* to be mistaken about Teacher Scotes—a sentiment of mine that even Teacher Scotes would have considered incoherent. For him, a proposition was either true or false or mixed; it did not *have* to be anything.

Father said, "The evidence in support is very simple and clear. And this is it: it has been related to me that Teacher Scotes openly likens democracy . . . to hemlock." Again he paused, and even louder murmurs rose. When they ebbed, he added, "Apparently, our beloved system, the greatest in the world, the greatest ever known to man, is no better to him than a deadly, poisonous, rapidly spreading weed."

What hit me was that spinning sense of unreality that often filled my head and stomach when faced with something that seemed both to be happening and not happening at the same time. To my knowledge, Teacher Scotes had never said those words—*Xephon* had, on the day I caught up with them. But that was not why I jumped up. Since *I* had not described our exchange that day to Father, how could he have known? No one had been near enough to overhear.

Apparently I had stood so abruptly that everyone, including Father, the chief magistrate, and Teacher Scotes, regarded me. Even though Father's expression was unaffected by my antics, I knew to sit immediately, at which point the proceedings recommenced and people turned their attention back to Father. Only Teacher Scotes watched me, a look of heavy wonderment upon him. I wanted to shout that I was as puzzled as he.

"These words you heard directly?" the chief magistrate asked my father.

"Not directly, no."

"And you intend to produce the witness who did hear these words firsthand?"

"I call Alcidia to testify."

CHAPTER 16

I t is still intensely painful to relate what happened next. Alcidia stepped forward and did not look at Teacher Scotes. When in position, he began to recount Xephon's quip about democracy and hemlock. He accurately attributed the words to Xephon but declared that Teacher Scotes had neither contradicted nor discouraged the view, not then and not later, and that Teacher Scotes never contradicted such views. This comment reminded me of Xephon's other quip, about the constitution, at Teacher Scotes's house. Alcidia pointed out that Teacher Scotes did exclaim in response to Xephon's words, but that this was likely because I, Representative Antonyn's son (he indicated me), was present and might attribute Xephon's view to him.

Just days before, I would have considered this an outright lie. Alcidia, having no direct knowledge of *why* Teacher Scotes had exclaimed (he had only uttered Xephon's name), had no basis to suggest a reason. The likely explanation was a desperate concern for Xephon's health and an attempt to convey dire urgency. I did not know Teacher Scotes intimately but knew enough to wager that his priority in that moment was his protégé's well-being, not the appropriateness of some political proposition. But there was also Father's account of Teacher Scotes's views. And here was Alcidia, making just that case.

I wondered why Father had asked Alcidia to testify and not me. I was relieved that he hadn't, for the impossible situation that would have put me in. But Alcidia must have been the one to tell Father of what had happened since it would never have been Xephon and certainly had not been I.

When the chief magistrate asked Alcidia for other examples of Teacher Scotes's nonresponses to attacks on our ideals, Alcidia claimed to be unable to recall specifics, and so the chief magistrate recorded just the one. Perhaps Alcidia had forgotten what Xephon had said at Teacher Scotes's house, though this seemed unlikely, given the gravity of the comment. Finally, when the questioning was over, he ceded his spot at the front and, rather than return box-side, came to take the chair beside me. Approaching, he did not look away, and I perceived no discord in him. But we each said nothing, and seated, he leaned forward comfortably, his hands upon his knees.

For a moment the chief magistrate appeared to be reflecting on what had happened and, in the delay imposed by his contemplation, trained his eyes on Alcidia. The small observing crowd murmured plainly. As if to assist the chief magistrate, my father prompted Mathias to stand again, which he did, offering with greater confidence than during his own testimony that he had no further witnesses. The chief magistrate refocused, thanked Mathias, and bade him to resume his seat.

Then he turned to Teacher Scotes, as did we all.

Have you ever noticed something for the first time only by its absence? The pleasures of health, perhaps, once you are afflicted or your need of air when trapped in a cellar? Though it sounds paradoxical, this was the moment that I appreciated just how strong a presence Teacher Scotes was—how strong a spirit—when I studied him in that courtroom, after hearing Alcidia speak. Though he had hardly flinched all morning, something now had left him, some invisible thing that before had animated him so consistently you never fully saw it. It was unlikely that others in the courtroom recognized this. Only I, Xephon, and Alcidia, perhaps—I know that Xephon did because, near tears (and likely wracked by guilt, he having been the speaker of the comment just entered as evidence), he seemed fixed on Teacher Scotes, rather than angry at Alcidia—and I know that Alcidia saw it, because he never looked at Teacher Scotes again.

People sometimes say that those who think most logically love less, but that was not my experience of Teacher Scotes or of myself when I endeavored to be like him. He loved Alcidia deeply, had seen in him the best of a new generation and the expectations of a better future. He had pushed himself at seventy to push Alcidia at thirty, ever eager to help the deserving young, and Alcidia had seemed more deserving than most. I sensed that Teacher Scotes had reverence for every soul but especially for Alcidia's, who was like a sunflower standing singly in a barren field, awaiting its chance to transform that field into something beautiful. I believe he struck Teacher Scotes that way.

Teacher Scotes still had not moved but stood vacantly, focused on seemingly nothing, in a different kind of reverie from his usual exploratory one. What Alcidia had done had stopped him, as if some gear had slipped and would not advance without repair.

Quietly the chief magistrate said, "How does the defendant answer?"

Teacher Scotes did not reply and had not yet looked in the direction of the man addressing him. The courtroom had grown quiet. Gently again the chief magistrate asked, "How does the defendant answer? How do you answer, Teacher Scotes?"

Still Teacher Scotes did not respond. Like Xephon I wanted to cry because I caught what appeared to be the glint of moisture at the tip of Teacher Scotes's beaked nose, though it was likely perspiration.

"Answer, Teacher Scotes," someone at the back said.

The chief magistrate raised his chin. "Ladies and gentlemen, please do not address the defendant directly."

When still Teacher Scotes stayed silent, Xephon addressed the chief magistrate. "I would like to testify," he said firmly.

"I am sorry, sir. You may not testify unless called by the defendant." In the ensuing silence the chief magistrate added, "Teacher Scotes, would you like this gentleman to testify?"

"Let me testify," Xephon urged the profile of Teacher Scotes.

"Sir," the chief magistrate said to Xephon. "Please."

It was difficult to watch. Even Father, seated opposite us and more forward in the room, turned stiffly to regard Teacher Scotes. Xephon, only a foot from Teacher Scotes, remained silent, though he clearly wished to speak.

At last Teacher Scotes exhaled, in the manner of a deep release. The effect was of a reawakening. From his box he turned in our direction and, clear-eyed, regarded Alcidia. Then he looked at me, clear-eyed and for an extended moment. Then he faced away and toward Xephon and, judging by Xephon's brightening expression, regarded him too. Then he looked back at Alcidia. His great brain seemed to be calculating something. Perhaps he was assessing where he could best turn. Still looking at Alcidia, he plainly said, "I call Xephon to testify."

Xephon fairly jumped three steps loudly in his boots to stand before the administrators' table and the hovering chief magistrate.

Like a plowshare, Xephon's archaic beard slanted forward from his chin. "Chief Magistrate," he said, "as this man Alcidia has just told, I was the one who made the ill-conceived joke, and Teacher Scotes did yell my name in return, and Palleias was in fact present. But what this man Alcidia did *not* tell you was that at that moment I was holding stalks of hemlock in my hand, something I hadn't known and that Teacher Scotes yelled because he was desperate for me to fling the plant and rush to cleanse myself. That was the reason for his exclamation and why there was no time for him to reprove my indiscretion. Thanks to that exclamation, I ran to the river and nearby tavern for assistance and never did suffer any effects of my stupidity. He saved my life, Chief Magistrate, and that alone is the significance of the event that the prosecution would have you believe is otherwise."

He had spoken so quickly that he had to catch his breath upon stopping. At that moment I admired him more than ever: being himself over thirty meant that, by admitting to such words, he was exposing himself to the very charges that had been leveled against Teacher Scotes.

Hands folded, the chief magistrate spent a moment in stocky repose before questioning further. Then he asked, "Once you were out of danger, did the defendant question your remark? The prosecution has testified to the contrary."

"No, Chief Magistrate," Xephon eventually responded, then added forcibly, "I believe he was in shock."

"And did you witness other occasions when the defendant similarly did not respond to such comments? The prosecution has alleged that too."

"Never, Chief Magistrate." But he said it altogether too quickly and without even the appearance of consideration, and the chief magistrate regarded him dubiously. I think that Xephon sensed his mistake, because he shifted in place. Teacher Scotes reacted not at all, having regained his former firm but passively observant stance.

"I have said the truth, Chief Magistrate," Xephon said.

"I thank you for your testimony, sir," the chief magistrate said. "You may step back."

"But you believe me, Chief Magistrate?"

"If the witness has no further testimony, nor anyone to call, he may step back."

At these words—"anyone to call"—the light of strategy came to Xephon's face. He immediately turned to me and, in that solemn room, in the presence of the chief magistrate, Father, Teacher Scotes, and the assembled people, seemed to weigh a choice.

Because our eyes had locked, I tried to say to his, Don't.

"I call Palleias to testify," Xephon said.

As if a pump were shooting water to all my extremities, a rush of warmth filled me, along with that familiar sensation of unreality, again, that something ill was both happening and not happening. For a moment I think I lost sight of Xephon and everything around me.

The standing onlookers faced me. At the front the chief magistrate peered down. Sitting with Mathias, Father regarded me impassively as well, giving away nothing—not of what he wanted me to do or of how I might avoid this burden. I wanted to shout for help, but of course there was nothing he could do. He stared calmly, as if there were but one option and that he could count on me to do it. Even bent Alcidia at my shoulder twisted to register my presence. At last I looked at Teacher Scotes, not twenty feet from me and latched into a box that enclosed half his body but that soon might enclose the rest of him—imprison if not entomb him.

I'm not sure how long I hesitated, but it must have been too long, because the ever-patient chief magistrate addressed me.

"Young Palleias," he said. "Kindly step forward, sir."

I imagined childishly that if I did not move, I would not have to.

Now Father did betray emotion—a vague irritation that perhaps only I could detect. Perhaps he expected me to aid him eagerly, or perhaps he simply didn't want me to embarrass myself by sitting there indecisively in front of this small group of prospective voters.

Finally I stood, because there was nothing else to do.

I loathed being gawked at, which is comical to say given that in not two years I would be running for national office and, if successful, would spend nearly every waking hour being gawked at by thousands. Sometimes I thought that if Father's bedroom were on the first floor of our house, people would stand at his window to watch him sleep. For me, a crowd's eyes fell upon me like a heavy cloak, confining and immobilizing. Others remained a blur, a pressure, and to break that feeling now, standing before the hunched administrators, Father and Mathias at the table to my left, Teacher Scotes behind me, I focused on the robed and red-faced chief magistrate above—on speaking just to him, the man who then counseled me to "relate all you know that might pertain to the matter at hand."

Here is what I should have said. I should have said that my memory of that day was exactly as Xephon had recounted and—simply, plainly, without equivocation—that on no other occasion had I heard any untoward beliefs expressed by Teacher Scotes, nothing about flaws in our system or our national ideals. All of which would have been true. Sometimes it had been maddeningly true: I wanted Teacher Scotes to state directly what he thought about diverse philosophical issues, rather than pickax us repeatedly with his cutting questions. If he ever did, he only did when there seemed no other way to raise some significant point.

But no sooner had I taken my place to testify than I recalled again what Father had said about Teacher Scotes's views. Father, who was invariably correct in his appraisals, would never have invented such an accusation and must have experienced such views firsthand. I again recalled Xephon's comment about the need for a new constitution, that day at Teacher Scotes's house. I loved Xephon, but standing in that courtroom, with the obligation to testify, I found it impolitic that he was inclined to blurt such things. And what had Teacher Scotes done? He had changed the subject. It was sudden intuition only, but right then—and I cannot fully blame myself for this—I became more suspicious still, being myself aware of two examples now of Teacher Scotes's unresponsiveness to an impropriety by Xephon, and I couldn't help wonder whether Teacher Scotes's exclamation on that first day had indeed meant something other than concern for Xephon's health. Twice I had witnessed such an exchange and in a span of only weeks. Might not these have been glimpses into a pattern? Absent my company, who knew what those three discussed? And I couldn't dismiss, though legally it was irrelevant, Teacher Scotes's dubious questioning of the crowd in Assembly. Everything seemed suddenly unsettled.

Then I remember thinking, Should this case go to trial and the conversation at Teacher Scotes's house be revealed with my never having mentioned it though under oath to do so, I myself could be liable for withholding material information. I knew our system well enough to know that if you were not careful, it could quickly turn on you.

And throughout I was aware that my father was keenly watching.

All this occurred to me, whiplike, inside that courtroom, in the presence of that congregation. It hit me as a single emotion, not these separate thoughts that took reflection to untangle. Was it ultimately an honest way of thinking? Looking back and once again, I cannot say. I cannot say whether in fact I was searching for a reason to do exactly as I must—avoid defying my father.

So what I actually told the chief magistrate was that Xephon's account was consistent with my recollection and that on the question of other occasions, I had less experience than did he. Then I mentioned the day at Teacher Scotes's house, what Xephon had said and what Teacher Scotes had not said. Though I was aware that Teacher Scotes might in fact be guilty of the crime as charged, still the words were burdensome, and as they left me, I could tell, as if listening with others' ears, that they were damning. The will of our minds, or lack of it, often becomes the weight of our bodies.

Once dismissed I regained my seat, instantly horror-filled at what I'd done.

CHAPTER 17

S ufficient evidence, the chief magistrate said, for the case to proceed to trial. He appeared to say it reluctantly and was followed by a stir of carnivorous anticipation at the back, which likely previewed what was to come in the newspapers. Like Teacher Scotes, the chief magistrate was of another era, and he was known to judge with an eye to those past times. But before he gave his ruling, he had invited Teacher Scotes to make his final arguments, setting him free to speak from the dock in a way that he was not on our populated streets.

He did not speak for long and, to my mind, spoke little to the purpose. Not to mention that I listened through a fog, distracted by a kind of perspiring queasiness. He did confirm that his exclamation to Xephon that day was, as "his friend" Xephon had inferred, out of concern for his exposure to the poison (the only time he referred to anyone as friend). He did not address my testimony regarding his nonresponse to Xephon's comment at his house—and how could he? The moment it had happened, he was obliged to correct Xephon or be open to the charge of corruption, and because plainly he did not correct him, there was nothing to say now. Of course, the issue was not corruption of Xephon, who was over thirty, but of me. It was my testimony, then, that despite his or my father's reassurances later, likely sent him to trial. This fact I must live with for the rest of my life.

157

What little else he said was addressed to the chief magistrate himself, or at least I think it was. He spoke of men and women of great experience and intellect who thought deeply about the issues of the day, who understood what most people could not devote the time to understanding, and who had taken up the big questions and had judged for themselves the truth or error of others' answers. These men and women had a special responsibility, he said, not primarily to the nation—although the nation could benefit greatly from their abilities—but to themselves. For what was justice and goodness but following with your footsteps the path envisioned as right by your own mind? Most citizens were at risk of being swayed by rhetoricians and demagogues. Though capable of understanding, they were still at sea, buffeted by changing currents. But those with understanding could guide the rudders of the fleet. Whether they did so was their choice, a choice not without consequence for their own souls.

It was a strange speech, and most people in the room appeared bewildered. Perhaps not the chief magistrate, who kept his silence and his calm and from what I could tell, took no account of Teacher Scotes's words in rendering his verdict. I did notice, however, that Father never looked in Teacher Scotes's direction but sat facing forward, immobile as a milestone.

When we adjourned, Alcidia left before the crowd, who then pressed through the doors, in a froth at what they'd witnessed. For a moment Teacher Scotes remained. He stood in his box between me and Father, causing both of us to pause before proceeding. But the next case was due, so the administrators ushered him and Xephon out. Then it was only Mathias, me, and Father, and though I wished to depart unaccompanied, I did my duty and joined them at the exit. As I did, Father glanced at me with unconcealed affection. It did not assuage me.

On the steps outside, we encountered a crowd comprising the next defendants, prosecutors, and onlookers, all waiting to go in. Teacher Scotes and Xephon were already heading north on Fifth. East, down Chestnut, walls of brick buildings converged distantly on the bare masts at harbor. I had planned to head that way myself, toward home, and expected Father to head west, toward Assembly, but in stepping down, he said, "Gentlemen, please join me," and Mathias and I obeyed.

As was always true, the waiting crowd eyed Father dramatically, and some me also. But we headed off briskly, with an air of urgent business, and they respected our need to leave them.

We did not go far, just to the other end of the block, to the west wing of the building we had just occupied and to the room where Teacher Scotes's trial would soon take place.

Just after drafting our National Constitution, while the amphitheater and VOP were still being built, the representatives met here for several years. Upon their departure, this wing was renovated to house our major trials. Two floors became one, and the walls were extended out: west, flush with Sixth Street, and south—all to create a second amphitheater, this one indoors and wooden. It could seat a thousand people, sufficient to house our largest juries, with a stage at the western wall for the bailiff, accusers, and defendants. The stage had a podium at center, flanked by two large white statues at the wings, one of General Washington and one of General Pericles. While most trials waited months to be scheduled, trials of capital crimes were expedited and could occur within weeks of the preliminary hearing. This was why Father wasted no time coming here; in just days, he and Mathias could be called to make their very public case. And Father was never one to leave anything to chance when having to express himself formally before the people.

There were no trials scheduled on Mondays, so we stood virtually alone in the massive hall; only a few scattered laborers did their work, ignoring us. Father fairly leaped to the stage. We followed. Presumably I was the reason for his cheer. My face and ears still blazed.

Not having considered clearly what had happened up till today, I had been thrust into a situation to which I could but react, could then choose based only on that blur rather than on thought. As a result, I would now live with my impetuous choice and its vast consequences, for good or ill.

As would many others. As would Teacher Scotes. And whether for good or ill in the end, I did not want to choose or feel this way again.

Father and Mathias spent a moment admiring the architectural achievement that was this place. The high walls just below the domed and massively chandeliered ceiling were plain, but most of the room was seating, shaped as a half dodecagon, all in dark shiny wood, in both lower level and balcony. To face it from the stage before the shouting masses had to be imposing. The Pit below was of plain wood, divided horizontally by two long troughs. To vote, jurors left their seats and weaved past both troughs. Every vote required two ballots, each a small tin disc with a short rod through the center, like a two-sided mushroom. The rod of one ballot was hollow and indicated a vote for the plaintiff; the second was solid and for the defendant. Voting consisted of casting both: jurors dropped the one to be discarded into the first trough, farthest from the stage, and the one to be counted, in the trough closest to the stage. The ballots in the closest trough were then released and collected, in dramatic fashion and in a manner of which we were proud, by a team of clerks who arranged them for all to see and easily be counted. They were implanted on the front wall of the stage itself, into which a thousand circles had been cut across its entire length, each circle with a center hole, creating a kind of mural of crops growing in the fields from the perspective of birds who flew above it. With skilled hands and moving quickly, the clerks secured the ballots into these holes. On the right side as you faced the stage, they placed the solid ballots for the defendant. On the left they placed the hollow for the plaintiff. In this way everyone could quickly see which side was more numerous, and the vote could be corroborated, visually and immediately. Then by summing rows and columns for each vote, the clerks obtained the formal count as well.

"I have sat in jury," Mathias said, "but I have never stood upon this stage. Someday I would like to recite my poetry in such a glorious place." I wondered whether he was making some sort of request of my father, because in fact Mathias *could* one day recite in such a place: at the theater across the street—the very one that had performed *The Clouds* some years back—which in fact sometimes held trials, when the docket was overflowing and the theater not in use. These days, the docket was fuller than ever before.

Then Mathias regarded me. "Are you quite well, Young Palleias?"

Father, too, was observing me, more searchingly than before.

"Where is Alcidia?" I said.

Mathias continued to watch me closely. Father smiled and patted my shoulder. "Who needs Alcidia when we have you?" He winked at Mathias. Even with an audience of one, his manner could be different from that at home. Then he asked, as if reminded of a thought that was also a trifle, "By the way, that day at Scotes's house, was Alcidia present when Xephon made the comment that you testified about, or had he left you for the moment?"

"He was present," I said.

My father considered this and chuckled wryly.

We approached the podium, our footsteps echoing into the vast and empty room. Only the muted sounds of squeaky carriages, clopping hooves, and intermittent shouts reached us from outside. In the Pit, before the stage, three ragged men swept randomly until they took the hint to labor farther away, though no matter how far they moved away, they would be able to hear us.

Despite my stricken state, I saw that along with his ebullience, Father was ill at ease too. His movements quickened, a quirk I don't believe I had witnessed since I was very young, before he had perfected his skill at addressing an audience. Mathias didn't notice. I wondered what concerned him. Perhaps it was the obvious: that opposing him on this very stage, in front of hundreds on that day and thousands more in the accounts to follow, would be Teacher Scotes himself, a man whose capabilities we both knew intimately.

Father invited Mathias to take the podium first, arguing that the sequence they had used at hearing would also work at trial: Alcidia would follow Mathias, then I would follow Alcidia, then Father would summarize. He was planning that I testify. At nine o'clock in the morning of the scheduled day, the trial would commence. The prosecution would have until eleven, the defense from then till one, all governed by a large clock at the back of center stage. After that came voting and sentencing. Father's plan was that we would practice in the coming weeks to master our respective parts. We would meet at our house and gain confidence as a team in this worthy endeavor. Mathias scribbled everything Father said in a small book.

"And now, Palleias, you step forward," Father said, indicating that I do so.

I did not.

He observed me, then smiled conspiratorially to Mathias. "As you will no doubt one day witness regularly, my son is a brilliant man and is reflective in temperament." He turned to me and appeared not eager for whatever I might say. I was fortunate that his delight at what had happened at the hearing still bathed me in a glow. "Come," he said, warmly, "stand at the podium and feel the possibilities of this position."

I stepped forward, putting them behind me. I grasped the smooth wood. Still the laborers swept and polished at a distance, and the dark shining pews rose to great heights. Then I turned to face them.

"It is an astonishing space, no?" my father said.

I am not sure how Mathias was judging my behavior, and I could sense that Father wished to protect me from embarrassing myself before a man who tomorrow could recount what he saw to any who would listen: "We brought Palleias to the court, and he stood upon the stage looking sickly." Or perhaps Father feared that I had become unhinged.

I cleared my throat and asked my father, "When will the date be set?"

"Very soon." He appeared relieved that I still functioned.

Then, because I offered nothing else immediately, Father said, "Well, gentlemen, I think we've done enough for now. Let us rest, enjoy the fruits of our good labor, and reconvene later."

I turned again to face the room. Whether my actions had been right or wrong, I *felt* they had been wrong, and the longer I remained there, the more I regretted them and the less I wished to take that stage again.

Father stepped up to my left, Mathias to my right. Together we spent a final moment taking in the massive space.

"Teacher Scotes," I said to the emptiness at large, "is accused of not believing in our ideals and of corrupting the young."

Quietly my father said, "We will have ample time in days to come to examine that further." I noted his use of Teacher Scotes's word, "examine." "For now," he said, "let us leave the law alone. It will preoccupy us soon enough."

A group of four men in coattails entered by a side door and gathered at our feet before roving in the Pit and inspecting various sections from a distance. When another group followed and stood immediately before the stage, we dispersed.

Something urged me not to testify for Father's prosecution. But this time I resolved that I would not decide by urges alone. As Teacher Scotes said, just because you feel that you are right or wrong doesn't make you so—the only way to know is to understand. Father had accused him of something truly vile, Alcidia apparently agreed, and the chief magistrate had seen enough to dictate a trial. Should I come to agree with them, even Teacher Scotes would say that I should testify against him. He himself sometimes heard an inner voice that warned against some action; he called it his demon. His practice was to examine its advice till he grasped the reasons to heed or ignore it. Now it was my turn to understand my inner voice and become clear about what to do. Father could not have been more pleased by my behavior at the hearing, and until recently, that response alone by him would have been enough.

CHAPTER 18

For as long as I could remember, I found the greatest pleasure in solitude. It wasn't a pleasure I could mention, let alone write about in university essays, because those whose votes I would seek one day might assume that I disliked people. Which was untrue.

Many people I in fact admired. One type especially intrigued me. Whether living roughly in the wilderness or among the din of our city gatherings, such people had friends, family, colleagues, and neighbors all, as everyone did, yet were also somehow separate. Not physically so or socially. Just separate, in a way. That's imprecise, I know. But their numbers were small, so I had little chance to study them.

The older generation may have shared my intrigue, considering their accounts of how the populace had changed across the years. I do not know if what they said was true. I did know that my attitude was a danger to me. Better for my future was to profess equal reverence for all, as most representatives did, which I rather think was genuine, given how they met the crowds and burst to life before an audience, whether at podium or parlor.

Most of all I could not mention the fear I sometimes felt in the presence of some citizens. I don't exaggerate to call it fear. To be alone on some secluded road and be recognized, to find half a village running toward my wagon, *was* fearsome. If their manner was gesticulating and angry, I anticipated pleas for this or that—more money, more grain, more land, more access to physicians—and accusations that we were blackguards for depriving them. It wasn't their behavior only that frightened me but also that it issued from the brains and brawn not of children but of men.

I had not always felt this way. When I first traveled on behalf of my father, I felt honored to be inquiring about their problems, proud to pass their messages to him, delighted to have played a part. Their gratitude made satisfying days spent being jarred on rutted roads, buzzed by mosquitoes, and terrified of being robbed. But gradually I learned that meeting their demands only brought forth others and not just from the farmers, who with their implements really could threaten, but also from the merchants and mill owners—men and women of every means. Upper, middle, and lower—it mattered not (though there were more, then, of what we called middle). It was the manner, not the caste. I saw that Father's job, and by association mine, involved a precarious balance: meet the people's demands, yes, but not so as to bankrupt the country, impoverish them, and ultimately incur their wrath. For their wants and needs were bottomless.

The trial was set for Thursday, June 30. The *Peep Hole's Daily* ran the story, the other newspapers followed, and for days it was all that was discussed. We even dampened talk of hardship, prices, foreclosures, and the upcoming weeklong celebration of the Fourth, which officially would begin the day after the trial. The trial, I think, became a kind of national distraction. When people struggle, they find relief in scandal. Anger seeks a villain, and I won't deny that some representatives, to deflect the people's anger, decried this or that group to offer someone other than themselves to blame. The rule was if possible, scapegoat the Brits or Europeans; if not them, then our wealthiest citizens, such as the merchants.

Once word had spread, I learned how famous Teacher Scotes really was and that Father was likely right in saying that to associate with him meant recognition, for good or ill. Letters and pamphlets arrived from every state, and many were reprinted with speed. Even the letters Father received, which I helped sort, addressed the trial. Many thanked him for leading the effort to uphold our standards; some criticized him. Though since the Jury Payment Act, we no longer struggled to panel juries, for this trial we probably would not have had to pay at all. For this trial, people would have volunteered simply for the spectacle.

There were not three weeks to prepare. Thus, the very evening of our visit to the courthouse, Father summoned Mathias and Alcidia to our house, where we would meet several times more.

I wanted badly to speak to Alcidia. Father had confirmed that Alcidia had been the one to tell him both about the hemlock and about my rejoining them after Simon's, and he had agreed to testify. In exchange, Father agreed to assist in his ambitions—an arrangement that struck me as unseemly, even if Teacher Scotes *was* guilty. When he arrived that night, he stood boldly down the hallway in my sight, and in him I saw no shame or guilt, just confidence, even friendliness, both of which persisted during our group discourse at table. Unlike me, he seemed certain of the rightness of his action. Unfortunately, there was no opportunity to be alone with him, so my questions had to wait.

Father still appeared nervous. Just after we adjourned, he scolded Mother for something petty, which he never did. When I tried to console her privately, she seemed amused by my attempt and ended up consoling me for some apparent emotion on my face. To me, Father's being worried was distressing in itself. His anxiety made me anxious in a way that had naught to do with preparing for the trial. It was that simple: when he was anxious, I was anxious. It had always been so.

He gave me an assignment: walk the streets and eavesdrop to discover people's opinions of what was coming. Of course I withheld my own opinions—or rather, my uncertainties—especially from my father. Teacher Scotes would have disapproved. His call was to think deeply, debate openly, and test one's assertions in conversation. It was, he thought, the path to learning. There was never shame in being wrong, unless arising from your refusal to see, think, discuss, act.

The city grew red in the June sun's high bright heat upon the brick. Birds twittered in the trees, and the trees themselves were shades of green: a darker, older undergrowth beneath a lighter, fresher tip, as if they had been frosted. May fragrances had yielded to the odor of manure, with fewer farmers arriving on market days to remove it. "Goods in, waste out" had been the longtime arrangement of mutual benefit.

I began meandering among the crowds near home, where I'd be less of an attraction, dressed modestly in work trousers and without a collar, with the flapped hat that was a farmer's gift. Most jury members resided in the city, though the more we paid and the fewer people were employed, the farther did they come. And with fewer people working, more could be found milling about, dressed not unlike me. So I loitered, outside shops, public houses, park gates—wherever a crowd assembled. I visited taverns and especially printers, who were most attuned to the people's sensibilities. Whenever talk turned to the trial, I leaned in to catch the sentiment.

Half the conversations included words like "dangerous," "immoral," "an affront to everything precious"—all condemnations and spoken in a personal tone, as those confronting Teacher Scotes often did. The other half were reticent, either silent or offering quiet questions designed to calm the rising emotion that was saturating the discourse.

"He has violated the law," one might say. (He likely has, I thought.)

"He has flouted the people's will." (Possibly this too.)

"Oh, he is harmless. A comical, questioning old man. Take no heed of him." (Old and questioning, for certain. Harmless? A few weeks ago, I would have readily agreed.)

"But what if his ideas spread? What will happen then? Especially since he targets the young and impressionable."

"What ideas? I have more than once been in his presence and have hardly heard him assert anything."

"And that accursed, self-deprecating irony." (Valid questions and observations all.)

Once I heard, "Well, the truth will out at trial."

I wanted to question them, these people that I overheard, as Teacher Scotes might have done, so that I could better understand what was at stake and how to think about it. Or perhaps I'd simply anger them for exposing what they thought they knew but did not. No matter; I was angering myself. For once I wanted to choose by reasoning, but all I truly knew was that events were rapidly progressing and that soon the trial would be upon us.

CHAPTER 19

The last day I went out to gather people's views was the Friday after the preliminary hearing. That same day Xephon tracked me down a second time, in an isolated alley off Seventh, north of Market. I had made it my practice to proceed by alleyway instead of street to avoid being approached. It was one thing I was glad of that week: my purpose in traveling was other than to be approached.

At first I did not recognize him. When I was halfway down the alley, the sound of boots behind me echoed. The number of thefts had been increasing, and not knowing the intention of this stranger, I judged how far I'd have to run to reach the next cross street. I glanced right and left to look for residents at their windows, people whose presence might deter an attack, and found only one large orange cat sunning itself between glass and closed curtains. Then the man called my name and began trotting. I turned and noted his size, his gait, his high riding boots, and most especially, his beard, which jutted from the hood of his military-style cloak. Recognizing that it was Xephon did not completely calm me.

Reaching me, he looked around and said, "Step in here" and steered me into a cramped archway on the cool, shady side that led to an inner courtyard. It was too small for us and almost insufficient for his height, and he crouched a little to match the angle of the arch. Almost knee to knee we stood.

"You are brave," he said. He let me relax in response to these words. Then he added, "My intention might have been to do violence."

"Once you began running," I said, "I saw that it was you."

"That is why I say you are brave."

I gave him a sheepish look. "So, then, you don't intend violence?"

"Palleias, I wish to speak to you." His manner was of urgent business. Across the narrow alley, the sun shone white upon the opposing wall.

"Because if you did," I added, "I would not altogether blame you."

He regarded me. "It took some doing, Palleias, but he convinced me that you are not to blame. You were called and were required by law to be truthful or be guilty of a crime yourself. In fact, as he would not let me forget, I was the one who put you in that position."

It was everything I could do not to slump with relief. "How is he?" I asked.

"He is *too* well, if you ask me. He does not take the danger seriously."

"He is preparing his defense night and day?"

"I tell you truly, I have been with him nearly continuously since then and have seen him prepare nothing. He hardly thinks on it, as far as I can tell. He seeks no counsel, consults no speechwriters. When I object that he must plan his words carefully and anticipate the prosecution's arguments, he only makes light and tells me that his whole life is his defense, as if that answers it."

"I imagine he knows what he is doing."

"He does not. This time I have the advantage on him. He believes that people never knowingly do wrong, that wrongs are innocent and are corrected the moment the error is seen. He does not prepare because he places too much confidence in the jury." I thought this over. "He is too benevolent for his own safety," Xephon said.

"At least you are hard at work in preparing *your* testimony."

"He will not let me testify. No one is to testify. He did not want my testimony at the hearing even, but once Alcidia did what he did, he needed someone to rebut Alcidia's account."

"Have you seen Alcidia?"

Xephon's face colored. "No—luckily for him." He turned his head and spat. "But I imagine you have."

"He has since been to my house, but I have not spoken to him. . . . He has not explained himself to Teacher Scotes?"

"He has not, and what he is doing brings Teacher Scotes almost to tears."

"Because Teacher Scotes saw him as a friend?"

"Not for that reason."

Then he proceeded to question me further, asking me to describe Father's preparations for the trial. I understood that he was testing my allegiances and whether I regretted my role in what had happened, and though I hesitated, I freely offered all, thinking that my report was betraying Father nothing. Our second meeting was scheduled for this evening, where I was to relate what I had heard during my wanderings.

"Surely," I said, wanting to direct us back to the topic of Teacher Scotes's preparations, "he will introduce his wife and daughter to the jury. Every defendant does that, and there is not a jury who fails to take them into account."

"That, too, he refuses."

Somewhere down the alley came the slow clopping of a horse. Shortly, it ceased. When certain of quiet, Xephon lowered his voice. "There is little time," he said. "Little time today, little time before the trial."

"To do what?" I asked too loudly.

"What we can."

So we had come to the purpose of this meeting, and I wasn't certain I wanted to hear it. I recalled his request two weeks before that I get Father to withdraw the complaint and said, "The trial can't be stopped, not even by my father. There is nothing to do but await the verdict."

"There is always something to do." He spoke with that calm self-confidence I always associated with him, a genuine man of action—and not Alcidia's showy kind of action. This in part is why I had admired Xephon from the beginning. His nature was jovial and kind yet also powerful and decisive, and he was not naïve. He saw for himself, and he acted accordingly. He was a true friend of Teacher Scotes and of mankind.

A breeze flowed outward from the courtyard, where I hoped that none could hear us. The breeze was cooler than the alley air. "Xephon," I said, "you are a loyal friend to Teacher Scotes, but you are imprudent."

He explained his plan. Over the next ten days, we would solicit volunteers to join the jury pool, people who knew Teacher Scotes and loved him. In our judicial system, juries were chosen by lot. Citizens could submit their names to the Court Commission and be chosen as needed to fill the juries of the cases scheduled for trial. To proffer your name meant that you could be called for any upcoming trial, which you could accept or decline, and at any time you could leave the pool. To be most efficient, Xephon (and others) would cover the city and I, the country, where I was expected to travel anyway and where my father could not observe me. Together we could reach a hundred people, some of whom might submit their names. From there, it was up to luck and Teacher Scotes. Just a few sympathetic souls could make a difference in the verdict. It was an unlikely assistance, Xephon said, but it was legal and it was something, and when faced with the opportunity to act, however tenuous, that was what one did.

I listened, rather incredulous. When he seemed quite finished, I said, as much to avoid answering directly as anything else, "Your zealousness does you credit, but your plan will not work. When I travel, people approach me, and those who do so are not the ones you want for this jury. The people who love Teacher Scotes are not the people I encounter."

"That is why I will carefully direct you. I will tell you where to go."

"What you ask is impossible, not to mention futile."

"Impossible, why? It will require little of you. You explain the idea and move on; they choose what to do from there. Futile? That remains to be seen."

"Sometimes action is futile," I said, rather pedantically.

"Action is never futile. Only action toward a particular goal may be." I got the impression he was referring to something other than Teacher Scotes's trial. "The more people who volunteer," he said, "the more likely his acquittal. This trial is not about justice, Palleias. It is about the mood of the moment, a mood that is not good. People are seeking someone to blame for what they suffer. They understand our problems well but as yet do not understand the solution. How could they?"

"What is the solution?"

He frowned. "Let's leave that for another time."

"Does he know that you are asking for my help?"

"He does. After he refused to let me testify, I insisted on doing something and shared my plan. I said perhaps I should involve you. After all, you did promise to help, that day he was accused by Mathias on the street. I also wanted to test his resolve in being right about you."

"And what did he say?"

"He did not respond at all."

I looked off, then offered tepidly, "Perhaps he is wondering what to make of me, as I am of him."

"What are you wondering about him?" he asked sharply.

Does only confidence produce calm? Perhaps so, because at that moment, the sense of being both challenged and uncertain caused me to bark right back, "Why does he not argue with you when you say the things you do? Why does he not make his views known? How can I assess what he believes? I don't know what to make of it. I don't know what to make of him."

He tilted his head and stared. "You know enough," he said. As before, he waited for his words to register. "You have spent months in his company across two years. What more do you need?" This criticism stung. He stared again. "Have you not learned from him?" he asked.

"Yes," I admitted.

"Have you not valued what you learned?"

"Yes."

"As a result, have you not improved in some way?"

I nodded.

"Have you been corrupted?"

Oddly, I hadn't considered this before. "No," I said.

"Whatever he believes, are you obliged to believe it too?"

"No."

"Are you compelled to do as he advises?"

"No."

Then he said, more reasonably, "He asks us only to think, Palleias. What about that is corrupting?"

For a moment I had difficulty eyeing him. Then I said, "May I consider your proposal overnight?"

"Do that. Then do the following. Tomorrow morning, Drover Wilson will be herding to the city and will arrive at the Market Street Bridge by eight o'clock. Meet him there and discuss the plan with him. I am to meet him shortly after, in City Centre. If he reports no conversation with you, I'll take your answer to be no. If you have spoken to him, I'll take it to be yes. Then I will ride out to find you—you head north along the river and find a spot to rest, somewhere past the upper bridge—and I'll bring a list of people you can solicit."

Then he sidled from the archway. In the alleyway he glanced in both directions, taking up position there and blocking my exit. "I assume you will be testifying," he said.

In other words, he was implying that I would acquiesce to what my father desired of me, no matter what. I shot back, "The only reason he's in this situation, you know, is that you don't mind your tongue."

"Yes, *that*," he said, "and your father's laws."

Then he left. Leaning out, I glimpsed his large cloaked figure turn the corner and disappear.

CHAPTER 20

T hat evening, after a quiet supper with Mother, I took a different chair in the library than I had before, by the window. Below, the back lawn sat peaceably in orange light, and beyond the walls, at the end of the long, shaded pass-through, was busy Chestnut Street. Father was elsewhere.

Alcidia arrived first, which was fortuitous. After my encounter with Xephon, I had cut short my planned meanderings and gone straight home to think on what he'd said and, now that Alcidia had come, could question him at last about everything he had done.

I heard Mother lead him up the stairs in quiet conversation, then the sound of her more muted steps descending. In her respectful way, she would leave us to it. Alcidia must then have hesitated, because there was a delay before he appeared in the doorway and located me across the room.

"Am I disturbing you?" he asked.

Atypically, he was dressed simply and in brown; perhaps his garish wear had only been to pester Teacher Scotes, or perhaps he felt this outfit would more agree with Father. The afternoon still lingered, the lamps were still unlit, and I could not, in my distracted imagination, help seeing him as a paean to the day, his golden curls the sun above the earth of his attire. He was equally at home in a library as in an athletic competition, and I understood why he had been a favorite of Teacher Scotes. Yet Alcidia had testified against him. Had it only been to curry favor with my father? Or did he, like my father, consider Teacher Scotes the threat his views suggested he might be?

In a way, he had always frightened me. I sensed he saw me clearly, as few did, as did Teacher Scotes. Yet where Teacher Scotes eyed me charitably, Alcidia's eye was accusatory. At least till now: today his manner was almost demure, and I was pleased to read friendliness in him, if a probing one.

"I am sorry that my father is not yet home," I said. "But no, you are not disturbing me." I stood. He remained where he was, for I had yet to invite him in, and Alcidia was nothing if not well mannered. "Please come in," I said.

He did and looked around at our vast collection of books.

"Has my mother offered you refreshments?"

"She has, graciously."

I indicated two leather chairs before the silent hearth and moved to join him. He lowered himself with such control that his chair did not slide, unlike mine, which scraped. Something in me wanted to tell him of my exchange with Xephon and of what Xephon and Teacher Scotes now thought of him—or at least my guess at what they thought of him. But he would understand that. His would be a clear-eyed venture; he would not be acting without thought.

He sat tall, regarded me amiably, and left me to lead the discussion. Usually every moment for him was an adventure in a ceaselessly adventurous life, though in this moment, there was an air of self-possession about him. Rather disingenuously I did not question him straightaway but began by raising middling topics. I spoke of western outposts in a number of our states; of reports of railways spanning Britain; of our decline in banking, seemingly worsened by the recent vote on debt forgiveness. In all he appeared interested, though my observations, I suspected, demeaned me in his eyes, for why trifle when battles wage? I had never sat with him alone, and I was nervous. Then, because time was short and he seemed content to sit till Father and Mathias arrived, I pressed more boldly.

"Alcidia, if I may, I would like to make an inquiry of you. Our time with Teacher Scotes has encouraged me to initiate more investigations with others. And since you and I both appreciate the importance of this approach, I wondered if I might engage you in a matter of some interest to me."

He bowed agreeably.

"I know my father has promised to assist you in campaigning when the time comes. I would like you to know that I do not begrudge you that. He would not do so if he thought you unworthy. And speaking for myself, I look forward to our future collegiality."

He waited, as if ensuring I was finished, then said, "As do I." Then he added, "And may I say, Palleias, that should I be fortunate enough to be elected, I would certainly do whatever is in my power to assist you in your election, when the time comes. Not that you require it."

"I also believe you to be an admirer of Teacher Scotes and that the choice to prosecute must have been difficult for you."

Again he waited. "I imagine we both found ourselves facing similar difficulties. We weighed them and decided upon the proper course."

From our meeting with my father and Mathias, he understood me to be testifying, and I was not about to acknowledge my uncertainty—though by not explaining the reason for my inquiry, I risked making him wary. At that same meeting he had said, when we were discussing strategy, that only after I had testified about Xephon's constitution comment did he himself recall it and that once he did, he was pleased that I had done so. I had not quite believed him. In speaking now, he was likely being politic, having assumed that I was testifying just to please my father and not because, as he said, I had "weighed" anything. I began to see why he was sometimes referred to as a chameleon.

"Perhaps we chose for different reasons," I said lightly. "If you will allow me, I am interested in yours."

He smiled gently. "Like you, perhaps, I felt it to be my duty."

"Why your duty?"

"The law is the law. I possess material information in a lawful trial . . . and your father asked me to testify."

"Both reasons, then?"

"Perhaps the same for you?"

I smiled. "Another question. Would you help prosecute any lawful trial? Were my father not involved and had Mathias asked instead, would you have agreed then too?"

He good-naturedly snorted just a whiff, which I took to be an admission. I appreciated his candor. He said, "Mathias might have had a harder sell."

"In making your decision, did you consider anything else?"

"Such as?"

"Such as whether the act under which he is prosecuted is a good one?"

"You mean the act your father sponsored?"

Obviously he was teasing me, and I acknowledged the humor. "Bear with me," I said, "for argument's sake."

He smiled. "You're in an inquisitive mood today."

"I intend it as an improvement of my character. I hope you approve."

When ready, he answered, "I would not presume to doubt your father's acumen. Plus, the time for such considerations has passed. The law that guides this prosecution is duly made. Not to enforce it would be lawlessness, and no rep, current or future, can countenance that."

It was a valid point. If you thought a law had been broken, perhaps you *should* prosecute, for the reasons he had given. The implication made me uneasy, so I went elsewhere and asked, "Why had you been following Teacher Scotes?"

Though the question must have seemed aggressive, he budged not the slightest, and I noted then how startling had been his affability, given how like an enemy he had treated me before. Then it occurred to me: he would likely answer anything I asked because of who I was to Father and what Father was to him. To him, speaking to me was the same as speaking to my father.

This time he answered more attentively. "Again for reasons probably similar to yours: to learn from him."

"And what did you learn?"

"How our system works. How to argue. How to win people over to your position. That most of all. When you and I are in Assembly and are expected to influence other representatives and the people at large, will there be a better skill to have?"

"But that is *not*," I said, more vehemently than I intended, "what he tries to do." His allegation was unjust: Teacher Scotes sought answers, not to convert others to his positions. But he stayed silent, so I said, "So you've benefited from knowing him."

"In some manner."

"So, in all, you consider him a good influence, not bad."

"I don't see anyone as wholly good or bad."

This struck me. "Do you consider him to be a corrupting influence, as the law alleges? Whatever he believes, we seem free to take or leave him."

Finally he compressed his lips sardonically and shifted in his chair. "Palleias, perhaps if you elaborated the nature of your interest, I could better help. Do you mean to question the validity of the prosecution?"

"I am just examining some issues of my own."

I'm not sure he believed me. Eventually he resumed, "I suspect we have to leave that for the jury to decide." It sounded insincere. Then he added, "But not to worry. He can defend himself and will suffer no worse than banishment." My father had alleged the same. And I noticed he had not answered the question directly.

"Why do you want to be a rep?" It was a question I had not intended, but I recalled what Teacher Scotes had said about examining one's ambitions, and Alcidia was sitting there, captive, and I wanted to understand him.

He burst out laughing. "Why do you?" When I didn't answer, he added, with a softer smile, "That's not a question I would have expected from you." Then, likely registering some frustration on my face, he answered, "Is there a greater ambition? What higher aspiration can we have?"

"All your life, people have said you were destined to be a great rep."

"The greatest." Then he caught himself.

"I imagine you have sought it for a long time," I said.

"You and I both?"

I didn't like hearing it. I said, "Your whole life you have been proving yourself, dizzying the multitude, and now you're on the verge. . . . What do you hope to accomplish?"

"What do I hope to accomplish?"

"Yes."

He squinted. "To serve the people. To be their voice. To provide the leadership they need. . . . Is this a trick question?"

"To what end?"

There was a long pause. "You are making an effort, but you are not as good at this as he."

"I know well I am not." Though my behavior seemed ridiculous even to me, and I knew that we were lurching in many directions, still I felt compelled to draw him out. "Forgive my lack of focus," I said. I looked off, to reestablish some equability, then added, "Do you think Teacher Scotes believes in democracy?"

"I am certain he does not."

"Do you believe in democracy?" Gradually he smiled faintly, but not without exasperation. Father and Mathias could not come soon enough for him. "In all your years," I said, "of anticipating your election, have you ever questioned the nature of what you would be joining?"

"What *we* will be joining?"

"Yes."

"What is there to question, Palleias?" Finally he spoke freely, and I liked that he kept saying my name, as if we were equals, though I felt ashamed of liking it. "Philosophizing is fine," he said, "but not a soul would deem our inquiry to be anything but frivolous. You and I can discuss this only because we are friends. When we are reps, everyone in the nation will know our names and seek us out on every matter. And I don't believe that we can achieve our ambition by being anything but single-minded. If you waver, do you not fear losing your chance, even with your father's help?"

They were words my father could have said. To my father, Alcidia must have seemed a more worthy protégé than I. But his answer troubled me. Having been so "single-minded" for so long, he was explaining himself, but with a tinge of dogma. He was equating questioning with wavering. In fact, his justification seemed to rest solely on the idea of its being beyond examination. On the other hand, he might have only been explaining in a way that, should I have related all this to Father, would have reflected well on Alcidia.

"I am not trying to trick you," I said. "I hope you know that I am genuinely interested."

He allowed us a tranquil moment. Then cheerfully he asked, "So why *do* you want to become a rep?"

Though my mouth opened in response, no sound emerged because I had no answer—nothing genuine, nothing firsthand, nothing but the repetitions of my youth. And in this I saw that I was in no position to criticize Alcidia.

At that moment we heard the front door open and the sound of Father greeting Mother, Mathias immediately following, and their own faint exchange in the entryway, and we were compelled to drop our mutual interrogation.

I never resumed it. For all our back-and-forth, I understood little more about his reasoning. He would prosecute any law, though it might depend on who had asked him. He thought no one good or bad. He believed that philosophy was fine but irrelevant to judging one's ambition. This much was clear: he desired to be a representative. But my ambition was no more laudatory than his. Every day of every year, I had lived to please my father, and not only for help in my advancement but for help in everything. Perhaps in courting my father's favor by prosecuting Teacher Scotes, Alcidia sought nothing but advancement; if so, he was doing for that end only what I had done for all.

CHAPTER 21

Our meeting with Alcidia and Mathias was mercifully brief. I related what I had heard, and Father complimented me on my efforts and assured us that the people's sentiments reinforced our strategy.

Standing shoulder to shoulder in the doorway, Father and I watched them depart. The night air was warm and still, and the sounds of travel reached us through our tunnel. He did not seem in a hurry to go back inside.

I asked him, "What do you think of Alcidia?"

"As I said, a dangler and a fox." He looked over at me and winked.

"There is something about him I do not trust."

He patted my shoulder. "He will deliver what he promises. And do not worry, there is room for both of you in Assembly." I was sufficiently astonished and hurt not to speak. Then with all pleasure he said, "You did well this week, gathering information for us. What you shared will serve us ably."

We went inside and sat upon the sofa in the entryway. He seemed relaxed. With the trial now less than two weeks away, he might have been experiencing a kind of calm before the storm and wanting to savor the quiet. Of course I myself was still in storm, which he perhaps sensed, because, leaning back against the wall, he turned his head only and said, "You are pondering something."

It was unlike him to acknowledge my desire to speak when I was not insisting. He was never eager to draw me out, which was yet another contrast with Teacher Scotes. The likely difference now was our seeming alliance in his cause. If he knew that I was considering helping Teacher Scotes instead, through Xephon's plan, it might crush him. All of this, I feared, could be read upon my face, I was so unskilled at hiding it.

"I am thinking of the trial," I said, by way of cover.

"You and I both."

"It is an extraordinary thing, the passing of laws, the enforcing of them."

He compressed his lips in profound agreement. "It is that," he said. "Which you and I can never forget. Most people pay our laws no mind until they violate them and learn their meaning. That is why ours is such a profound responsibility, being the legal shepherds we are. How we perform our role has great effect on the lives of those around us."

He spoke as if reflecting on his life and reminding himself of the nature of his calling, while also counseling me as well. I felt the power of his position and his concern for how he wielded it.

"I hope I never lose that sense of responsibility," I said. "Or of how my actions affect the lives of others."

He regarded me with a look that might have been from long admiration, had I not known better. Then I thought, Perhaps in some way he does admire me.

"I know you well enough to know that you will not," he said.

The stillness of the house, the night, and the moment hung about us. I gathered that he wished to say more but was not at ease with his intention. This gave me leave to press ahead.

"I've been considering the issue of 'corruption' in our act," I said. I spoke again as if my sole objective were to learn. "Your observation about the consequences of our laws brought it to mind." Of course this was untrue, but it could seem as if the topic had arisen from our pleasant discourse.

"It is a damning accusation, I know," he said.

"This trial has made me reflect upon my future role as legislator, as you have said."

"And you continue to analyze the various elements of the act in question, as any good legislator must." He was referring to our conversation from before the preliminary hearing, though now he seemed more open to examination. More open even than Alcidia had been. I felt almost as free to question him as I did Teacher Scotes.

"Here is what I wonder. Teacher Scotes appears to reject our deepest ideals. And for that, he may deserve condemnation." His eyes lit on the word "may," but he did not object. "But having spent time with him myself, I cannot say that I feel corrupted, if I apprehend the meaning of that charge. Now that I more fully understand his views, I feel at liberty to disregard them, pay them no mind, and still think as I please." I glanced over to observe his reaction, and though he may have disagreed that I was uncorrupted, he did not oppose my reasoning and gave only the thinnest of smiles. "In fact," I added, "I have been thinking that you yourself once followed him and were exposed to his thinking yet walked away and, I know for certain, were not corrupted."

"And from this thoughtful consideration you conclude?"

"Not only were you not corrupted, you ended up with antipodal views."

"So you are wondering how the first part of the act necessitates the second." I nodded. That was a good way to put it, and he was not afraid of the question. "You wonder how his not believing in the ideals of the nation necessitates corruption." I nodded. He ended with "So perhaps the law mistakenly condemns a behavior that in fact is of no harm?"

I nodded, hesitantly.

He turned away and gave a thoughtful look, though he did not appear happy about what he was thinking. I worried that I had gone too far and soured our exchange. Then he said, "Not everyone is like us, Palleias." He turned back and watched me gently.

I was not entirely certain of his meaning. "We listened to him and walked away," I tentatively repeated.

"You and I are different."

Then I understood. The better among us, like he and I, *had* the capacity to judge, but the multitude, for whom exposure to falsehoods *would* necessitate corruption, did not. *We* could reason; they could not. He watched me sit with this. Still I had the feeling that he was reluctant to broach some topic and that my questioning had made it harder, not easier, for him.

Whatever it was, he did not raise it, and we shortly went to bed, parting on better terms than we had in weeks.

Upon waking in the morning, as when coming face to face with your own shortcomings can push you past your hesitations, I resolved to profess my doubts about testifying, to be as upright as that. So at breakfast, fairly shaking and in an effort to appear most manly—absent preamble, circumlocution, and hedges—I was at the point of admitting my deliberations when Father rose, having hardly eaten. He was due shortly in Assembly, so he dabbed his mouth and said, "Come outside with me."

We walked across the stretch of grass and dirt and stood before the pungent doors of the carriage house. As always, early sounds of man and beast beyond our walls were amplified through the tunnel.

"While I'm gone, please see that the gig is repaired," he said. "Arrange to have Wheelwright Bolton take it to his shop. That is, unless you'd rather spend the morning at Assembly with me?"

Before going down to breakfast and while planning my confession, I had also decided that I would meet with Drover Wilson—to at least take that step. Though I had never met him, he was someone I admired by reputation, and it had occurred to me that the meeting itself might clarify whether I should help Xephon. Perhaps it was also a way to delay deciding. "I will see that the gig is repaired," I said. "As much as I would like to join you, there are other matters I should attend to first."

"As you wish," he said. Then he said, "I have been thinking, Palleias. I believe it best if you do not testify." I just looked at him. "I know you want to assist," he said, "and for that I am grateful. But weighing all, I think it better if you don't."

He watched me as if expecting my objections, which would please him, even if he would not yield.

"Why?"

"There are risks in getting close to this. Risks not worth taking." Then, because I was clearly at a loss—at least that's how he would have taken it—and he was anxious to depart, he said, "We can discuss this later, if you wish." He touched my arm and left.

I felt lighter than I had in weeks, though aware that I myself had still not chosen what to do. But there was no time to deliberate further. Straightaway I drove the gig to the wheelwright's, returned and harnessed Betsy to our wagon, and prepared to head out for the two-mile ride to the bridge as I had a thousand times before but also as I never had before: while contemplating a personal rebellion. That, at least, is what it felt like, and I wanted no possibility of arriving late to meet Drover Wilson.

CHAPTER 22

It was Saturday, June 18. Because our house fronted the last of the permanent stalls that covered the three most eastern blocks of Market Street and by now would be surrounded, I left by the back for Chestnut, where I turned away from the morning sun and into its smooth light. A few blocks later, I returned to Market.

Though still our principal thoroughfare, Market had for years been more sparsely trafficked than when, as a boy, I would watch the wagons pass. Its two red sidewalks reached distantly to the faraway permanent bridge, blade-straight and up and down a gentle slope, brick buildings yielding to clapboards then to chestnuts and oaks, from east to west. Perhaps one day buildings would connect the rivers, if we progressed to that degree. Soon it would be the Fourth and the week of our annual celebration—the twice-daily ringing of the Democracy Bell, the banners, the flags, the fireworks, the reenactments—which was as close to sacred time as our nation had, Philadelphia being the altar of our national church. As was customary, all would commence the Friday before the Fourth and end the Sunday after, which happened to be the week that followed Teacher Scotes's trial.

Most everyone headed east, opposite me. The approaching wagons would have been crossing the bridges since daybreak—some from their homes, some from where they had camped on the western banks. Many would be farmers transporting their own foodstuffs and wares, especially since passage of the act bestowing wagons to most; some would be larger farmers paid by neighbors to transport their goods as well, as in the old days, and who therefore were merchants of sorts themselves; on foot would be the merchants proper. The wobbly wagons with their angled wheels tilted front to back like crouching cats that crawled behind the horses they pursued. The wagons seemed an army not of warriors but of makers, each to be met by those who came to buy and then, refilled with purchases of their own, to return to homes, farms, and shops and then repeat the process for, they hoped, a lifetime. In their presence I thought of Teacher Scotes.

I had topped off Betsy's bucket, which hung at the back of the wagon, and loaded extra grain into the small barrels I carried for her, not knowing what I would need or where I might end up. In her snorts and steps, she seemed excited. I had donned my best waistcoat. Shortly I might be meeting with the men and women who befriended Teacher Scotes—meeting with them, siding with them, and for a few days, joining them.

First to Drover Wilson. He was one of the largest drovers in the country and certainly in the state. He himself led massive herds of cows, sheep, turkeys even (he had invented a way to boot the birds so they could travel the rocky roads on foot), and he employed others who did the same, from Pittsburgh to Philadelphia or all the way to Baltimore, where the market for meat was greatest. To converse with him as a peer would be an honor.

On the western half of Market, I could better see the distant oncoming traffic disgorge from the covered bridge. More and more the land opened up; nearly there, I passed the shot tower and got my first clear view of the amphitheater, downriver to my left, miniature in the distance, white and semicircular, facing the river on the bluff, with the small brown scaffolded head of VOP facing back. An early Assembly had convened. Father would be there. Then the noisy muted crowd arose, followed by a long, deep, reverberating "Aye."

At the mouth of the bridge I stopped. Across the wide river and next to the road that fed the other side, standing in a grassy patch, was Drover

Wilson. Even at this distance, he was unmistakable. With him were ten or so horned and dappled steer, three men, and two dogs, who circled and yapped unmolested. The herd lowed distantly. Drover Wilson stood at their head, grasping a tall whip and looking vaguely in my direction. I assumed he was awaiting my arrival, and I headed across, the sounds of vehicles and animals now rumbling under cover.

I had been unsure whether he would know me but soon presumed he did, because once we exited the bridge, he sighted us and studied our approach till we finally reached him.

Remaining on my perch, I smiled grandly. "If I may introduce myself," I said, "I am Palleias."

He was short and thick, imposing—mostly grime, with a long black beard, tall felt hat, neckerchief, and jagged face that was tanned nearly the color of his beard. His eyes were black and steady. Even Betsy seemed a little taken aback, for she stepped to the side and positioned me to look down upon him. His tall whip was planted emphatically into the ground.

"I am Wilson," he said, without a smile, grand or otherwise.

For some reason the cattle behind him also stared, their ears splayed like their horns, except when individually flipping back. One or two heads peeked around the rest. They made no sound till one called out and bowed to nibble at the grass. After that, others followed. The two dogs lay in watchful passivity. The three other men stood one at either side and at the back.

"Xephon asked me to meet you here," I said and smiled again.

"And so you have."

He seemed prepared to receive me, but only that. When he spoke, his mouth appeared, then disappeared into his beard. I said, "Xephon tells me that you will be meeting him shortly in the city."

"And there I must be headed."

In part I could appreciate his manner. His was a dangerous profession, requiring vigilance, toil, and risk, and he was known not to suffer fools. But I also knew that in recent years citizens had proposed laws against him that Father and the representatives were under pressure to consider. Apparently he had found a way to deposit animals in the east that were somehow healthier and fatter than at journey's start—presumably by the arrangements he made with those who bedded them—but he would never tell of how, nor would those who aided him tell, nor would they shelter anyone else. This infuriated some, especially other drovers. What aggravated matters was that, with the decline that had befallen us, drovers had been disappearing, and Drover Wilson had been absorbing their remainder. This only intensified the push to compel him to explain.

In anticipating our meeting, it had occurred to me that I might befriend him by suggesting that should such legislation reach Assembly, I could use my position to try to mitigate it. I could play the role of advocate on his behalf, knowing that few would likely take his side.

"Please wait a moment longer, if you can," I said. "I was hoping to relate that I have heard a great deal about you." It was a ridiculous thing to say, and I colored. As if sensing my frustration, Betsy whinnied and stepped in place.

Drover Wilson's scraggly face compressed enough to indicate amusement at my words. He replied, "And I have heard much of you as well." From the way he said it, I gathered that he hadn't liked what he had heard. I noticed, too, that he began nearly every sentence with "And," then repeated much of what you said, as if from insufficient practice in speaking. Or perhaps he just didn't want to speak with me. Then he said, "Were you interested in becoming a drover? From what I gather, a rep would make a good one."

One of his associates chuckled.

I said, "Drover Wilson, I understand from my father that there is pressure to pass laws that could reasonably be construed as against your interests." I paused, allowing him to adjust to my more earnest tone. "I want you to know that I consider that to be regrettable, and should the occasion arise, I would endeavor to see that it does not happen." In response he only darkened, as if clouds had suddenly come, though if anything they had thinned. "I do not know how successful I might be or even the course I might take. But, like you, I would think it unfair should such bills become law."

He eyed me levelly. "Am I to consider that a threat?"

"No! Sir. I assure you. It is the opposite. It is a pledge of my assistance." He did not so much as blink. I went on, "Please consider me a friend. After all, we are both aligned in the same noble cause, are we not? That of helping Teacher Scotes in his time of difficulty." I was aware that my words implied a commitment I had yet to make but perhaps had been approaching all along.

He continued to stare. I realized why: he knew me in the only way he could, as my father's son, someone who traveled the state for a powerful representative, doing his bidding, serving his causes. To him, I was the enemy. And in a way, I was. Whatever I said today, he would see me as siding with those who wished to restrain him. That he stood with me at all was attributable to Xephon's request, and he was no doubt wondering if the too-benevolent Xephon hadn't miscalculated and invited a traitor into their midst.

I found it difficult to speak again, so he took the opportunity to excuse himself, recharge his team and move off, eventually swaying noisily onto the bridge, rumbling through, emerging smaller on the other side, and ambling toward the brighter eastern sky. I eyed his progress for some time. Around me at the mouth of the bridge, traffic flowed, though more lightly. Breezes swirled. I let myself feel them.

What Xephon said was true: I knew enough. Teacher Scotes had helped me greatly. However mistaken he was about our nation, he pressed those views on no one, and no one was forced to follow him, could take or leave him, as they had—ironically, by using the very thinking method that *he* taught. And I found it difficult to accept my father's claim that the multitude could be swayed against its will and therefore required protection from an alien idea. If anyone did the swaying, it was the multitude. Something seemed amiss about this law—my father's law—though I was unsure as to its fault. Duly made it was, as Alcidia had said, but that fact alone seemed an insufficient defense.

The time had come to choose: I would join Xephon and his plan to solicit sympathetic jurors. Downstream and across the river was the tiny amphitheater. From this angle I saw into it, upon a section of the colorful crowd, whose voices rose and ebbed for indiscernible reasons.

CHAPTER 23

A s much as I had experienced the great cities of the world, visiting
London and Paris when very young and of course living in Philadelphia, I had never felt comfortable in them. I found the sounds, the smells,
and the press of people all around to be anything but inspirational. This
is why, when roaming on Father's behalf, despite the hardship, I liked best
the roads west of the Schuylkill—such as the one that intersected Market
Street at the bridge, where I had just left Drover Wilson. The road followed the river, sometimes on its shoals, sometimes on its highest banks,
and was secluded, the colors and sounds of nature abounding. It was
peaceful and less traveled than many others and therefore relatively
smooth, our predominant traffic being east-west.

I passed the mouth of the Upper Ferry Bridge, which rose like a hollow mound over the wide sliding river, careful not to be seen, and continued north to my resting place, a spot where the river swung wide.
There, Betsy and I settled at the modest promontory across from Lemon
Hill (Merchant Pratt's old seat), with a clear view in the northern distance
of Eaglesfield (Merchant Rundle's old seat), which itself sat perched on a
bank across from Segdeley (Merchant Fischer's old seat). I liked the view
of all three from this one location, though absent the delight that had
filled me as a boy. Each was a National Park now. For a time, after becoming national property in one of the Distributions, and after their owners
had fled (rumor was to England, their ancestral home), the houses took

in indigent boarders. But today they were in too much disrepair for that, so people used the once-landscaped grounds instead for walking and relaxing, though the grounds were overgrown.

Betsy took some water and ripped the tall grasses, and I sat on a fallen trunk. I would not have minded the wait even had it been hours till Xephon reached me. Instead it was but half an hour, and he arrived with speed, alert to where I might be waiting, and did not miss us when he reached our quiet gathering. Betsy seemed to recognize him and nodded at his dismount.

"Palleias," he said.

There was no need for chatter or thanks, and he proceeded, militarily, to instruct me. He had written a list of names on a map, with marks for their addresses, and drawn a line through them in the order of most efficient travel. There were nearly thirty names, and he was magnanimous in saying that I might not reach them all in the time available. He understood that I must be discreet and spend but one night away from home at a time. In addition to him, there were two other trusted fellows who would assist; at their request, he would not name them. When he finished, he asked if I had questions, and when I did not, he slapped me on the shoulder and remounted.

Before he galloped off, I said, "I want you and Teacher Scotes to know that I will not be testifying." This, I thought, in addition to my help, would impress and gratify him further.

Instead he looked perplexed. "But you will be at trial anyway?" he asked.

"No. Only those who participate can attend."

His horse turned a circle. "You must attend," he said. "Teacher Scotes was pleased that you would be there."

"Pleased—why?"

"He did not say."

"Did he say he wanted me there?"

"No, but I could tell he liked the idea."

I looked at Xephon. "But I can't attend. Not unless I testify."

To this he replied nothing, gazing down upon me. Then he rode off in the direction he had come, without regard for the burden left behind. Betsy and I stared after him till she glanced at me and resumed her nibbling. I let her eat a moment, then climbed aboard the bench, not wanting to delay what I had pledged to do. With one twitch of the reins, we headed north, and I thought, After this I can't go back—not to my old ways and plans.

My first stop was about a mile farther north, beside a robust tributary, where the water dropped and was partially diverted to a man-made basin. There Machinist Clark lived, in a small white clapboard house set in the shadow of his manufactory, which stood behind the house much the way a cliff bestrides a boulder. It was three stories, long and many-windowed and also white, a large clock tower at one end. It lay not a quarter mile from many smaller cloth mills that had sprouted in this area, largely because of Machinist Clark, who manufactured and repaired parts for their looms. If not aware of the presence of the other mills already, one wouldn't become so from this setting, which was sequestered by wooded undulations to the north, west, and south. I found the small compound through a shaded narrow road, which opened upon the house. There I secured Betsy and sought the owners.

Out back I found Mrs. Clark, I presumed, standing with a small boy amid tall wispy plants in a garden that sat between the house and factory. They must have heard me arrive, because they were facing me when I appeared around the house. Mrs. Clark had been smiling, until she wasn't. I imagine that she recognized me, because I detected a suppressed alarm in her mien. Sensing the change, her boy regarded her.

I introduced myself in a friendly manner and asked after Machinist Clark, who, she warily informed me, was hard at work inside. She seemed unenthusiastic at the prospect of my meeting him but of course invited me to do so. I attempted further pleasantries, smiled at the boy, and complimented their hearty though modest crops. All of this she accepted with refinement but without warmth. I felt a chill, as I had with Drover Wilson. Then I excused myself and proceeded toward the factory.

I had to enter through a stone and dirt basement and was smothered by the rain-like sound of water passing from the outside basin through a gate. The water struck a massive vertical wheel of broad wooden buckets, and its powerful roll spun two large metal gears and ultimately a vertical shaft, which disappeared into the first floor of the building. The sound of this false rain mixed with the grinding of metal, and the gears steamed and smelled of some sort of fat that had doused them. I had to take this in. Most ingenious was what turned the wheel: not the river flow itself but the manufactured drop of water into the basin. It was thus the weight of the water and not its natural force that did the work, and this impressed me as an efficient use of power and a reliable means to drive it upward.

The shop upstairs smelled of sawdust and oil, which seemed to have permeated the floor. The room was high-ceilinged, long, and thin, the reason for its design being apparent. Against either wall was a long row of machines—lathes, drill presses, table saws, punches—all connected by leather bands to a central metal rod beneath the ridge, which spun by gears that converted the movement of the vertical basement shaft to horizontal. The leather bands were divided by interlocking teeth, and large wooden sticks hung from the ceiling next to each machine. The sound was thunderous, and four men—and one young woman—stood intently at work, having not heard me climb from below.

Three of the men were armed with pistols, and this, too, I understood and did not fear. The price of metals had risen so much recently that marauders had taken to raiding shops like this, in greater numbers than the authorities could defend.

It was the presence of the young woman that held me. Though time was short for me to talk with Machinist Clark about the jury pool before I need depart, I could not help staring. One rarely found women in such a place, their work typically being as weavers, bakers, teachers, or in the professions, such as banking. She was early twenties, tall, thin, and as grimy as the men she matched in energy at attending the machines. A small cap covered most of her short dark hair.

She was so focused on her task that she became aware of my presence only when one of the men finally noticed and approached me, causing her to leave her station and approach too. The man was also tall and very thin, middle-aged, with jagged cheekbones over a low narrow chin. He was as lean and lanky as any man I ever saw.

"How do you do, sir?" he yelled, nearing me. He told me that his name was Clark and when the young woman reached his side, that she was his daughter. "What may we do for you?"

"I am Palleias," I said.

"We know of you, of course, sir."

Knowing I should not, I took the measure of the woman to assess her degree of welcome. It was nominal: clear-eyed but neither friendly nor unfriendly.

I came immediately to the point, prompted by the plain efficiency of their manners. Knowing them to be friends of Teacher Scotes and possibly desirous of helping him, as I put it, I explained what they could do: Though we might not successfully influence the ultimate result, it was our best option, and the action was fully legal. I and other friends were traveling the region, sharing the idea. Of course, everyone must decide freely whether to act, and such busy people as they, I understood, perhaps could not afford to spend a day in court. We each had our constraints and must help in our own ways.

Machinist Clark took this in. His daughter continued to regard me. Her intelligent eyes shone.

Machinist Clark said, "I gather that time presses upon you so that you may not take refreshments with us?"

"I regret that it does, sir. My intent is to reach as many as I can in the little time we have. But I thank you."

He nodded but added nothing, and a silence set awkwardly upon us. I addressed the woman. "I regret, Miss, that I may not enlist you in the same proposal." I hoped she would take my attention as a compliment. "As you know, jury positions are open only to those aged thirty and above."

She was almost as tall as her father yet with features much softer and more beautifully apportioned. But in manner and dignity, she matched him. Though I knew her not at all, my impression of her was soaring, and this alone discouraged me, for I had once or twice become acquainted with women whose seeming spirit and strength of character enchanted me. I did not pursue them. Such women, I believed, could never admire me since in character I did not match them, and the women who pursued me, and there were not a few, did so less for my character than my station.

"Thank you, sir, for thinking of me," she said.

Once again I faced their simultaneously warm and cold reception. They offered neither that they would or would not volunteer, nor even that they would mull the option. Indeed, they hardly acknowledged it. Our exchange was reduced to mutual staring till I could only excuse myself with thanks for granting me their valuable time.

Mrs. Clark, still in the garden, watched me pass out of sight, and I was back at the property's front, organizing Betsy, and ultimately on my way.

CHAPTER 24

Westward and not far was my next stop, a small farm run by Farmer Foulke. Teacher Scotes had mentioned him. Though the farm was not a hundred acres, it was prosperous, with the largest piggery in the state. He had also built a bottle kiln that he ran year-round and operated a grist mill in which he worked his own grain and that of many neighbors, who paid him from the grain they brought for milling. In this way he could grow primarily wheat yet still acquire oats and barley for feed and food. The redware pottery he sold locally; it was inexpensive yet known to be reliable and of a glistening hue, made from the plentiful clay dug from a large pit not far from the kiln itself.

The thin path to the main house split a low open field, which was marked by jagged fences. It passed the bulbous kiln and shop, circled the mill and pond, and ended at his porch. Visitors must have marveled at his diverse operations. No sooner had I reached the steps and dismounted than a goat raced around the house, followed by a small, aproned girl. Fearful more of the girl than me, the goat scraped by, and I grabbed its scruff and held it. Foiled, it bleated.

"Oh thank you, sir!" the girl cried and grabbed the scruff. She addressed the animal directly. "You come with me," she said and pulled it back around the house.

A tall hatless man pushed open the front door and took a clumpy step onto the porch. He was dusty and scratching his thick tousled hair but was not unfriendly looking.

"We do thank you, sir," he said, still scratching. "We have been chasing that animal all the way from the barn." He must have seen what had happened, and I was glad of it for how it might influence my reception.

"I am pleased to have been of service," I said.

He introduced himself and invited me to take the rocking chair next to his, which I did, and as I sat, his wife came out to join us, taking a chair on the opposite side. She was half Farmer Foulke's size, rounder, aproned, and bonneted, and where his expression was affable, hers was not.

Rather than identify myself, I said, "I am a friend of Teacher Scotes."

This elicited a warm response from Farmer Foulke, who brightened before darkening again. He knew of the trial, of course, as would anyone who read the news, which by now had reached the remotest settlers. He expressed dismay and despair at this turn of events, and I heartily agreed. "We are simple people, young sir," he said, "and cannot understand such laws and why they would touch a man like Teacher Scotes." We all three rocked energetically, though Mrs. Foulke eyed me.

Farmer Foulke continued to wonder about why anyone would trouble a man like Teacher Scotes till Mrs. Foulke said, "You have not introduced yourself, sir."

"My name is Palleias," I said.

Though I gathered that neither of them had recognized me, Mrs. Foulke said at once, "Representative Antonyn's son."

"Yes, ma'am."

"Antonyn," Farmer Foulke said. "*The* Antonyn?"

"Yes, sir."

They stopped rocking in unison. Then they resumed, and for a time, there was rocking and no speaking. Not identifying myself had probably been a misstep. At this point all I could do was explain my mission and my reason for visiting. In doing so, I realized that they could never spare the time for a trial anyway, and I wondered why Xephon had directed me to them.

I had taken a liking to Farmer Foulke and would have liked his wife as well had not she seemed so wary. But once they knew who I was, any possibility of conversation, let alone friendship, seemed lost. Three times today this had happened. Likely it would be the fate of all my visits. My endeavors yet again appeared to be unprofitable, and I thought it best to take my leave.

Then Mrs. Foulke stopped rocking and said, in a more fawning manner and seemingly out of the blue, "My husband and I deeply appreciate this political system of ours and are happy to have someone like yourself to converse with about it." The teeth of her smile were the color of Indian corn. When her husband appeared confounded by her words, she said, "Isn't that right, Chickens?"

He looked at me, stopped rocking too, and his face appeared to elongate.

"Madam," I said, trying to assuage them, "I assure you I come only as a friend, both to you and Teacher Scotes."

Still smiling stiffly, she resumed rocking, and as if following her lead, he did too. Likely they were fretting his comments about the law and trial, especially knowing who the prosecutors were, which also had been reported. We were at an impasse, and they would trust no complaint from me against my father's action. To them I was first and last the representative's agent, the man who rode on his behalf and aspired to his position. I was the princeling—in their eyes, the man as much responsible for Teacher Scotes's predicament as was my father. And so, in a way, I was.

I had begun the day thinking I could make a start with people I admired, a small population whose affection I would cherish. But no matter my desire to aid Teacher Scotes, to them I was someone else, because while they were unknown to me, I was known to them. By my actions across years, they knew me. Then I realized something. Having always tended toward uncertainty and indecision, I had assumed that I was not yet somebody, not yet formed—that I was still to be. But in this I was in error. I *was* somebody: I was my father's son; everything he was I had by default become. Who could know differently? No one-time action now of mine could convince them otherwise.

A few others on Xephon's map lived or worked nearby, so I finished the afternoon by visiting them: the itinerant brickmaker Grellet, on the site of his latest job; Carder Morris; Miller Offley; and Weaver Logan—all of modest means and honorable characters, and I without hope. Then I gladly headed home, into the same flow of traffic, now reversed, that I had split that morning.

Every visit had been similar. No one had embraced or rejected me. None promised to join the jury pool. Some, like Mrs. Foulke, took pains to register how much they loved our Assembly, and I could scarcely hide my disappointment at their need of telling me. They almost seemed to fear my prosecuting *them*, that my true intentions were clandestine.

Perhaps some would join the pool, anyway, and in this I took solace. Yet they would also know that if I wished to track their actions, I could, that I might monitor the pool and if they volunteered, somehow use that against them in the future. Of course I would not. Again I wondered why Xephon had sent me on such an errand.

Travel home that afternoon was long. Betsy, too, seemed weary.

The next day, Sunday, I made two more visits and no more after that. They were doing, I feared, more harm than good.

But I was not yet finished. If what Xephon had relayed was true and Teacher Scotes preferred that I attend, then I wished to be there. I would take this up with Father, despite expecting his refusal. And I would have the opportunity because he had invited me to discuss my role further when he asked me not to testify.

That next Tuesday, I tried. We were dining together in a committee building near Assembly, Father having forgone invitations with colleagues that day: he wanted to avoid subjecting me to questions about the trial from important men. We ate quickly, and upon our leaving, I asked to raise the matter of my attendance. We were in sunshine and in public, with the people's gaze upon us (as always it was, but now with even greater reason), so we walked the sidewalks briskly. An approaching woman, not much older than I, eyed my father steadily until she passed. When another did the same, I said, "I think they like you, Father."

He seemed amused. "When you are a representative," he said, "you will receive like attention. But I can pledge to you that I have only ever been true to your mother." Then, as answer to my request to discuss my attendance, he said only, "Later."

Later turned out to be Friday, the day before he was to leave and not return until the trial, which was the following Thursday. At dusk, Alcidia and Mathias arrived for a last rehearsal. With every meeting, each had dressed more simply, as if having gleaned the importance of this manner of presenting themselves at trial. Mathias usually dressed that way, and Alcidia could be prodigious in his changeability. As usual we enjoyed wine, desserts, and tea before formally convening.

This time, however, rather than remaining downstairs, Father led us upstairs to his study. He often retired to his study after supper, on nights when we had no visitors, and even then would sometimes settle there after Mother and I retired to bed. It was a large room with high ceilings and a grand desk, behind which he sat, after lighting a lamp, and before which we three took chairs. The fresh light illuminated the remaining red leather chair in the corner. Above it, as a reminder to himself, Father had years ago suspended a large sword by a single horsehair, blade pointing down, directly over the chair, which of course was never used. More than once these past weeks, Alcidia had asked my father to describe what it was like to play the role he did in our nation, and Father had usually warmly replied something to the effect of "You'll know soon enough." But perhaps by bringing us here he wanted to complete his answer, because no sooner had we sat than my father smiled at the sight of Alcidia inspecting the sword and chair.

Alcidia said, "I recognize that."

Father said, "Would you like to sit there tonight? It will answer your favorite question better than I have done so far."

Alcidia chuckled and remained where he was.

During the meeting, which was brief, Father mentioned me hardly at all and delegated to Mathias and Alcidia much of what had been my testimony. Most of all he asked Alcidia if he would relate what had happened at Teacher Scotes's house, and Alcidia assented, assuming, I expect, that his testimony would simply corroborate mine. If Father worried at all about what Teacher Scotes might do, he didn't let on. He projected confidence, as always, and I believe this reassured Mathias, who needed reassuring. Alcidia seemed confident. There was little Teacher Scotes could say to refute the evidence of his guilt, and victory (which is how they thought of it, not I) was assured. We agreed again not to discuss anything with anyone outside this house, a policy we had vowed since the hearing, and at about ten o'clock, Alcidia and Mathias showed themselves out. Father and I remained upstairs to finish our wine.

When we were alone, Father said, "At last we can complete our discussion, and I can explain myself. The audience, I have confirmed, will be five hundred citizens, some from neighboring states, and you have no experience in front of such a large and diverse group. They can be unruly and the proceedings unpredictable. And Scotes is nothing if not master of the sleight of hand in oration. Given this, I feel that the possible benefits of their seeing you are not worth the costs if the trial goes badly. I have no doubt we will win; still, there is always the possibility of embarrassment. Mathias is no orator. And neither are you. Alcidia, being known and admired, will persuade them sufficiently. I have also invited Representative Lycon to join. And I will bolster all as necessary. . . . Well," he said, upon my silence, "is my thinking still agreeable?"

"Will I still be able to attend?"

"You wish to attend?"

I nodded.

"Why?"

"It is a moment of massive import that I should witness," I said. It was all I had come up with, and it was true.

He pondered and nodded tepidly. Then he said, "But if you are not part of the proceedings, by law you cannot be there."

"Then I shall testify."

"You want so much to attend that you will testify?"

I nodded, unconvincingly. He frowned and watched me, though still pleased, I think, by my willingness to side with him. Then he shook his head and said, "It is too risky."

"Perhaps there is another way?"

"What other way?" I felt it best not to respond. He was obviously bewildered. "Let me think on it," he said. But he looked doubtful of a solution.

I was truly grateful. "Thank you, Father."

Then he said, "I know why you want to be there." He said it gently.

"You do?"

"Yes." He held a moment. "Because you love him." I was shocked. Though his eyes were steady, his mouth bore a touch of melancholy. "It is all right," he said. He gave a look of acceptance at the necessity of having to discuss this with me. "I did also, once. But you have to believe me that you will outgrow it. You will come to see him—and me—differently. One day, you will."

That Father might be jealous of my feelings for Teacher Scotes had never occurred to me, but as we were together in that dim room and on that quiet summer night, that is how I read him. Up welled a tenderness that of late I had not been feeling. The combination of his anxiety about the trial and his acceptance of my feelings toward Teacher Scotes made him seem vulnerable in a way he never did. The effect of this change in him was disorienting but not displeasing.

Because he then reclined and seemed at peace and indifferent to our many recent battles, I took a chance and said, "Am I fair in assuming that you had considered my not testifying from the beginning?"

A slow small smile formed. "Perhaps you are more astute than I sometimes give you credit for."

"You didn't want me to testify?"

"I was proud of what you did at the preliminary hearing." Again I warmed at "proud." "You were called upon and told the truth. That could not have been easy. But a trial is different. The people can be unpredictable, and I do not think it wise, on balance, to have you before them just yet. One never knows what might happen in their presence."

Hearing him express this fear again made it more real. "But what about you? Are you not concerned for yourself?"

"Whether I am or not is beside the point. One day, when you are a father, you will understand. . . . Are you prepared for a guilty verdict?"

I nodded, though weakly, for I was not at all prepared.

"Not to fear," he said. "As I've said, it will not come to death. These cases rarely do, and Teacher Scotes is regarded highly enough that the jury will show mercy. His record in the war alone will protect him. Whatever alternative punishment he proposes, whether prison, fine, or ostracism, they will second. All they'll want—all any of us wants—is for him to desist."

"Then perhaps the law should be amended to change the penalty?"

"No. The behavior is too dangerous and needs to be discouraged. But it will not come to that." He looked off, in the direction of the chair in the corner, and I interpreted his restating the point about the unlikelihood of death to be more for his benefit than mine, for he said at last, "It can't."

CHAPTER 25

In the almost three thousand years of human history there are a million days—days of births and deaths, with battles won and lost, in which joys and sorrows ruled. Each had its occasions, and many were momentous. But some stand above all others, have left impressions on the earth, like paths upon which we walk forever. For me, June 30, 1831, is such a day.

I don't believe we appreciated it then. I don't believe we appreciate it now, though I hope for this to change.

Does the weather of that day matter? When its events are studied years from now, will it be noted that the sun shone and the sky was blue? If such facts mattered to anyone, they mattered to the jurors who streamed from their lodgings, having taken sustenance enough to last till afternoon, and to the crowds that clogged Sixth, Chestnut, and Walnut, despite pressure from the authorities to dissipate, despite knowing that from outside they would only hear the indecipherable shouts of speakers and jurors.

To me what matters most is what happened in that courtroom: what was said and done. That is what I will attempt to relate.

We arrived early, before the jurors were let in. "We" meant me, Father, Alcidia, Mathias, Representative Lycon, and Founder Haydock. Founder Haydock was a late addition; Alcidia had suggested him just days before. The only reason I was there was that Father had listed me as testifying, though we both knew I would not. This was Father's solution;

remaining silent on the stage would mark me as a son supporting his father but not as an active prosecutor.

The courtroom was empty, cavernous, its great chandelier high above, its high east windows streaming sunlight upon the stage. Only a small group of counting clerks waited in the Pit, along with the bailiff, who would keep time and announce the results; no other magistrate would preside. The dark wood from floor to ceiling glistened, and our footsteps reverberated. We had entered at the south door and now stood in the Pit at one end of the stage, facing up at the row of chairs awaiting us. Behind them towered the white statue of General Pericles, who over two thousand years before had innovated to pay his nation's jurors. His was the prosecution's side. At the other end of the stage was one chair, for Teacher Scotes; behind and above it stood the white statue of General Washington. In the center was the podium, and on the back wall was the clock, which told that in half an hour, the proceedings would begin.

We took our seats on stage. Mathias sat nearest the center, as the lead prosecutor, then Alcidia, then Lycon, Haydock, me, and Father. The row of chairs was angled slightly, so we could all comfortably see the podium.

Not long after, the jurors began to stream in, less noisily than I'd imagined. Perhaps they moved with the solemnity of knowing their purpose. All five hundred would fill the mezzanine, and the balcony would remain empty. Upon entering they had each been handed four tin ballots, and when seated, they fingered these or set them into the designated slots on the bench-back at their knees. Gradually, the noise of their conversation swelled and would only intensify from there. When seated during the proceedings and before they rose to vote, they could speak without restrictions and in the manner of their choosing. They were the people, and this was one of their houses.

This was my first trial, in any role. Father also rarely went to court. He thought that prosecutions should be left to the people, and he especially cautioned against a representative enforcing his own laws. He himself had only prosecuted one, many years ago, a law that he had actually opposed in Assembly. Doing so, he believed, demonstrated his commitment to our laws and modeled for other representatives that they should not be overzealous. That he now was prosecuting his own law was an exception to his long-held rule.

Twenty years before, trials drew mostly older jurors because the pay did not supplant a day's lost wages and there were fewer people idled. This was not the case this day. The men and women filling the seats were of every age—that is, from thirty on up. Judging by their attire, most appeared to be of the lower or middle sort, or perhaps former middle sort. They formed a colorful and voluminous wall, rustling in anticipation. A sheet explaining the day's agenda had been placed on every seat; some jurors were reading, some not. I wondered what they thought of us, aligned upon the stage. Though our dress was also plain, still we must have struck them as a peculiarly varied group. I wondered, too, what they thought of Teacher Scotes, who had not yet arrived—if they knew him, if they had only heard of him, what they knew, what they had heard. Had many of them reflected on the act that governed this trial, understood its meaning or significance? Perhaps they simply sought the pay and had been randomly selected. In their faces I searched for the familiar; none I recognized from my travels. Were any friends of Teacher Scotes? At most a few could have been approached by Xephon or the others in the two weeks prior.

Just before nine, when the jury was nearly seated, Teacher Scotes appeared. He had entered by the north door and for a moment faced the jury from the Pit. Upon noticing him, they quieted. Then he turned and climbed onto the stage.

He was dressed as on any other day: same white shirt, same worn breeches, same bare feet. Though the pants and shirt might draw favor from this crowd (for being plain, not for being unfashionable), the lack of shoes might unnerve. Teacher Scotes was not one for convention, and usually this worked against him.

Whatever solemnity might accompany the sight of a man threatened with possible condemnation, a solemnity that had quieted the jury upon his entrance, seemed to vanish, because once he was seated, their noise swelled again, this time with occasional laughter. Likely the laughter pertained to their private affairs, not to us and not to Teacher Scotes. I would like to think so.

A few seats to my left, Mathias seemed especially nervous, mouthing to himself, as if rehearsing words he had hoped to read rather than recite. But Father had advised against it. Juries didn't like prepared remarks. Representative Lycon sat stiffly—he at least was used to crowds, though perhaps, like Father, not to juries—and Founder Haydock kept tilting his neck and crossing his legs. Even Father, next to me, seemed tense. He eyed only the jury and did not look across at Teacher Scotes. As well as he had prepared himself and the others, with a jury, one never knew. And one never knew what Teacher Scotes could do. Father understood this as well as anyone.

Teacher Scotes also watched the jury, but to me he seemed calm, the kind of calm, he argued, that came from knowing what you plan to do and why and knowing what you can control and not. I rarely saw him otherwise. Yet Xephon claimed that Teacher Scotes had not prepared. I confess, with due regard for the others on stage, to more than a little curiosity as to how this battle between my father and Teacher Scotes would unfold, and the sight of Teacher Scotes, hands folded quietly on his lap, calmed me some too, at least in a way I hadn't felt since the day I encountered them above Gray's Ferry.

At nine the bailiff approached the podium and raised his arms. He at least was dressed formally, in greatcoat. The crowd quieted, and he described his role, the sequence, the timing, the ballots, the voting process—everything that was provided on the sheet. That took but minutes. Then he read the charges, bowed, and retreated. The crowd remained quiet, as if hearing the words spoken—words they had no doubt read in the newspapers or on the courthouse wall—had given them new meaning. The bailiff called Mathias forward.

Mathias rose, hesitated, then proceeded to the podium and, at the podium, hesitated again. The jury chuckled. With a breath he began, and when he finally reached full stride, he moved apace much better than he had at the preliminary hearing. His presentation was so improved, I think it amazed his fellow prosecutors. His tone was of modesty and respect for the law and gravity at the nature of the charges and the penalty, but he recounted with felt emotion and poetic flair what his son had related to him about the confrontation with Teacher Scotes. Evoking much detail and nearly performing both his son's conversation with Teacher Scotes and his own with his son, he left a strong and unflattering impression of Teacher Scotes. It was the very story that the chief magistrate had dismissed as irrelevant, but this was a trial, and nothing was inadmissible. The jury could decide what to weigh and not.

Not only did the incident reflect badly on Teacher Scotes's political views, it also unfortunately reminded the jury of the play that had been written about Teacher Scotes, when Mathias mentioned his son's apprenticeship with the playwright. He warned the jurors not to be swayed by Teacher Scotes's eloquence, as he called it. In the end he spoke the longest of any prosecutor, and even I, as irritated as I was with him, had to acknowledge his capacity for presence on a stage and the fact that someday he just might recite a poem before an audience. I myself had once dreamed of doing just that. The jury listened, their sounds—mostly respectful of Mathias's presentation—rising and ebbing like waves.

At well past half an hour, he summed up, then ceded the floor to Representative Lycon, whose height and grave demeanor must have buttressed his words. He used his turn to describe Teacher Scotes's presentation at Assembly, the day that I was there—how Teacher Scotes had suggested the impropriety not only of a law to forgive debts but of the very act of voting on that question. I had recalled the day minutely and frequently since, so I could contrast what I remembered with Representative Lycon's account. What truly happened was that Teacher Scotes had posed some questions and mostly, in turn, had been shouted down. Hardly had he *suggested* anything, unless we interpret questions to be answers. It was also true that anything he said in Assembly could not be considered criminal, and Representative Lycon was conscientious enough to remind the jury of this fact. But he also said that in assessing a defendant's overall views, such speech could be weighed as background, as corroboration of other acts and transgressions. This was why he chose to attend the trial and attest to the events of that day.

Founder Haydock was next and was mercifully short. Alcidia must have aided in his preparation, because I did not deem him capable of relating the conversation we all had witnessed at Simon's, later that same day, nearly three months ago, but he did so with some accuracy, at least by my recall. This was another conversation I had recollected many times, as I recollected most that I had witnessed, including from the year before. I did so nightly, when I should have been sleeping. Nighttime for me was the best for thought.

Conveying too much emotion, Founder Haydock characterized his experience, alleging that Teacher Scotes had advocated the destruction of his ironworks and questioned the generally accepted meanings of the concepts of the right and good. As always—Founder Haydock here invoked the defendant's reputation—Teacher Scotes had suggested that nobody knew anything. This portrayal of Teacher Scotes elicited a murmur of recognition, and the conversation described by Founder Haydock, like the one described by Representative Lycon, seemed to impress the jury, because everything Teacher Scotes had said—both what and how they said he said it—smelled of impropriety.

The more I listened, the more worried I became—and frustrated, because I knew the truth was not so simple and that what the jury seemed to think it understood, it did not. But that is the nature of argument, and it would be up to Teacher Scotes to remedy their impressions. He was going to have a difficult time of it.

His situation worsened when Alcidia spoke. There were many reasons: Alcidia was known and well respected; Alcidia was a friend of Teacher Scotes, someone not likely to wish him ill; Alcidia was eloquent; and Alcidia was, well, Alcidia. His bearing at the podium was better than regal: it was both of the people and yet above them at the same time. He struck the jurors, I could tell, as one of them yet also as more skilled and brave. Truly he had the potential to be a famous representative, perhaps even equaling Father's stature. Some superiorities the people will condone.

By the time he had finished, it was past ten thirty. At eleven, the prosecution's time would expire. But Father hardly needed what little time he had. All he planned to do was summarize, explain his role, and position himself as a supporter of this worthy cause.

At first he did not rush to move, then raised himself by placing a hand on my shoulder, not conspicuously but not briefly either, and I believe the jurors noticed. Up to this point, none of the prosecutors had been applauded, not even Alcidia, but Father lightly was. The jurors' applauding hands fluttered like a meadow full of gently feeding butterflies, modestly consistent with the gravity of the moment. Watching Father settle at the podium, the way he placed his hands or looked from side to side or high to low, without hurry and with presence of mind, hearing his voice fill the acoustically powerful hall, I was reminded that every time I saw him speak, in groups large or small (though it had been some time since I had witnessed either), he impressed me with his skill—a skill that seemed the output of a great recipe: voice and body control, intelligence, humor, compassion, attunement to an audience. He spoke as if he knew his listeners' very thoughts and could blend his words with their desires. I do not know how he did it.

Most of what Father knew firsthand of Teacher Scotes's views had come well before the passing of this statute, so he could not dwell on that. Instead he framed his role as the statesman who had proposed the act, why he had done so, and why he thought it important to bring offenders before a jury of their peers to enforce it. This nation being theirs, he reminded the jury, it was only right that they maintain its standards. Such was the responsibility of citizenship, and he knew well, after long acquaintance with them, that they were capable of such a role. He need not remind them, he said, of hardships they suffered daily—hardships exacerbated by ideals that were critical of the nation. And no one had been more critical than Teacher Scotes. Maintaining our ideals is essential, he said, because the day we lose faith in them, we lose faith in ourselves. Would that day be today? It was one of his best lines.

By appealing to their sufferings and blaming Teacher Scotes, he empowered them to remedy their plight, to transform their sense of futility into force. And where, he wondered aloud, *are* we, if we cannot govern ourselves? That question, we all knew, they could easily answer, so he waited for the shout, and when some jurors did, he affirmed their response: we are back in Monarchy and no better than Britain. He also explained the history of the day's proceeding. He told of how he had heard from Alcidia the story that was just told them and that he'd felt duty-bound to consider prosecuting. Then, soon thereafter hearing similar accusations from Mathias, he knew the case was just.

In that way and in minutes, he lent the broad sweep of history and the heavy weight of coveted values to the facts that had been asserted in the two hours before and in so doing transformed the case (had any jurors been leery) from the taint of a merely vindictive persecution to one of collective and idealistic urgency. Teacher Scotes's behavior jeopardized fifty years of building and a future of prosperity, and as much as we appreciated his role in our founding struggles, we could not condone his behavior since. Perhaps, Father said, he should have argued for the passage of the act years ago, but he had waited till the need was greatest.

At that he left the podium and sat, and even the bailiff paused before advancing, as if stilled by Father's words. A similar feeling flowed back from the crowd before us, who had quieted. In the chair next to me, he bent his neck in solemnity, and I studied him.

Then the bailiff summoned Teacher Scotes. Judging by the mood in that moment, that Teacher Scotes would end this day punished in some fashion for the crime he was accused of now seemed virtually inevitable.

CHAPTER 26

Words pass to us from the ages, the remnants of the minds that originated them. Why some survive for a single generation, let alone a hundred, I cannot say, given that they are splashes in the streams of what has been written and spoken by all who came before. I suppose they touch us in some way, each generation's esteem building upon the prior's, such that some particular words endure.

Teacher Scotes was a lone man, and he spoke at trial on a single day, and I cannot claim to have understood every word he said or why he said it. But I will write his words with hope that they survive long into the future and that people study and debate them. Which makes me, I suppose, his scribe.

Like Father, Teacher Scotes did not hurry to the podium but stepped deliberately; his were the only footfalls that did not reverberate. He seemed to float in our direction, and from the angle I viewed him, he faced the audience, as did the shiny white colossus of General Washington not far behind him and in the corner. Our one hope now was that General Washington would save him again, as he did when Teacher Scotes fell at Princeton. In saying "our" hope, I admit my intuition back then that mankind itself would suffer a great loss should Teacher Scotes be found guilty.

Before he began speaking, the immense hall quieted again, but it would not remain so for long.

"Ladies and gentlemen," he began, "I must confess at the outset that I find myself unused to being in such a position. I hardly ever address you in this way. Never before have I faced a trial, and I am rarely at Assembly. As a result, public speaking is not my strength, so I ask your forbearance if I fail to communicate well."

A modest murmuring arose. I peeked at Father, who was facing not Teacher Scotes but the jury, with the blandest of expressions.

Teacher Scotes said, "I don't mean to credit myself alone for not having been accused before, for the law under which I stand accused is new. Throughout history nations like ours have had such laws. And like me, you who can recall the early days of these United States might have opposed such laws back then. I imagine that our long experience before the Revolution restrained what elsewhere seemed rather commonplace. Still, we can wonder, despite his explanation, why the esteemed representative felt the need to propose this act last year rather than several years ago. But I am not here to waste your time quibbling."

Though he spoke to an audience of hundreds, he was not in manner speaking differently than he would to five or even one. This had not been true of Mathias or Alcidia—or even my father. In tone and style, he was the same that day as on any other.

"In fact," he continued, "I am inclined to say that out of respect for your intelligence and your time, I should waive my chance to make any defense at all, since my accusers seem hardly to have called for one. I don't know about you, but all I heard were allegations, not about what I *did* say but about what I *might* have *suggested*. Or what I *didn't* say in response to what others said. Or what I *don't* believe. Or how words of mine intended one way might have been interpreted another. Never have I encountered such a litany of negatives."

At this there was some chuckling.

"Perhaps then, ladies and gentlemen, given such allegations, we would all be better served if I allowed you to vote immediately." At this he showed his palms and stood through a hesitation till a slow protestation began.

"Speak!" they yelled. "Explain yourself! Speak!"

If anyone thought otherwise, they did not call out.

"Very well," Teacher Scotes said. "I see that I must address you."

Without delay he stepped out from behind the podium and clasped his fingers.

"I applaud your respect for our procedures and your oath. So I will speak and, out of respect for your respect, will keep to the purpose. Still, I do ask your forbearance, for, as I say, I am not accustomed to speaking in this way."

For a second time murmurs arose, as if the jurors rejected any proclamation of his inadequacy. But he continued, "It is true, ladies and gentlemen. My audiences, such as they are, are always quite small, and the people I encounter talk more than I do. So please do allow for some lack on my part, especially when compared with my accusers, who daily exclaim before you and perform their arts or are practicing to."

This comment elicited a weak roll of laughter directed at us.

"Though most of you have never met me, I fear you are inclined to distrust my words. Some apparently consider them diversions, when in fact I only ever mean what I say."

Teacher Scotes had a reputation, which was that he often meant other than what he said, that one could not be certain of what he meant, and that he frequently cloaked his speech in irony. Perhaps it was not the fairest of criticisms, though I, too, sometimes got the same impression. It was an approach that bothered people greatly. For this reason, I did not see how calling attention to it helped.

"Ladies and gentlemen, you are entitled to question why the prosecutors have brought this case when their charges are so weak, and I believe I can answer you. I have been aware for many years of a prejudice against me. This fact, I believe, is what they are counting on and why they feel no need to offer any substance. Perhaps some of you have experienced prejudices against yourselves. Certainly I am not special in this regard. Normally they are harmless. But they can taint our reputations."

This point seemed to register, as indicated by some nodding.

"I can even share the source of this prejudice against me and would like to take a moment to do so.

"Following our revolution and the hard-fought war that nearly bankrupted us and in which many gave their lives, we began as a people to discuss a way forward, and our nation, newly independent, took shape. What emerged was the form we have known for fifty years. Living in this city, then, I overheard the discussions that sprouted daily, and I wanted to learn and understand. Because the conversations I happened upon did not enlighten me fully, I sought out my own. I questioned politicians, poets, and craftsmen—anyone who claimed to have knowledge and was willing to speak. Perhaps out of sympathy for the afflictions I suffered during the war, many welcomed my inquiries, and I was grateful. But the more I questioned, the more I found they didn't have the knowledge that they claimed. I, who was ignorant and who recognized my ignorance, repeatedly encountered men and women whose answers grew more contradictory, and they themselves more confused, with every question.

"At one point I described my encounters to a pastor I knew, who said to me, 'Young Scotes, you are wiser than the rest of them.' At first I did not understand his meaning, but I believe I understand it now: I was ignorant, yes, but at least I *knew* that I was ignorant. I knew I didn't know. They, who offered many answers yet seemingly could defend none, nevertheless claimed certainty in everything they said. This puzzled me, so I pressed on. After a while, their receptions, once warm, grew cold, then hostile. This puzzled me further, for I merely sought to learn. Still, I questioned, though risking ill repute. But what else could I do? Like each of you, I have but one mind and can only think with it.

"Well, I admit that a certain amount of scorn and ridicule did eventually follow, tempered somewhat by knowledge of my past, and the prejudice I now speak of was born. Some even wrote unflattering plays about me, which no doubt many of you have seen. They continue to be staged."

I had never heard this story and always had been drawn to hearing about Teacher Scotes's youth. Then and there I wished I had inquired of him further.

"This was the origin of the prejudice against me," he said. "The origin, but not the only cause. There is a second one yet.

"As time passed and my questioning became a way of life and the mantle of 'Teacher' found me, I obtained a modest following—young people who attached themselves to me and, emulating my example, examined themselves and others as best they could, even their parents, who in turn also became annoyed with me and began accusing me of tainting their children with wrong ideas. This at least is what they asserted. In fact, I believe they were less angry at their children's thinking and more angry at having their own confusions exposed. Nevertheless, again I became their target.

"I present all this as background for you to consider. It is settled smoke you must disperse in order to see me clearly. But come. You have requested that I argue the present case against me, so let me do so now." He paused just long enough for quiet. "I have been accused by these men of not believing in the ideals that the nation believes in and of corrupting the young. Very well, to these charges we turn directly." He faced in our direction. "Poet Mathias, kindly stand, if you would."

Mathias, at the end of our row, nearest Teacher Scotes, startled. His hair was somewhat longer than was the custom and today was wet and combed, thereby causing it to swing with every jerk of his head. From the moment he had completed his statement, he had been smirking—but no longer. Teacher Scotes returned a friendly gaze, and Mathias sneaked a look at Father, who still faced only forward. Apparently Mathias had planned his speech but nothing more, which was understandable, given that usually the defendant addressed the jurors, not the prosecution, though this was permitted. When seemingly convinced there was no option, he stood.

"Thank you," Teacher Scotes said. He paused before taking up his questioning. "You say before these people that I corrupt the young."

Facing the jurors with a soldier's bearing, Mathias said, "That, I believe, I have proved."

"Please explain to these jurors what you mean by 'corrupt.'"

Mathias blinked, held a moment, and blinked again. "It is not I who use the word, but the law. Unless you are questioning the law?"

Teacher Scotes smiled softly. "I understood that the law was left deliberately vague for the people to fill in and only wanted to ascertain your meaning in bringing this charge. I assume that you have thought carefully and deeply about these issues and would not prosecute a fellow citizen unless you had."

Mathias reset his bearing. "By 'corrupt,' we mean that people are harmed by believing in your bad ideals."

"And what makes these ideals harmful is that they are false?"

"Yes."

"Very well. Now, in accusing me as you are, is it your claim that I corrupt intentionally or unintentionally?"

Mathias's eyes went back and forth. "I strongly claim intentionally," he said.

"Strongly claim. I see. So by 'intentionally,' you mean that I deliberately discuss ideals that I know to be false and therefore harmful?"

"Yes."

"Meaning that I myself, knowing them to be false, disagree with these harmful ideals?" After turning a puzzled look toward Teacher Scotes, Mathias immediately thought better of it and did not answer. By way of explaining, Teacher Scotes added, "You accuse me of corrupting intentionally. That would suggest that the harmful ideals I discuss I myself believe to be false."

"No, you believe them to be true."

"I thought you said I believe them to be false."

"You deliberately confused me. I meant that you believe them to be true." A few people chuckled.

"Very well. So if I believe them to be true, then I consider them to be beneficial and not harmful? . . . Is it possible, then, that whatever harm I cause is unintentional?"

To this Mathias answered nothing, and though rigid of body, he appeared to be faintly shaking. Teacher Scotes must have observed this too because he said, "Good Mathias, you needn't fear me. You and I are only sharing arguments, nothing more."

"I do not fear you, have never feared you, and never will fear you," Mathias said, in a manner that elicited even louder chuckles. There also followed a smattering of boos, perhaps arising from the bias that Teacher Scotes had claimed was against him. Normally a man on trial for his life was given a certain deference, which most would spend in supplication, pleading for mercy. Few, likely, would engage in syllogisms.

Teacher Scotes addressed the jurors. "I am sorry, ladies and gentlemen, if you disapprove of my methods. But they are the only ones I know for arriving at an understanding." The jurors settled. Teacher Scotes turned again to Mathias. "I ask again. Might whatever harm I cause be unintentional?"

"You corrupt intentionally, I say."

Gently, Teacher Scotes said, "It would seem, then, to be both." By his expression he did not appear to be relishing his questioning. Then he said, "Now my good sir, there have been so many men and women, young and old, happy to keep my company over the years. If it is true that I have corrupted them, where are they or their families today? Why have they not joined your prosecution and testified?"

"That only shows that they agree with you. That you have succeeded in corrupting them."

Teacher Scotes tilted his head and appeared to ponder. Then he said, "Now, these young people that I corrupt, how do they become corrupted?"

"What do you mean? By listening to your bad ideals."

"Just listening to them?"

"You are playing tricks. By believing in them."

"So they have made an error in accepting these bad ideals and can rethink and correct their error?"

"No."

"No? They must accept the bad ideals and act on them?"

"Yes."

"Can we not inoculate them against their errors?"

"You know we cannot. That would mean exposing them to corrupting ideals."

Teacher Scotes nodded. "If they should happen upon bad ideals, then, can we not help them examine what is wrong with their way of thinking?"

"I just answered you that."

"Why can we not help them?"

Emboldened, Mathias slumped theatrically and raised his hands to the audience, as if to appeal, How much shall we tolerate? Some supportive grumbling returned. Finally he raised his chest and said, "Because that would mean discussing the corrupting ideals with them, which will corrupt them further, obviously."

Someone yelled, "Keep to the point," apparently in support of Mathias.

"But if they could see the errors in the bad ideals," Teacher Scotes said, "they would not be corrupted, no?"

"They cannot see the errors. Being young, they are as yet unable."

"Unable—because they are young?"

"Yes."

"Only when of age do they become able?"

"Yes."

"When over thirty?"

"Yes."

"So they are unable till aged thirty; after that they are able?"

"Yes."

"Then they can think?"

"Yes."

Teacher Scotes held a long moment, and the longer he held, the more the jurors murmured. I doubted he was influencing them for the better. He held so long I wondered whether he had forgotten Mathias. As if eager to take advantage of the pause, Mathias moved to sit.

"Please," Teacher Scotes said, extending a hand. "We have made such a good start, and I have very few questions." He waited, and as he did, the bending Mathias straightened, and the murmuring subsided. "Shall we proceed?"

"If you wish," Mathias answered, but in a way that suggested he wished not. Perhaps he feared that whatever benefits he had sought from helping Father might soon be overshadowed by the opinion that could form of him the longer this went on.

"Thank you," Teacher Scotes said. "And how do they become able to think? How do they go from being unable before thirty to being able after thirty?"

Mathias paused. His eyes went back and forth. "Age," he said. A few people chuckled.

"As if a kind of lever has been pulled."

"Yes."

"Like corn that goes from seed to stalk in an instant."

"That is not my analogy."

"Then I withdraw it. Would you like to offer one?"

"No."

Teacher Scotes nodded. "It occurs to me then to ask a different question. I assume by your charges that individual citizens can be wrong and not believe in the ideals the nation believes in."

Mathias looked at Teacher Scotes. "Of course, as is the case with you."

"And from our discussion so far, you believe it may be possible to persuade such persons of their error—if they are over thirty."

With hesitation Mathias answered, "It is possible."

"So perhaps if I am wrong, I could be persuaded of my error."

"No, you are not open to persuasion."

"I'm not?"

"No. You have proved your intransigence by persisting in not believing in the ideals of the nation."

Teacher Scotes feigned enlightenment from the assertion. Again some people chuckled. "And if other individuals are wrong, it might be appropriate to prosecute them?"

"That would be justice."

"Such as some of the jurors here, for instance?"

Mathias paused. "No," he said.

"No? All of them believe as the nation does?"

"Yes."

"Should we poll them, as a kind of experiment?" Mathias did not answer. "Perhaps you are right," Teacher Scotes said. "Perhaps it would be dangerous for them to join in our discussion, given, as you say, that you might prosecute them for their errors." He held a moment. There arose another murmur, which this time did not seem wholly antagonistic to Teacher Scotes. Mathias shifted in place and glanced at Father, who still had not looked at him.

"So," Teacher Scotes resumed, "if some individuals can be wrong, how then do we determine what the nation's ideals *are*? How do we know which individuals to believe?"

"By vote."

"So whatever the majority believes to be good and noncorrupting, *is*?"

"Yes."

"And the majority could change its mind?"

"Of course."

"A corrupting idea one day becomes uncorrupting the next?"

"Yes."

"So if we took a vote and the majority agreed with my so-called corrupting ideals, then I would no longer be guilty in your eyes?"

Here Mathias gave the first relaxed answer in many minutes. Smugly, he said, "Is that not what we will be doing very shortly?"

Teacher Scotes smiled. "Yes, we will. . . . Now," he went on, "if it's possible for an individual to be wrong, could that individual also be a father or a mother?"

Mathias looked mystified. "Of course," he said.

"And as fathers or mothers, if they happened not to believe as the nation does and were inclined to teach different ideals to their children, what should they do?"

"That could not happen."

"I'm a father. According to your charges, it has happened to me." Mathias did not answer. "Could it happen to you?"

"No."

"Meaning that whatever the majority wanted for your son, you would accept, even if you disagreed?"

"I would not be in that position. I agree with the nation's ideals."

It took a moment, but some jurors laughed. Mathias did not respond. When the laughter quieted, Teacher Scotes assumed a somber tone and resumed his questioning. "What about these jurors, then, Poet Mathias? As fathers or mothers, might they not wish sometimes to instruct their children on something other than the majority's view?" Mathias did not answer, and into the silence the murmuring returned—this time because the jurors seemed unambiguously to be considering the implications of what Teacher Scotes had asked.

Then Teacher Scotes faced the jury squarely. He extended his arms and, in a more conversational voice but distinct and amply loud, said, "Let us sum up, ladies and gentlemen. We have established a great deal and very quickly. First, that I corrupt the young both intentionally and unintentionally; second, that all the people I corrupt are so corrupted that they continue to value my influence; third, that the young have no choice but to believe in false ideals when hearing them; fourth, that they are able to think only when they are thirty, not before and without ever having examined falsehoods; and fifth, that we determine which ideals are right by vote." He turned to Mathias. "I thank you, Poet Mathias, for such an illuminating demonstration."

Laughter broke out along with the stamping of some feet. Mathias glanced again at Father but getting no reaction, visibly inflated his chest instead. He seemed ready to end the interrogation however he could.

"One last question, Poet Mathias, and I will let you sit." Mathias did not respond. "May I ask you to clarify your point about these ideals that I allegedly do not share with the nation? For instance, is it your view that I have no ideals myself or that I have the wrong ideals?"

The answer Mathias selected was the one I suspect he could best defend, because he said, "I believe you have no ideals."

"None? But I understood that others were corrupted by believing as I do."

"They believe, as you do, not to believe in what we believe."

Teacher Scotes squinted and pretended to parse that statement with his fingers. Some people laughed. "And on what do you base that allegation? You and I had never met before you brought these charges."

"I base it on the fact that you have written nothing, and everyone knows that you are sly in expressing your beliefs."

Teacher Scotes frowned and asked, "So every citizen, including all these good people here, who has written nothing and doesn't run around professing his ideals necessarily has none?"

There was a pause. "It is not necessary for me to know what your ideals are. All I know is that you do not share the people's."

"Hmm. I don't myself quite follow that, but let it be. So," he added, "I *do* have ideals. It's just that they are different from the nation's?"

"Yes," Mathias said. Someone whistled. To this Mathias raised his chin and added, "All that matters is that you don't believe in the ideals of the nation."

"Yes, you said that." There was faint laughter, but less than before, as if exasperation were setting in. "But have *I* said that?"

Mathias did not respond.

Teacher Scotes repeated, "Have *I* said that I don't believe in the ideals of the nation?"

"You never say anything directly."

"You mean that I question others?"

"That is exactly what I mean."

"I see. In that case, would you like to question me? Would that assist you?" Mathias hesitated, and his eyes went back and forth. "Dear Mathias, for some reason you wish to prosecute me with respect to how I think but at the same time seem indifferent to how I actually do think. What would you like these jurors to make of that?" Mathias stood defiantly. The murmurs swelled. "What if I told you," Teacher Scotes said, "that I do have ideals and that they *are* shared by the nation—would that be of interest to you?"

"Yes!" someone suddenly yelled.

"Ask him!" someone else yelled.

Mathias glanced one last time at my father. "I see you looking at Representative Antonyn again," Teacher Scotes said. "Perhaps you would rather question him?"

There was laughter, and when Mathias remained stony, shouting began in earnest. "Question him! Question Teacher Scotes!"

Teacher Scotes said, "I find myself perplexed, Poet Mathias. On the one hand, your very presence today suggests that you have an interest in understanding my ideals. On the other hand, here you have the opportunity to discuss them with me but seem reluctant. Therefore, again, I extend the offer. I am ready. . . . No?"

Now the hall filled with boos and further calls for Mathias to respond. When he did not, Teacher Scotes said gently to Mathias, "You see, this is why I sometimes find it necessary to question."

Mathias stiffened. If his paralysis began with Teacher Scotes's offer, it hardened with the crowd's reaction. I wanted to cheer. At that moment, had a vote been taken, Teacher Scotes might have been acquitted.

Mathias, the chief prosecutor, had been made to appear ridiculous—without facts, without plan, without command of what he meant or thought. Even if the jurors were prejudiced against Teacher Scotes, I don't think they would have convicted him based on what they'd heard. Teacher Scotes seemed to sense this too. He seemed ready to release Mathias and relinquish the stage, though a goodly time remained for his defense. Of course we'll never know, for at that moment and just as Mathias was about to sit, Father rose and turned to Teacher Scotes, he, too, standing tall and at ease.

"Teacher Scotes," he said, with a slight bow. "If it is acceptable to you, I am willing to intercede and question you, as you request, on behalf of the prosecution and these good jurors here."

Though he held a beat, Teacher Scotes smiled ever so slightly. "I do accept," he said, and Father bowed more fully. And from there the trial, which moments before had seemed near ending, proceeded and did not stop till time had formally expired.

CHAPTER 27

Because our row of chairs was angled, Father could stand in place and address both Teacher Scotes and the jurors simultaneously. For me it was a question of where to look: up and to my right, at him; or left at Teacher Scotes, half across the stage; or at the jurors. I chose none of those but focused on a patch of stage just ahead and at the edge. Listening alone would be taxing enough.

For all the time I had spent in Teacher Scotes's company, I had never heard him say what he was about to. It was stunning. Whether Father coaxed it out of him or whether he had planned to do it all along I do not know, but for the next hour, the more Teacher Scotes spoke, the more I was compelled to watch him after all. At times I even forgot that we were not alone in that vast hall.

In bearing, Father matched Teacher Scotes: calm, steady, unemotional, cordial. He even opened by complimenting him. "You are a man of precise language," he said. When Teacher Scotes did not react, Father began his interrogation. "You wish to have the accusations clarified. I am inclined to say that this is unnecessary, that they have been well established by our testimony, and I believe that these good people have understood and are not fooled by your deflections. It is simple: your ideals, your beliefs, undermine the nation's; you teach them to the young; for that you are on trial."

"I note," Teacher Scotes said, "that still you do not question me my ideals."

"You do not believe in democracy," Father said. This statement elicited a collective breath that resolved into a steady murmuring, though I was inclined to agree with Father that this charge had been implicit in what the jurors had been hearing. Or perhaps the point was clearer to me because Father had been alleging it for weeks. The murmurs faded, and the jurors seemed to ponder Father's words, which were grave. Whether they were true I, too, was primed to learn.

"That, too, is not a question," Teacher Scotes said. "But let that be. We will begin as you wish. You accuse me of not believing in democracy. Very well. We have a basis for proceeding."

"We will hear your answer, if you have one."

"I will answer, if you will permit me a question or two to clarify first." Sounds of impatient irritation rose. "Now please," Teacher Scotes said, "I asked at the outset for some forbearance and to be allowed to speak in the only manner I know." Father raised one palm no higher than his chest, and the crowd calmed. Father nodded at Teacher Scotes. "A question first, then," Teacher Scotes said. "By 'democracy,' you mean our current system?"

"Our current system, our past system, and our future system," Father said.

"The system in which we have a single legislative assembly, staffed by representatives who are elected by the people, with the power to enact any and all national laws?"

"That is it. And though we representatives are known to disappoint the people from time to time, and perhaps more frequently than from time to time"—here there was some benevolent laughter—"it is an exalted system at that."

"Hear! Hear!" someone cried.

"The system in which those representatives may act without limit?" Teacher Scotes said.

"Not so. The people are our limit. If we displease them, they replace us."

"The system in which you may legislate the repeal of slavery?"

"As we proudly did. You do not object to that, surely."

"And could legislate its reinstatement at some future date?"

"The people would not condone that," Father said.

"One in which you may nationalize all businesses, shops, and manufactories?"

"That, too, the people do not support."

"But it is within your power, should they support it?"

"It is within our power because it is within *their* power. The people's will is supreme, as it should be."

"A system in which a man's savings may be taken for any purpose, at any time?"

"You engage in fiction, Teacher Scotes."

"His property and income?"

"I repeat—fiction."

"Is it? Is this not what happened to your own father in the first Distribution? Is this not what you witnessed when you were but a boy? Is this not the pattern you yourself have repeated in many acts subsequent to your election?"

At these words Father seemed to stiffen, but not obviously so. "I have never acted but in accord with the people's will," he said.

Gently, Teacher Scotes replied, "I do not doubt it." There was a pause and some murmuring, as often happens in the presence of open conflict.

Now Father did color faintly, though perhaps only I could see it. "Teacher Scotes, as I said before, these deflections will not confuse this jury. Your sophistry has no power in this building. The jurors are aware that they are not here for a primer on political systems."

"But perhaps they would like a discussion of my ideals and how they relate to the nation's? Unless you would rather not proceed?"

Father said dismissively, "Go on. You are only wasting your own limited minutes."

"Thank you. So, acting on behalf of the people, you may one day take every last demos owned by these five hundred good men and women here, the next day return it to them, and the next, increase theirs by taking the savings and income of a different five hundred?"

"You may characterize my role however you wish. These are not my words."

"If you have more accurate ones, I will gladly use them."

"These jurors know that I embody their will and provide them a voice."

"Very ably put, if abstractly so. I was endeavoring to be more concrete."

"I see that you have successfully steered our conversation toward an interrogation of your own. I understood I was to question you."

"I gathered that you did not wish to."

"If you are endeavoring to show that you do not believe in democracy, as we allege, you are succeeding."

"You say 'we,' Representative Antonyn, but are you not the only one here who has openly alleged that?"

Stiffly Father said, "These are the allegations of the prosecution, and I stand behind these good men here."

"So you agree that you are part of the prosecuting team. You are one of them?"

This I thought an odd and obvious point. Was not Father with the prosecution? But Father only said, "Continue with your defense, if you have one."

"I will now endeavor to explain my ideals," Teacher Scotes said, "and how, contrary to what you yourself allege, they are in fact in accord with the nation's."

It was here that the day turned. It was here we began to hear words from him that we had never heard, and in this I include Father, for I do not think even he anticipated what was coming. I can only summarize as follows: Teacher Scotes admitted the charges while simultaneously denying them. He began speaking and went on speaking, disturbed by nary a question or pause, speaking as he never did, as he normally seemed opposed to doing, and he left us reeling in the end—the prosecutors, the jurors, and most especially myself.

He first acknowledged that he and Father agreed on the nature of our system. He granted everything—the power of the legislature and the supreme will of the people. "It is true that this is our system," he said. But then he asked, "Is it, however, our ideal? Is it what we fought the Revolution for?"

I believe by invoking the Revolution he was firing two pistols in his defense, because the Revolution was our most cherished event, more cherished even than building the amphitheater and VOP, and because Teacher Scotes himself was admired for his role in it. Though the Revolution was ever-present, to hear him name it in that setting, on a day more than fifty years later, when his life was again at stake, with the now midday sun streaming dustily from the highest windows, gave the jurors pause and Teacher Scotes room to speak, at least for a moment, with fewer jeers and cheers and, except early on, hardly a call to interrupt him.

"Back then," he told them, "we spoke of liberty and rights. *These* were our ideals, as they are mine." He was using words—judging by how young many jurors seemed—most had likely never heard expressed. "Democracy," he said, "was no part of that ideal, except as a contrast to it. Rather it was a system to be avoided, along with monarchy and aristocracy, the three options bequeathed to us from ancient times. Since each of those systems we understood to be the negation of liberty and rights, each decried for twenty centuries, we sought another way—a different structure for a different purpose. And for that we fought the Revolution." And he began to elaborate as he never had, especially for those too young to understand his generation's past.

But before he got much further, Representative Lycon yelled with unrestrained outrage from his seat, "The defendant is referring to works that are illegal to obtain!"

Teacher Scotes calmly proceeded. "Thankfully I am in court," he said, "and am duty-bound to speak freely." He regarded Lycon. "I do not refer to the works the good representative reminds us are prohibited but to the very discussions I myself heard firsthand, in my youth." He regarded the jurors squarely. "From whom did I hear them? From General Washington, with whom I served. From Lawyers Jefferson and Adams, Scholar Madison, Assemblyman Mason, and many others. When they spoke, they spoke of the blessings of liberty, of a life spent guided by one's own lights. Alas, we lost them too soon, most to the war they had championed, though they understood the risks when they championed it. We lost them before they could help put the ideals I speak of into practice."

By the time Father stood, Teacher Scotes had just time enough to finish with this: "So when my prosecutors ask whether I share our ideals, I do not know how to answer since we seem to have two sets, which are at odds. This, what the prosecution claims to be our ideals, and that, what I understood to be ours from inception."

With not a little animation, Father called out, "Shall I tell you, good people, what he has said in my hearing? Because Teacher Scotes raises views held only by rich oligarchs from a distant past, shall I tell you what I myself heard him say, also in the past?" Without waiting for an answer, Father boomed, "I have heard him refer to democracy as one of the three forms of tyranny. *Tyranny*, he called it." Following this came some uncomfortable murmuring. "Let me add that I have also heard him quote approvingly the adviser to Charlemagne who supposedly said, 'Do not listen to those who say the voice of the people is the voice of God, since the riotousness of the crowd is always very close to madness!' *Approvingly*, I say!"

Again the murmuring came, only louder and accompanied by more distinct objections. But these, too, did not fluster Teacher Scotes, who waited for calm and then calmly said, "I seem to have once again agitated the good representative."

Father almost let this go and began to sit, then nearly down he shot up and raised a finger high. "If I am agitated," he yelled, "it is because I hear you defile our history and our ideals before these good people!" Then he did sit, to some acclamation.

Again upon waiting for quiet, Teacher Scotes said to Father, "I will now proceed to complete my defense, unless you wish to add anything further?" Father from his seat extended a palm in exaggerated deference. Teacher Scotes said, "Very well" and raised his chin and regarded the crowd.

Then he set free the following words, words that would settle his fate. I cannot claim to cite them verbatim, but I cite them faithfully.

CHAPTER 28

This (he began) is the distinction as I understand it. If we want a democracy, we have exactly what we want. But if we want liberty, then ladies and gentlemen, we do not have what we want.

If you ask me to state the difference between the two and how, if we so desired, we would transform one into the other, I would point to one feature—that the power of the Assembly must be limited. To what? To protecting individual rights. By what? By clearly defining those rights in writing, in our Constitution, and by defending against anyone who violates them—any person or group—even the Assembly itself, should it pass contrary laws. That defense would be secured by checks among the branches, especially by our courts, who would treat such rights as principles of law that govern everything the Assembly does.

I know this approach sounds alien, for it means sharply limiting what the representatives do. Indeed, I would not even call them representatives, which implies a responsibility they should not have: to legislate on behalf of any interest or desire their constituents happen to hold. Any wish, any preference, any goal. Rather I would call them legislators or senators or members of Congress or of the Assembly, whichever you prefer. A delimited purpose requires a careful title.

A minute ago I named some men who shared this view. "Rich oligarchs," Representative Antonyn called them. I would call them pioneers and brave soldiers. Doubly so, for they fought not only an actual war, which is dangerous enough, but also one more difficult to win: a war of ideas.

For them, the opposite of liberty was the state of having no rights—none recognized in principle and none protected in fact. The state of forced obedience. The state of submission to the restraint or command of authority.

It was precisely against such submission that we fought our revolution, against the restraint and command of the British Monarchy. In this we all agreed. But to the men I named, monarchy was but one form of authority that could enforce obedience and therefore not the only one to be opposed. Using their knowledge of history, including of the ancient world we so revere, they did not confuse the principle of authority with but one of its manifestations. They did not conflate the fight against monarchy with their desire to eliminate obedience in political life. They recognized other forms of oppression too.

And this led to their criticism not only of monarchy—rule of the one, as they called it—but also of aristocracy, rule of the few, and of democracy, rule of the many. Please do not shout, ladies and gentlemen! Each form had existed and each, in their view, negated the liberties they sought to protect. In fact they opposed *rule* of any kind. Unlike us, they did not equate law with rule but considered them opposites. For them, to rule others was contrary to proper law. To rule was to command, to grant whim a seat at the political table, to make desire the standard of political power. To them, it did not matter whose desire ruled—whether a monarch's or a vast majority's. They did not judge by counting heads. They did not argue that a monarch's act was wrong but the same act taken by the majority was right. For them, if monarchy meant arbitrariness, democracy meant arbitrariness writ large. This is why they did not refer to their ideal system as a democracy. The system they pondered, a system that constrained the legislature and therefore the people's will, required a different name.

I said they advocated liberty and rights. In so doing, what exactly were they promoting? Something akin to this: as a competent adult, innocent of any crime, you should be free to think, judge, and act accordingly, so long as you respect the equal right of others to do the same. To act without obstruction, according to your will, within the limits drawn around you by the equal rights of others. Colloquially they called this the right to pursue your own happiness. I call it your right to independence. Not national independence, which we did win, but individual independence, which we are far from winning. Or, another way I think of it: you should be free to decide for yourself and provide for yourself.

Specifically this meant, to them, protection of your person and your property—of your person to banish violence and restraint, of your property to secure you in producing and keeping what you produce. In fact, they thought the two could not be separated. Whatever you produced, they argued, should be yours by right because it came from you, from your person, which itself is yours, by right. You being the cause, your creation is the effect and hence your property. Be it a crop, a tool, a service, or the simple output of your labor, you produced it and so should be entitled to use or dispose of it however you wish, as others may with what *they* produced.

Protected in your person and your property, you are then free to create the means of your existence and that of your dependents. That is, to create wealth. To grow a bushel of wheat is to create wealth, which you can either eat or trade for what others have to offer, on what terms they wish to offer it and you to accept. Once traded, your wealth takes on new forms—perhaps you trade for clothes and then for seeds for planting in the spring, or perhaps you trade for money that becomes a bank account—but whatever form your wealth takes, its source remains the same: your productive action and hence your property. In this way you can survive and prosper according to your success at it, a success that need know no limits. By right. The more you produce, the greater is your confidence and your pleasure, because of what you make available to others. The more others produce, the greater is your confidence and pleasure, because of what they make available to you. Your life improves the more you produce *and* the more others do as

well. In producing, together we make life easier and more secure. There is
no other way to do so.

But in describing this process, I have not mentioned a third way to
obtain goods and services, other than by producing and trading for them.
And that is by theft. Goods and services can be obtained in this way too,
but doing so does not make them your property, because of how you
obtained them. To obtain by production and trade is to obtain by right;
to obtain by theft is to obtain by wrong.

In a free society, one that protects your rights, you have only the first
two options open to you. If you produce nothing, you own nothing, unless
others bestow gifts upon you, giving freely of what is theirs. But in our
present democratic system—perhaps it will offend you to hear this—you
may obtain wealth not by producing it but by this third way, by taking it
from your fellow citizens. In this way you gain goods and services that
were originally and by right the property of others.

I would even go so far as to say that such takings are the essence of
democracy, that democracy necessarily becomes the means of transferring
wealth in just this way. Why? Because whereas in a free system, wealth is
considered privately owned, in a democratic system, wealth is considered
collectively owned. No longer does your property belong to you unambiguously; instead, it belongs to everyone, to the people. This explains why even
today we do not tolerate private theft, no matter a person's need: no one
may legally trespass on your land and rob you of your possessions just
because they need to. Publicly, on the other hand, following a vote in
Assembly and under the banner of a legal statute, that same act *is* thereby
tolerated, even celebrated. What makes it not "theft" is the premise of collective ownership. This is also why we say, "We are managing *our*
resources," as if those resources belong to us collectively. Or why we say,
"We must spread the wealth around," as if the wealth is ours collectively
to spread. To hold what you individually own to be sacrosanct, unable to
be confiscated even by those who wish to vote it away, is consistent with
liberty and rights. It is inconsistent, however, with democracy.

So under our system, you are not free to use or dispose of your property as you see fit but instead must cede it for collective purposes. Perhaps you are allowed to hold it for a time, but only so long as the Assembly permits, because it is not yours by right—not yours to use, trade, or give away how and when you please.

And these restraints on your action do not apply only to what you have already produced. They also apply to what and how you produce in the first place. You all well know the laws that dictate what you must and cannot do—what you must and cannot buy or sell, what you must and cannot pay to others, whom you must and cannot hire. Myriad ways in which your action is controlled, regardless of your wishes. Regardless of what you believe is right. Regardless of what you judge to be best for you, your family, your craft, your farm, your manufactory. Such laws arrest action, bleed joy, and undermine will. They are the opposite of what we need in order to live.

If you see some truth in what I say, you may wonder how we arrived at such a place. How did we stray so far from implementing the ideals of those men I named? I believe this happened because fifty years ago we misunderstood what we were fighting for. Inspired by Lawyer Jefferson's words in our great Declaration, we mistakenly conflated two things: a government derived from the consent of the governed and legislation that secured our rights. The first called for popular sovereignty, making us a republic, which we are and should be—we the people have the ultimate right to form, dissolve, and reshape our government. But the second pertained to the standard of legislation, which should have consisted of rights but became instead the popular will.

We then compounded the error by applying the term "self-government," not to ourselves as individuals but to "ourselves"—as if this has meaning—as a nation. By a choice of words, we conflated millions of selves into one. Since then, your right to decide and provide for yourselves has been aggregated, pooled. It has been joined, to make the democracy.

In a democracy, the meaning of elections becomes not, Who should defend my rights? but, To whom should I cede my judgment? Wittingly or not, you have delegated this responsibility to your representatives: *they* now decide and provide for you. They decide what jobs you may take and under what conditions; whom you can employ and on what terms; what food you may eat and what medicines you may take; what contracts you may sign; what you can read and hear; what products are good and bad, safe and unsafe. In short, they can prescribe what you must do, proscribe what you cannot do, and confiscate what you have done. Empowered by you, they pass two sets of laws, one relieving you from having to think for yourselves, the other from having to produce for yourselves. In sum, from having to live for yourselves.

For those who accuse me of irony, here I could accuse them also, because at the core of this choice—whom to vote for—is a greater irony than I could ever invent, even were I so inclined. That is: while voting to make myself dependent on the reps, I assert that I am independent because I am the one who voted for the reps. Without acknowledging that I have done so, I cede my agency while claiming to keep it, in the form of my vote. My logic is this: I have voted for the reps who vote on my behalf, therefore I am self-governing. Meanwhile, those reps are free to pass any laws at will, in the very name of my will, laws that in fact restrain my will by replacing it with this mythical, collective one.

If such a role sounds parental, it is, and precisely so. It puts us in the same relation to our legislators as are children to their fathers and mothers. Children, unable intellectually and physically to decide and provide for themselves, require their parents to guide, even compel, them. Citizens, by delegating such parental powers to the reps, exchange their role as adults for that of children. Were we free, were we living under what once were called the blessings of liberty, we would be protecting the rights of adults and parenting children. But we no longer recognize that distinction.

I once heard someone say that to teach a man how to grow independently and for himself is the greatest service one can do for another. It is perhaps the profoundest principle I have heard and one I have tried to make my own. As a father and as someone who has observed parents for fifty years, I have come to think of parenthood in just this way—that a parent's essential job is to make him- or herself no longer needed. That the best time to learn independence is in childhood. That it's the very purpose of childhood. As the Proverb says, "A wise son maketh a glad father."

Most of you, I expect, agree with me and see this principle as natural and quite plain. Nature bestows upon the very young the desire to be independent, long before they have the ability to be. Despite their lack of knowledge, they want to act and to help, and they resent being controlled and commanded what to do. Guided appropriately by their elders, they thrive and beam with accomplishments which, however small those accomplishments seem to us, are large to them. And gradually they acquire the knowledge and abilities to one day stand on their own, as adults, ready to think and act for themselves. To decide and provide for themselves.

Given this, how should we judge a political system that reverses this glorious process by claiming that the very same adults who have developed over years into independent beings can no longer be defended as such but must be treated as no better than their earlier, juvenile selves? And to the extent that they wish to remain independent, defying laws that compel actions they prefer not take or prohibit actions they would, deems them not as praiseworthy but criminals? I speak here, of course, not of those adults who tragically *are* dependent because of an affliction and are judged so in a court of law and assigned a needed guardian, but the rest of us.

I myself am a case in point. Under the law that brings me here, I am deemed a criminal because the reps have ruled that certain things are bad for me—no matter what *I* may believe—and bad for you—no matter what *you* may believe. Such a law would be impossible under liberty but not so under democracy.

For those of you who do hate irony, I apologize again, for here is a second example at the heart of our current system. As citizens, you are deemed incompetent to judge your own interests. Yet as voters, you are deemed competent to judge whether your representatives are serving your interests well. You can't judge for yourselves, but you can judge those who are judging for you.

When I consider our history from start to present day, I regrettably come to this conclusion: we are a nation that won its independence collectively only to cultivate dependence individually. We separated ourselves as a nation only to chain ourselves as individuals. In fact, the more like dependent children we become, the more like overindulgent parents our elected representatives become—parents who compete for our affections based on how well they take care of us. This process has been going on for fifty years and is now accelerating at great cost.

Ideas alone did not make this possible. It also took the National Bank, which controlled our coins and now controls our currency. Only because of the National Bank can the reps spend what they spend and do what they do, which is for anything and everything we want. Clothed with unlimited power, the reps propose new acts each day that purport to solve our problems, without a thought as to whether those problems should be solved by legislative act, can be solved by legislative act, or whether the acts themselves may be the cause. You know the outcomes well. You've seen our prices and our manias, such that in every state there are fewer people working, fewer goods and services available, and we suffocate with worry over the future.

In forcibly undermining your independence, then, our democracy does you great harm. I said this happened because we misunderstood what we were fighting for. It persists today, I fear, not just because of that misunderstanding but also because many citizens now value the very dependence that is harming them—without admitting this value, even to themselves.

They wish to take what is rightfully others' and control what others may do, without acknowledging those wishes. To be funded, without naming the true source of that funding. To buy products with features they want or at prices they prefer, regardless of what the sellers might say, ignoring that those products, until freely sold, rightly belong to the sellers. To be hired on terms they dictate, ignoring that the money for their salaries, until freely paid, rightfully belongs to others. Being unwilling to see these policies clearly, they cannot see themselves clearly. Rather than seek insight, they resent it—and abandon the very independence that could save them.

But independence is our natural state, and the consequences of losing it are grave—so grave that it can only be surrendered by degrees. This gradual surrender is what masks the danger and clears the road to ruin.

The transformation might occur like this. Struggling under burdens imposed by your fellow citizens via their laws, you might one day come to resent both your fellow citizens and your own labors. Being independent is difficult enough when you are free; how much more so does it become when you are not? Then, seeing others capitulate, amid the steady national decline and alleged national beneficence, you question the wisdom of your struggle. Exhausted, finally you cede your independence and actively undermine others'. When you tell yourself your choice is right, your soul is lost, whether you walk among us still or no.

Yet, though living the very life you now extol, you come to feel that it is not the good life after all. Thinking you have freed yourself, you instead are trapped, for you still value being alive—not wanting actually to perish—but you no longer value living. To live is to think and act on that thinking. To think and act for yourself.

Why is independence our natural state? Because the reasons for your actions can be of just two kinds: those that are the product of your honest judgment and those that you *pretend* to believe in because you desire to take the action anyway or because you choose to uncritically follow others' desires or directives. The first are healthy; the second are not. To adopt pretend reasons is to make your mind your enemy, to direct it away from understanding the world around you and yourself. And the longer you pretend, the greater is your need to pretend, to protect your prior pretenses. Instead of spending years at becoming better at understanding— your most important skill—you undermine that skill and cause your own decay. In other words, while *what* we choose has consequences for our well-being, *how* we choose does also. Much of what happens to us in life comes down to this: Which kind of reasons guide us—real or fake? That is what most determines the fate of our souls.

This is also why those who seek to help others by compelling or manipulating them not only are not helping but are actively harming. They deny their victim two choices: one, whether to seek help at all and, two, if they do seek help, from whom. If you substitute your mind for others' on the theory that you know better, you weaken them and push them toward dependence on you. You also push them into pretense, which is all they have when obeying without understanding. Of this you are aware, for had they honestly agreed with you, you would not have had to compel or manipulate them.

Here, then, is a final irony to consider. Encouraged by our democracy to evade the nature of our policies, how can we have the supposedly beneficial dialogues that must precede our votes? The dialogue of a democratic people ostensibly is predicated on openness and reason but instead becomes closed and rigid, guided by pretenses, wishes, and desires.

Understanding full well the system under which we live, some reps claim to have put themselves above it and be in a better position than all of you. Indeed, I suspect that is why many of them became reps. Seeing no alternative to either ruling or being ruled, they chose the former, thinking it safer. But here they are mistaken. Knowingly or not, they are victims of their own unlimited power, for they can exercise that power only at the whim of those who grant it.

A representative has no more will left than you do. Alas, poor soul, he is doubly separated from himself. He cannot think and act on his own but must seek the approval of the multitude and spend his days serving their desires. And how does he serve them? By giving to them. Giving what? What he takes from others. He produces nothing but postures as a benefactor—as if he himself had produced what he distributes. After some years of this, he has only this false and concocted image with which to regard himself, an image that he must diligently seal off from his true nature.

In speaking of how central independence is to the good life, though, I do not mean to imply that we should be alone. To judge for yourself is not to isolate yourself or disregard others' judgments. Question, advise, and challenge others when it is requested—that is, by appealing to their judgment and honoring their independence—and ask others to do the same for you. Indeed, in judging what is good in life, you are judging others too. You ask, Is this a person I can love or befriend, associate or partner with, sell to or buy from, teach or learn from? Similarly do they judge you. What is best in life requires others, for others enrich our lives and we theirs, according to who they and we are. Just think of all that others have done for you, personally and professionally, and you have done for them.

This means that the only way to properly relate to others is freely: you choose them, and they choose you. Anything else is slavery and violence. An independent man on occasion may require the charity of others—whether family, friends, associates, ministers, or philanthropists—but he seeks it voluntarily, protecting their independence and ultimately his own.

Thus the benefits of independence are many—in relationships, character, knowledge, skills, results. But its ultimate benefit is knowing your own worth, judging yourself appreciatively, taking pride in what you do and why you do it. Having judged what is good and then acted to achieve it, you can see yourself as good. The proof is in your choices, but only those that you yourself believe in. To esteem yourself is to esteem the reasons for your actions.

If you ask me what I want most for myself and for all of you, it is that we each operate under full motive power—a confident and energetic power—crippled neither physically nor mentally. I wish each of us to believe that "Good things are possible to me" and be confident in knowing what is both "good" and "possible." What you see as good and possible you want to do. What you do not can only leave you indifferent or antagonistic. But to "see" anything is an act of independent judgment.

Thus the fight for the best political system is a fight for our very lives. Nothing less and nothing more is at stake. Those of you who know me know that the individual human life has been the object of *my* life's study and my greatest interest. You know the explorations I have devoted myself to. What it means to live a human life. What it means to live a good life. How our decisions affect our bodies and our souls. Today, my prosecutors are telling you that living your lives depends on me not living mine. Of course I cannot accept that. I accept nothing less than that we all should live our lives, every one of us.

I am nearing the end of my time, and though I could talk with you at great length on this subject—indeed, I have been doing so for fifty years—I must now summarize. Let me end by saying that this is the good life: achieving what *you* believe to be good, by offering what *you* think will be valuable to others, for them to accept freely, because they also see its value. In this way both you and they preserve integrity. Integrity is a precious state; it is the state of internal harmony. I have long said that I would rather play an out-of-tune guitar or sing in discord with a chorus or contradict the whole of mankind than be in contradiction with myself.

I hope I do not find myself so today.

CHAPTER 29

I do not need to explain that by the time Teacher Scotes had reached this point, there was a kind of emotional engorgement in the hall, and not necessarily of a good kind. The jury's intensifying agitation knocked me out of my reverie, from being transfixed on him to being transfixed on them. He had gone to some length to accuse them of being children with endangered souls, and because of both this and another argument he would shortly make, Xephon would later claim that Teacher Scotes must have been courting death, though I myself cannot accept this.

On me his words had the opposite effect. I could have listened for hours more. For a time when he was speaking, I had forgotten the moment, forgotten the danger, forgotten why he was there. I wished then and forever after that we had spoken of the matters he had raised, just he and I, at every one of our meetings. I wish still to be speaking with him. Just as he had said, I had made myself dependent, but this fact led me to accuse myself, not him. I regarded the massive jury. Did they understand? How could they not, having just received the benefit of his sight?

The time was fast approaching for the vote, so Teacher Scotes made a last plea. He said, "In considering my testimony, am I asking you to judge according to what many outside this courtroom might believe? Or am I asking you to decide what you believe? Deep within you, do you answer *to* others or for yourself?" Then he added, "Throughout my life, I have stayed at my post. Whether in the war or for two generations since,

I have done my duty according to my conscience. But I have spoken long, and the clock's arm climbs high behind me. I wish we had more time together and a different venue, for the discussion I attempted here does not lend itself well to lectures and crowds. But alas, our laws do not allow for such discussions beyond these walls."

Here Father stood. Surprisingly, Teacher Scotes allowed him a final comment, but I suppose he could hardly have refused. Gradually the crowd quieted, at which point Father said, "You have heard from the antidemocrat. . . . No doubt Teacher Scotes is worthy of some respect, but it is that very respect that makes him dangerous to our young, who are thereby more inclined to listen to him." Here he paused dramatically, as only he could, till his voice filled the space above. "Do you *want* them to listen to him?" A tepid "No" answered. "You have heard him insult you by saying that he would rather you each stand alone than we stand together. Is that the nation you want?" This time a firmer "No" answered. "You have heard him wish to take away your support when you need it, your relief when you struggle, your income when out of work. Is that the nation you want?" An even louder "No" answered. "Well, ladies and gentlemen, that is the nation you will have if you allow him to seduce our young with his poisonous way of thinking, which you heard today is clearly not ours."

With this short speech, Father once again had the crowd seemingly in no mood to be lenient with Teacher Scotes. To this day I wonder whether the outcome might have been different had Father not made this final comment.

Teacher Scotes seemed to acknowledge the turn but was dismissive. "In closing," he addressed the jury, "I feel bound to say that if you decide to condemn me, the harm will be more yours than mine. You will find it difficult to replace me, ladies and gentlemen. Who else will do for you what I do? I am like a gadfly, pestering you with questions you otherwise do not ask. That makes me your benefactor, though you are accustomed to seeing only political leaders in that role.

"Why, then, you may ask, have I worked only privately throughout my life and not in Assembly? Because had I done so, I should long ago have lost my life. No one who conscientiously opposes an organized democracy can escape condemnation. Today, a champion of true justice must leave politics alone.

"No doubt at this point you expect me to make the usual appeal. You expect me to beg for my life for my family's sake, to let them weep and plead before you. But I will not insult you or myself by doing so. Yes, I had a father and a mother and know what it means to have lost them, and I do have a wife, Ansea, and a daughter, Sophia, who may lose me. I see some of you smiling at Sophia's name, and so you should. Ansea and I can take some credit for what our daughter is becoming, but not all. Of this I would wish to speak further, but the bailiff is signaling, and you are becoming restless. So I will stay myself and await your judgment."

Teacher Scotes sat.

After the bailiff resumed the podium, he explained again the voting procedure, and as he did, the four ballot counters rose from their benches in the Pit and assembled at the troughs. Then there was hardly a pause before the jurors rose with a collective creak, one ballot in each hand, though hiding which was which: solid for innocent, hollow for guilty. Like water cascading over stones, they left their pews and descended. Initially the ballots hit the wooden floors inside the first trough with a thud, but soon the room reverberated with the pinging of tin upon tin. These were their discarded ballots, the ones that wouldn't count. The same sounds followed in the second trough, the one nearest to the stage. Orderly and quickly the jurors passed one, then the other and, having dropped both ballots, returned to their seats.

Had they understood what Teacher Scotes had said? Had his words affected them as they had me? Teacher Scotes watched them throughout, as if studying something he had never witnessed. Little could I read in their faces, these men and women, of multiple generations, stoic in their duty. Some appeared hesitant or even anguished, but such feelings revealed nothing because they might accompany either verdict. Most instead wore the look of certainty, not the calm clear-eyed certainty that Teacher Scotes often noted in others but one of rigid features. People sometimes have a way of deciding they are certain even when they are not.

I myself was no more certain now than before, but I was more prepared to question than ever. His words were like a window on the world and his clarity an invitation to question with him. They energized. They gave power. They turned the wheel and set the machinery spinning. Clearly there was some truth in what he said. Perhaps not all, but some. It was undeniable.

The ballot counters in their stiff coats waited respectfully with their hands behind their backs, allowing the jurors to vote in privacy while being responsible to see that each person dropped ballots into both troughs. In performing this duty, they were expected to be inconspicuous and not to notice which ballot was which; anonymity was strictly observed. In truth they likely could not have figured anyway, for as the two piles rose within each trough, the ballots mixed haphazardly like an unruly pile of children's jacks.

The counters also wore gloves so as not to cut their hands when the time came to count the ballots. This step would wait upon each juror's being seated, though everyone was anxious for the counting. When it began, they first unlatched and lowered the trough wall closest to the stage, not to the floor but far enough to give the counters better access without the ballots spilling. This left but a narrow space between the ballots and the stage, just wide enough for the counters to pick the ballots and begin inserting them into the façade. Those for Teacher Scotes would fill the holes beginning at his end of the stage; those against him, at ours. Then they would progress toward the center. Two of the counters worked below Teacher Scotes, swiftly sorting and picking out acquittal ballots and twisting to insert them, then twisting back to repeat the process, again and again; votes for conviction they slid to their colleagues across the trough. The two below us did the reverse. Quickly they converged, and the jurors could monitor the accumulating results. Heaven forgive me, but I couldn't help think of the counters' impressive skill, and I wondered if Teacher Scotes admired it too. It wouldn't have surprised me if he did.

Judging by the stippled light that now filled our side of the Pit, someone had lit the lamps beneath the stage. Everyone knew that if one side filled faster than the other, that was how the verdict would go. That it took some minutes for the jurors to react, beyond staring at the front of the stage, meant that the vote was close. But at some point, they began to lean into one another and whisper.

"Guilty, guilty."

When done, the counters faced the stage at attention, their hands behind their backs. Only the lead counter moved to write upon his ledger, which he then lifted to the bailiff, who had come forward and bent for the exchange. Standing where he was, the bailiff read the ledger silently. Then he returned to the podium. As he did so, the counters returned to their benches at the base of the first row of pews.

"The defendant will please stand," the bailiff said.

Teacher Scotes stood at his seat.

"By a vote of 280 for and 220 against, the defendant is guilty as charged."

Some sort of liquid flushed inside me and rose warmly to my neck and ears, but I stemmed any outward reaction. Teacher Scotes did not so much as flinch, looking out upon the jurors. I looked to the bailiff, not knowing what else to do. Before he had spoken, I had prepared myself for the verdict. Still, what had happened did not seem real.

After a pause, the bailiff said, "We will now begin the sentencing phase of our trial. The proposed penalty of the crime is death. However, ladies and gentlemen, under the act governing this prosecution and according to the procedures that have been explained to you, the defendant is granted the opportunity to request an alternative punishment, which you are duty bound to consider. He will have fifteen minutes to speak, after which you will vote on which of the two punishments you believe to be appropriate. . . . Teacher Scotes, are you ready to address this jury?"

"I am, sir."

"Take the podium, please." At this, and with much dignity, the bailiff stepped back. Teacher Scotes resumed his place, center stage.

"I cannot say that I am surprised, ladies and gentlemen," he said, "for your verdict was not unexpected. What does surprise me is how close it was. With a change of but thirty votes, the result would have been different."

Though he spoke evenly, his voice began with a hint of gravel, which quickly cleared.

"The law asks that I propose an alternative to the punishment of death. Very well. What alternative should I propose? This is not an easy question, for it requires me to consider what is just, given what I have done. Allow me to think, then. What do I deserve for trying to give you moral encouragement?" He struck an almost theatrical pose, with hands folded and eyes looking to the heavens, as if he were reflecting but not really so. And something jarred in the tone he had taken.

"What would be fair, given the lifelong assistance I have offered?" He asked this as if to himself. Then he shrugged. "I cannot say. Unless you'd care to make a statue of me, to replace the one of Pericles here?" and his hand reached out to the side, in our direction.

Someone near the stage gasped. It wasn't Father, but it may as well have been, for I caught his profile fixed on Teacher Scotes and bearing the oddest expression—more of shocked alarm than anger. It was what I felt too, and I turned to Teacher Scotes, hoping to catch his eye, but I could not. Instead he persisted in that air of reverie, as if still pondering alternatives. Then he said more assertively, "I do not wish to propose anything of much expense, given conditions today, though I do consider my service to be of great value. Let us say then that this modest token of appreciation in the form of a statue, to adorn this great stage, will suffice. There, ladies and gentlemen, is my proposal."

The jurors must have been stunned, because they remained silent till they released a violent murmur, as if obliged to fill the silence but not knowing how. It was not a pleasant sound.

I turned to my father and whispered, "What has happened? What is he doing?" He did not respond. "They will kill him for certain," I said. Hunched and staring ahead, he turned his gaze inward. "Father," I said. He looked pale.

I turned back to Teacher Scotes, who now was eyeing me. From my seat I presented him with my most forlorn expression, begging for some understanding, but the look he returned was only blank.

The murmurs grew intense, ugly. Yet some of the jurors' round-eyed faces suggested a bewilderment as great as mine and that the amplified irritation was felt by only segments of the crowd, not the whole.

"Propose an alternative!" someone yelled.

Teacher Scotes answered, "I have proposed one."

"Propose an alternative punishment!" came again from a different section.

"I can think of no other," Teacher Scotes answered.

Seconds more of murmuring passed. The bailiff seemed uncertain of what to do but hearing nothing further from Teacher Scotes, hesitantly approached, I assumed to call for the vote.

I stood. I had no thought of doing so, and the hand that grazed my arm must have been my father's, but I did not remain to look, and then I myself was beside the podium, facing Teacher Scotes.

"Young Palleias," a soft voice said, though Teacher Scotes had not spoken. It was the bailiff, who now stood intimately in our circle. "Sir," he said quietly, "you may not approach. Return to your seat, and I will recognize you there."

I ignored him. "Please," I said to Teacher Scotes.

Being somewhat taller than Teacher Scotes and standing close to him on that stage, with hundreds before him empowered to decide his fate, I for the first time saw how vulnerable he was, in a way I had not before. For me his presence had always meant strength, though it was a different kind of strength compared to that which threatened him on this day. In answer to my plea, he but smiled kindly, as if one could do naught else in that moment except bestow affection, and on me, the most undeserving of friends.

"Your words," I said, taking a different tack, "have reached me."

He regarded me with an unreadable expression.

"Sir," the bailiff repeated, a little more forcibly.

"Palleias." A hand touched my back; it was Father's. "Return to your seat," he commanded without anger. "I will speak for us. We will not let events proceed in this way." I did not respond immediately, so he added, "Do not remain here. The jurors will not understand."

"Propose a fine," I said to Teacher Scotes. "I will pay it. Of any amount."

Teacher Scotes said nothing, and as I only looked at him, he only looked at me.

"Son," Father said, his hand now pulling my shoulder gently, "return with me, and I will address the jurors."

"Gentlemen, please," the bailiff said.

"*Sir*," my father now addressed the bailiff, "a moment only, please." The steady grumbling of the crowd must have swallowed our words. The bailiff relented.

"Propose three thousand demos," I said to Teacher Scotes. Teacher Scotes did not answer.

Then Father addressed Teacher Scotes. "You have calculated wrongly," he said. "They will vote for death. You don't know them as I do."

Teacher Scotes did not answer.

"Propose ostracism," Father said. He stepped forward, beside me, as if shielding me from the crowd's view. "I myself will arrange for your family's transport to wherever you wish to go." Teacher Scotes did not respond. Father whispered harshly, "Think of your family, Teacher Scotes."

Then Teacher Scotes did address Father. "But the prosecution calls for death," he said. "You do not agree with your own prosecution?"

Father glanced at the bailiff, who looked as if he'd never encountered such an exchange.

"If you ever had affection for me," Father said quietly—odd, jarring words coming from him, the kind of words that draw your attention from all else—"then listen to me. You are wrong. They will vote death. It will happen."

"Is that not what you proposed?" Teacher Scotes asked.

"I beg you," Father said. Father's tone contradicted any sentiment I would otherwise have attributed to him.

Two of the ballot counters joined us on stage, and the bailiff reasserted himself, insisting we return to our seats. When the audience gleaned our reluctance, they contributed additional pressure. "Sit down!" a few yelled, and their noise swelled again.

"Please," I said again to Teacher Scotes, before the counters stepped between us and began guiding us away. Father's demeanor was of a far-away anxiety that made it appear he did not see where he was going. I had to coax him into taking his seat before I took mine.

Teacher Scotes addressed the jurors, and the bailiff did not intervene. "For those who support me, you may wonder at my choice of alternative punishments. Understandably you may ask, Why *not* a fine? And I will answer that I do not have the money and while paying a fine would save me today, it would not eliminate the threat of my returning to you and being prosecuted again for the same reason, poorer only in the bargain. Imprisonment, then, you suggest. It is true that my feet are calloused and tired but not so much that I could willingly confine them to our dingy cells and less space than you provide your hogs. But there is also, is there not, banishment to the West? There is, but would you knowingly subject yourself and your family to the daily threats of violence and hazards of deprivation that would follow such a course? Not to mention that beyond our borders exists a conception of society too alien to mine. At last, you say, then pay a fine and promise your silence, and by this means preserve your life and freedom. But here, ladies and gentlemen, is where I least follow your reasoning. For silence to me is neither life nor freedom. Because my greatest good, and yours, incidentally—order, please, ladies and gentlemen!—because pursuing my greatest good and yours *is* my life. I have never wanted wealth or fame or power but just to meet with anyone who wished to discuss issues of justice and goodness and the related questions of our lives. To me, a life not spent examining such issues is not worth living.

"No," he said, after a moment, "I think the statue is the best alternative."

"Ladies and gentlemen!" I said, standing. "I propose a second alternative: a fine of three thousand demos. I myself am good for the money." It was only after the words were out that I realized I was speaking. Of course I possessed no such funds but would compel Father and Mother to provide them.

At this, several members of the jury jumped up, arms raised, and yelled, "Sit down!" You had to admire their respect for procedure. For myself, I am certain I appeared ridiculous. But Father saved me from further embarrassment by gently guiding me down. That instant I saw how futile my outburst had been, that there was nothing more to say, though a few hundred pale ovals stared back at me, awaiting my next utterance: any proposal now could only come from Teacher Scotes, and he had already settled the matter.

Seated again, I allowed Father to hold my arm. What the jurors made of this I do not know, but in pieces their attention shifted away, and the ballot counters removed the first set of ballots, and the process was again orderly and calm, and the jurors once again composed themselves, and the bailiff kept repeating that a hollow ballot meant a vote for death, solid a vote for a statue—he somehow avoided tripping on the word "statue," though I could tell it was a labor—and when the jurors confirmed that each possessed a second set of ballots, the bailiff called for the vote, and the jurors rose and descended for a second time. Past the first trough and then the second they filed, then ascended again, and the counters again began their work. Lamps were lit again below us, and the stippled light returned, and the jurors leaned in to await the count. When the verdict became inescapable, the murmurs resumed, just as they had the first time.

I do not like it that when life presents me with threats and things to fear, I disengage, my vision blurs, and though I stand bodily in the presence of others, in a sense I am not there. I wish to change this fact about myself. I wish to effect the opposite, in moments of greatest danger, my mind becoming most acute, my senses sharpest. As if it were not happening, the bending bailiff again received the official account, again read it, and returned to the podium. Teacher Scotes was back to standing before his seat, not having to be instructed.

"By a vote of 270 for and 230 against, the defendant is sentenced to death."

Two ballot counters climbed to the stage and stood by Teacher Scotes. The bailiff said, "Jurors have completed their duty before this court and nation. Upon hearing any final words by the convict, you are dismissed."

Teacher Scotes spoke one last time, standing where he was. Some of the jurors, not granting him the courtesy, rose and began to depart.

"Let me first address those who voted for my guilt," he said. "Though I do not know you personally, I expect that some of you might hate my words because you fear your independence and feel better as a member of a herd. That you'd prefer any decision to your own. If so, that is a shame, because what you fear you need not fear, and what comforts you, you should fear greatly. Your independence is your route to joy, and you are capable of more than you imagine, if only you'd embrace that route. I have seen young and old alike reform their lives with this one embrace; I have seen how quickly their lives change. Which is ultimately the argument for freedom and for rights, and why our present system must perish. And along with it, you. If you survive that long.

"Being near death, I find myself now moved to prophesy. To those who voted against me, if you thought that by eliminating me you'd escape my criticism, I predict the opposite, that my criticism will grow louder and more numerous. Shielding your mistaken ways by putting people to death is not possible. Instead of stopping the mouths of others, you would do better to improve your own.

"And regarding my accusers, I say pity them, for while they have convicted me, truth herself will convict them soon. Soon thousands beyond these walls will point their fingers and say, 'There go those who killed the wisest of them all,' whether I am that or not. And they will seek justice for their action.

"To those who voted for me, I thank you and consider you friends. Though I do not know your reasons, I can only hope, for your sakes and our nation's, that they had something to do with agreeing with my words. If so, I wish you the best. Yours won't be an easy life, and any challenge you make to our policies will be met with venom. But you will have the satisfaction of confidence and the pride of self-regard, and who knows? In time, you may also experience the pleasure of newly won freedoms."

The jailers arrived. "I see," Teacher Scotes said, "that it is time for us to be going, I to die and you to live. It will be yours to decide which is the happier prospect."

Perhaps out of respect for Teacher Scotes, the large jailers, in blue army-style coats, laid not a hand on him but followed him toward the back of the stage and down a set of stairs to a back exit, where they needed only to cross Walnut Street to enter the jail and cell that would confine him for his remaining days.

CHAPTER 30

"What has happened?" I fairly yelled.

Mother, Father, and I were in his study, he at his desk, we standing before him, and I was trying to reach him, talking *at* him, really, in a way I never had because I had taken as my opening that he appeared weak, slumped, and nonresisting, not about to do what he normally would when I disrespected his authority: correct me. For reasons I cared little to discover, the verdict seemed a calamity to him too, and he was distracted, perhaps uncertain even. I cared for none of it. Though Mother was present, this confrontation was between him and me. Perhaps she knew not all of what was between us. Her hair was up; she was dressed for an evening out. Observing Father's reaction, she may have been more worried than I. Nothing in me wished to release him from my grasp.

"You said it would not come to this! Did you not tell me? Did you not *assure* me?"

"Palleias," my mother said softly.

He may have been waiting for me to storm out, but I deprived him of the satisfaction. The moment the trial ended, we had dispersed. Father had enjoined me to return home with him right then, but I refused and began wandering. Nearby, behind the prison walls, they would be bathing Teacher Scotes, cutting his hair, replacing his white shirt with their gray linens. I wandered not long, however, for being met by knowing stares. Whether of blame or credit I did not know, but I was indifferent to anyone's feelings but my own. When I returned home, they were in his study. It was late afternoon and the sun had reached this end of the house, but the color had not warmed the mood.

"Mother," Father said gently, for he always called her that in my presence. I only ever heard him say "Permelia," her actual, beautiful name, when I was eavesdropping. "Would you allow Palleias and me a moment? Then you and I will depart for our engagement."

"You are going out?" I yelled more than asked.

Before my mother left, she turned to me and said, softly but firmly, "Palleias, whatever happens in your life or will happen, you know that your father only does what he believes is right. He is a man of character and ideals, which is why we both love him, for you and I are that way too. It is also why I always stand beside him. When you disagree with him, please remember the spirit in which you should raise that disagreement."

After she was gone, Father exhaled as if he hadn't for some time. Despite my mother's counsel, I could not relinquish my aggressive posture. He regarded me just long enough to register my attitude. Then he spoke, quietly, hands folded before him.

"Here is what must happen." That was it. No "I'm sorry." No "I have erred." No acknowledgment of his failed assurances before the trial. He said, "I will do all the preparation, but you must play a role. Are you willing to assist me?"

His desire to move immediately to action infuriated me. At least he should have addressed what Teacher Scotes had said. Never mind what Father had said to the crowd. That was for effect. That was playing a role. *What*, I wanted to know, was his honest answer to Teacher Scotes's charges, now, with only me to hear? We both had heard the same words, words that we could not unhear.

I yelled, "Everything he said was true! *Everything.*" I wanted the hyperbole to wound him. "Your answers were no match. Tell me now, without the show, what is your response?"

"Palleias."

"You are ruining the nation!" I yelled.

"Palleias," he said again, quietly, without a shift in posture.

"You are the reason everything is so horrid!" This caused him to close his eyes, but only that. "Teacher Scotes explained it all. *You* are to blame. You and all the rest. How can you act so callously and destructively? How do you justify yourself?"

Stiffly but calmly, he said, "Are you nearly finished?"

"I am just trying to understand you!" I yelled as loudly as I could.

He exploded. "Well, stop trying to understand me!" This shocked me into silence. It was only what he had before demanded, yet this time it struck me as something to take hold of, as additional words I must not dismiss.

As if regretting his outburst and sensing my reaction, he calmed. Then he said, "You are speaking from anger. Calm yourself, and please answer my question. We have but little time."

"What question?" I shot back. He only stared. "Assist you with what?" From this point I knew the conversation would alter permanently and revert to his agenda.

He wasted no time. Eyeing me, he said, "You must visit him in prison and offer him a means of escape."

For a moment I almost forgot my anger. I thought perhaps he'd gone mad. To deflect that possibility, I yelled again, "You said this would not happen!"

Having regained himself, he could now ignore my outbursts. "I will arrange for it," he said. "You may tell him that I have. That will secure his confidence in the plan's success. Then, when all is ready, you will be the one to let him know."

"What are you talking about?"

"Palleias, times like these require men like us to be calm and to act."

I knew what he was doing. He was avoiding what he would call "wasting time fixing blame"; he was focusing not on the past, not on what had happened or why, but on the future, on what to do about it. It was his favorite stance. He had been preaching so to me and publicly for years.

"Father," I said, "I do not believe you are thinking rationally. I believe you are speaking heedlessly because you wish not to face what you have done, having expressly said that you were not doing it."

"Do you wish him to live or to die?" he said simply.

It was my turn to exhale. "How is he supposed to escape? And why do you care? You are the one who put him there."

"Palleias, I tell you truly, if you have ever trusted in my judgment, hear me now. If Teacher Scotes dies, I will soon follow. Or if they don't actually kill me, they'll banish me to where no one can survive. This evening they might revel in the prosecution, but it won't last, not once the judgment is carried out. Only then will it be real to them. And for them, *I* am the prosecution, despite how we arranged things." He must have noticed my shocked alarm, because he went on, "For yourself you needn't worry; they will not associate you with the outcome or my role. But what happens to your mother if I am gone? You value thinking? Think of that. Think also whether you wish to live without a father." Throughout my silent unresponsiveness, his eyes held mine. "However," he said, "if he lives, none of us need worry. There may be anger at his banishment, but no vengeance. Eventually, all will return to normal." Whether I had understood or not, he finished with "So will you help?"

"If they blame anyone," I said, "they will blame themselves. They were the ones voting!"

He pressed out the smallest smile—not a happy one—as if resigned to my impenetrable ignorance despite years having apprenticed at the highest levels of state, though my naiveté may not have *only* displeased him.

"But they voted!" I repeated, to deflect the coming ridicule.

"They will not blame themselves," he said, as simple fact.

So ludicrous was his statement that it caused me to question again his saneness, but he was Representative Antonyn, and whatever I understood about our nation's politics he understood a world better. Then I said, "So this is about saving yourself, not about saving him."

"I never sought his death. You know that."

"You just sought to ruin his life."

"No," he said. "To save yours."

This was yet another of his perennial claims, once again hitting me as if newly profound. I could have continued interrogating him, but however long our back-and-forth persisted, I would but arrive where Father had been, at the outset of our meeting: that our energy must now be spent on freeing Teacher Scotes.

"Would it not be better to approach him yourself?" I asked.

He softened, as if appreciating my finally joining in the solution. "It would appear suspicious. Whereas for you it will seem a simple visit from his friend and recent companion."

"I thought no one knew I was his friend and companion." I hoped that by agreeing to this characterization of our relationship I would wound him again.

"Of course they do." He frowned. "You still do not understand. No matter how often I remind you that your life is not your own and that there is nothing about you they cannot learn, you resist me."

"Will they even allow him visitors?"

"He is allowed some, but I will make sure that you, Xephon, and others who will aid in his escape can come and go freely."

Toward the end of the trial, when Father and I had found ourselves standing at the podium, Teacher Scotes had sardonically asked Father whether he agreed with the proposed sentence. That question I am certain was for my sake. Father had argued for what the act stipulated—a conviction of death—but suddenly, faced with its achievement, he was renouncing the very thing he fought for. Obviously I was aware of that, but Teacher Scotes was not allowing me to shun that awareness. He was asking me to consider the implications of Father's action. What did I think of it? What did it say about Father? Was it a behavior to emulate? Questions of that nature.

I am not so top-heavy as to lack comprehension of why Father acted as he did, why he now opposed the very verdict he had pursued. Having sought Teacher Scotes's ostracism all along, he had used the threat of death to compel Teacher Scotes to propose the only real alternative, ostracism—Teacher Scotes would want to live, but not while imprisoned or muzzled by our laws—leaving him at least free to philosophize elsewhere and leaving us, and me, alone. And he knew that the jurors would accept the alternative and spare a man of Teacher Scotes's age, family situation, and historic contributions.

But what Father "knew" turned out to have been wrong, and his plan had miscarried. By proposing a statue of himself instead of ostracism, Teacher Scotes had all but commanded the sentence he received. As a result, the very power Father had trained on Teacher Scotes, the power he had harnessed all his life—the power of the people—would now, he feared, be trained on him. In a way, he had lied: he had *not* wanted the thing he claimed he did. He had expressed one goal yet sought another. By insisting I see that, Teacher Scotes was suggesting that this was not an isolated case with Father, that this somehow *was* my father. *That* I could not accept. Still, I knew how Father would defend his actions, had I pressed him. Many times I'd heard him say "I don't really believe that. It's just politics." Even to me he'd say it. But I had never considered the implications of that phrase.

Now, in asking for my help, he was warning me of politics again. Judging by the extent of his anxiety, I expected to find visitors at our door at once, wishing to seek him out. But the people are a cauldron, and if boil they will, they still require time to heat. As Father said, Teacher Scotes had so far only been convicted, not executed.

In the end, visitors did arrive, later that night, though they were just newspaper reporters (having awaited Father and Mother's return, while I cowered out of sight), and Father, standing in our open doorway, talking as they scribbled, monitoring the archway, gave them what they wanted. "Condemning a man is never to be celebrated," he said. "But justice is our currency, and the people have spoken."

Home in solitude and awaiting my parents' return, I had felt my anger go the other way and become relief because I'd realized that the best thing that could have happened had: that Father himself wanted Teacher Scotes's release and that whatever Father wanted, however extralegal and otherwise implausible, was achievable. That under Father's direction almost anything was possible, for his authority and influence made events. Teacher Scotes was saved, and though in mere days he would be leaving and I would never again see him, he would survive. Me, I would inform him of this plan; *I* would turn his despair to joy. Father and I had different reasons for wanting him to live, but our goals were joined. Of course I agreed to assist him. Wholeheartedly so.

That night, in black and stillness, during one last stretch of peace before the pomp of the holiday week to come, I slept not at all. Hours slowly passed, and I kept turning from one sore hip to another. My small metronomic clock ticked. The quieter the hour, the louder our thoughts. Eventually I lit a small lamp. Teacher Scotes loved the company of his thoughts, but I had never felt the same about my own. I retrieved a notebook and pencil from my bed table and sat up in the dim light. Across the room the light flickered on the high blackened panes.

Released now from anguishing over Teacher Scotes's fate, I considered my own. His words were overtaking me. I would tell him this tomorrow. I wouldn't say that I now doubted his strategy of discussing ideas in intimate gatherings only—for though addressing hundreds from that stage, as he never would have chosen to, he had also addressed just me. Now, for me, there was everything to think about. His words were to be reckoned with, not to be dismissed, forgotten, or redefined away. Perhaps this is all we can ask of ourselves, to face the questions that arise and answer them as best we can rather than pretend that none was asked. It was time for me to answer: How well had I been living? To what extent was *I* decided and provided for—by Father or any others? Of course I knew the answers, knew from the sudden taxing of my spirit at the questions' very posing—at the thought of who I was.

But to rouse a deeper analysis, I decided not to just recall but document his speech, as best I could, for myself and for the day it might be shared. Lead in hand, my lamp within reach and ready to be extinguished if need be, I spent the remaining blackest hours recording every word that came to me—his and my own.

CHAPTER 31

W hen the light outside whitened, I rose, locked the pages in my trunk, and descended. Mother and Father were not yet down. The house was quiet, except for the creaking floorboards underfoot and the front door's hinges when I retrieved the dailies, which we paid a boy to purchase and deliver to us.

Each blared the story. The account in the *Peep Hole's Daily* ran a full sheet and quoted several jurors. Reading the quotes, I wondered if they had attended the same trial: their characterizations of both the prosecution and defense did not accord with mine. Father would be eager to read them and would not be displeased by the portrayal of his role as "measured" and that of Teacher Scotes as "reckless." Alcidia fared well; Lycon and Haydock were scarcely mentioned; Mathias was lampooned. My name arose in passing only. Officially, the transcript of the trial was eventually to be published, but I was doubtful, given the ideas professed in Teacher Scotes's speech. Some excuse would be made. Some administrative failure alleged. Some clerk would be reprimanded unjustly. This day I would not have to travel to neighboring states to know that by tomorrow their newspapers would share the story too. And I needed neither coach nor vessel to know that in a few days' time, all the nation would learn of Teacher Scotes's fate.

When my parents awoke, we breakfasted together, quietly. We did not discuss Teacher Scotes, and I assumed that Father and Mother had conversed exhaustively last evening and had nothing further to work out. She would be concerned for Father's safety too because she was astute, with long experience of his labors and his pressures. In this situation, as perhaps in few others, she might have insisted on knowing, and he might have shared, the details of the escape plan so that she would be assuaged. I myself knew them not, and Father would not tell me, lest they go wrong, lest he be called to account and forced to testify against those who had also known.

I stepped out into the cool morning. The heavy sky ached to rain and would for days. My priority was to make the few minutes' walk over to the prison to inform Teacher Scotes of our plan—my first mission in some time that Father both knew of and agreed with. It was Friday, July 1, the opening day of our annual celebration, and this perhaps explained Father's reference to celebration the night before, when speaking to the reporters; perhaps he was attempting to shift attention away from the trial, as naturally might occur.

The festivities were clearly imminent. As far as one could see, a hundred flags slumped high above Chestnut Street, which was also strewn with red, white, and blue paper. Parade-goers were amassing. At the docks by now, steam-snorting horses, harnessed to decorated wagons, would be idling in the mist, preparing to proceed all the way to the Schuylkill and Gray's Ferry, where actors would recreate General Washington's entrance to the city, and starting this day the fireworks would light the masts at harbor, ships would sail and battles be recreated on land and river, and raucous bands would march and commerce cease and speeches follow, one upon another, atop erected platforms.

Though on Saturday we would celebrate the fifty-five-year-old signing; on Monday its proclamation; and next Friday, the final day, its reading in the square, the entire week to come was really one event, a once-a-year reliving of the achievement of our independence. Assembly would be closed, so the only collective noise would be that of collective jubilation. We were a nation freed from the tyranny of a king, and we never wanted to forget it. For all our differences, for all the turmoil and factional agitation that was our politics, this week still had the power to unite and calm. Normally unity and calm eluded us, but for one week, we could forget that fact.

In years past I would feel a child's delight this time of year. Not today. Not after Teacher Scotes's speech. What exactly were we celebrating? We had gained our independence—and for what? Not lost on me, or I'm sure on Xephon or any of Teacher Scotes's friends, was the irony that at this moment of our celebrating freedoms, Teacher Scotes had lost his. And yet our revelries were also his respite, because by law no capital executions could occur during this our holy week. Had he been convicted any other day, his death would have come the next. Instead it would wait till Monday, July 11. Oddly, now knowing of Father's desire that Teacher Scotes escape, I wondered if this timing was not accidental, if Father had taken this precaution, not expecting a death sentence but accounting for its possibility. He had some influence over the schedule. None of this had he mentioned. But his was a chess-like brilliance, that of move and counter-move. Would anyone suspect him? Certainly not the buffoon Mathias. Likely not even Alcidia. No, there was but one person who perhaps had anticipated Father's intention, who had the alertness and intelligence to match Father's, even in guile, and that was Teacher Scotes.

A block from home, I crossed to Walnut, and above the trees and buildings, the high white prison came into view. Its operation made us proud. Forty years ago it was reformed on humane principles, and officials traveled from other states and even nations to study it. Father himself had chaired committees on criminal punishment and had reported their deliberations to Mother and me. Its buildings were daily cleaned and yearly whitewashed. Prisoners bathed in the mornings, ate well, and wore clean clothing. The women and men lived separately, and most learned trades in the yard for which they would be paid upon release, less the cost of their keeping. (This of course would not apply to Teacher Scotes or those awaiting execution.) Keepers were unarmed and trained to speak gently, and inspectors regularly visited to monitor prisoners and keepers alike. For the few days of his stay, Teacher Scotes would not suffer.

The main building fronted Walnut and stretched the block between Fifth and Sixth. It was two stories and of stone, with a handsome roof and cupola, elegant perimeter walls, and a grand staircase that beckoned at its entrance. Were it not for the two long rows of barred windows glowering high above, it might even have seemed inviting. Its two main wings extended back from there, southward.

The gates were already open, and the massive stairs awaited. Those passing, if they recognized me, likely wondered at my purpose. Gray clouds scudded over the weathervane. Across the street and through the leafy park was the distant back of the Statehouse. A cool breeze rustled the branches of the trees.

I climbed to the entrance, where inside it was darker still. There I was greeted by Jailer Douglass, who himself, not the turnkey, admitted me and guided me through the narrow passageway. He was tall and plainly suited, somewhat bent, with angled sideburns, and he seemed to have been expecting me, seemed even pleased that I wished to visit Teacher Scotes. We crossed the wide echoing aisle, exited through an iron-grated doorway, and descended steps to a short, pleasant, tree-lined path. This was the courtyard, where the gray-clothed prisoners were assembled for their labors, silent in the open air, before the two-storied semicircle of workshops, which backed piles of cut stone, marble, and nails. The effect was of a well-organized manufactory, not a jail. To our left was a small brick building, also of two stories, atop a raised foundation of three arches. Jailer Douglass led me to it and unlocked the gate, and we entered.

Years ago, following the reforms, we had built this separate wing, designed to hold the most rebellious prisoners in solitary confinement. Father and I had toured it. Its cells were small, each having no bed, no bench, no chair, just one small window too high and narrow to see out of, the prisoners given only modest rations, delivered in the morning. None but the most brutal and merciless offenders lasted more than a day in this building, before swearing off their disobedience and begging to return to the main wing. The method, inspired by the Quakers, was so successful that we eventually requisitioned a new prison at Cherry Hill, in our northern wards, to house hundreds in just this way. Though but one wing of it was open, with the rest still in construction, that facility had already attracted much attention too.

This was another fact that before my talk with Father had puzzled me. Why had Teacher Scotes, convicted of a capital crime, been brought here, to the older, less secure facility, where escapes had occurred as recently as last year? But to ask that question was to answer it, given the suspicions I had. Not to mention that this prison was nearer to our house and the harbor. Other than the belligerents, those awaiting death were also placed in solitary, and this, too, facilitated Father's plan. Of course, most of those awaiting death normally suffered solitary for one day only, but I worried not for Teacher Scotes's heart and mind: unlike the others, he would have visitors, and even absent visitors, even alone with just his thoughts, he was at home.

We climbed the cool stairway to the first floor and held at the landing. A small wooden chair guarded the doorway to the inner chamber, and Jailer Douglass regarded it with what seemed consternation. Then he noisily pressed open the unlocked doors, one of iron, the other of wood, and he entered so that I might follow.

At the end of the murky hallway stood a keeper, who noted us. Above him was a small softly lighted window, like the small high windows in each of the cells we passed. All the cells were empty, their outer wooden doors slid open, their iron grates locked. Four cells to our right, three to our left, all but one being of the same size, for two had been combined at the end, the thick wall separating them having been taken down some years ago. This would be Teacher Scotes's cell, and it was the one the keeper guarded. The keeper was a young man, large, with prominent chest and arms. The hallway was dim and could not have been six feet wide, but the whiteness of the cells brightened the passage.

Jailer Douglass had informed me that Teacher Scotes alone resided on this floor—that the others had been moved upstairs, to avoid their becoming jealous of visitors; their torment, though deserved and presumed to benefit their souls, was sufficient without the reminder that none could come for them.

We congregated closely at the end of the hallway. I could not yet see into Teacher Scotes's cell because the door was blocked by Jailer Douglass and the keeper. Jailer Douglass appeared stern, and the keeper, as if chastised, lowered his chin, pressed by, and returned to the entrance. When he had reached the door, Jailer Douglass said to me, "I will return shortly" and indicated that I could take his place. Then he left, following the keeper, and I stepped into the open doorway, barred only by the iron grating.

Inside stood Teacher Scotes, his back to the door and facing the high deep narrow window, through which not a sliver of sky was visible. He was dressed in coarse gray linen but was still barefoot beneath his massive calves, which were almost too big for his trousers. In the cell was a small brick privy and, unlike in the others, a small bed. Seeing him thus, I had to grasp the grate of his door.

He turned. His face lit. "Palleias!" He approached and placed his fingers onto mine. "How good of you to come. You are my first visitor." When I did not respond, from an emotion he certainly detected, he said, "Xephon will bring Ansea and Sophia shortly." He released my hand. Then he said, as if to make normal the situation, "It is a pity you did not arrive fifteen minutes earlier. I was conversing with Keeper Daniels, who is an interesting young man. He reminds me some of Xephon. He loves his books, which he resourcefully borrows from the prisoners. Escorting me here yesterday, he got us talking, and we continued our discussion this morning. He even left his post outside the chamber so that we could. Imagine that. We were conducting the most interesting examination of the issue of justice."

That Keeper Daniels had left his post might have explained Jailer Douglass's agitation and might have also suggested that Keeper Daniels was not involved in Father's plan. Jailer Douglass himself would have to be involved, and if Keeper Daniels were as well, there'd be no cause for the reprimand. On the other hand, perhaps he *was* involved and Jailer Douglass was just maintaining appearances, even for my benefit. Human machinations often require such performances.

I knew that Teacher Scotes was speaking so as to calm me, but his manner had the opposite effect, because I was still angry at him for taunting the jurors and bringing the sentence upon himself. So impulsively I said, "I am glad you are so merry, in light of the circumstances."

This subdued him. "Come, Palleias. Do not chide me. I fear I have insufficient time to deal with my enemies, let alone make reparations with my friends."

"Am I your friend?" I asked, less angry.

"I do hope so."

I gesticulated wildly at our surroundings. "But it is I who have brought this upon you!"

"Why ever do you say that?"

"It is not *just*," I said, with excessive animation; then I recalled the jailer and keeper, who were likely positioned outside this tunnel, so I proceeded more calmly. "It is not *just* for you to welcome me. Were it not for me, this never would have happened."

Instead of replying, he regarded me further, as was his habit when I hadn't fully answered. So I added, "Father never would have brought the charges had I not rejoined your company."

"That would suggest that your father is the cause, not you."

"I should just have listened to him."

Softly, he responded, "Should one ever 'just listen' to anyone?"

"But I rejoined your company."

"I wanted you in my company. Do you still feel that you must flout my wishes, solely to protect me?"

"I gave evidence at the preliminary hearing, which brought you to trial in the first place."

"You only told the truth and testified as the law required. You were author neither of the law nor of those procedures, and you were compelled in the matter. Besides, you cannot fully know the reasons the judge approved the trial, those being internal to him, whether your testimony played any role or whether he would have done so anyway, which I expect is the case."

It was brighter inside the cell than where I stood, and I again glanced down the passageway at the opened door. If either jailer or keeper *was* waiting just outside, I had no doubt they could hear us; hardly thirty feet spanned from here to there. When I looked back at Teacher Scotes, he was eyeing me, and under the pressure of his gaze, I reverted to being his pupil, though he was the one confined and I the one who would help free him.

"I have been thinking at length about your words from yesterday," I said. "In addressing the jury, you were also speaking to me."

"Those whom I speak to are those who wish to hear."

"I have been examining myself since that hour. I did not sleep, for thinking. I cannot respond for the five hundred, but I can for myself. Just as you described, I have been that child. Please don't answer," I said, though he had not moved. "I wish to tell you what it has meant to me to be with you this year. Watching you, listening to you, being in your presence—it has been a kind of liberation. The feeling you've given me is of an open road. Observing you, your method, and your way has shown me what is possible, that I can understand, that the world is there to be understood. That good can be achieved. Then yesterday, when you spoke as I have never heard you speak before, I felt transported down that road and saw why I have had such difficulty moving. *I* have been that dependent man. God help me, but I fear I was approaching the day of no return, when I would be the one to tighten the noose, not only on myself but on the rest of us as well."

Having taken in my words, he seemed to shift just slightly in his manner, which became more earnest and less playful, though his expression hardly changed. He said, "Palleias, I tell you truly that I do not know the answer, but I have long suspected that there is no point of no return. That the noose is not the right analogy, for in the situation you describe, it can always be loosened, whether around others' necks or one's own."

I thought of Alcidia. I thought of Father. But I said, "Though I try, I can recall few decisions for which I took genuine responsibility. Few in which I tried to understand rather than simply go along. I cannot say that I have much experienced the judgment you spoke of. It is unfamiliar to me. But observing you and Xephon and others I have met through you, I sense now what it must be like. It is a feeling that I want." Still he only regarded me. I said, "When I testified against you, it was only because I had not analyzed for myself what was right to do. Even as the hearing neared and I weighed the chance of being called, I did not so much as wonder what to do. Then, when the moment came and I *was* called, I had only impulse to govern me." At this his eyebrows raised just perceptibly, as if he were impressed by my reflections, and I continued. "I had no framework to call upon—I hardly have one now—and I am much uncertain about what life requires me to know. I have been poorly served by my passivity, by my wishing not to need to know, by my shirking of the least effort. That still is true. There is no one I can blame. Not even my father can stop me from considering my options. Only I can choose that."

When he could tell that I was finished, he said quietly, "You *have* been long in thought."

"I tell you this now so that you know what you have given me."

He smiled. "Thank you, Palleias. I am glad to know we part on the best of terms." Then he asked, "Why are you also smiling, young friend? Are you so eager to be rid of me?"

I had not known I was smiling, and under his observant eye, my smile widened. Both my fresh unburdening and his words had redirected me toward the purpose for which I'd come. I thought, As thanks for what he's given me, I can give something in return. I said, "Because perhaps I know something you do not."

"Such an occurrence would likely have become ever more frequent. Come, what is it that you know that pleases you? Tell me and make my final days here brighter still."

I rechecked the entryway and lowered my voice. "What I know is that these will not be your final days."

He, too, glanced sideward, toward the entryway, though futilely and from inside the cell. Briefly he regarded me, almost with suspicion, but this passed. It was freshly strange to be facing him closely but separated by bars. Then, knowing full well that I was not, he said wryly, "I see. You are speaking of an afterlife."

I answered more softly still. "No, Teacher Scotes. Only of this one. Your time is not as short as you think." Again I glanced down the hall. "I have spoken with my father. He no longer believes your sentence to be just. It weighs on him. He does not wish to see it carried out." Having raised the topic, I felt an urgency to explain before Xephon, Ansea, and Sophia arrived.

"I am glad to hear of it," he said, after a pause and without animation. "Your father has always been a reflective man, one open to seeing the error of his ways. Alas, if I could compliment him I would, but the verdict is in and not even your father can undo it."

"Undo it, no. But he can offer another remedy."

"Pray tell. Can he return me from the dead?"

I grabbed the bars and pulled close, though anything Jailer Douglass might have heard he likely knew already, and if Keeper Daniels had not been privy to our plan, Jailer Douglass would have likely asked him to withdraw. I whispered, "I tell you this on his behalf. He has devised a plan for your escape. He is in charge of it and has asked me to convey this message. When the time is right, I will notify you. You will be afforded passage to any land you choose, with your family, where you can take up residence as a free man. Or as free as is permitted on that soil."

I expected to witness his body lighten in relief, because even Teacher Scotes, as controlled as he was, was capable of displaying deep emotion. Instead he only watched me closely, as if seeking further information. "I see," he said.

"You are to be freed," I said, more loudly than intended. "I have no doubt he will make it happen." Still he did not respond. "You do believe it possible?"

"I have no doubt it is."

"You seem troubled."

"Troubled? No. I deeply appreciate your telling me."

"What, then? You do not trust him?"

"I have no reason to question his intentions. Nor need I fear repercussions in praising his plan to you. One thing about a man in my position: he cannot be tricked into losing what he has."

"I swear to you that I would never trick you."

"You would not, no," he said.

His reaction confounded me. Likely he mistrusted Father—anyway, he should have—but he was sentenced to die already, so there was no basis for a trick. I hesitated to beseech him for his thoughts directly. I said, "Perhaps I was not plain. Unlike at trial, ostracism here means not banishment to the wilderness but paid transport to any nation in the world. You, Ansea, and Sophia can thrive."

"Your father has arranged this for me?" he asked, somewhat off the topic.

"Now you see the reason for my demeanor."

Looking off, he asked, "Involving whom? How does he expect to achieve such a feat?"

"He has not informed me of the details."

"You are supportive of this plan, then?"

This jarred me. "Of course I am supportive. Did you think I wished to see you die?"

"But I am justly convicted," he said, looking back.

He seemed suddenly to have switched to examination mode, which angered me, but I held firm. Only after a moment could I speak. "You know I do not believe so."

"How would I know that? This is the first time we have spoken since the trial."

"I do not believe you are justly convicted," I said, somewhat stiffly.

"But the procedures were followed impeccably."

Why he was subjecting me to this interrogation now I could not fathom, but if this was what he required of me, I decided, I would comply. I said, "Procedure is not the only standard of evaluation, as you have pointed out."

"What of your father? What of his abandoning, at the moment of its achievement, the very goal he had been pursuing for weeks?"

Not entirely truthfully, I said, "He has seen his error. You said yourself he was capable of that."

"Is that the sole reason for his change?"

I held a moment. "Perhaps not only that."

He nodded. "And yourself, what do you think of his reasoning?"

"I understand it."

"And you believe it sound?"

"He wishes for his own preservation," I finally had to say.

"So he desires a better outcome for himself?"

"Yes."

"I understand," he said, softening. He looked off one more time for just a moment before looking back. "Then I wish to aid him in his desire. Tell your father this. Tell him I will consider his kind offer, but on one condition: that he come and discuss it with me himself, alone."

A squeak of hinges announced the return of the jailer and keeper, who appeared in silhouette in the white opening. Remaining where he was, with Keeper Daniels behind him, Jailer Douglass asked if I required more time and informed me that other visitors were waiting in the main building. I requested a minute more, mindful that Teacher Scotes would be eager to see his family. The men withdrew.

"I fear he will say he cannot come without jeopardizing the plan," I said. "He is leery of the suspicion his visiting might cause."

"He is wise in matters such as this," he said. Then, with not a flutter of emotion, he added, "Kindly inform your father that I cannot accept his proposal and will serve my sentence as commanded. It is good to see you, Palleias. I sincerely hope that you will visit as often as you can. There are a handful of people I wish to see this week, and you are one of them."

With that he turned and stepped away and, hands behind him, studied once again the deep rectangular window at the top of his cell wall, through which he could see nothing.

CHAPTER 32

KKKKKK

When Father heard me tell of Teacher's Scotes's "one condition," he was sitting outside, secluded on our property, where he had placed a chair. He loved summer months. He said they reminded him of his childhood on the farm, where he rode or walked the acres every week, tending things for his father, in meadows, in plowed fields, among crops, in woods. Even today he preferred the open air of the amphitheater to any courtroom or committee room.

When I approached, his eyes were closed to the warm gray sky and he was leaning back, hands folded on his stomach. It was not a pose he could indulge in often. Even during this week of no official business, he would attend gatherings and celebrations, cutting ribbons and making speeches to the glory of the Revolution, to our collective lives together, to the ideals I was reconsidering—or considering for the first time. Dressed in vest and plain trousers, he heard my steps and regarded me with equanimity, knowing I had returned from my visit and my mission and awaiting what I had to say. When I told him what had happened, he gave a wry smile, as if having anticipated the answer, though it was not the one he wanted.

I have come to believe that thoughtful men and women react in just this way—react least to the gravest information and most to the least consequential, as if the first engages their faculties and the second relaxes them. In this my father and Teacher Scotes were similar. Knowing my feelings for Teacher Scotes, my father likely wondered whether our confidential exchange that morning had brought us closer together or further apart, but if he did, he did not question me. He only asked whether I thought that Teacher Scotes would accept our plan if he, my father, were indeed to visit, and I answered that it must be so, for life was surely his one option. My father absorbed this, too, with hardly a reaction but thanked me again for my assistance and told me that he would go to the prison that very hour.

If Father had otherwise been a stranger to Teacher Scotes, I could have resisted the temptation to overhear their conversation and would have remained home, awaiting his report of the only answer that was possible. But knowing their history, I had to hear their words, and though Teacher Scotes had stipulated that Father visit alone, it would be simple enough for me to follow him by fifteen minutes, travel such that I remained unseen, and arrive in time to catch their conversation in the main. This I did.

Of course Jailer Douglass for a second time welcomed me at the entrance and did let me pass to the courtyard (despite the fact that Father must have requested privacy, which in the jailer's mind would not apply to me), and hefty Keeper Daniels, for his part, standing guard at the entrance to the solitary building, bade me hello in a friendly way and gestured that I could enter. I did and stepped softly up and, arriving at the second-floor hallway entrance, which was open, I heard Father's voice from inside, at the door, presumably, of Teacher Scotes's cell. Gently I lowered myself onto the keeper's chair and gently reclined to secure it—all out of sight but within hearing. I did not risk peeking. At my right shoulder was the doorway, and across it were the stairs to the third level. It was a warm, tight, and uncomfortable space but not one I expected to remain in for as long as I ultimately did. I should have known better.

Settled then, I leaned toward the opening.

There was a hollow, echoing quality to their voices, especially Father's, as their words traveled the tight hallway to the door where I was sitting. Arriving I must have been sufficiently silent because their speech had continued unabated. The first words I caught were Father's, something about how it needn't have ended this way, if only Teacher Scotes had stayed away from me, and Teacher Scotes replied that I had sought his company and that he, Teacher Scotes, was never one to turn away those who wished to join him, just as he had not turned away my father decades ago. Teacher Scotes shared his memories of back then, of Father's brilliance and his promise. To this, Father said little. Teacher Scotes commented that Alcidia today reminded him of my father then, and my father agreed without apparent anger, even though to me Alcidia was now the archetype of disloyalty and betrayal. Their exchange proceeded in this way, like idle chatter, though also with the quality of a matador sizing up a still placid bull—my father being the matador. It was heading somewhere and both knew it, though I as yet did not. At last Father sought to progress things, perhaps mindful of the want of time to carry out his plan. He said, "My son tells me you wish to speak to me before we free you."

I would have expected Teacher Scotes to speak ambiguously, as was his practice when hesitant to reveal his purpose, but instead he said, "I asked to see you, Antonyn, because I wished to learn something from you for my own purpose."

When Teacher Scotes did not elaborate, Father said, "What purpose could supersede your own survival, since we are but days away from the execution if we do not act quickly?"

Teacher Scotes said, "I wish to understand the choice you made all those years ago to leave my side, speak against me, and seek political office. I wish to understand whether it was right, whether it was best for you."

When again Teacher Scotes did not elaborate, Father said, "Perhaps I treated you too harshly in prosecuting you and misjudged the effect of age on your judgment. Perhaps confinement in a medical ward would have been more humane, for you seem to wish to play games when your very life is at stake."

"You of all people know that I do not play games, despite what you told the jurors at my trial."

There was a pause. Then Father said, "How can you be sure that I need not act this very moment in order to free you safely and that but one hour's delay could be your ruin?"

"I am asking for one conversation."

There was another pause. "You wish to discuss why I left you," Father said.

"And whether, looking back, you believe that choice to have been right. Though I have since thought about it carefully and at length, I cannot better analyze this matter than by speaking with you directly. That is why I requested this last opportunity. Come, Antonyn, you are not afraid of a few words with a caged old man?"

"I fear no conversation with you."

"For me," Teacher Scotes said, "this will be a kind of final examination."

"Not so final," my father said. "Once you arrive at your destination with your family, you will engage in many more, I am certain."

Cryptically, Teacher Scotes said, "Where I am going, I am not certain such examinations are possible." I thought, Is he speaking of death or of some strange location he would choose? After a moment he added, "Is this agreeable to you?"

"You wish to ask me questions for which you already have answers?"

"No, that is not true. I have suppositions, but I am not certain of them."

"This is what you require in order to partake of my offer?"

"This is what I require in order to consider whether I'll partake of it."

"I offer you life," my father said, "and you question whether it's a worthy option? Perhaps, if you are unsure, I should withdraw the offer." There was the sound of feet scuffling—shoed feet, therefore Father's. I prepared to flee. Then my father said, "So I must pass this 'examination,' as you call it, for you to want to live?" I calmed.

"Something of that nature," Teacher Scotes said.

After a beat, Father said, "As I said, I do not fear your examinations."

"No man should, so long as he seeks truth. And you, Representative, I believe to be a man who seeks truth."

I had read in my school days of the ancient gods and their feuds and battles. I know my imagination to be excessive, but the somewhat altered voices from that hallway evoked those stories and the strength of the combatants, their courage and their valor. Sitting there rigidly, secretly, in the warm, echoing stairwell, I felt again how much I differed from them both, how timid I was compared to their force. They were the oaks and I the sapling, at risk of encountering the least grazer's jaws and being lost before I spread my roots. They lived by reaching skyward and, though capable of being toppled like even the mightiest of trees, could withstand all but the fiercest storms. At my age I esteemed them excessively, more so than I might have had I progressed at a more appropriate pace.

Sometimes we judge others with a kind of facile certainty, thinking we know them better than they know themselves. I once, for example, laughed in the presence of a merchant—who quietly withstood my ridicule—for charging prices so far below what others charged, as if he did not know his business, only to realize later that he understood his position well and, for reasons of his own, had chosen as he had. Teacher Scotes did not make this error, being one to reserve judgment till effecting much consideration. He assumed that men and women had good reasons for their actions, no matter how odd those actions seemed to him. So as their discussion progressed and he questioned my father, I took this now to be his mode. He had long pondered their separation and had formed hypotheses, but these were insufficient: he wanted to understand; in so doing, he would not presume illogic on Father's part, but logic. He would presume that Father had calculated carefully his path in life based on reasons not easily shaken now. Such would be consistent with what Teacher Scotes had said earlier, that he believed Father to be brilliant, formidable, great.

"Why I left you, all those years ago?" Father said again. "I would not have expected it to be mysterious."

"Like Alcidia," Teacher Scotes said, "you were there one day, gone the next. One day espousing one set of views, the next, espousing their opposite. And as with Alcidia, I did not think your disagreement with me could be so total and of a sudden. Disagreement alone could not account for the change or have been the explanation. One's views do not change so totally so quickly."

Teacher Scotes recounted what he had observed, as he put it. That my father had shown an early erudition, had made original and compelling observations about the nation, its laws, and its political system—observations that even Teacher Scotes had absorbed. That within their circle, Father had been an eloquent spokesman against the evils of unfettered legislation, using the experience of his own family but also of many others he had witnessed. That of all Teacher Scotes's students and young friends, my father had evinced the most independent of minds and mastery of the epistemological process. He could cite theories and examples. He had read widely, but his reading did not supersede his own perception.

For me it was stunning, this characterization, this portrait of Father's beliefs, given how different they apparently were back then to those he held now, but for the moment, I attributed their transformation to simple youth and an ability to grow and change. Still, his change *had* been radical and swift, and this is what Teacher Scotes wished to understand. Shortly after their break, Father had called upon the services of my mother's cousin, a printer, and begun writing. He published regularly in the gazettes and dailies about the virtues of democracy and our young system, and even wrote a pamphlet. At age twenty-five he ran for representative and won.

I imagined Father listening to Teacher Scotes now with a kind of placid impatience, resigned to the fact that his own purpose required him to accommodate Teacher Scotes and listen, though he himself would learn nothing from the exchange. But I was intrigued because such a change in beliefs seemed incomprehensible to me as well; that Teacher Scotes could not comprehend it only heightened the intrigue. My own transformation would of necessity be different from Father's, for I, by contrast, would begin from the point of holding no views at all.

Then the conversation altered, in a way that made it difficult for me to stay silent. Instead of explaining his past actions, Father said, "You are a brilliant man, Teacher Scotes. I knew it then; I know it now. Though perhaps thinking you odd, I considered you exceptional. As did many others. You could impress a crowd even as you angered it, and this is even truer today. You were and likely are my superior in many ways, and I regret that I've had to oppose you, then and now. But you are also naïve and, in at least one principal respect, I have been right and you wrong. . . . You believe that I underwent a change, but I underwent no change. Being with you then only deepened my understanding; it did not alter it. I believe then as I believe now. No, the difference between you and me is less in how we think than in what we do based on what we think. The difference is that I inhabit the world as it is and you, in fact, as others have alleged, do inhabit the clouds."

There was a long silence, and I worried momentarily whether I had made a sound. Then Teacher Scotes said, "You are saying that we agree in what we think—that we did then and do now—and yet I am wrong about some matter?"

"Yes."

"That would seem a paradox," Teacher Scotes said. Father did not answer. "You say that we agree about our system, about the injustices I claim, about the evils I chronicle—about all those things you have publicly lauded and supported as a representative?"

"Of course."

"I do not understand," Teacher Scotes said. Neither did I, and I felt a kind of numb tingling in my hands and a moist chill at my neck, where the cloth pressed against the chair. The act of listening was itself becoming difficult.

"But you do understand," my father said. "On the one hand you admit my brilliance; on the other, you need only perceive where you are now and where I am."

This to me made little sense, till Teacher Scotes said, matter-of-factly, "You have succeeded, and I have failed. Yours has been the efficacious strategy." There was a pause and Teacher Scotes continued, "From the beginning, you knew your path, even before you joined me."

"What I learned from you I could hardly have learned as well else-where. You taught me more about our history and system than anyone else could have. You lifted the fog from the world, past and present. And you were a war hero."

"You could use the best of my reputation and knowledge while also distancing yourself later, and easily so. But why? What was the mistake in my strategy and the superiority of yours?" There was another pause till Teacher Scotes himself offered, "I sought—and seek—to change the system."

"Whereas I understood that it cannot be changed. That it *is* rule or be ruled, despite what you said at trial."

"That is why you say you inhabit the world as it is and I inhabit the clouds."

"As I must sometimes remind my son, when floodwaters rise, it is best to be on top of the mountain."

"And you are on the top of the mountain."

"And you are drowning and need me to save you."

And I was drowning, too, lost like Teacher Scotes, but for the opposite reason. For twenty-eight years I had been warm and dry, till this day, when father opened his mouth and said that he in fact believed what all my life he had steered me from believing, and the floodwaters came and took me.

CHAPTER 33

But it didn't end there. I thought to leave, not so much to avoid being discovered but more impelled to saddle my horse and race to some faraway inn and then another. Of course this would have meant abandoning Teacher Scotes, which I wanted least to do, but right then I was not thinking in such terms; something had possessed me. Then, no sooner had I begun pressing myself up, likely risking my discovery, than Father said, "So will you now let me save you?" I eased back into position.

"Perhaps," Teacher Scotes said quietly, "but a few more questions suggest themselves."

I imagine it was Father who exhaled. I remained seated, heavily so. I did not wish to listen further, and yet I could not stop.

"It is true you have been successful," Teacher Scotes said, and he proceeded to recount the ways: Father was wealthy, famous, in good health, married, and a parent. In all, he was beloved—by the people, by his family. "And yet," Teacher Scotes said, "you are here, seeking my escape, for reasons beyond your concern for my well-being. You are here because you fear the people's wrath should I be killed. You do not know for certain that their wrath will come, but you fear it likely will. You fear that you yourself will be ostracized or worse. So it would appear that their regard for you is precarious."

"The people's love is never unconditional," Father said, "and I never saw my path as without risks."

"In fact," Teacher Scotes said, "the people's love is highly conditional, conditioned on whether you grant what they wish and want—is that not true? Even I who am not in your position can see what it requires—what you must say, regardless of what you think; what you must do, regardless of what you desire; how you must weigh and balance and calculate what is ever-changing and fickler than anything in nature. How on one day you are *for* a policy and on another day against it. That to one group you extol the policy's virtues and to another you promise its curtailment. To behave otherwise is to give up your position and return to a life of plain citizenship, the outcome you cannot abide. Thus, at every turn you can only do what will keep you in your position, which means what will keep you in their favor."

"It is better to be loved than reviled," Father said.

"But I am not reviled only, Representative. And you are not loved only, no? The difference is, perhaps, that I am loved by those who admire my virtues, whom I admire for theirs, while you are admired for your posturing and by those whom you despise. You understood this thirty years ago. Do you see it differently now? You said that it is rule or be ruled. It would seem to me that you *are* wrong: you do not rule but are ruled in turn. They dictate to you as much as you dictate to them. You obey as much as they do. It would seem that, contrary to what you say, the choice is not to rule or be ruled; rather, it is to be ruled and be ruled. That one entails the other."

"So you understand, then," Father said, "that you *are* ruled. In this you are correct. As I said, you have failed. In fifty years, you have achieved nothing. You have changed nothing. The restrictions on you now exceed those at the beginning. For myself, yes, I grant the existence of the pressures you describe. But at least I can control what happens to me. I have what I have and know how to keep it. No one can take it arbitrarily, of a sudden, for mysterious and undefeatable reasons. At least I am above that."

"You admit that such arbitrary taking is the citizen's fate?"

"I don't admit it; I face it. I accept it as fact."

"You have worked for twenty-five years to advance a system that you yourself consider to be unjust," Teacher Scotes said. "You speak, you travel, you labor, you sweat, you think, and for what? For nothing that can bring you joy, for no goal that can honor or excite you. Your life instead is a game of whom to please and how many. Your moral compass is a survey. Your action is dead action, in which each day you must tread water furiously—the same water you claim to rise above—with the lone intention of surviving to tread another day. Meanwhile, whatever you might have been, whatever truly productive skills you might have developed, whatever real achievements you might have earned, even *if* limited by our laws and rules, daily recede further into the distance, into the never-will-be. You must be aware of this. You must daily compare what you are to what you might have been. In this, whom do you blame more, them or you? To me, you seem no less a prisoner than I, with this difference: that what I've been allowed to do I have done with pride and with the belief that I could not have done better, that my actions were as good as I could make them, mistakes or no. At least I can do something, whereas you can do nothing—nothing that is not designed to please, that does not subordinate you to them. Me, I may soon be murdered, but you, you are a suicide."

"You may well consider me ignoble," Father said, "but I of course do not. I have made my choices knowing the costs, and even knowing them, I still prefer my life to yours."

"Let us consider a few more of those costs," Teacher Scotes said. "You are married and to a woman that you seem to love. To that extent you are happy. But are you loved in turn? My own wife, aware of my foibles and weaknesses as well as my virtues, loves me knowing who I am. Does yours know you? Do you speak with her privately as you speak with me now, contradicting everything you say and do in public? . . . You do not answer. Is that a no? Then what she loves—the great Antonyn, the man of the people, the public benefactor, the champion of our system—she may love genuinely, but it is not you. What she loves is the public you, the fictive you, the facade. Like the people, she must be fooled in order to be kept. Like the people, she must see only the portrait, not the man who posed. She loves you not for your ideals but for hers. In betraying yourself, you have betrayed her. That, I imagine, is another of the costs you bear."

There was a long pause till Teacher Scotes added, "And the same principle governs the love between you and your son."

Then Father did respond, and there was a thick, gravelly quality to the voice that carried it. He said, "There is nothing you can say to me that I don't already know. You may seek to reveal to me my errors, but you cannot. I do not act without thought; I never have."

"I seek to reveal nothing to you but to understand for myself."

"I do not say," Father said, "that my choices have not sometimes been painful, but I do say that given the nation we live in, they were the best choices open to me or anyone."

"To what end? What could have made it all so valuable?"

"Because what I am and what I have become have made it possible for me to offer the same position to my son, so that he, too, need not be victimized. He need not go the way you are going or the way my father did or countless others but can remain above it, can survive. Because of my life, he will have his."

We were but three persons on one floor of that building. I knew that I was silent. Teacher Scotes—his voice I recognized. But the other voice I was having difficulty recognizing as my father's. His being had been transformed, from that of my closest intimate to someone unfamiliar to me. As seemingly had been true of every person on our streets, I had for my entire life known only his appearance, not his person; only his outer, not his inner, self. He had made himself a kind of Trojan horse, delivering in secret what was needed to those that he deemed needed it. The difference was that what he delivered to me he considered my salvation, not my destruction.

In the silence that followed, I imagined Teacher Scotes to be mulling what my father had confessed to, for at last he said, "Your love for your son is very deep. And the burden you have shouldered for him is great. I do not know whether the costs you acknowledge have on balance, in your mind, benefited you personally, but I do believe you deem them beneficial to your son."

"I have given my life for him, and I will continue to do so."

When I followed Father to the prison that morning, I had not known that I myself would become the topic of conversation, that whether Teacher Scotes would live or die rested on the nature of the discourse about me. Had Teacher Scotes not been involved, the conversation could have ended there, but his nature was to seek each logical conclusion and abandon no question that arose, no matter how uncomfortable. All he needed was a willing party. In that he had Father, who would stay till Teacher Scotes agreed to flee, and me, who could not have moved had I wanted to. Yet for all I'd heard so far, the rest to come would dwarf it.

Father was quiet. Eventually, Teacher Scotes did resume his questioning, but gently so.

"Does Palleias share your strategy and your views?"

"You know that he does not."

"Does he profess outwardly what he opposes inwardly?"

"He could not."

"Does he damn our system, as you do, and therefore seek to rule in self-protection?"

"Perhaps under your influence, he now questions it. And if he does come to damn it because of you, he will be unable to participate in it in any way. Rather, he will shun it. Such is his nature. This is exactly what I fear. This is what would ruin him. If he does not stop questioning, he will throw away everything I have prepared for him."

"But why?" Teacher Scotes answered. "Could you not convince him of the rightness of your strategy, to see the world we live in—as you say—face it, and make the same choice as you?"

"Never," Father answered without hesitation. "He is too idealistic for that. The day he sees an alternative ideal, that is what he will pursue, however impractical. No, to become a representative, he must hold our existing system to *be* the ideal. He must love the system he will run. Otherwise, all is lost. If it is not lost already because of you, especially that speech at trial. I did not expect you to be so foolish as to argue as you did, to so offend. Virtually no jurors could you have influenced speaking as you did, but I fear you may have influenced him. Or begun to. Now you must leave, before it is too late. He is my son. His well-being is my responsibility, not yours."

"His well-being, it is true, is not my responsibility. But is it true that you could not explain to him your thinking, that you could not admit that you in fact share his emerging judgments while still persuading him to choose as you did? Might he not find the same arguments as compelling as you do?"

"No. He could never seek what he condemns. He could never speak what he decries."

"Then how have you persuaded him to follow the course you suggest and become a representative?"

"He is a good son. He does what I require of him, for no other reason than that I require it."

"He does not question his future role for himself? He does not judge what surrounds him, seeking effects and causes?"

"He did not do so before he met you. His has never been a questioning nature."

"And now that it is becoming one?"

"I discourage it."

"How?"

"By reminding him of the nobility of service and that he has few alternatives, and that he needs my help. He knows the path to fame and power is open to him if he but heed my guidance. And he knows what will be lost if he does not. My son is an intelligent young man, but there are few practicable professions that attract him or that he may confidently pursue. Thankfully for me, he has tried his hand at many and has seen the results. Instead, he knows what can easily be his because of me, if he but follows."

"I am not certain that I myself follow, Antonyn. You say that he does what you require of him for no reason other than that you require it. And yet you offer him reasons. You argue for the nobility of the system and how easily he can attain this career, given your stature, how easily he may establish himself there, in contrast to other fields. It would appear, then, that while you claim no need to give him reasons, in fact you do."

"Of course he requires reasons and would not act long out of simple obedience, even of his father."

"I will tell you why," Teacher Scotes said. "Because no man—not even one of limited intelligence, let alone the intelligence of your son—could act while telling himself, 'I do this only because my father has directed it and for no reason else.' Oh, perhaps on occasion he might, when he grasps no other option and the need to act is pressing, as in, 'I will attend this event' or 'I will read that pamphlet.' But not as a course of life or a guide to decisions that cover years and must be daily reconsidered. 'I became a representative because my father directed it.' 'I married this woman because my father directed it.' He would never openly abide such an animating principle of his adulthood. No, he will need reasons, even if they are false. What you provide are words that he may claim guide his actions, though they come not from him but from you. In truth he is propelled by uncertainty, obedience, and the fear of deciding and acting on his own, but because of your words, he need not face this fact. The reasons you provide he can pretend to see as valid. That is all you and he require for him to follow your advice."

"These," Father said, "are simply additional costs that you describe, costs I understand and grow weary of hearing you recount. What I do, I do for my son's good, and if my guidance appears outwardly false, it is in fact true. The end result is that he will act in his own interest."

Looking back, I give myself this credit: rather than condemning my father for his lies, for his manipulations, instead I condemned myself, for his strategy would have failed without my aid. Every reason he provided I could have challenged. Every choice he offered I could have questioned. Whatever pressure he applied I could have resisted. Knowing me, he may have expected my docility, but my docility is what *I* provided, not he. It was my passivity he counted on and that I proffered.

Softly, Teacher Scotes asked, "*Have* you acted for his own good, Antonyn? Are you confident in that assessment?"

Father did not reply.

"Is it possible," Teacher Scotes asked, "that your claim is instead false, that your policy is one of harm rather than good?"

Father did not reply.

Softly, Teacher Scotes asked, "Shall we direct our final questions to that end? Shall we close our conversation by examining whether in so acting, you do in fact benefit Palleias and not harm him?"

For a long time, Father said nothing. Then he said, "Yes."

At that moment, had someone entered the building and begun to climb the stairs, I would have silently pounced, strangled him, and returned before another word was said so that I would not miss a one. There was another pause, then the shuffling sound, I imagined, of Teacher Scotes pacing, then an indistinct call of some official outside, of muffled rhythmic hammering.

"I am thinking of a future time," Teacher Scotes said, "when Palleias sits beside you in the amphitheater, having arrived, he thinks, to serve a noble cause. What does he witness, day to day? Take, for example, the day he is begged to vote to furnish debt. Will he question the justice of his choice, or will he calculate the requirements of his own political survival? And the next day, when he is begged to forgive that debt, how will he answer? Which would you have him dwell on? The question 'What is right?' Or shall he subordinate that query—in order to survive—to the act of counting the heads that beg of him? And what of the next day, when other questions arise, and countless policies, and to-and-fros, hardly any of which satisfy his reason and excite his spirit?

"True, from time to time, he may take pride in a decision well taken, say if we are invaded and must fight and all agree on the course. But day-to-day and year-to-year, for as long as he endures, how many such decisions will he take, and how noble will the calling seem? Do you not project like me that the day he insists on honesty is the day it all evaporates, that the day he sees clearly is the day it crashes, that on that day VOP itself will be for him a crumpled hulk? Though he might defer the coming of that day, the longer he defers, the greater will be the crash; his pretense for following your guidance will be lost, and he will lose all energy to play his role; he will be defeated and left to wonder where the years have gone and what he should do now."

Father did not respond.

Teacher Scotes said, "And what if instead of honesty, he shuns all questions regarding the nobility of his acts and whether the availability of your assistance was a sufficient reason for choosing his profession and instead embraces the game you wish him to, preserves the pretense, and thereby continues on his course? What if he persists as he began, telling himself that his cause is noble and his choice was sound while never truly testing the truth of those propositions, perhaps even fearing such tests? Will he not have created a life tethered to his never knowing? Will he not sense this bind? How will he then exist in the world with its voluble masses arguing every which way, its events and consequences, its myriad examples and truths? Could he assess them squarely, or at every glance would he fearfully anticipate the pin that might burst his pretensions, the spoken or written word that would reveal his contradictions and bring disaster? How will he relate to others when each person could inadvertently shatter everything he pretends is true?

"For him, all men and women will become threats, and the better their characters, the more devoted to truth, the greater the threat. For him, there will be comfort only in the insipid, the unquestioning, the blindly agreeing, the vapid. The best people will shun him and the worst will flatter him for what he can bestow. And he will gladly bestow it, if only to preserve his fictions. Having chosen his path by pretending, by pretending he will travel on, with this difference: staying his course will require an ever-greater blindness and an all-encompassing fog. Choosing his path with eyes closed, he will never be able to open them. Is this what you consider to be for his good?"

Father did not respond.

"And should that day come," Teacher Scotes said, "when he does wish to open his eyes, what will make sight possible? Or rather, not sight but clear thought, about himself and the world. What will make that possible? For the eyes are automatic but the mind is not. On that day, if you are gone, who will guide him then? Not himself, surely, for his judgment will be an untrained one. He will have spent from youth to middle age avoiding thought, not developing it, and it will be a heavy affair to begin then what he should have begun in childhood and to undo what he spent his life doing. Will he even survive the fear and anxiety, or will he be paralyzed, dependent, calling out for your guidance—you who are no longer there—and, calling, dependent instead on whoever answers?

"But here is another difference. Whoever answers will less likely seek his interests and more likely seek control. At that point we could ask, Who has made Palleias so? The answer, of course, will be, He has. But you, Antonyn, his father, will have encouraged him from his earliest days, by means of your love and affection and by stoking his fears. Is this the policy you consider to be for his own good?"

There again was a long silence, and I feared that the conversation had finally ended and that Father would suddenly appear in the doorway, having silently passed the hall. When the moment became unendurable, I almost peeked because I could not conceive what was happening, what Father was doing. All was still. Then, when the quiet began to seem interminable, Father said, "You never intended to accept my offer of assistance in your escape."

"You have done me a great service," Teacher Scotes said. "And I will pass my days here knowing that I have spent them well."

CHAPTER 34

U sing the railings, I swung all the way to the bottom of the steps and out the iron door. The white light struck, and it had begun to mist. Before the workshops, the men were working, though few so much as glanced over. Keeper Daniels was still at guard. I put a finger to my lips, took three steps toward the main building, turned, and stepped back, as if I were just arriving.

Father appeared at the door and almost bumped me before noticing and pulling up. "Palleias," he startled. "Why are you here? What has happened? Here, walk with me," and I followed him through the courtyard and up into the dark echoing hallways, out again into the whiteness and down the broad front steps, across the street, through the tall gates and into the park, where we sat on a bench in the drier shade of the leafy trees.

Behind Father, and some distance across the park, was the tall back of the Statehouse, its cupola above the trees and its clock marking the afternoon. People clicked by on the pathways before and behind us, and raindrops tapped the leaves above. At a distance, from the other side of the Hall, came the muffled sound of brass and winds and calling crowds.

Father paid the bustle no mind and studied the moist earth at his feet. He looked dazed. We were sitting close, but I felt the distance. I felt ill. Here was the man I thought commanded events. The one I had trusted with my future. The one who had lied to me about his beliefs, had seen me as someone who complied and had used this fact to implement his plan for me. Sitting there, I felt the cold blank of my future, a nothing where my whole life had just been.

We sat like that till Father placed an elbow on the back of the bench and looked off, rounding the muscle of that shoulder outside his vest. People continued to pass on the walkways on either side of us. I did not want them there. I did not want to see them. If ever he and I needed seclusion, it was now, yet we sat in the open, among the crowds. At any moment one of them could invade and command our attention. Then, with but a glance at me, he said in solemn tones, "We must prepare to leave at once." His voice was still gravelly, but his thoughts seemed in the present.

I knew he was not speaking of the park, but I feigned misunderstanding by beginning to rise.

"He refuses our plan," he said louder. I sat. One of Father's offices was in the Statehouse, and this is what he was referring to when he said, "I will visit my office. When I return home, we can inform Mother and begin preparations. We have the week." He said this matter-of-factly, as if having anticipated that this action might be required and now that he faced it, was resigned to it.

But instead I thought, He has known of my frailties all along and has accepted them, even used them—for my good, as he conceived it—but nonetheless used them. I wished angrily that he had loathed my weaknesses and combatted them. He might have held my interests dear, but the success of his method depended on my failures. Despite what I had heard, even now I felt myself resisting what I knew: that he saw me as susceptible to his influence, that he would not have wished me otherwise, that my defects were an asset to him. But all of it was true. And he was right at least in this: I was precisely as he saw. I was an accomplice in his plan. His purpose had required mine, and we each had served the other.

A wet breeze arose and swirled. "He will not leave?" I asked. "He wishes to die?"

Just then a well-dressed man in hat and blue dress coat stopped before us and bent toward Father. His prominent sideburns tilted.

"Representative," he said, not asking whether we were free to speak, "I am glad to have found you. It was arranged that I see Representative Lycon, but neither he nor his assistant was at his office, where we were to meet. It is imperative I speak to someone."

Father squinted into the mist and slowly met the man's gaze. The man seemed to note Father's hesitation and more firmly said, "I am Shipwright Hardwick. I request to meet with you on urgent business."

"What can I help you with, sir?" Father softly said.

"Sir"—and here the man crooked his elbows and fanned his fingers— "my business is in peril, as are my hired men and my suppliers. We cannot bear much longer this ban on imported iron. The price of the domestic supply is prohibitive, and we must purchase from elsewhere, as I could do before the latest acts. We have attempted to endure the current arrangement, but we cannot survive indefinitely and require relief."

Father said, "I will be at my office shortly, Shipwright Hardwick. You may go ahead of me, and we will talk there."

"There are many in the manufactories that share my troubles," the man said, sternly and as if in warning.

Reassuringly, Father said, "We will speak soon." The man regarded Father, then me, then strode off toward the Hall.

Given the circumstances, I was astounded that my father could reply so cordially. But he had taught me that in conversing with one citizen, you are in fact conversing with many, for they often share their experiences with associates, friends, and family. Normally he would have introduced me, taking every opportunity to spread my name and ambitions. This time he had not. Instead he said to me, "You return home, and I will join you soon," and he rose, stood, and scanned the park for the first time. Then he touched my head and walked off toward where the man had gone.

For a moment I sat in dampness. I did not return home, but to the prison.

There, Teacher Scotes sat on his mattress, unmoving, looking inward, though he must have heard me coming. I stood before his door some time before he caught my presence. "Palleias," he said but did not rise.

I laid one hand on the cold black bars. "Father told me what has happened," I said. This caused him to eye me eagerly till I said, "He told me you refused his plan." At these words Teacher Scotes relaxed his expression and did rise, with some effort.

"I am glad you have come," he said. The tan of his skin was darker and his eyes whiter in the flagging light. "I hope you will visit every day. As much as you can."

"You have refused his plan," I said.

"I have."

"Why?" I did not attempt to conceal my vexation.

In considering his response, he winced and placed a hand on his lower back, and I realized he had not been fully upright, for now he straightened gingerly. "I have been here but twenty-four hours," he said, "and already I feel my lack of mobility. To cage a man is most severe."

"You can say that knowing we can get you out? In a day or two, you could be free."

"Do you mind if I walk while we talk?" He began to circle the cell, a soft sound of suction from his feet on the concrete, around and again, like a penned animal, his hand still pressed to his back. Between myself and Father, we had kept him half the day, and I wondered where his family and even Xephon were. He said, "Is your father upset with me?"

This I thought an odd question, but I said, "He is talking of taking us away. He is convinced that you will stay and die, but I do not believe that you really wish to give up so. Your love of life is too great to accept defeat and leave it."

"I hope you will consider seriously your father's advice about departing as well, Palleias, at least for a time. He is right. One cannot know for certain their reaction when I am gone. You have seen yourself that I am loved as well as reviled."

That Teacher Scotes's assessment of the danger was similar to my father's made me even more afraid. "Teacher Scotes, please answer. I cannot understand what is happening."

Softly, he apologized. Then he said, "Would you allow me not to answer though I know you question only out of affection? Can I satisfy you with knowing that I have reasons of my own?"

I thought this over. "No," I said.

He stopped pacing, seemed to peruse me benevolently, and said, "Thank you for your friendship."

I said, "What are your reasons?" for I had hit upon a strategy: I would do to him what he did to us. I would examine his reasons, reveal his errors, and convince him of the illogic of his choice. There had to be illogic because life was better than death. Seeing his error, whatever it was, he would have to accept rescue. This was not presumption on my part, because a man condemned to death was surely prone to heedless thought.

"You will not accept my silence in this matter?" he asked. I shook my head. He said, "Then I see that I am not at liberty and must defend myself."

He sat, expressing regret that I could not sit also, and I stared, thinking I might quicken my wit and sharpen my discourse by speaking less now rather than more. He began.

At first his words were about admiring me my youth and recalling his own—the quarry work with his own father, the soldiering, his early days teaching and meandering, the simplicity of his life then, his meager possessions, his days among people and his nights alone, except when invited to lodge with strangers on his travels, his reading in their libraries or his borrowing of their books, his long hours spent at market and his visits to artisans and manufactories of every kind. He had sailed the northern coast and then the southern, and he still received (though did not answer, never himself writing) letters from families in every state.

Hearing him recount his life, I saw it as early filled with travels and tra-
vails, the opposite of my own, his life being like the roads of our
nation—long, well-worn routes and tiny branching footways, a life spent
with purpose and, like the roads, leaving impressions, large and small.
Sitting there, he showed his age, as if having concealed it before by striding and debating in the open air.

He gave a long account, some of which I knew and some I didn't, and
before he even reached an explanation of his choice to die, I found myself
envisioning his final years, and I anticipated his pain. For him, a slow
decline would be cruel and unendurable. Then, when he said as much
himself, arriving at his point at last, I was not surprised. "I am old," he
said, "and do not have long before the ravages begin. So you see, Palleias,
the nation has done me some service after all and has freed me and my
family from inevitable burdens. Burdens that I don't believe we could have
borne."

"You don't know that," I said.

"No, I do not. But neither do I wish to gamble. What I do know is
that there is no easier way to die than has been granted me and that it is
a poor wager not to take it."

"You could have many healthy years."

"Do you know me better than I know myself? At least the poison is
quick and painless. One stiffens, hardly more so than I feel right now,
and then one sleeps."

I remembered his friend. "Look at Merchant Girard. He survives ably,
ten years beyond you."

At the name his glance sharpened, and he said, "He suffers greatly
and has for some time, despite the benefit of his unsurpassed wealth."

"It is a sin to take one's life," I said.

"Being alive is not the same as living." I recalled his words from yesterday. When I didn't answer, he continued, "We all must choose our
path, Palleias. I, mine; and you, yours. I am sorry our relationship will
end so abruptly, having hardly begun. But all in all, I am glad you returned

to us this spring. I mean that most sincerely. You are not to blame for what has happened—that you must accept or know that I know it—and to not have had the pleasure of your company would have made these months much poorer. I think well of your future. It will be bright. If you wish to honor me, honor me by making it so."

I tapped the bars nervously and at length. "I will find the words to change your mind."

He smiled. "In the meantime, allow me to rest." Then he lay upon the bed, facing up, and placed his hands across his chest, and he looked for all the world to have expired.

I departed quickly in order both to plan what I could do and not absorb that image a moment longer.

CHAPTER 35

I suspect that much of what happens to us in life is a function of what we attend to. Three fates collided that week: Teacher Scotes's, my father's, and my own. To these I could add "the nation's," but perhaps that overstates the case. After some hesitation and some musings about how he might prevail with Teacher Scotes, Father dropped the effort and put his energies into planning our escape. For me, the future had evaporated in two cataclysmic blows: first, the trial and speech, which stayed my sails and altered my direction; second, the conversation between Father and Teacher Scotes, which shattered my pier. I was freshly adrift, and had I focused on that fact, I would have become obsessed with groping for a shore.

Saturday became Sunday. Beyond the news reports elaborating the trial, no one—no crowds, no dailies—yet agitated over Teacher Scotes's sentence. No one begged for his life or condemned his prosecutors, as Father had feared. Instead our national celebrations continued. Both days I visited him, though I was too preoccupied to visit long and hardly able to speak before his stubborn immovability. "Palleias, I greatly desire that you stay," he said on Sunday. "We have much to discuss." But stay I could not.

Monday, Independence Day, was the day we honored the signing. The Democracy Bell rang hourly, in three reverberating chimes—one chime each for the letters of "Aye" or "Nay"—though to me the toll felt ominous.

Twice I questioned Father about the necessity of fleeing, but he and Mother persevered in their preparations. Our journey was to last until word arrived that all unrest had dissipated, perhaps up to a year. As a destination, Britain was out of the question; no American representative could shelter there and return to govern honorably. Truly, most of Europe was a risk. The exception, perhaps, was France, or perhaps Poland. In the end we chose the detached, the tropical, the nearby—the French West Indies. Rumor was that Representative Lycon had sailed already but on the very public pretense (this was Father's assessment) of being a foreign emissary.

I say that three fates had collided, but none commanded my attention more than Teacher Scotes's. In this I give myself no credit. He did not deserve to die and must be saved; justice demanded that someone make it right. Even so, the verdict vote kept resurrecting my subordinating tendencies. Who was I to question so many others? What permitted me to say their judgment needed remedy? But that is what this year had been about. There was no escaping that fact, and I could no longer hide behind such formulas as *Who was I to*? Plainly, I should have examined more intensely the justice of his trial from the outset rather than idly wishing it away. I should have remained with him last year, despite Father's orders and his reaction were I to disobey. I should have questioned Father's tactics. These would have been the right actions.

I was beginning to agree with Teacher Scotes that the law, not I, had brought this fate on him. Yet who was the law? I was, in part, but Father more so, and the people mainly. In thinking this, I headed in a dark direction, for such thoughts were heresy. I was hardening, like the hull of a newly minted ship, against everyone: against a people who clamored for everything but what was theirs by right; against representatives who saw their role as doing the people's bidding, on the justification that "you can't change the system unless you're in it, and you can't be in it unless you accommodate the people"; against my father, who believed that deceiving me was in my interest and thereby treated me worse than he might a child; against myself, who chose as I did, who *was* worse than a child. At least a child, though unable to achieve it, yearns for independence. I, by contrast, was able though afraid.

It had come to this: events had piled upon events in a way I had not anticipated but once completed seemed inevitable. For all this they felt no less sickening.

On Tuesday I encountered Xephon on the front steps of the prison, as he was leaving. He did not seem pleased to see me. I presumed he had been avoiding me since the trial and by now had been told of our desired plan. He was dressed in military coat and boots and descended noisily and rapidly. At first I was not certain he would stop, then he did.

I asked him what we could do. Was there no way to convince Teacher Scotes to escape or something else? Xephon was scornful. "You would like to help him? The best you can do now is be his friend and grant that he spend his last days as he wishes. I myself will be departing shortly. Unlike you I am over thirty and could myself soon become a victim of their laws. I do not wish to remain to see whom I'm accused of corrupting or what so-called ideals I am betraying. Damn their 'will' to hell," he said. "I want no part of it any longer."

I looked around to see if anyone had heard. Of the few men and women skipping up or down the wide steps or passing the open gate below, no one had.

Then he was gone. I was only to see him once more, on that last day, when we congregated at the cell.

I did not just then visit Teacher Scotes as I had planned. Instead I sat on the hard steps and took to reflecting, uncomfortably, but no less uncomfortable than Teacher Scotes must have been at that moment. His life's goal had been to better himself and others. Right or wrong on any given point, that was his intention. And now, when he was most in need himself, who would aid him, against the odds, as he had aided others? Who had the means and methods? There must be someone who was willing to repay him, if only from love of his character.

Then I knew. That April day, when I had joined him, Xephon, and Alcidia in Assembly, Teacher Scotes had stood at someone's request, stood to address a body he had long avoided, stood for a friend, because he could not sit idly by. He had risked himself, asking nothing in return. He had done so with Father present and me observing. He had done all this when Merchant Girard had asked him to.

Merchant Girard would stand for him now. He would have to—there was no one else with the resources and inclination—and I must be the one to beg him to.

To those who did not know them well, their friendship was a puzzle. Merchant Girard was among the wealthiest in the country, Teacher Scotes among the poorest, yet their mutual affection seemed real and strong. To many people, the upper sort was a separate kind of human being, the middle sort another, and the lower, another still, and never would they meet, nothing could they hold in common. It was a misperception that many representatives exploited. Hardly a speech left their lips that did not profess their backing of the lower sort, who were most numerous, and their censure of the upper sort, who were few.

But for me, the reason for their friendship was evident. Excepting his family, Teacher Scotes valued nothing greater than an individual's capacity to build—the imaginative, industrious acts, large and small, that he saw as possible to everyone. In no one was this capacity more evident than in Merchant Girard. His ships sailed the globe, at great risk to his crew and fortune, transporting our goods to markets abroad and returning to us theirs. It seemed at times that we owed half our imports and exports to him and that without him, we either must forgo the goods or obtain them at a dearer price. Once a captain himself, he had for nearly fifty years directed his vast enterprise from his home and public office near his wharf, where he famously worked from dawn till dark, except for hours spent daily on his farm, at least before much of it was taken in the Distributions. At eighty-one, he kept to the same schedule. Each morning, he read newspapers from around the world to assess markets; wrote voluminous and minute instructions to his captains, supercargoes, and agents; fought legal battles to reclaim goods taken by pirates and foreign governments. He had even taken to arming his own ships, given our struggle to fund our Navy.

Especially in recent years did he venture his fortune beyond these regular occupations, extending loans to companies and individuals alike. For a while he operated his own bank, till the Banking Act prohibited private banks from competing with our national one. When exposed to new prospects, he often risked enormous sums, as he did on canals and turnpikes, and sometimes lost, as he did on coalfields and railroads, when the Assembly disapproved those ventures earlier this year. More than once since the Revolution had he financed the government itself, paying its debts or, from time to time, its profligacies. A generation ago we had almost warred a second time with England, and had we done so, no doubt he would have supported that too, but we had insufficient ships at trade then to justify opposing British harassment. He was the man most sought in need, one who was disposed to help. It was even rumored that he had planned to rescue General Napoleon from the British, but the emperor had died in captivity before the mission was launched. (This rumor I cannot confirm, but it was one reason I thought of him in connection with my own plan.)

Yet for all his wealth, his greatcoat was worn; he walked the city, end to end; and when ride he must, it was not in four-horse coaches, as did some merchants and some representatives, but in a one-horse gig he drove himself. This quality, too, I am certain Teacher Scotes enjoyed.

Nor is it difficult to understand why Merchant Girard liked Teacher Scotes. Many of his reasons would be the same. Though not wealthy, Teacher Scotes evinced equal industry and zeal for producing what he could. And the kind of wealth that Teacher Scotes produced—in thought, ideas, knowledge (though he himself would deny this)—Merchant Girard was also known to covet. He, too, loved philosophy, with special knowledge of the French, even naming four of his ships in their honor: the *Rousseau, Voltaire, Helvetius,* and *Montesquieu.* I could imagine the two men encountering each other over the years, each doing what he loved and what we needed, whether we knew it or not.

I would be lying if I didn't say that in asking Merchant Girard for help, I was mindful that he was likely at this moment most displeased with Father. On that day months ago, he had visited our home to complain of recent acts, and I am certain that he viewed Father as something far from friend. Thwarting Father's prosecution, then, might be yet another reason he would agree to be of service now.

The morning was again overcast, cool with drizzle, as it had been all week, and aptly so. The far-off birds called above the piers. From blocks away and inland, I heard the Bell ring, as it would less frequently than it had the day before but regularly throughout the week. Fewer ships would be sailing; I wasn't certain whether this helped or hindered the prospect of finding Merchant Girard at home.

His house sat, four stories tall and two-chimneyed, brick itself in a row of brick buildings, a block from the river, beside a narrow alley that led to his private wharf and storehouse. Because I both liked observing ships at pier and was anxious about our meeting, I took a moment to pass the alley and his garden and found a bustle at his beach and wharf where his great gold-banded ship *Good Friends* was docked. It appeared to be in loading. Chests and barrels were amassed and awaited carry. Men shouted. A few open chests at water's edge revealed their contents—books— before someone closed them and passed them over the walls. This I thought odd, unless the supercargo of this vessel was a great reader. But time was short, and much as I enjoyed the sight of men at labor, it was time to arrange for a different journey and a cargo more precious than even this.

I returned to the front. There I encountered two attached buildings and three doors: one to his public counting house, the building on the right; the others to his private counting house and the main entrance. The last was to his home. I chose the private counting house door, hoping to catch him before he moved to busier quarters.

I knocked, expecting to be greeted by a servant, a family member, or an assistant. My palms perspired. Once again, as with Teacher Scotes's friends before the trial, I would interact with someone who likely thought ill of me, more so to the extent that I admired him. All I might offer was the possibility of political influence, but such an offer men like him loathed and considered fraudulent. To join them ever, they asked only after your character, and of that I had little yet to give.

Then the heavy door receded, and the man in the opening was Merchant Girard himself.

He released the door and stood at the threshold. His short stature calmed me some, though I recognized this thought as inappropriate. He wore his usual black coat and white cravat and stood erect, his right eye closed as always. His left, however, shone upon me, even seemed to beam with recognition and something else—perhaps a flash of disquiet in its round intensity—though his face was only stony. But my silence was relieved when he said, "Young Palleias." It was not a pleasing sound. With that, the fact of being in his presence hit me fully. Then he peered over my shoulder and invited me inside, where the street noises quieted.

We stood together, just we two. The room was spare. The floors were wood and uncarpeted. There was a desk and chair and thick safe, atop which towered crisscrossed volumes; the few spines I noted were of Voltaire. In the corner was an open coal fire, now dark, a possession of his that people gossiped about. In his warehouse he stockpiled coal from England, and he heated all his buildings with it, insisting it was superior to wood. Even Father had expressed a desire to obtain a hearth or two for our home, along with the sheet-iron shutters that Merchant Girard had himself designed. The room's only ornamentation was a Chinese drawing of a ship of his and two canaries in swinging cages. From elsewhere I heard bustling, and I assumed that his assistants were awaiting him next door.

He observed me regarding the room. Politely he said, "Please forgive the lack of comfort. I am transporting some items to my farm." I nodded. With a smooth formality, he added, "How may I be of service to your father during this week of celebration?"

"Sir, I have not come on behalf of my father."

Whether or not he believed me, he only made as if to bow and said, "Then how may I be of service to you?"

"I am here on behalf of Teacher Scotes."

To this he neither responded, moved, nor even blinked, and I could not help admire his control. Then, knowing by reputation that he was a man who coveted his minutes, I leaped to my purpose and said, "In fact, he does not know that I am here."

There was a pause. "What of Teacher Scotes?"

"I wish to save him," I said, suspecting that the simpler and more direct my speech, the more receptive would be the hearing. To this he gave no answer, though my words had likely startled even him, such that I needed to speak further and at length. I said, "I know, sir, that I utter strangely. But I am sincere and wish to be direct with you."

"You wish to save him in what manner?"

"I wish to save him from his fate."

He stared. Reflected in his all-seeing eye was not just my outer but my inner self. Eventually his eye looked away and back. "He has not asked you to come?"

"That is just it, sir. He has friends who wish to help him, but he refuses their assistance. In fact, to the contrary, he seems set on perishing." This required some elaboration, so I added, "He claims that he has not long before the sufferings of age hit him and that his present fate is preferable." Then I remembered to whom I was speaking.

Merchant Girard relented somewhat. "He is correct on that account," he said. "Though I cannot complain of too ill health, I cannot claim good feeling either."

"So I am here to beg your assistance, knowing you to be his friend."

He resumed his formal manner. "Assist in what way? What may I provide him?"

"I am requesting that you help free him."

"Free him from what?"

"To assist in his escape."

His unblinking eye regarded me, then he turned, stepped toward the brightness of the window, and clasped his hands behind his back. Beside him I glimpsed the passing vehicles of Water Street.

I said, "As you know, he has but days before the execution. There is little time."

Still facing away, he said, "Do I understand that you are asking me to assist in freeing him from prison?"

"Yes, sir."

He turned. "To violate the law?"

"I beg forgiveness for doing so, and I would not make such a brazen request were there another way. But if I may assert, there is no other way. I am certain of it. . . . No one need know," I said. "You have my word that I will never divulge your role, should you grace him with your help. I will not speak of it to anyone, not even to my father. And I am confident in saying that if you are successful, my father will not inquire into the case, for he would not disapprove of learning that Teacher Scotes is saved. Of this I can assure you."

I thought he might inquire as to why, but he only turned away again. After a moment, he said, with some emotion and an even stronger accent, "I will tell you frankly that Teacher Scotes did not deserve this fate. Least of all him. Yet he stands in prison awaiting execution. If, however, you and your father now regret your actions, I can only pity you. Unfortunately, you have but one choice now, and that is to live with their consequences."

The justness of his speech restrained my pleading, and I said, "You are right to chastise us, sir. But I do want you to know that I never did seek his prosecution."

He turned. "No?"

I felt my own deep lament and the futility of argument. "I will not dispute the matter." Then, after a moment in which I sensed that he was eager for my departure, I said, "As I say, I believe this to be his only option." I waited. "Is there anything I can offer in return?"

"Even should I wish to violate the law, which I do not, you yourself have said that Teacher Scotes does not wish this."

This time I could not restrain myself, and the words poured out. "Merchant Girard, I know that such a man as yourself has no reason to countenance pleas from me. But I intend, over the course of my life, to think of men like you and Teacher Scotes as models, in character and consequence. I know also that such intentions to you are mere words. But they are not mere words to me. I do not seek your action as a gift to me or Teacher Scotes, and I pledge whatever collateral I can raise. I will place myself in defense of your person and your property, in whatever capacity I can. I know that my father has failed you and you have suffered things that in justice you should not have. I understand that now. Teacher Scotes has helped me to understand it. For that, too, I wish to stand by him, and could I, by myself, I would do so and involve no other. But the means are not at my disposal. Please, may I request the honor of your consideration at least?" At this I stopped. I felt I had entreated far too much.

Though my words did not reach him, he did seem of a sudden to engage a purpose of his own when he said, "You still have not made it clear. Teacher Scotes, you say, has no desire to be freed. What, therefore, can anyone do?"

"Abduct him," I said, "and extricate him from this peril. He may object, but later he will see that right was done by him." The narrowing of his one pupil suggested that this point fared worst of all, so I added, "Sir, I do not believe that he is thinking sensibly. I believe that, ultimately, when freed, he will see the matter differently. I have spent long days in his company and believe I know him well. I suspect that his current wish arises more from desolation, perhaps from a fear that flight could not succeed, and that to attempt and fail would jeopardize his family. But presented with success, he may turn." Then I added heedlessly, "You could take him to your beloved France." I said this despite having read that Merchant Girard had no desire to ever leave our shores, yet I pressed on. "France is our oldest ally," I said, as if he did not know this. "Under your wing, he would be more than welcomed."

He removed a watch from his pocket and glanced at it. "I regret that urgent matters beckon," he said. He replaced the watch. "And I regret that I cannot be of assistance."

"I wish to impress upon you that this act would be for his own good."

"For his own good, you say." His otherwise genteel intonation seemed momentarily reproving.

Sensing defeat, I awaited words that did not come and said, "I shall take my leave" and moved to go.

But he extended our meeting by saying, "Even were I friends with Teacher Scotes, as you say, and desperate for his safety, I still would not violate the law. I have never done so, and I will not begin now. You may inform your father to that effect."

I wanted to protest again that I was not there on behalf of Father. Instead, for the first time since the trial, the slump of resignation hit me, as it must have hit Teacher Scotes at the moment of his conviction—he who could see so far ahead and with such dispassion. I wished Merchant Girard good morning and thanked him for the unscheduled interview as courteously as I could, and he seemed in that moment not unkind. I wondered then if he expected me to punish his noncompliance. Perhaps he did.

I heard again the yells, clangs, and bustle from the wharf a block away and, before I got two steps, became curious about his plans. The activity I had witnessed shipside seemed feverish. So, because he had not left his stoop, I called, "Sir, I hope you will grant me pardon, but being deeply interested in seeing your men at work, I took the liberty, before calling upon you, to briefly observe them. I hope that was not improper of me."

He answered with a restrained though uncharacteristic anger. "I request that you not do so again, sir, for my men are easily distracted and I require them to be efficient in their duties."

At that I left him.

CHAPTER 36

I walked the block to Market Street and headed home. I could think of nothing else to do. Warm rain fell, steadily now. At the sidewalk posts, darkened horses bowed their heads serenely. The stones glistened.

Father and Mother would continue arranging their affairs today, four hands working methodically. There was little time. Trusted confidants would come and go. What I had thought would easily be remedied was not to be. From doom to salvation to doom, in days. I could beg Father to have Teacher Scotes abducted, as I had Merchant Girard, but he would never agree. No workable plan could be traceable to him, and if Teacher Scotes were abducted, what would stop his returning or getting word back of what had happened? Even I could project the dangers. No, Teacher Scotes had to go willingly or be abducted by a friend with means like Merchant Girard and reconciled, neither of which would happen now.

I entered our tunnel, escaped the weather, and held in the dimness there, my back against the brick. People passed by swiftly, made myopic by the rain. People walking, riding, driving clopping horses. The rain trickled like a stream, the sound echoing through the tunnel.

By week's end Father and Mother would be gone, and I would join them. He had lied to me for years, but he was still my father. To remain was to be alone, alone as I had never been and dreaded being. What occupation would sustain me? How would I answer for what had happened—I, who could answer nothing? Were I to insist on staying,

Father might arrange to have me watched over, but could any benefactor withstand what might befall him if the people's rage spilled over? Would our house survive or remain in our possession? At the outer end of our tunnel was the rising *human* river, with their preoccupations, their pursuits, their lives, and with little care for me; at the inner end was warm home and the two who placed my needs above all else and always would. Inside, Father and Mother were working for our survival; outside, the rest—*they*—were working for themselves.

I entered, dripping. In the dining room, Mother and Father wrapped the silver, which was laid out on the table. They calmed at seeing me, then glanced at each other, as if I had been the topic of discussion.

"How is he, dearest?" my mother said.

"I don't know. I did not visit him this morning. . . . What can I assist with?"

Father laid down the cloth he was using as a wrap. "Dry yourself and change your clothes—if you wish—then join me in my study."

I went upstairs to dress. My room was unchanged: nothing moved, nothing packed. When I heard him take the stairs, I descended and joined him, he at his desk, I before it.

I wondered what his plan was, how we could depart without appearing to be fleeing. Or perhaps this was impossible, and Father was only counting on the pacifying quality of time. This would not have surprised me. Often had he waited out the people, knowing that in time they would forgive and forget. After all, they still needed him. More than any representative, he got them what they wanted, and despite his role in Teacher Scotes's fate (assuming they would rage at this at all), Father's bounteous capacity would remain.

He observed me with what appeared to be affection rather than the restless purposefulness that earlier had been upon him. His ample hair was more disheveled than usual, and at his temples was a fresh patch of gray, or perhaps I hadn't noticed it before. He looked resolute but tired. The effect was disarming. I realized that to come was another solemn talk, adding to the many we'd had in only weeks, far more than in all our years. Events were that momentous. Perhaps I had matured in his eyes as well.

I assumed that we would discuss the terms of our departure. Thinking this, I imagined standing before the bars at Teacher Scotes's cell, where fresh guilt commanded me to stand, on the day of his demise. Like most such feelings, I dismissed them. Yet this was not the topic Father raised.

"What I am about to say to you," he said, "I expect you will find strange to the hearing, even odious. But I owe it to you to say it." With that he leaned forward, elbows on his desk, and made such statements of anticipatory apology that I knew right away where the conversation was going and that I was unprepared for it.

He did not mention the exchange he had had with Teacher Scotes, but that in fact was the topic he now raised. He characterized what he would confess as being something without remedy. He had committed, he said, a grave injustice against me—I fixed on that word, "injustice," a central concern of Teacher Scotes—one for which Father was deeply regretful. Out of love—he had acted out of love. Though more importantly, he had acted in a way that caused me harm. He saw that now. He had not before but did now. What remained for him was to describe his transgression and do all he could to help me survive it. He used the word "survive."

I could only let him speak. I imagined later that something about my expression—some lack of alarm or intensity on my part—had to have astonished him; but if so, he never mentioned it. He just proceeded with his preamble, leading to the enumeration of his crimes, as he put it, till he got to the words "I have lied to you, Palleias. I have been lying to you for years." He took a breath. "I have argued that certain things are true that I myself believe are false in the hopes that you would accept them as true. I have pressed you to believe things that I myself do not. I have done so since you were a boy. In other words, I have been a false father and have been so till this very moment. I have never been otherwise."

Then he quieted and, though he had not yet reached his point, seemed to grant me time to process what to him must have been a cannon shot across the desk.

I only blinked into the silence. My actual feelings were alien to me, and I'm not sure what he expected either: I felt a sudden warmth, a relief, as though a wall between us that I never knew existed had of a sudden crumbled. As though for the first time, I was seeing him and he me.

When I didn't answer he took another breath. He said, "You've known all your life that I wanted you to be a representative. I have made that clear enough. Even when I allowed you to experiment with different occupations, you knew—you couldn't help knowing—that I approved no other choice. That much has been clear, and it is not the lie to which I now refer. You knew what I wanted, but what you didn't know was why. You didn't know my real reasons for pushing as I did. This is what I lied about. Had I told you my reasons, I feared you never would have chosen as I wished. I never could have persuaded you. So I pursued other methods. I invented reasons to give you.

"*These* were the lies. I pressed upon you the nobility of the calling. I insisted on the virtue of the system you were to lead. I even threatened you—not openly, perhaps, or at least not usually; open threats were mostly not required—but I threatened nonetheless the withholding of my love and support. I made clear as only a father can that if you refused my bidding, I would abandon you in spirit and in fact. You are a sensitive young man, and I knew that you would receive the message. This was my solution. I was willing to do whatever came to me to do other than tell the truth. Perhaps I believed in part the lies I told, but that is no justification and is too facile for even me to accept as true. I have been sufficiently aware of what I was doing to execute my plan and continue it across twenty years, ever since questions about your future first left your lips."

He stopped, then closed his eyes, as if gathering strength for the worst of what he had to say. He said, "Palleias, what I am telling you is this. Instead of teaching you, I misled you. Instead of nurturing you, I stifled you. Instead of encouraging your growth, I encouraged your stultification. Instead of preparing you for life, I kept you as a child. I more than withheld from you; I thwarted you. I have been a father in name only."

Again he stopped, as if again allowing room for me to speak. Still I could not. This time he hardly waited, having, I imagined, achieved a certain momentum and determination to complete his mission. Shortly he said, "I have yet to broach any of this with your mother. That will be my next punishment. She may not forgive me, for I have lied to her as well. She may not even wish to flee with me, but she, too, will be in danger, and I have put her there, so I will beg of her to come, whether or not she remains with me thereafter.

"Here is what I believe," he said, and what followed was the core of what he and Teacher Scotes had discussed together in the prison: he loathed our system but believed it was unchangeable. Reform was not possible, not in his or my lifetime. It was rule or be ruled, and as such, we each of us had one true option. As difficult as it was to rule—and ruling was hardly the name for it, he admitted, being himself swung by the vagaries of the very people that he governed—to live otherwise was worse. Look at what happened to your grandfather. Look at what happened to Merchant Girard. Look at what happened to Teacher Scotes. And these are just the strongest among us; there are countless defenseless others. To be a citizen is to exist by the permission of every other citizen, whose voices project from the willing mouths of their supposed benefactors, the representatives. "This is what I believe and always have," he said. "We exist in an unjust nation, where anything can happen to anybody— such is the arbitrary nature of it. But," he went on, "given the opportunity to choose again, I would choose as I did. I still value my position over theirs. And I believe that you should do the same. Not for the false reasons I gave you in the past, but for the true ones I give you now. I hope for your sake you will choose as I have. Profoundly I do.

"But it is your choice, Palleias. Consider carefully, I beg of you. When you are past the shock of my confession, examine your choice for what it is. Not everyone has the opportunity you have. Let me be a father to you at last and explain my thinking and give you the best guidance I can. Not to manipulate you but to prompt your own thought. In the end, you will do what you believe is right, and you will be right to do it. Take to heart what I have said. Life," he said, now in a different, freer tone, a tone that oddly seemed more genuinely his, "presents us facts, and reality is immutable, and no man succeeds by evading what is factual and real. I am giving you the facts as I see them. I am presenting what is real to me. I acknowledge that my words may be too much to absorb at once, especially after years of hearing their opposite from me, the man you trusted most. Perhaps you will hate me now," he said. "If you do, your hatred will be fair. But my fervent hope is that this will not distract from the decisive choice that faces you. And I want you to know this: whatever you decide, so long as I survive and am able, I will love you and assist you. You are my son, and for as long as I have failed to be your father, for that long do I wish to be your father hereafter."

There was a pause in which his manner grew solemn, perhaps in the face of my continued nonreaction. At last he said gently, "I have given you much to mull. Remain in this room as long as you'd like. I will go down and continue helping your mother."

Before he fully rose, I said, "May I ask you a question, Father?"

He let his weight settle. "Of course you may. I hope you will question me freely and at length, whenever and for as long as you'd like."

"If you believe our system to be wrong," I asked, "what would be different under a better one?" He had told me what he hated but not what he favored.

"Each of us would be free," he said simply.

"If not freedom, then, what does our present system yield?"

"Restraint. Compulsion."

Then I thought of a question I had never asked even Teacher Scotes, a question that Teacher Scotes had not addressed, even at his trial. So I asked, "What, then, would a better system look like? What would be its procedures and its organization? What would be different from what we know right now?"

"I don't know," he answered quietly.

I sat with him. Then I said, "I will be downstairs shortly, too, to assist you and Mother."

He smiled, just perceptibly, and left.

In the space behind his desk, shelves had been installed to house his favorite volumes. He kept them close. All were on the topic of leading others, on the burdens of authority, on the intricacies of governing. There were histories and biographies, from ancient times till now. There were treatises and essays. It was a high wall of brown, red, and black bindings, and it was intimate to him; equally did his own life match the experiences that the books recounted. He as well as anyone could understand the stories in those pages.

In the corner to my left was the high-backed red leather chair that Alcidia had been enamored of, the long glistening sword hanging above it. For a generation Father had preserved it. He had understood what he was agreeing to all those years ago when he decided that as much as he despised what he must do, it was still for him to do it. He had decided with open eyes, eyes so open he understood that though he would rule, he would *be* ruled as well. That he was just exchanging degrees of capriciousness. To him, two paths had been presented; he chose the least debilitating. But debilitating nonetheless it was. The same dilemma now presented itself to me.

In the quiet of his study, even after hearing his confession for a second time, knowing the corruption of it, I felt closer to him than since my earliest awareness.

CHAPTER 37

⟪⟫⟫⟫⟫⟫⟫⟪

The downpour began in blackness. It splashed against my windows, charging and retreating, as if storming ramparts. Hearing it, I passed the night. Eventually black became gray, but the rain did not quiet.

Father's argument was that our national life from the beginning had been like a lit bomb and that the best we could do was to escape before the explosion. Or that we had set off on a downhill carriage ride without a team of horses sufficient to raise us again and what remained was to decide who would ride and who, for the duration of the vicious descent, would be struck bloodily from the road. Lying in the darkness and in the rain and sometimes thunder, I wondered less whether he was right and more what his theory might have done to him, to his life and spirit.

In confessing, he seemed to suffer, but he also seemed to blame himself too much and me too little; he seemed not to appreciate that for all the choices he made, I made as many of my own. In response to his behavior, he expected only anger, as if he were the sole cause of any outcome. Though I was grown, he granted me no responsibility. In a sense, he thought too little of me still, for in matters of the mind, the only destruction is self-destruction. As I pondered this idea, in the gray early hours, I wondered if Teacher Scotes would like it.

I did not wait for breakfast and did not don a coat but bent myself and ran the blocks from home to prison, when few yet were stirring in the streets. On the streets, water flowed with abandon at the edges but not upon the sidewalks. At the entrance to the prison, it spattered on the steps, and as I jogged them, drops jumped to dampen my knees. Inside, I came upon the jailer, who seemed startled by my dripping presence but who knew by now to admit me without a word. I passed the main building and yard and entered solitary, where Keeper Daniels stood at guard. He, too, let me pass.

No one else was present—not even Ansea and Sophia, whom I had yet to see that week, which surprised me, though I granted that it was beyond me to comprehend what they were facing. I found Teacher Scotes lying on his mattress, eyes closed and hands folded at his belly, which rose and fell in rhythm.

I did not speak but waited for him to open his eyes and see me, whereupon he turned his head just enough to regard me standing at the bars. On this occasion, though, he did not brighten, did not call my name, did not react the slightest to my being there, other than to slowly fold himself and sit to face me. Sitting, he waited patiently, as if to grant me first words, but because I had none—I had come only so as not to miss a moment of seeing him—I gifted back the opportunity to speak, with my silence. This opportunity he eventually took, saying, "I understand you visited Merchant Girard yesterday."

His words stunned me. He let me sit with them. His manner was stern, and I knew at once that I had committed folly, as one grasps the nature of one's actions only when suddenly having to defend them. I should have acknowledged my error immediately but chose instead to compound it by delaying an accounting with a question of my own. "Did Merchant Girard come to see you?"

"Is that relevant, Palleias?"

I bowed my head. He stood, stiffly, straightened to full height, and strolled unsteadily to the side and back. Then he sat again but did not speak. Neither did I. Neither did he. He only regarded me attentively.

"I did visit Merchant Girard yesterday," at last I said.

"For what purpose?"

"To arrange to free you."

"Against my will?"

My reaction was defense, but I caught myself and offered, "Yes." He did not answer. Neither again did I. He waited. A tremendous rush of wind and rain crashed against the outside wall. "I am sorry," I said, at which point my body relaxed, and I fully accepted the error of my plan, having been conscious of that error from his first question. Apparently, there can be degrees of our awareness.

"What are you sorry for, Palleias?"

As penance, I was now to be examined. This was just, for my actions exposed the sometimes gap between what we "know" and what we feel. If I had truly questioned myself before visiting Merchant Girard, likely I would not have visited. Instead I had followed an impulse that had been core to me, before my time with Teacher Scotes.

"I am sorry for interfering," I said. "I should not have visited Merchant Girard. It is your life and your choice." In my eyes tears followed upon my words, which carried the certainty of his demise, and I was not able to suppress them. They came, and with them, no further words.

He regarded me a moment longer, then looked down and to the side, as if releasing me. Still he seemed displeased. Rarely was his disappointment obvious, rarely worn upon his face, except perhaps in the dulling of his eyes. I could have departed then. By looking away, he had given me leave.

"Please forgive me for what I have done," I said. "I wish more than anything to spend this time with you."

He looked up. "Forgive yourself, Palleias. There is no injustice we commit that does not harm ourselves as well. If you've chosen poorly with respect to me, consider how your choice affects you also."

I took this pointed lesson as impatience on his part, which it likely was. Otherwise he would have questioned me, as was his wont. I wondered if he preferred I go. I almost did. But something in his manner did not repulse me entirely and bade me prove my regret, if I could, to "consider my choice," as he put it. I felt I owed him that.

I thought a moment and let it come. "I recall the time with Xephon," I said, for I had been thinking about this memory recently, "when we came upon a young man who was flailing grain in the white sun. His family was poor and could not afford a thresher. He had told us of his long-ago ambition to be a tailor and how he had sought apprenticeship as one but could find no place, being without experience and without means of introduction. So he had offered instead to apprentice for a man for no room or board, for no compensation whatever, just to acquire some skill, experience, and reputation upon which he might build. He saw far into the future and was willing to gamble on his ability to impress whichever master took him in. And no sooner had he found a place and worked for some months in this arrangement than the Assembly passed an act barring uncompensated employment. I recall that act myself, having read of the proceedings. The victorious majority had argued, they said, on behalf of those who would be abused by such arrangements. There was no debate, the act easily passed, and VOP announced it into law."

I observed Teacher Scotes. Still hunched upon his mattress, regarding me less dully. I took this as an invitation to continue.

"I recall, too," I said, "the time we came upon the group of rough cabins, far west and south of the bridges, on routes to neighboring states." This was another memory that had arisen after Teacher Scotes's speech at trial. "The farmers there were struggling, especially from the increasing cost to transport their crops to market. So they sought additional sources of income and had stumbled upon—or were stumbled upon by—travelers seeking lodging and meals, for single nights, year round. They took them in, sometimes having little more to offer than straw in crowded rooms and day-old breads and pies, for which they charged meager fees. Many travelers stayed, particularly those who could ill afford the taverns or were too fatigued or broken down to reach one. Sometime after, however, the Assembly passed an act mandating that any dweller who wished to offer beds or food for pay must meet the same requirements as did the inns of that time, such as by providing certain types of mattresses and comparable space. The cost of these requirements the dwellers found prohibitive. The act also mandated that the farmers post reports about their lodging trade. This, too, the farmers could not afford to do. The result was, they said, that anyone seeking lodging in their vicinity would have to use an inn, though there were none for miles. I remembered this act too, for it was renewed at least once in my memory."

I stopped, and Teacher Scotes continued to observe me. I said, "In both cases, supporters of the acts said they wished to protect the people from buying lesser quality products and services, from harmful or insufficiently beneficial offerings. But by my recall, those same supporters never asked the buyers what they considered valuable, what they perceived as harmful or beneficial. Indeed, even those who deemed their purchase as more than worth the money charged were not allowed, because of the acts, to make that trade again."

These were visits we had made last year, not this year, and I had forgotten them till recently. Teacher Scotes and I had never discussed them, though perhaps Xephon had mentioned something about them once. I don't recall. Whatever had prompted me to consider them further, Teacher Scotes looked at me now as if he had guessed what I was thinking. This is how my mind sometimes works. Sometimes the slightest agitation over some experience opens windows onto novel vistas. Sometimes if I allow them to, new connections stand upon old.

I went on, "It has occurred to me also that such acts characterize us citizens in two very different ways. As *buyers* of goods and services, we lack sophistication and are ignorant of what is valuable. But as *sellers* of goods and services, we are cunning villains who can successfully profit at others' expense. In other words, as a populace we are both incompetent and sophisticated cheats. Neither assumption seems correct, but if one is, the other would seem contradictory."

At this Teacher Scotes finally softened his countenance, though just so. Whether he agreed with me or not I don't know, but I do know that he liked it when we engaged in intellectual exploration. I raised my hand

and wrapped my fingers around the cool bars. Present were just we two. To my left the darkened narrow corridor was quiet and cooler than it had been all week. Outside the rain continued noisily. I became aware that I was doing all the talking, a first for us; usually he would question and I would curtly answer, no matter how long the conversation. Once again the rain splashed against the outer wall. The light around us pulsed.

"I understand that you wish to die rather than to live," I said. "I understand that under certain conditions, that outcome might be preferable. Perhaps a time will come when I feel similarly. It is not for me to judge. Or, it is, but only on my own behalf."

He stood, approached, and placed the fingers of one hand through the bars and over mine. A rising bustle came from the stairwell. Keeper Daniels appeared and held in shadow at the entrance. Behind him peeked a darkened head or two, and the gathering noise suggested more on the stairs, below.

I turned to Teacher Scotes, who smiled, anticipating my question. "My following of late seems to have increased," he said. "They come each day and are allowed to stand in the cell opposite, to converse with me for a few minutes. Then another group arrives. The jailer inquired of me, and I agreed. At least for a brief time each day, when I can spare it from family and friends." He let me consider this. "Perhaps I am a curiosity," he said, "and they wish to glimpse me, before I am gone."

I looked to Keeper Daniels, whose large frame detained the pack and who waited upon me.

"Go home for now," Teacher Scotes said to me. "But please return tomorrow, and we will talk some more." Relief and joy must have filled my face, because he said, "I am glad for your friendship, Palleias."

CHAPTER 38

A t home I encountered visitors who had been speaking with Father in preparation for our time away. These were men he trusted to keep him informed, watch over our interests, and vote on his behalf when he was absent. Father would not be resigning his position but traveling on official business and thus could designate a proxy for the time he was away. These men, in formal dress, left as I arrived, and passing through the doorway, they bowed and tipped their hats to me and used them to defend against the rain.

I assisted Father and Mother for a time, then took leave to organize my own affairs. Under pretense of doing so, I arranged some clothing and dragged a chest to where I could better fill it, but in truth I did little.

Perhaps, I thought, Teacher Scotes is right. Judging for ourselves may be *the* most fundamental personal choice; freeing everyone to do the same may be the most fundamental social one. I was anxious to discuss this further with him tomorrow and, in that moment, forgot his fate.

Thursday morning's daybreak lit the fog. When it cleared, joyous clouds ran across the sky, having shed the weight of yesterday's deluge.

Again I beat the crowds to Teacher Scotes's cell. But apparently I was not his first visitor.

"Palleias," Teacher Scotes said the moment I appeared. He had been standing, facing away, and hearing me, had spun around. "I had the most extraordinary visitor just now, a young Frenchman. He is here to make a study of our prisons. He really was quite intelligent, though a bit melancholy, and about your age."

I knew to whom he referred. His name was De Tocqueville. He had earlier been in New York, where it was reported that he was next to visit Philadelphia. I confess to momentary feelings of jealousy that Teacher Scotes was struck by the intelligence of another young person. He had never expressed such enthusiasm for my abilities.

"He also tells me," he went on, "that he is making notes for a book about our system. On this we conversed at length, and he has made some excellent observations. He even flattered me by seeking my advice about the book." In telling me this story, Teacher Scotes had resumed his mischievous mood. It seemed that in his estimation I had already recovered. "Do you know what I advised him?" he asked.

"To define his terms?"

He threw his head back laughing. "Palleias, that is wonderful. You tease me well." He sat, smiling brightly.

I enjoyed the change of mood, and I wanted to resume our conversation from yesterday, but the awareness of his fate intervened anew. I think he saw the change upon my face, because his own smile dimmed. I assumed to free my spirits he kept his humor and asked how my preparations for traveling were going.

"What makes you think I'm traveling?"

"I assumed your parents were."

I was embarrassed to be confirming our plans. "It will be for a short while only."

"Good. A foreign land can be difficult." With this comment, he became reflective. "When will you be leaving?"

"We sail Sunday," I said, conscious that I would not be with him on his last day and that he was thinking this too.

"It is well," he said.

I took this opportunity to raise again the injustice of what was happening to him, the great loss that we—his friends—and the nation would

suffer, and how deeply I regretted my role in it all. He would have none
of it. "Come," he said. "This is old, well-traveled ground." I did not
object. It was not for me to compel him now to speak of things he did not
want. The conversation stalled when he suggested no further topic.

Being with him was enough. I had finally grown accustomed to his
appearance through the iron, his body framed in shifting rectangles.
Oddly, though caged, he did not appear at all confined. Perhaps he had
survived so long and traveled so far that he could live expansively in
imagination. In his mind, he still beheld the world.

The cell was quieter this morning from the change in weather. Peace-
fully, he sat, and he seemed as comfortable with me as I was with him.
Strange, for all his powers and his superiority to me, I did not experience
his presence as a threat or weight and never had, not as with others I had
come to know through Father. Or even Father himself. With them I so
expected intimidation that I had forgotten I expected it, until with Teacher
Scotes I was astonished by its absence. I don't know how he did this, but
if others should ever admire me, I hoped that I could make them feel the
same.

We stayed companionably in our postures for some time. When still
he did not speak, I abandoned my reticence and took our pattern from
yesterday as my guide to initiate topics myself.

"I have been thinking about what you said about our being decided
and provided for," I said.

"Yes?"

"I don't think I agree with you." At this his eyebrows raised but he
seemed pleased. I said, "I mean to say that I agree with the 'provided for'
element. Surely many laws do that. What I question is the 'decided for'
one."

"You don't agree that many laws decide on our behalf?"

"I don't believe that any law can do that, or any person either. That
is, if we seek precision in our words." He left me to continue. "I mean, I
can see that a law can prohibit me from doing something I otherwise

would or punish me if I do something prohibited, and to that extent it 'decides for' me. Such laws do interfere by interjecting considerations other than my own. But they are not, strictly speaking, deciding *for* me. I am still the agent who decides. I still am choosing. Is this not accurate?" I paused to await objection. Receiving only thoughtful consideration, then a kind of pleasant alertness, I continued, "The problem, I think, becomes clearer in the moral realm, where no laws are involved. There, no one can 'decide for' me in any sense I see. Not even my father, who others—even he—might say has been doing that for years." I paused again. "It is true that he told me what to do, as have others. Advised, insisted, sometimes insulted me if I chose otherwise. But for all that, they could not *make* me choose, and whatever I did, for whatever reasons—even of obedience or pretense, as you like to say—I still chose. The choice to act and the reasons for it were still mine. *I* did this or that, not they."

By this point I was speaking quickly and becoming mindful of the arrogance I felt when asserting anything, so I slowed to breathe and added, "At least I wish to distinguish finely in this matter. I grant how people likely understand your words, and I don't mean to be pedantic. But I wish to guard against this: lamenting that my father all these years decided for me, that he caused what I did. But that is untrue. Whatever he said, I still chose and could have chosen differently. Yes, he pressured and encouraged me, for good or ill, and that dominated my considerations. But everything I did I initiated, and I don't see how pretending otherwise helps me now in any way."

This time I stopped in earnest, having exhausted my analysis, then immediately conjured ways in which I might be speaking nonsense. But Teacher Scotes only looked at me with calm regard and said, "The distinction you make is an important one."

I felt elated. It was not often that I had seen that look, and he did not give it lightly.

After that, he gave his own examples and agreed that it was indeed vital never to disown one's agency—not because we could, but because we couldn't. Pretending otherwise, like any form of self-deception, caused harm. We continued to investigate in the manner he preferred, by raising example after example, real or imagined. We talked, I felt, collegially. To me it was the first time we had done so to that extent, though he might have claimed otherwise.

When we both seemed tired of our analysis, he asked, "Anything else?"

"I have also been examining the proposition that we have reasons for our actions, that that is what independence consists of." I assured him that I was not ascribing this view to him but only clarifying my own.

"What of that proposition?"

"I am wondering if it too is imprecise. To proffer that we should have reasons for our actions suggests that it is possible *not* to have them. But if such a state is not possible, then being independent must mean something else." At this he seemed especially interested, so I continued musing. Again I used the example of my father. Though I had acceded to his desire that I become a representative and in doing so was acting dependently, it was not true that in choosing so I had no reasons. In fact, to win my obedience, Father had supplied me many: that it was a noble calling, that I was weak in other fields, that my success would be ready-made. All these I adopted. So though having reasons for my actions, I could not claim to be acting independently.

"Please continue."

"In fact, having those reasons was essential," I said. "Without them, I could neither have obeyed *nor* disobeyed. I could not have acted at all. Ultimately, *they* explain the choice I made." Then I recounted similar examples from my life, of choices large and small, remote and recent: to try an occupation; to study for exams; to respond to some young woman's interest in me; to follow him, Teacher Scotes, that day we crossed the bridge. Whatever I did, I had reasons for doing it. Yet by itself that fact did not make me independent. True, I was on occasion less aware of what those reasons were, but upon reflection, sometime well after, I could identify them.

"Continue."

"I can't add much more than that. But I've been thinking that my *dependence* has therefore consisted not in whether I had reasons for my choices but in something else, in the nature of those reasons, in how they existed in my mind. Here is how I think of it: the reasons that moved me I could not have defended. I could not have explained why they were right or wrong, even to myself. They were just words that helped me do what I otherwise wanted. In this they supplemented my desires and fears. I desired and feared, but it took the words to get me moving. They justified my choice, but falsely so. They were 'reasons,' I suppose, but empty ones."

Here I stopped, having offered all that I had pondered. Teacher Scotes reflected. I took this as a degree of victory till I began chiding myself that the purpose of inquiry is not to please but learn. But he asked me to take another step. "So what then *is* dependence?" he asked. "And what, by contrast, independence?"

"To be independent," I said, "seems to mean not allowing your reasons, as the cause of your action, to lead you blindly. To be independent is to attempt to see before you act. We must act; from this we can't escape. And we must have reasons for our actions; from this, too, we can't escape. The issue is not whether we have reasons but how we arrive at them." Then I recalled his speech at trial and said, "This applies especially to how we judge ourselves, as good or bad. We cannot judge ourselves without understanding what 'good' means—not what we are told it means, which again would just be words, but what we are convinced it means. I better comprehend today what you said last week: that a life spent without examining questions of justice and goodness is not worth living."

Months later, with some shame, I realized that I was expressing views that he himself had raised at trial and was only making them my own. He never mentioned this but began another course of example-raising and exploration. We took turns embellishing what each proposed. It was a joyful experience that lasted half an hour more, till visitors came, including a fresh group of strangers that would gawk at him from the cell across. Why he had agreed to see them I could not fathom, and upon their arrival, I left.

Home again, I packed. There was little I felt the need to bring, so it wouldn't take me long to finish. The rest of the week I would spend helping Father with our plans and visiting Teacher Scotes.

On Friday I began the day as I had the prior two, with an early walk to the prison. Heavy clouds had returned and seemed to sit upon the city like gray inverted hills. Again I found him standing, having awakened before dawn. The corridor was dark. I wondered if he had slept at all this week, though physically he appeared alert. Only his body had progressively stiffened. I imagined that when free of visitors, he likely strolled the cell, that having spent his life in motion, he could not easily remain stationary now. Seeing me, however, he sat again, and looked up in that same direct and silent posture of the last two days, his hands extended to his knees, his back straight. By now I understood I was not to mention this coming Monday or his choice but could raise what other topic I wished. Having spent last evening mulling our conversation and recording passages, as I had each night this week, I knew the subject I would broach. For me it was a logical extension of yesterday's.

"You spoke at trial of the concept of 'rights,'" I said, without so much as greeting him. "It is this topic that I wish to raise today."

"It is of great interest to me as well."

I described rights as a kind of protection, not recalling all of his assertions. I hadn't told him of my recording his words for posterity, but I expect he wouldn't have objected. I also cited his reference to Lawyer Adams, Scholar Madison, and others who had discussed the term in works that no one could lawfully read. Though our library at home held such books, I had not read them either. And though this very afternoon our Declaration would be publicly read, to us the words meant something different from what Teacher Scotes claimed they meant.

"But if a kind of protection," I continued, "it is not the kind we usually legislate. Though the laws we pass ostensibly protect us from others, such as the laws we examined yesterday—against being paid a certain wage or being offered a certain product on certain terms—really, these are misnomers because rather than protect us from others, they in fact protect us from our-selves. As we discussed, they disallow our entering into agreements we oth-erwise would choose or risk what seems worthwhile. As such, they replace our judgments with the reps' judgments, judgments enforced in our name for having elected those reps." Being pleased with how this left my lips, I kept going. "But this is not the kind of protection you described when *you* invoked the concept. In fact, it is the opposite. Rights, you said, protect us in acting on our own judgments, equally so for all. Every man and woman must be protected in this way. Doing so, you said, frees us and honors our capacity as adults. Not doing so treats us as children."

In the opening I provided, Teacher Scotes asked, "And in a particular situation, if the majority disagrees with you and fears that you will harm yourself?"

"They can seek to persuade me, but ultimately it should be for me to decide."

"Why?"

"Because preserving my independence is core to my well-being, as preserving theirs is core to theirs."

"Why?"

"Because *how* I decide—whether from thought or pretense—is as important as *what* I decide. To decide by thought is healthy; to decide by pretense, harmful." I realized later that this was another formulation from his trial that I was just securing as my own. But articulating his views did help me transcribe later what he'd said.

He inhaled and exhaled fully, and only then did I register that his mind seemed partly elsewhere. I wondered whether my speaking had distracted him, or whether he simply wore events more heavily today.

"Are you feeling unwell?" I asked.

"No . . . I am quite well. And I have been enjoying our conversations, Palleias. They are very instructive to me." He gave a muted smile.

Something about his more serious mood dampened my enthusiasm for philosophy and steered me toward more intimate topics, though for him philosophy likely was the most intimate topic of all. Our connection these past days had deepened, and I was grateful. In that moment I no longer felt like a pupil to be kept at arm's length by his questioning. Emboldened by this feeling, and though I had not planned to, I changed topics. "Last Friday, I overheard your conversation with my father."

He looked straight at me, then he barely nodded.

"I was sitting in the stairwell. I am truly sorry for listening when not invited to."

Again he nodded, just perceptibly.

"Father has told me about his strategy all these years to get me to become a rep and why he was not honest with me."

Teacher Scotes asked, "He told you this when you confronted him with having overheard what he said?"

"No. I have yet to tell him that I overheard. He told me without knowing that I knew."

At this moment I expected Teacher Scotes to criticize Father, despite Father's noble act in telling me unreservedly, but he did not. All he said was "I am glad." Again there was a pause. "So what are you going to do?" I presumed he meant for my profession, whether or not I'd be a rep.

"I don't know," I said. He nodded, accepting my uncertainty. That prompted me to say, as earnestly as I could, "I was hoping *you* would tell *me*." At this he could but stare, and not without concern. "I am only kidding," I said, and he broke into the greatest smile, and it was as if the light of the lost summer sun had filled his dank cell. For once, I had surpassed even him in teasing humor.

By the time I left, the rain had overspread us. The sky was nearly black. At a street corner, I overhead two ladies and a gentleman, crouching beneath a domed umbrella, talk of a coming storm. I thought, If they only knew.

No sooner had I removed my soggy shoes at the entry to our house did I realize that something was amiss. Perhaps it was the unusual quiet, in a week of comings and goings, of scraping chests along the wooden floors, of cries from top to bottom. One look into the dining room told me what had happened.

Father never sat alone in this room, but today he did, slumped at the far end of the table. I approached him gently. He looked up. His collar was undone, and his eyes were dry but red. I pulled the chair next to his, turned it to face him, and sat. The room was dull, unlit.

He watched me settle, then held another moment before saying, "Your mother will be leaving to stay with your uncle in Boston." He blinked. "She will say her goodbyes to you later. I do hope she will travel safely in this weather."

"For Boston?"

He said, "I have told her what I told you." I supposed he expected me to answer, but all I did was stare. "It's funny," he said, in a muted way that projected anything but humor. "I don't believe she ever suspected, all these years, what I truly thought. Though day and night we spent together, she never read my true heart. Yet she is a wise and perceptive woman. It has made me realize"—and at this he chuckled morbidly— "just how skilled I was at fashioning the mask. I was that good." He shook his head, as if the judgment were still seeping in. Then he placed his arm upon the table for me to clasp, which I did. "I do not know whether I can ever win her back. But whatever happens, she is still your mother and, in time, she will return to be near you." Having heard these words, I must have visibly relaxed, because he leaned back then. "We should continue preparations," he said. "There is much still to do before we go. This time Sunday we'll be at sea."

I knew what this meant: that though she would not be traveling with us, she expected me to travel still, that it was best for me to do so. Otherwise she would have claimed me and taken me to Boston. She, too, feared the people's reach, feared that even in Boston I might not be safe.

Which is what in fact she tearfully said when later she returned from some final errands and Father gave us privacy. We spent a quiet hour together, then she was gone. I wondered if she feared for her own safety but would rather risk her life than spend another day with Father.

That evening thunder and lightning came. The storm flashed and boomed and shook the house. I was glad of the roar, which no doubt made inaudible my groaning sobs.

On Saturday all that remained of the storm were clouds and drizzle. Our annual celebration was almost over. Shops would ready for the coming week and for Market Day. Decorations would fall. Yesterday the Declaration had been read in rain and under heavy skies. Perhaps people were eager to resume their lives. Perhaps that is why they started walking differently, at least those I saw on Chestnut and on Walnut. On the sidewalk near the prison, I came upon a pile of dampened, darkened sheets of the *Peep Hole's Daily*. All week, distracted by the festivities, the news had only mentioned Teacher Scotes. But the front sheet of the pile ran a synopsis of the trial, the opening lines of which referred to Monday's scheduled execution. I imagined pages north and south featuring similar articles this day.

When I arrived, Keeper Daniels was escorting someone out of solitary, a man I did not know. He gestured me in at the entrance and closed the bars behind me. Teacher Scotes was already sitting, ready for me, when I appeared.

"What shall we discuss today, my friend?" he asked.

"I have a ready topic." I told him what it was, using an introduction I had rehearsed and trying to forget that my minutes with him were dwindling. "We have considered independence," I said, "and what it might consist of. This took us to the concept of 'rights' as being the protection of that independence. There is, therefore, a topic that follows from the prior two."

"And what would that be?"

"The form of government necessary to implement this idea of rights."

With sudden animation he exclaimed, "Take care, Palleias—you have developed a true passion for these inquiries!"

In no mood for teasing, I continued. He seemed regretful of his outburst and matched my serious tone. I put the question to him baldly, in a way he never liked. I asked, "So if democracy is not the proper means, which form of government is?"

He feigned reflection. Then he said, "You have demonstrated such an excellent capacity to analyze these matters, I am inclined to boomerang the question back to you."

"And take great joy in doing so, I'm sure," I said. "Still, I'd rather you address it because I have no answer and am impatient of one."

"Impatience is an unproductive quality where philosophic inquiries are concerned."

"Yes," I said, somewhat cruelly, "but we have little time together." To this he answered nothing. "I fear I will not be able to answer it," I said, "though I am eager to."

"I believe you, that you are eager."

"Please then, indulge me."

"Very well." Then he said, just as Father had, days earlier, "Regarding your question, alas, I have not answered it myself," upon which I likely appeared incredulous. Later, after he was gone, I considered these words anew, as I did much of what he said that week. He was a man whose sentences sometimes could be deciphered variously. With the benefit of hindsight, I came to believe that I misinterpreted his claim that he had not answered the question himself. At the time I thought it meant he did not know. "Come," he said, "let us take up the question together."

We spent the next half hour going back and forth, he interrogating, me answering, sometimes in a word or two. He put questions to me like, What would such a system have to be? And, How would that be done? And, To whom would we assign that role? By the end, my passion for answers, as he called it, was more aflame than ever yet I was hardly more informed.

Had not a group of reporters arrived soon after, announced by Keeper Daniels down the hall, I could have kept him at it. I think he might have liked that. He seemed invigorated and, as on the day before, approached the bars to stand near me. Just then it hit me, as if I *had* forgotten—this would be the last I'd ever see him.

Tears welled, and he smiled in answer. "I wish we had more time together too," he said, knowing it would decrease my pain to hear it. "But time is finite for us all, and in the end, I had the pleasure of far more time with you than I ever anticipated having, last year, when you left me then." I withheld speech in order not to weep; to have opened my mouth would have been to release a torrent. He went on, "And had I not ended up here, who knows? We might never have had these marvelous conversations, you and I. I can think of no better way to have spent the time. You have made this week bearable to me." My eyes streamed. There was not two feet between us. I began to shudder exhalations, and still I could not speak. He regarded me warmly. He put his hand through the bars at shoulder height and bade me take it, which I did. "I predict great things for you, Palleias."

I burst out tearfully, "I feel that I am losing a father!"

He squeezed my hand. "Be a father to yourself."

At the finality of his words, my knees almost gave. I knew that I should leave him then, but I could not, so he withdrew.

"Goodbye, Palleias," he said.

CHAPTER 39

I exited the small building, the place other than our house where I had spent the week—in person and in spirit. But for a few brief excursions westward—during which I had felt the silence not of life but of VOP, this being the lone week in which the air from the Schuylkill to City Centre was not regularly sounded with the calls of "Aye" and "Nay"—I had confined myself to the city's east.

Left to do was just walk the short distance home, yet I could hardly place one foot before the other, as if dragging a chain. The drying skies would mean an easier time loading today and sailing tomorrow. By evening the possessions we were taking would be dockside, where the merchant ship awaited. Most everything we would leave behind, secured by people Father trusted and who would benefit from his gratitude, and we would travel free of charge. In fifteen days we would set up residence, and for months, at least, we'd stay away. Such was my course. It moved me not at all. Each step I took was one away from where I wished to be and toward nothing that drew me. So instead I wandered, as if to forestall that course. Eventually I went home.

There I encountered Father, who seemed of similar mind. He reported that he had met with Dean Albright, who had agreed to stand in and vote on his behalf. Being a friend, head of the State University, and Professor of Law and Philosophy, he was most qualified. He and his family would occupy and maintain our house, enjoy access to our library, and, I had to believe, curry our favor. It was a sensible precaution because an empty house invited mischief, no matter how watchful the police. These days, there was more mischief than they could contain.

For some reason, Father felt the need to explain this arrangement to me again, and in his labored movements throughout the house, he, too, seemed drained—he gestured sluggishly; his expression was not lit in discussing what would stay and go. Like me, he seemed to feel not the animating power of a purpose he embraced but the forced propulsion of bitter duty. How clearly do our bodies know our minds, for how dead or driven can be our actions according to our thoughts! The cause of his ennui was his break with Mother and the confession of his approach to guiding me. Nearly thirty years of life and vision had dropped away. For me the same. Blocks away Teacher Scotes neared the end of life, and here mine was ostensibly just beginning. But it did not feel so.

That evening, in the darkness, our trunks would be collected by a crew of stevedores sent on our behalf. There was little more to do till then, so Father left to perform some final errands and take a last look around. This city meant as much to him as to anyone. I might have done the same but instead retired once more to the library, which almost beckoned, and took the high-backed chair adjacent to the shelves. The room was bright, though the sun remained enshrouded. The tall windows drew gray ramps of light across the walls. Being there, I wished I had—and wondered why I had not—spent more time in this very spot. It was not that I was disinclined, but perhaps I had not sufficiently valued my own inclinations. At any rate, Father would not have approved.

Next to me were shelves of heavy volumes that had rested side by side for two generations, since being placed there by Doctor Franklin. I reached for one and realized that the impulse sprang from the first real desire I had experienced since leaving the prison. The book sat heavily in my hand. I breathed in waves of loss and loneliness.

To let the feelings come where normally I would turn away, I returned the book and just sat. I feared the evening's too-quick passing. In a way, my task was simple. All I had to do was not think, to distract myself and let time pass, and the dark would come and then the light, and we would board the vessel, and all would go as planned. This, after all, was how I usually settled matters, large and small, but sitting there, the chair against my shoulders like a cloak, I knew that I could not behave that way again. There was a decision to be made, and it was mine to make.

I straightened and scanned the volumes again. One caught my eye. Incongruously thin, it sat in a row of compilations of the legislative proceedings of our states before the Revolution. Its spine said *Essays of John Adams*. I pulled it and read the table of contents. At the bottom was the last essay Lawyer Adams had written before his death in the Occupation of Philadelphia in '77. It was entitled "Thoughts on Government."

Teacher Scotes had met Lawyer Adams and once, during our travels, had mentioned him respectfully. This should have prompted me to seek what we possessed of his writings, but I had not.

According to the scholarly introduction, Lawyer Adams in his day had been considered most knowledgeable on the topic of constitutions, and many compatriots had solicited his opinions. Given the exchange that Teacher Scotes and I had had that very morning on the hows of state as against the whys, on the necessary institutions and their responsibilities, I considered it serendipity to have found the book, and I read until the ambient light had dimmed. Outside of university I was not a frequent reader and was often slow about it but today went slower still, reconstructing sentences, seeking almost to converse with the mute pages. After some time, having finished with the first essay, I read others in like manner. I admit that even on that somber day, it was a pleasure to be sitting so, alone and absorbed. Perhaps, just perhaps, for that one moment, I felt as Teacher Scotes daily did. Words are like a window onto understanding, and the words on those pages addressed the very questions I had raised with him. But they offered observations only, fascinating ones, though with few specifics.

They were not the observations that were debated at our founding conventions in the eighties, where all talk was of constitutions—nearly every word of print and chatter. We had instead based our National Constitution on the most democratic state constitution of the time: Pennsylvania's. We considered it the most Athenian. But the words of Lawyer Adams contradicted what we'd done. His vision was of a legislature checked, its powers dispersed and greatly limited, not coalesced into one center and made total, as was true of our Assembly. This was why his words likely were proscribed; they were not unlike those for which Teacher Scotes had been condemned. From then till now, such ideas had frightened us—threatened, we thought, our traditions and our lives. And so perhaps they did, because if the words were right, then we were wrong, and if we were wrong, Teacher Scotes would die an unacknowledged savior, rejected by the very people he might have saved—perhaps just as Lawyer Adams had and the others whom we could not read.

Some time had passed before I realized that a touch of weight had left me and some energy returned. Soon after, I heard Father unlatch the door below. When I heard him climb the stairs, I replaced the book, but he proceeded to the third floor and did not see me. To my surprise and pleasure, I found myself thinking that it would not have mattered to me if he had.

After dark we passed a quiet dinner. Our trunks had been taken. He encouraged me not to worry, that all would be well. My equanimity comforted him, and I let on nothing of my day. Neither of us spoke of the recent changes in our feelings. When he inquired about whether I predicted I would sleep, I lied and said I would, and in response to the same inquiry from me, he lied that he would also.

In fact, I slept not at all. There was a decision to be made. Words to that effect had formed themselves within me. Only days ago with Teacher Scotes, I had argued that others cannot decide for us, in any meaningful sense. Thus, Father had not decided that I depart with him tomorrow—I had. He had not decided that I be a representative—I had. He had not decided what I should say and do—I had.

First at midnight, then upon every hour after that, the Democracy Bell chimed its standard three times, signifying the final twenty-four hours of our yearly celebration. At its fifth occurrence, the windows brightened, and I rose and leaned to see the view. Beyond our secluded courtyard, the distant ships at anchor pointed their dark and naked masts to the pale sky, while the patchwork of brick rectangles between me and them obstructed their massive bellies. One of those ships awaited. It quartered our possessions and reserved cabins for us both.

But it would carry Father only. It would not carry me.

At six, as he had promised, Dean Albright arrived. Father embraced him at the door. I watched them from the landing one floor up. When Father eyed me there and saw that I was still undressed, he bade Dean Albright wait below, then calmly climbed the stairs. Watching me and not the steps, he reached the landing safely nonetheless, and I could tell from his benign expression that he was not anticipating what I was about to say. I backed into the library to give us privacy, and we moved no farther than the threshold.

"We must make haste, Palleias," he said gently. "Our ship is set to sail."

A faint tremble filled my arms, but I forced myself to say it. "I am sorry, Father, but I won't be going with you."

He blinked and stared, as if he had no option but to wait upon my speaking.

I told him that I had lain awake all night considering and had come to a conclusion: I did not wish to abandon Teacher Scotes but wanted to assist him however I could. I was in part responsible for what had happened, and justice demanded of me some recompense. I did not know, I said, whether he would care to see me further, but I would present myself and accede to his wishes. Most of all, I said, I sought his presence, even if for one more hour.

He took this in, eyes wide. Then he said softly, his eyes still wide but dimming, "I had told myself that hereafter I would leave you to your own resolve. I did not expect to be tested so severely and so quickly."

I did not respond.

"Please reconsider," he said. "I could not bear it if something happened." It was difficult, but I channeled all my energy into projecting firmness. Silence was my answer. A sadness overcame him, as if it had resided just below the surface. "When losses come," he said, "they come in barrels."

I told him that I wished to visit Mother, that I would stay in Philadelphia just till Tuesday or so, when I would leave for Boston, so we would still require the services of Dean Albright. I offered to arrange to receive Father's letters if he would rather address them here than there and that I would reply with haste.

"You will be no safer in Boston," he said, "and you might lead the clamor to your mother."

I hadn't thought of that, which he could tell from my expression.

"I will try to hold the ship till Monday night," he said, "and perhaps you and I can depart then—after he is gone."

I admit that for another moment I was tempted, but I said, "No. You must depart today. You may not get out tomorrow."

"We will take that risk together."

"Father, you know they cannot hold the ship."

"For us, they may." With every line, he seemed more cheerfully deceived about this change of plans.

"Go, Father," I said. "I cannot leave on Monday or any day thereafter."

He eyed me at length. Gently, he said, "I fear more for your safety than my own." He spoke as if considering his own words. Then his glance turned inward, as if he were witnessing the play of some internal, private theater. He said, more firmly, "I have no advice to give you, Palleias, with respect to the dangers you may face. They might be extreme." I did not answer. At last he said, with a kind of forced bravado, "If you will stay, then I will stay. At least we can defend ourselves together."

In his voice was hesitation. All along I had believed him when he said that staying could lead to his arrest and trial, and I did not doubt it now.

He was at far greater risk than I, and we both knew it. For me, the moment was bizarre. Insisting as I was on hewing to my plan, I was experiencing a kind of frightened exhilaration at the prospect of for once being on my own, as if I both wanted and did not want it. Then it came to me, what I could say to make him leave. I said, "Father, if you stay, it will only give them greater reason to link me with what you did and it will endanger me even more."

After a long moment, he exhaled. "What are you going to do?" he asked.

I knew he was referring to the coming months, but I responded otherwise. I told him that I did not want to be a representative and, consequently, it no longer mattered how I was perceived. I said I did not know yet what I did want but that when ready, I would set a course. I asked him not to worry about my future.

He said, "It is mostly all I've ever done."

He held his ground, when he should have gone. Delay only imperiled him. In contrast to the day before when parting company with Teacher Scotes, it was not lost on me that I would have to end the meeting.

"Goodbye, Father," I said.

Then he was out the door, beneath a broad-brimmed hat, and I went down to find a bewildered Dean Albright in the foyer, awaiting me. He was a heavy-lidded, heavy, round-faced man, in too thick a coat for summer. He seemed at a loss for what to say. I thanked him for his service and reassured him that he could bring his family presently, that I would not be in his way. He demurely nodded his understanding.

I am not sure why, but before I left, I mentioned what I had been reading—I knew that he was aware of the contents of our library—and of my interest in philosophy. I went so far as to suggest that I might someday wish to earn a position at the university, where I could likewise investigate and teach subjects similar to what I had been reading. Dean Albright seemed supportive of my interests while being noncommittal. This was not surprising, given who I was and who my father was, and who had inspired me. He did explain (regrettably, he said) that the topics I described were of course prohibited but that there were many related ones that I might teach instead. I thanked him for his advice and candor.

I left for the prison and, with each step, walked into a kind of void, away from everything I knew and toward I knew not what. I became unusually aware of my surroundings. The air was cool; the sky, freshly blue. Groups of early churchgoers passed, bonneted women and necktied men, the particulars of their appearance registering as they brushed by. Beneath my feet the sidewalk rolled. On the street bridles jangled and hooves clapped hard upon the shining stone. I had walked these streets for years without the walking ever feeling like this.

At the prison Jailer Douglass raised his head from his ledger and seemed startled by my presence. "Young Palleias," he said. "I did not expect you here today."

"Nor did I," I answered.

After an energetic shuffling of pages on his table and a straightening of his coat, he led me as he had each day down through dark and into light and over to the forbidding door of solitary.

Today a group poured out as we arrived. I recognized none of them. When they had passed, he held the iron and said, "We can go in, but there are others there."

A group of men and women with Keeper Daniels crowded the landing. They struck me as of the lower and middle sort, dressed plainly and partly soiled. Keeper Daniels heard us climbing from the entrance and, when we reached him, prodded the rest toward the upper flight so that we could pass. I held the landing. At the far end of the narrow hallway, from the cell opposite, others peeked out. Above them the small square of light through the far window shone brighter than it had the days before. Jailer Douglass bade me go ahead, and I arrived at Teacher Scotes's cell, between him and the group that had been conversing with him, cell to cell. He himself was standing at the bars, so as to minimize the distance to the others.

"Palleias," he said. There he stood, a kind of apparition that I had not expected to see again. I could tell at once that he knew not what to make of my appearance.

"I have come," I said, "to spend more time with you, if I may."

He regarded me, seemingly perplexed. A man behind me said, quietly but gruffly, "Wait your turn." Then Teacher Scotes looked up beyond my shoulder. "Friends," he said, "this, as you may know, is my friend Young Palleias." I turned and greeted them perfunctorily, thankful, as I sometimes was, for my political rank.

When I turned again, he said, "I did not expect you today." I could tell that he was speaking obliquely, mindful of the others. When I hesitated for the same reason, he addressed the group again. "Good people, would you kindly leave us a minute? I will ask Keeper Daniels to allow you back, and we will resume our conversation."

They grudgingly squeezed behind me. One man muttered that he had waited days to be granted entry. When they were gone and Keeper Daniels had herded them and the others who were waiting down the stairs, I faced Teacher Scotes.

"I am not leaving," I said. "I was hoping to see you today and be with you tomorrow."

"So you are leaving on Tuesday, then?"

"No. Nor any day thereafter." Not an hour before, I had said the same words to Father.

He regarded me further and without apparent joy. It seemed a second moment in which he and Father had reacted similarly. "And your Father?"

"He left this morning."

He stepped away from the bars and sat upon the bed. He seemed to think a while.

"I wish to spend as much time with you as you will allow me," I said. "And I wish to be of service, if there is anything I can do. Even if you don't accept my guilt, I wish to be of service anyway." He seemed to take this in. "You're not worried about me, are you?" I asked.

"The reasons your father chose to leave are sound," he said.

I nodded. "Who are all these people who continue visiting?"

"Strangers, mostly. They are the people, Palleias, who for some reason have taken a fresh interest in me." There was a pause. Finally he gave a smile but did not rise. He looked very tired. "Please do visit as often as you'd like. It will be a welcomed comfort."

I left him then so that the others could return. All day they came, in groups of eight or ten. Apparently they had been coming all week. I myself returned a few times that day and spoke with him for as long as was possible. We talked of nothing, really, just of what he had been discussing with his visitors and his thoughts on his confinement—nothing like our conversations of the last few days. I told him that Dean Albright would be staying with me at our house. I had the urge to tell him of my reading and how it bore on our investigations, but this being his last day but one, I felt that all topics were for him to raise. At one point Ansea and Sophia arrived, and they, too, seemed surprised by my presence.

That day the prison was to me like the hub of some great wheel. I would leave it, venture off to home or tavern for a meal or just to walk, and return. The beauty of the sun-filled day was incongruous but not unwelcome. As I ventured, I tried to glean reactions from others to my presence, but I detected little. They recognized me; this I can always tell. But perhaps they knew to conceal their reactions. In a way, it was the first day I had ever spent alone, free of obligation or anchor. Away from the prison, I could drift at will, not unlike Teacher Scotes once had.

Though I had earlier offered to assist in any way, that day Teacher Scotes mentioned my offer not at all. Only on the next did he ask of me something that, at the time, I could not understand.

CHAPTER 40

The day had come. I left the house at dawn and, despite the hour, still passed through the back gate, cut over one last time to Fourth by Chestnut, then to Walnut—from there, a single block to go. As quiet as the house had been, so was the city. The light was gray; the trees, still; the air chilled, almost cold. Nothing moved, as if to match the disposition of the massive prison that lay ahead, awaiting my last approach. Jailer Douglass had approved my coming early today. That meant the chance to be with Teacher Scotes from dawn to dusk, when by law he had to drink.

I stopped, however, when I reached the opening in the wall.

On the grand steps above were thirty or so people, seated, standing, scattered, in groups of three or four or alone. I recognized a few. There was Miller Offley, Weaver Logan, Brickmaker Grellet. Mrs. Foulke, Farmer Foulke's wife, sat hunched on a step by herself, and not far from her stood Machinist Clark's daughter—virtually everyone I had met with just before the trial. Others I didn't know. They were waiting to be let in, dressed better than in work attire. It was a different crowd from the ones earlier in the week. This, seemingly, was a gathering of friends. And there, near the top and on the left, was Xephon himself, chatting quietly with a group of younger men and women.

At first no one saw me, and I hesitated to advance. Then heads began to turn. I thought to acknowledge those I recognized, but I saw no smiles, though certainly they recognized me. A few who had been sitting stood.

Finally Xephon saw me too and stepped down swiftly in approach. He gestured as he got closer. "Palleias, come," he said, then to my surprise embraced me. Over his shoulder I saw several others witness our embrace. He guided me up to where he had been. "I am glad to see you," he said.

He introduced me to the group he had been standing with. They all looked not twenty years old, and their eyes were red more from the occasion, I suspect, than the hour. We stood high upon the hard steps in the chill, before the grand door. The others, all around, still regarded us. Some appeared bewildered; some, distressed. I could tell that Xephon was aware of this, was not surprised, and anticipated no objections.

"We should be entering soon," he said to me.

"I am not sure I am welcome."

"You are most welcome."

"Who are these people?"

"Close friends, here at his invitation."

Then a latch sounded and the large doors swung, revealing Jailer Douglass in the opening. Without a word we entered, and the jailer led us for the first time not into the courtyard but through the front hallway and down a staircase, to one of the larger cells in a wing of the main prison. Keeper Daniels was at the open door and stood aside to let us enter.

Sitting together on a small bed at the back were Ansea and Sophia; they we filed in: Xephon first, ducking, then me, then the rest. There was no other furniture, but a blanket was spread on the floor. The walls were high and whitewashed. The eastern light from the hallway was not unpleasant. Teacher Scotes stood beside his wife and daughter. He embraced us each in turn and said our names. Xephon and I circled to the back.

When everyone was in, he said, "Friends, thank you for being here," and he sat upon the blanket, followed by Sophia on the bed, in the arms of

Ansea. The rest of us, even the ladies, sat upon the floor. Shoulder to shoulder, front to back, we filled the space before them. Ansea and Sophia appeared remarkably at ease. Perhaps Teacher Scotes had implored them to be so.

He had been moved from solitary, allowed to spend the last night with his family and his last day among friends. Such leniency for a capital conviction was rare. Father may have even approved this arrangement before he left. I didn't know. At the sight of Teacher Scotes, some appeared to be restraining tears. Those who outside had been eyeing me were doing so no longer, as if Teacher Scotes's acceptance of my presence negated their right to be concerned.

Sitting, Teacher Scotes looked us over. He seemed tranquil but watchful. The rest of us, I could tell, were at a loss for what to say. Someone sobbed. "Please," he said. "There is no need for that." Then he said, "You honor me by coming. And your distress is proof of your love. But I hope you will believe me when I tell you that I am calm and now that you are here, feel greatly heartened." He showed his palms. "Come, let us use this occasion to do what otherwise might be forbidden. We have an authorized gathering, a chance to speak together in a way we otherwise could not. A chance to speak our minds and share a last exchange, with no worry of who might be listening to approve or disapprove." Though no one looked my way, I wondered if they agreed. "Rather than mourn," he said, "let us glory in our final meeting. So," he ended, "what shall we discuss today?"

People looked around. That question at that moment from this man caused two of the younger boys to wipe their eyes. "Friends, friends," Teacher Scotes said. "Please do not weep for me."

"We weep also for ourselves," a man in the middle said.

"I could not remain with you forever," Teacher Scotes said, gently. "There had to come a day when we would part. But if you choose to remember me, I will remain with you for as long as you wish."

There was a pause. "How can we be of service to you?" someone asked.

"You are, by being here," he answered.

A man, in a low but urgent voice, said, "Perhaps it is not too late to free you, Teacher Scotes. Please, I beg you!"

"I thank you for your friendship, which I know is true." Teacher Scotes addressed the man. "But please, let us not spend our last day discussing what I do not wish to."

The man bowed his head, and I could feel the resignation in the room.

A white-haired man said, "Can we assist with arrangements for your burial?" at which I blurted, without a thought for what I was saying, "I can assist with that." I don't know why I said it; it may have been a kind of boast about my influence.

Teacher Scotes looked at me and smiled. A few others turned their heads, but just in profile. "Not all of you have met Palleias," Teacher Scotes said. "He and I are old friends, and I hope you will get to know him better soon."

"With respect," a woman at the front said to Teacher Scotes, her voice restrained, "is it wise to have him here?"

Teacher Scotes spoke over their heads to me. "Palleias, is it wise for you to be here?"

Now a few heads did turn. I wished for them to see me differently, but I knew this was unlikely, at least right then. I said as humbly as I could, "So long as you wish it also, there is nowhere I would rather be."

"Then I think the question answered," Teacher Scotes said to the room at large.

Xephon, sitting next to me, turned and, in as low a voice as he was capable of, said, "Teacher Scotes will be cremated." Cremation as a means of disposal was new. There was but one crematorium in the state, and apparently the man who founded it was in the room. Even in death, Teacher Scotes valued innovation.

As if to relax the group and bring good feeling, Teacher Scotes addressed us individually, recounting particulars of our lives or virtues he admired. On occasion he would say, "Ansea, Sophia, you may not know this" and then tell of something one of us had done. When he got to me, he said, "And Palleias here has risked his safety to be among you one last day." I thought it an exaggeration but was pleased to have his praise among this group.

When he had mentioned everyone, he addressed all of us as one. "Now tell me what you have been working on."

One by one the others answered, discussing projects underway at work and home—tests and trials and investments. When the chain reached the young Clark woman, she told of an upgrade to the turbine that drove the main shaft to their manufactory, which she was overseeing. Xephon, who was last before me, said that he was outlining his work on household and business management. I touched his sleeve, planning to whisper that I would like to read it someday, but he did not acknowledge me, as if dividing his attention just then would have been disrespectful. Then it was my turn, and I was forced to say, "At present I am contemplating what to take on next."

About midmorning Ansea and Sophia left and returned with some apples and bread for refreshments. At midday they brought meats and cheeses and some cider. Teacher Scotes ate nothing, as he sometimes did when wanting to remain alert. But he seemed to enjoy our eating together, and as the hours passed, the mood lightened and became more like that on any day of following him.

Eventually the conversation turned to the injustice of what had happened and to how any of us, or anyone, could survive given how things were going—the decline, the restrictions, the hysteria that daily slid around us.

"That seems a worthy topic," Teacher Scotes said. "One on which I'm sure you all have much to share."

Then began a kind of orderly confessional, with everyone speaking of how they coped. It was astonishing to hear and most illuminating. As I listened, I tried to commit their words to memory. "I go about my business," one man said, "and choose my friends wisely. And I never ask my rep for anything."

"I improve the running of my farm as best I can," another said, "and do not ask whether what I do is allowed. If challenged, I deal with the consequences, but till then I do not worry."

"I spend each day honing my craft. No matter what's to come, my skill will always serve me."

"I congregate each week with those I love—friends and family who share a bond—and together we describe what we aspire to, no matter the world around us."

"I assert what's mine and make them steal it openly, if they are willing. I say, 'This belongs to me, and if you think otherwise, you'll have to take it. I will not give it to you.'"

"I refuse to serve anyone who participates in the passing of some act against me, so when I discover them in my coffeehouse, I ask them to leave. I have since encountered several like-minded patrons who discovered me as a result."

"I do not think of such people too much. They can push for this or that, but most of it comes to little."

One man said, "I follow the example of Teacher Scotes and converse on like topics with others, from time to time—and discreetly."

A few when their turn came glanced at me, as if still uneasy about speaking in my presence, especially when confessing illegalities. I made a point of showing only camaraderie and no alarm. Teacher Scotes listened only, as if he had departed already and wished to leave us to ourselves. But he took pleasure, I could tell, in their company, in who they were.

They continued. "When crowds come to threaten my establishment, I block the door and shout that if rising prices are what pains them, then look to the Assembly and not to me, that the prices I pay to fill my shop are rising just as fast as theirs."

"If the reps transfer income back to me that they once took, I accept it but pursue nothing further from them."

When all but Xephon and I had spoken, Xephon said, "Perhaps more than most of you, I expect to be a target. Therefore, I will be leaving for a time but will return and hope that we can meet again." His words were received with only nods, in that same quiet acceptance in which others' words had been.

Then came my turn, and I knew that by holding off another moment, I might be spared. No one turned in my direction, as if to grant me leave either way.

Pressed together into this single cell, sitting cross-legged or with knees to chests, they had spoken without rancor, and their words had the timbre of the genuine. This was a different crowd, not only from those we encountered in the streets but also from those I had forever been engaging in my travels. Oddly, their air of individuality only seemed to deepen their connection to one another; their mutual affection and admiration was palpable.

They had followed Teacher Scotes after their own fashion, whether by his side or from afar. In their own ways, they were living as he taught, at pains to understand the good as best they could and to act on it. By example I imagined that they touched the lives of others, too, as they were touching mine. Yet so much had been taken from them, and so many rules dictated what they could and could not do. To hear them tell it, they engaged in politics only to defend their lives, not to take from others, and they lived as freely as they could within the constraints of our system. In them I saw a lot of Teacher Scotes. He as well as anyone had defined the life he wished to live, and he had lived it. This was his example; its greatest lesson was what his life had done for him, for him personally, not because of what *we* thought of him—God knows there were more who thought ill of him than well—but for what he thought of himself. By asking us, on this his final day, to discuss our lives, I think he hoped that we would inspire one another. If so, I wondered why he hadn't convened us earlier in the week and why he had invited those many groups of strangers to his cell.

These people who had come today—I wanted them as friends. I wanted to take a step toward things that were newly important to me. Something about their presence goaded me to challenge myself and take on problems that I wished to think about, goaded me toward better efforts. Thus I felt compelled to speak before the opportunity passed and made my best attempt.

"Your stories are an inspiration to me," I said. "As conditions have worsened, as the profits of your actions have become less your own, you have had fair excuse to stop and abandon your pursuits and use the laws to gain from others. But you have not done so. You have continued on. . . . I myself have accomplished nothing of note," I said. "I wish I had known you sooner and hope, for the nation's sake, that there are many like you. Here is *my* ambition, whether or not I can achieve it. I wish to understand the political system that can protect you from the votes that you endure today."

Whether they heard my words as friendship or as bluster, there followed a quiet that Teacher Scotes let settle. Then Keeper Daniels appeared in the doorway.

"Teacher Scotes, I am sorry to disturb you, but it is time to bathe." The light had dimmed and lined the cell in faint shadows. To the rest of us he said, "You may congregate in the yard till he returns."

A man implored, "Teacher Scotes, before you leave and then return to be subjected to this crime, I must tell you that I cannot stay to watch. I cannot do it. I hope you will forgive me. The law requires witnesses to the act, but I cannot be one of them. I humbly ask to take my leave and say farewell."

"Of course," Teacher Scotes said. "And any others who wish to go, I hope you will do so freely. Most of you traveled far to be here today, and Ansea, Sophia, and I love you for it."

A few others bowed their heads and expressed the same sentiment. But before we broke, and as if to delay the fateful separation, someone asked, "Teacher Scotes, is there anything we may say on your behalf to those who may ask after you?"

"The same as I always recommend," he said, "which is to profess little and look to yourselves. Let them see the goodness in you. Knowing that you were my friends, they will, justly or unjustly, associate your character with mine. I cannot think of a better way to be remembered." And as he still hadn't risen, we remained seated too, and he called across the heads to me. "Palleias, will you kindly remain with me, in this cell, before I leave to bathe? I wish to ask something of you." I nodded tentatively. Others looked around, as if surprised by this request and uncertain of whether they should rise.

Teacher Scotes saw their indecision. "Before you go," he said, "perhaps there *is* something more I can share. Keeper Daniels, may I delay a minute more?" Keeper Daniels withdrew.

"Our day together brings to mind a story," he said. "Or perhaps it is myth." He settled himself, and we did too. All was quiet. He began: "There was a village that long ago was threatened by its neighbor, a much larger nation led by a great king. The invading army approached, sending envoys to announce its intention and demand surrender. Facing subjugation or annihilation, the people trembled. All seemed lost.

"But then a man from the village, who had before kept mostly to himself, rode out alone to meet the army before the onslaught began. To hear it told, the man said to the warlike generals, behind whom stood a phalanx of thousands, tall upon their steeds, that the village they were about to overrun was small and poor. That their quest would therefore yield little in riches and less in honor. 'But,' the man said, 'I have heard much about your nation and the suffering of your own people on your vast but unprofitable lands, and I understand your passion to advance their cause. I know that this is what brings you here and to the other lands you claim. I imagine that your great king, whose unrestrained will governs you and every man here, who commands your forces and claims ownership of all your lands and dictates every word and deed to your people—this king, I imagine, is grateful for your noble service in furthering his desires. Still,' he went on, 'I cannot help wonder whether you have available to you another option, a nobler calling still, one that could enrich your own lives and those of your unfortunate compatriots even more greatly.'

"The lead general, bearded, dressed in mail and shining upon his barrel-chested horse, regarded the man impassively, as did his flanking officers, who were also plumed and bejeweled. 'What noble calling?' he asked.

"'I leave that for your consideration,' the man said, and he said no more but turned and rode back to the village.

"The army camped for three nights, not a quarter mile from the village. But it never attacked, and on the fourth day, it rumbled from the plain. The floating dust it left behind did not obscure what happened next, for some time later it was rumored that the king was overthrown, and his former nation forever lost its warlike character.

"Well, astonished by this turn of events, the people of the village bounded the man with revels. Where before they had hardly noticed him, they now pronounced him brave and wise and were loath to leave his side. More than giving thanks, they seemed in need of something further from him. This astonished and embarrassed the man, who could not calm or dismiss them. By the hundreds they gathered in the large clearing before his cabin where his cattle once grazed, and they said, as if beseeching him, 'Tell us what to do.' This happened almost daily, and as a result, neither the man nor any of the villagers could resume the business of their lives, even after the threat of subjugation was gone.

"Then, one day, the people gathered and waited for the man to fill his open doorway and, as they had each day before, said, 'Tell us what to do.'

"'I will tell you what to do,' the man at last responded. 'But first, to improve my counsel, let me make a study of the plants.' And he proceeded, over several days, to go about the village and its outskirts and examine the plants. Many of the villagers followed and observed him—touching, gathering, tasting by his side. When he was done, they regathered in the clearing of his cabin. 'I have made a study of the plants,' he said, 'and find that some can be eaten and some not; some are beautiful, some hearty, some grow large, some small. And I have noticed many other qualities besides.'

"In silence they considered what they heard, but their call did not subside. 'Tell us what to do,' they said.

"'I will tell you what to do,' he said. 'But first let me make a study of the animals.' And he proceeded over days to seek the nearby animals and examine them. Again the others followed and watched him and, when he was done, gathered again at his clearing. 'I have made a study of the animals,' he said, 'and find them to be of great interest: some friend, some foe, some strong, some weak, some a source of food and some of muscle. Like the plants, they too are various.'

"'Tell us what to do,' they said.

"'I will. But first let me make a study of the sky.'

"It went on like this for some time. When finished with the sky, he made a study of their buildings, and when done with that, their clothing. As he progressed, he noticed that the crowd was dwindling. One day he asked of the smaller group in his clearing, 'What has happened to the others?'

"'I apologize,' one said, 'but my son is among the plants, having witnessed you examining them.' 'I apologize too,' another said, 'but my wife and daughter are studying our buildings.' 'And mine, our clothing,' another said.

"Still, those remaining said to him, 'Tell us what to do.'

"In response he proceeded to a study of their writings and their art, their families and their associations. Then of their farms and crafts and fairs. At every gathering in his clearing, the group was smaller, which they explained as they had before: 'He is in our markets.' 'She is among our crops.' And still they asked him what to do.

"At last, one day a single man arrived at his clearing. He was young but not too young. He stood before the brave and wise man and said, 'Tell me what to do.'

"'Alas,' the other said, 'I cannot, for I have nothing left to study.'

"This response put fear into the younger man, who hesitated but persisted. 'Please,' he said. 'Tell me what to do. There must be something.'

"'I fear I do not know,' the man said. But seeing the other's look of anguish and not wanting to leave him in such a state, he added, 'Very well, do this then: go away and spend some time, and help me think of what else I may study.'

"So the younger man, hardly comforted but taking solace, went away and thought about the question he was asked. When he had spent what seemed a goodly time, though still without an answer, he returned to the man's cabin. But the man was gone and was nowhere to be found. Several times the younger man returned, but he never saw the man again. His cabin and possessions remained, but nothing else.

"For a time the younger man wandered aimlessly, anxious and uncertain. Of all the villagers, only he seemed at a loss. And this is what he noticed. In his wanderings, he observed the others among the plants and animals, the fields and farms and markets, together and apart, in work, in play, and in repose. They seemed to be thriving. They seemed happy. And he decided, That is what I will study: what makes them so, what makes it possible. Thus, at long last, after having begged the brave and wise man repeatedly to tell him, he knew what he should do. And that is what he did."

Keeper Daniels reappeared in the doorway. "Teacher Scotes," he said.

Teacher Scotes rose. "Kindly usher my friends into the yard, Keeper Daniels. I will be with you presently."

CHAPTER 41

The group filed out, Ansea and Sophia too. Those few who would not be returning embraced Teacher Scotes and restrained their tears. Xephon touched my back and left. Those remaining glanced my way before stepping into the hallway, leaving just us two.

We moved close together and away from the door. His eyes were moist, but he smiled. "This has been an illuminating week," he said. I could not speak. He added, "You might be interested to know that being alone with my thoughts, as you so often are in your travels, I, too, have taken to composing poetry."

This strange admission for a moment left me at an even greater loss. Then, to say something, I said, "Will you be sharing it with us?"

He chuckled. "Perhaps it is best I not be remembered for such amateurish dabbling."

"I myself am no longer writing poetry," I said.

He nodded and let a moment pass. More earnestly, he said, "I have thought much about what we have discussed this week. I have learned from you, Palleias."

"From me. That cannot be true. And anyone observing us would have said the opposite, I am certain."

He eyed me fixedly for what seemed too long a time. Then he said, "Things are sometimes not what they seem." I thought upon this and have done so many times since, as I have upon so many of his words. But

I gave no answer. Finally he said, "There is something I wish to ask of you."

Given Xephon's plan to leave, I had anticipated that he might request that I check on Ansea and Sophia from time to time, which I gladly would have done without his asking. And he did ask that, of sorts, though his specific request was much odder; he removed a folded sheet from his trousers, handed it to me, and said, "I would like you to purchase my house."

Just stunned enough to take the sheet, I unfolded it. It was a deed. I regarded it dumbly.

"The price I ask," he said, "is a single demos."

He explained: though the house could pass to Ansea legally, he did not trust its ownership to be secure because the representatives might take it for any number of reasons. But were I to own it, given my position and influence, her rights were less likely to be molested. Nevertheless, should something happen and I could not defend it, I was not to fret; he still thought this arrangement best.

I removed a demos note from my trousers and extended it. "Shall I pay it now?"

He took it. "Thank you, Palleias. For what you do now—and may do in the future." He reached and lightly cupped my neck. "Now I must go." And he left the cell.

I found my way to the courtyard, where his remaining friends stood waiting; only a few had departed. They eyed me as I approached. Behind them, the two-story amphitheater of workshops was quiet, and the early evening sunlight shone like fire upon the brick and grass. Perhaps they wanted to interrogate me my purpose or were waiting for me to offer, but they did not and I did not, and as it became clear that neither of us would, they returned to milling quietly or in silence.

Over to the side stood Machinist Clark's daughter, away from the others and by the tree-lined pathway to the main building, toeing the grass. Her cheeks were moist. I approached. She looked up and wiped her eyes, which were shining, dark, and round.

"It is a black day for us all," I said quietly.

She looked away. "Yes, it is. It is truly that."

"Have you been his friend for long?"

She took a breath. "He has known my father many years. It was he whom Teacher Scotes invited. But my father could not come and asked me to instead." She held a moment. "My father has taken ill and may not recover. I was thinking of him, too, just now."

"I am deeply sorry to hear it."

"You are kind to say so."

I recalled the day I visited. "What will happen to your factory?"

"He has left it in my charge."

This I found astonishing—given her age and gender—and simultaneously unsurprising, from the glimpse of her I'd had that day. Her situation brought to mind Teacher Scotes's concern about the fate of his own property. When she offered nothing further, I said, "Is there a way I may be of service?" In saying it, I did not expect her to want my help, and I only intended kindness, but hardly had I said the words than she turned and with some heat let out, "If you wish to be of service, you may leave us alone."

It was the reaction I was accustomed to—if not expressly, at least in sentiment from the people who had come this day and others like them. I was still my father's son and had as yet earned no other estimation. I understood the reaction well and did not begrudge it. It was for me, not them, to earn a different response.

Then she seemed to regret her words and looked up shyly. "I apologize," she said. "It has been an awful time."

To demonstrate my acceptance of her reaction, I returned what I hoped was a gentle reply. I said, "Having met your father and seen what you have made together, I find myself an admirer of you both, and cannot say I wish to leave you alone."

Gradually her expression softened, and she regarded me a moment. I smiled, and she did as well. "You are welcome to visit any time," she said.

Just then, from across the courtyard and the western wing of the prison came Teacher Scotes, escorted by Keeper Daniels, Xephon, Sophia, and Ansea. He was dressed in a fresh gray shirt and trousers, and his hair was moist. When they reached us, Teacher Scotes announced, "Ansea and Sophia will be leaving us now, in Xephon's care." They embraced, Sophia rising in her father's arms. Ansea's eyes grew teary, and in response, Sophia's did as well, as if she had been withholding so long as her mother did. Ansea took Sophia's hand and exclaimed, "Oh, Scotes! This will be the last you see of your great friends!" She appeared to be elevating our importance to him above her own grief, which I presume Teacher Scotes had asked her to suppress in public. They embraced again, and Xephon led them by the path to the stairs, where they disappeared into the darkness of the building.

The waning light of the enclosed courtyard told us that the sun had nearly set. We followed Keeper Daniels and Teacher Scotes back to the cell.

In our absence, someone had placed a pallet and the blanket on the bed. The overhead lamp was as yet unlit, and the walls were gray, as was our skin, which shone, like the whites of our eyes. No sooner had we assembled, all standing, than Jailer Douglass entered too, holding before him a pewter cup. We let him pass and make his way to Teacher Scotes, who stood with Keeper Daniels by the bed. Face to face with Teacher Scotes, Jailer Douglass said, "Teacher Scotes, you have been the noblest charge of any we have known, and it is with profound regret that I must announce to you that it is time."

"And you both have been honorable to me," Teacher Scotes said. "I have much valued our conversations and your gentle keeping. Had we met outside this place, I would have hoped to have been your friends." He placed a hand atop a shoulder each. "Now explain to me what I must do."

Jailer Douglass handed him the cup and instructed him to, once he had drunk, pace the floor until his legs grew stiff, then lie upon the bed.

He would feel the poison working but it would not be painful, and when it reached his heart, he would tranquilly expire.

But the moment the cup was in Teacher Scotes's hands, one among us yelled, "We will avenge your death! We will show no mercy to those who voted for it and to the people who defend such laws!"

Teacher Scotes addressed the man who spoke. "Good soul," he said, "if you assault the people generally, you will be avenging not a crime but an error. They have only acted on their ideals. Life itself necessitates ideals, and the people you condemn could only live by those that had been offered them." He addressed the rest of us. "Friends, if consolation will ease the pain of our separation, then remember that at last I will be free. Liberty has not been mine in life, but it may be yours. Look after one another and others like you that you will meet. For contrary to what is often said, the only true support is the friendship of an independent man."

And with that he looked us over once, raised the cup as if to toast, and said, "To a life well lived," then tipped the cup and drank. Seeing that—seeing that he had finished—we began to weep, despite ourselves. Teacher Scotes returned the cup to Jailer Douglass and walked some steps near to where he stood, and we gave him room. Then he lay upon the pallet, underneath the blanket, which he pulled to his chest. He looked to the ceiling and seemed in no distress. A moment later Jailer Douglass lifted the blanket from his feet and pinched his legs; Teacher Scotes reacted not at all. Then Jailer Douglass pinched his waist. In another moment he covered Teacher Scotes in full. We were led from the cell, and milling numbly in the courtyard, before we could bring ourselves to leave, we saw Teacher Scotes being carried toward the back of the prison.

I watched him go. When he was gone, what filled the emptiness within me was rage.

CHAPTER 42

Somewhere west of Haverford there is an unnamed stream. On one side is a yellow field; on the other, woods. The stream is traced by a narrow path, one person wide, though no one walks the path and would hardly have occasion to. A strong breeze ripples the grasses and rustles the leaves. Tall pines sway. Then there is calm. The sun is shining. Butterflies hover, settle atop thin stems, and pump their wings. Tiny creepers and nuthatches hop up and down the tree trunks. Another breeze arises, and the butterflies float and land again. When the breeze is absent, there is the soft burble of the stream. The sun is warm, not hot. It is afternoon.

High above, an eagle passes, floating upon a stream of its own; its white head can be distinguished. It traverses the field and disappears beyond the treetops. Then it returns and, even higher than before, circles above the field. It circles again and rises. A few more times it circles, then cannot be seen.

After it is gone, the strongest breeze yet arises and bends the grasses and the trees. The butterflies and birds fly with it.

First I registered the dimness and the fact of being in my own third-floor bedroom. Then I heard voices, agitated voices, as if coming from somewhere in the room. At the landing they were more distinct. I placed them at our entryway. In a hastily drawn pair of trousers and unfastened shirt, I went down.

In the doorway, his wife and daughter standing behind him and still in bedclothes, Dean Albright cinched his robe and nervously faced a group who were yelling to see Father. Hearing me on the second floor, they watched me descend and position myself beside Dean Albright. On our front steps stood four untidily dressed men, with perhaps another ten men and women below them on the lawn. Dean Albright turned to me and with a strained equanimity said, "I have explained to them that your father is not here."

A hatted, bearded man on the threshold yelled, so loudly it caused us to start, "We demand to see Representative Antonyn!"

Someone from the lawn called out, "Push in and let's see for ourselves whether he's at home!"

Before they could, a constable emerged from our tunnel and ran toward us. Two more appeared behind him, followed by a much larger group of citizens who spewed like sewage from a pipe. The constable pushed his way up the steps, yelling, "Get back or I'll have you arrested!" The group stepped off, and the constable turned to face them. "Anyone who wants to spend the day in prison, remain on these premises and you will be shackled immediately." They backed away but did not leave the yard.

The constable turned to me. "Young Palleias, sir, I apologize. My men are getting organized now, and I am posting guards at both ends. Remain here, if you will. It is safest. They may try to get over the walls, but I don't expect so. They are all over the city, and what you see here is not the main of it."

"Who is all over the city, Constable?"

"The people, sir."

Violent clops and squeaks came from the tunnel, and then appeared a police wagon, causing the crowd to split and run around the house, toward the back entrance. Two officers pursued them. One young man, who hadn't run, backed against the carriage house and began writhing when grabbed by an officer who muscled him into the wagon. Then the wagon itself lurched and pursued the others.

The constable, who had been observing this, turned again to us. "Mind yourselves and be well." He ran off.

Behind us in the foyer, Dean Albright's wife and daughter clasped hands. I thought of Ansea and Sophia. I wished Father had been there to direct our course of action.

"I must leave," I said.

Dean Albright asked, "What could they want?" He looked dazed.

I leaned through the doorway. One step down from the landing was the discarded front sheet of today's *Peep Hole's Daily*. A headline read, "Teacher Scotes, Rest in Peace." A kind of shudder threw me sideways against the doorjamb. I went back in, sprinted up to my room, dressed quickly, and returned to find that no one had moved. Watching me ready myself, Dean Albright said, "I am required at Assembly later this morning." It did not seem a happy thought.

"Your family will be safest here," I said. "The police will guard the entrances. . . . I am sorry I cannot stay." I assured them I'd be back as soon as possible.

I hitched Betsy to the wagon, thinking I might need it, and led her through the tunnel, past the guard and onto Market Street. Though it was not a market day, the street was early bustling. People leaned from windows high above; the sky was pale above them, the air as cool as at yesterday's dawn. No awnings shrouded the sidewalks yet, and groups of twos and threes scampered past, as if eager to reach some unplanned destination. Light traffic approached me. Much more headed west. Far ahead a crowd that spanned the width of the street, blocking passage, marched away. To bypass them, I cut over to Chestnut, which also had frenetic movement, though at corners here and there, small groups surrounded speakers who yelled as if addressing an audience blocks away. I asked of Betsy a more urgent pace.

What I witnessed should not have surprised me. Drifting home last evening, I had seen them, though in that way of not truly seeing past one's preoccupations. With clearer wits I might have registered those who walked too quickly in the dark or who seemed aimless at an hour when they should not be. Instead I was for bed, for returning to my home of strangers and passing without repast or discussion to my room where I could hide in sleep, which I did not do well, as exhausted as I was and accosted now and then by muted sounds that normally would not rise at such an hour and that I also did not trouble myself to hear. They must have been amassing in the night.

This is sometimes how it happened. What would start as common gatherings, even protests and marches—the regular push and pull of our daily discourse—on occasion could explode into uprising, into the pressing of the people en masse behind some issue. Such times could frighten even Father, who was quick to say that the people were the ultimate force, that no police or army could stop them if they yearned intensely enough, and that though the currency of his role as representative was reason, such currency was worthless when facing flames. He assured me that such occasions were rare and did not detract from the nobility of our calling. From what I'd seen, they seemed not so rare. When the people's will was unambiguous, it superseded all—all the laws, agendas, procedures that otherwise governed us. After all, their will was ultimately the point.

What did they want? I did not know, but if their anger had to do with Teacher Scotes's death, it was tardy, and I was in no mood to credit them. The laws that killed him were passed with their support; the prejudice against him was of their making; the trial that convicted him they had manned. I also did not believe it. Whatever had been lit today had been smoldering at length, for reasons having nothing to do with Teacher Scotes's trial: people were out of work and spending more and more for less and less. More likely his death was just the match to the tinder.

What I did know was that I owed it to Teacher Scotes to find Ansea and Sophia and assist if needed and that the shortest route, across the bridge at Gray's Ferry, was not the route today, for it could readily snarl when multitudes were on the move. Instead I would cross at Market, which I returned to after reaching Broad, and though Market was busy at this end as well, buildings were fewer and people could spread on horse and foot more easily. Far ahead the bridge was only somewhat active, mostly marchers crossing in this direction. Betsy trotted. Nearing the bridge, I saw the amphitheater to the left, about a mile away, small and pink in the early sun, and already I could hear its crowd—a highly irregular sound, this early. Its curved sides appeared banded by two rows of tiny windows and, at the bridge, the open, horseshoe end became visible, its miniature VOP backed by the faraway trees. Shifting crowds already filled the seats, a faint roar went up, and oddly, it appeared that the stage was full as well.

Then we rumbled through the bridge and, clearing it, could resume our trot and reach Teacher Scotes's house in twenty minutes. Across Mill Creek and along the way, some marchers on the Darby Road called for me to stop and let them ride. I had to yell that I could not. When I reached the side road, I was glad to leave the main. In the clearing at its end, Teacher Scotes's house appeared.

All seemed quiet. I hitched Betsy and knocked. No one answered. After I announced myself and knocked again without response, I entered. The house seemed undisturbed. I called again for Ansea. The table in the main room was set, though the oven was cold and Sophia's bed was made. I tried to assess whether anything had been stolen, but their few possessions seemed in place—utensils, chairs, plates and pots, a book or two. A cone of sugar and bowl of butter remained as well. I went into the second room, which appeared in order too, though there again the fire was out. Then I noticed that only one of Ansea's dresses hung on the hooks, where I thought I had seen three or four before. I peeked back into the main room. Same for Sophia's: some clothes were there, but few.

I opened the back door. In the outside corner where the two wings met and Ansea had nervously positioned me last time, the subtle mound of earth seemed also undisturbed. If coin was buried there, it was at risk, in a spot too easily discovered, which I would have to discuss with Ansea and remedy. Their fields extended distantly from their wooded stream to their far stone walls. Neither Ansea nor Sophia was in sight where they might be minding animals and crops, though from where I stood, not all their land was visible. I would wait briefly to see if they returned and if they did not, ride home, tend to matters there, and return later in the day. If I did not find them then, I'd assume they were taking comfort elsewhere, in the wake of their loss, perhaps with nearby friends.

Still standing at the open back door, I heard Betsy whinny, then a commotion at the front. I went to a window on that side. In the clearing were five or six work-clad men and an aproned woman. Quickly they approached the house. Ansea and Sophia were not among them. I returned to the back door and latched it, then scampered to the other end of the front room and took up position, near the chimney and with the large table between me and the front door.

Without knocking, they stomped noisily into the house and, with alarm, saw me. The first two stopped abruptly, causing the next two to collide, forcing the last to squeeze into what little doorway remained.

The first one gaped. "Who are *you*?" he called, in a tone both aggressive and fearful. He had a gruff appearance: short, with bushy sideburns and a leather vest, though his hair and spectacles were more a book-keeper's, or ex-bookkeeper's. He used his walking stick to point in my direction. I felt suddenly the smallness of the space we filled.

"I am Palleias," I said. "And who might you be, sir?"

One of the men peeled off, disappeared into the second room, and returned. "No one is here," he said.

"Where is Teacher Scotes's wife?" the first man demanded of me.

I read the countenances of the rest. I neither sensed imminent violence nor trusted that all was safe. Craftsmen and women, I thought. Politely, I asked again, "Who, may I ask, is inquiring?"

The first man poked his stick in my direction. "I did not know I was required to answer to you," he said with an edge of fearful bluster.

"I am the caretaker of this property, on behalf of Teacher Scotes himself."

"He is Palleias," a man behind him said.

The first man frowned. "Yes, he said that. We've learned he has a name."

"I saw him at the prison," the man behind said.

The first man crooked his neck while continuing to eye me. "At the prison, eh?"

"Teacher Scotes called him a friend," the second man said, before I could respond.

The first man looked me over and lowered his stick, and along with it fell the tension in the room. Whatever mission brought them here this morning sat with them uneasily, more so for having encountered me. Their unwillingness to identify themselves could either be from malevolence or ill manners. I was glad that Ansea and Sophia were away. For a moment the men before me looked around, as if about to leave, then the woman, who had kept back, said, "He was also at the trial. I read about it in the dailies." Her tone was less friendly than the second man's.

The first man reexamined me. "You were at the trial. What were you doing at the trial?"

"He was on the stage," the woman said. "I read about it in the same account."

"On the stage, eh?" the first man said. "Might this be true, Palleias, friend of Teacher Scotes?" Now his tone was sly and mocking; he resumed the poking gesture.

"Sir," I said again politely, though this time with a wavering firmness, in an attempt to establish some authority, "I have given you my name and identified myself as the caretaker of this house, yet you have not introduced yourself or your colleagues here or shared with me your purpose.

If there is nothing I can help you with, then I am obliged to request that you leave."

"Colleagues," the first man said and chuckled. He craned his neck toward the woman without turning. "Where did he sit upon the stage?" he asked her.

"With the prosecution," she said and nodded.

He faced me. "The prosecution, then? You sought to prosecute him as a friend?" As if in concert, they all took one step forward but did not round the table.

The man who claimed to see me in prison said, "I was present when Teacher Scotes called him friend."

"This is very strange indeed," the first man said. He scratched a bushy sideburn. Another man, who had a kerchief tied around his arm, went over and leaned into the second room, then came round next to me, eyed me warily, and peered out the window to the back. Then another man approached and looked out as well. I greatly feared that they would leave to scour the fields and would notice the mound beside the house.

The first man said to me, "Where is Teacher Scotes's wife?"

"Like you, I gather she is not at home. What do you require of her?"

"But you know where she is?"

"I do not."

At last he said, "I will tell you, friend of Teacher Scotes, if friend you really be. We are here to ask her and her little girl to join us at Assembly, where we can together make the case for retribution. Today the reps will hear us, by God, and they will answer for what they've done, and they will bring the prosecutors to justice, and they will act to make it right!"

"Hear, hear!" three of them yelled. Another came over to look out the back window when the first two stepped away.

"The people have taken to the streets and are converging on Assembly now," the first man said. "Those responsible—all of them—will have to answer to us shortly."

The woman said, "His father is Representative Antonyn, one of the accusers." She sniffed and wiped her nose. "I read about it."

"You don't say," the first man said to the woman. "Your father is Representative Antonyn," he said to me.

Father had been right to flee. Not one day after Teacher Scotes was gone, the very thing he feared had happened. Had he been there, his life would have been in danger.

The first man thumped his stick on the floor. "What are we to make of you, Palleias? You are friend of Teacher Scotes and caretaker of his house, you say. Yet you join the prosecution at his trial, and your father is Representative Antonyn. So which is it?" He laid his stick and placed his hands upon the table, which scraped the floor and bumped my legs. "Are you friend or foe? Make your case, and we will listen. We are a small and modest tribunal of the people and will be heard today." Upon saying this, he tossed his head to indicate the others. They all looked at me.

When I didn't answer, the man with the kerchief around his arm said, "What might he be doing here if he were not a friend?" He had short black hair and grime above his collar.

"Removing evidence of his crime," another said.

The first man eyed me. Then he, too, walked to the window and looked out. Looking out he said, more to himself, "What might be here that you could want?" Then he addressed me directly. "What to do with you," he said.

"Hey," the second man said, now standing clear of the rest, "let's bring *him* instead. If he truly is a friend, he can speak with us on behalf of Teacher Scotes. If not, he can be judged along with the rest." At this suggestion, the others made approving noises. The first man, who hadn't looked away, raised his eyebrows.

I could claim that terror did not fill me, but it did—at what they might intend, at the thought of Assembly itself, at what I had already seen this morning. I could have fled, but that would have been futile and, once I was apprehended, likely to make things worse. And I felt anger—not so much at this ragged band of criminals for breaking into Teacher Scotes's house, threatening me, and demanding I accompany them, but more for what they represented. And what they represented was amassing now at the amphitheater. Then I thought that leaving with them would actually be a godsend, just to get them off the property till I could later remedy its vulnerability and learn the whereabouts of Ansea and Sophia, whom for the moment they seemed to have forgotten. So I objected histrionically, knowing it would make them press me all the more. When this time I demanded that they leave, they announced, "Oh, we will!" and grabbed me by the arm.

"This is how you address a fellow citizen—with violence?" I screamed.

"When violence is the rule, violence is the answer," the first man said.

Out front they steered me away from Betsy, claiming to have their own wagon around the bend and telling me I could return and get mine later. She watched me leave, lifting and lowering one hoof.

We reversed direction on the Darby Road, from whence I had come. Two rode on the bench, a man who drove and the woman, with the rest around me in the wagon. By now the crowds were thicker still and nearly all on foot; because of them, we could not make haste. Our wagon jostled. Those we pushed aside looked up to see. "Palleias," I heard someone say. "Palleias is with them." More calls followed distantly. The driver snapped the horses, who fell into a trot, and the crowd split further. Sitting close, the man with the sideburns grinned. "It seems you are famous. Or is it infamous?"

We turned and pressed our way toward the floating bridge. The eastern sun above the horizon made it difficult to see, but we could not miss them, descending the near embankment and climbing the far, and from shore to shore, the bridge was full and had submerged into the water. It was as if the entire population west of the city had decided to visit the Assembly this morning.

Perilously, we crossed. Again I heard my name called, but with what intent I could not tell, so I kept my gaze forward. The river sparkled and pulled us sideways; its rush below the bridge was nothing compared to the sound from just ahead. We reached a green and yellow field; the road ahead was dry; and up the hill and past the bend and now not far away, the amphitheater came into view. A great roar went up.

I was going to it.

CHAPTER 43

We crested the hill, and traffic slowed. We ended up hitching the horses fifty yards away because of the expanding impasse. The early sun lit the high curved walls in soft yellow. Shockingly, the crowds encircled the amphitheater like a moat, streamed into every entrance, and were thickest at the open end. They even filled the area behind the stage, from the back of colossal VOP all the way to the bluffs, dispersed throughout the woods. A few sat among the limbs to get a view. From inside came another roar.

The crowd immediately around us yelled and jostled but hardly moved. The lead man took my elbow. "Come on," he yelled. He pushed ahead, calling out, "Let us through! I have someone here who can right this wrong!" He looked at me and yelled, "Should I tell them who you really are?" He seemed amused. Through the force of his intention, we gained a step and then another. He yelled, "Let us through, friends, this man can help!"

Someone called, "Let them through!" The rest of his compatriots were pushing right behind us.

Eventually we reached the open end. Being the entrance for the representatives, it was normally secured with ropebands. Today twenty guards dressed in blue stood close, more to watch the crowd than steer it; they seemed to have given up their duties. They stood against the high angled wall, in the cooler shade beside it, where just the other side the most southern staircase rose beside the Georgia section. All around the guards, people pressed and jumped to see. We forced ourselves ahead till all became so compacted that our movement ceased. Forward, back, and side to side we rocked. Ahead was the scaffolding of VOP, the remaining stage in front, and beyond, the throbbing northern sections. The other seats were out of view.

Another roar went up, even louder this time. Still the man pulled at me. "Let us through!" he yelled.

"Stop pushing!" someone turned and yelled. "We all want in!"

"This man is a representative and must get to his seat! He is with us!"

Just as it seemed we were stalled, a thickset guard approached, using the end of his club to part the bodies. When he broke through, he was pushed and almost lost his balance. "I can help escort you," he said to the man holding me. "Where is the representative?"

"This man here," the man said. The guard looked at me. "We must get through," the man said.

"This man is not a representative," the guard said, tentatively.

"Of course he is," the man said and tried to pull again. "Help us through. We have to get him through."

"This man is not a representative," the guard said again and looked at me, as if uncertain what to do. I could tell that he recognized me but did not know what I required of him. We still swayed in the throes of the crowd.

"I would like to assess the situation, if I could, Sergeant," I told him. He regarded me a moment.

"Follow me, sir," he said, and we filled the space behind his large back and let him plow the way.

We finally reached the end of the wall and could fully see inside. Rising high before us, the long curve of seats, still gray in shade, was more than full. The crowd was standing and in colorful disarray, including in the aisles. I doubted they had confined themselves to sitting with others from their state. The Pit, from stage to seats, was also full. The stage itself also remained in shade—the sunlight had only yet clipped the treetops behind it and brightened the bluffs on the other side of the river—and on the stage the representatives stood stiffly terrified among people who stood with them, some of whom were dancing. Behind them pieces of scaffolding from massive VOP were down, and its long brass speaking horn, which normally reached from its cradle at the back up into the gigantic mouth, was torn from its support; its mouthpiece lay instead on the stage itself, surrounded by the crowd; visible through the bodies was a crouching man trying to speak into it. Others continued tearing at the boards. If a few more were to join them, the whole VOP could crash upon the stage, the crowd, and the representatives.

It was a mass of people such as I had never witnessed, in number or in manner—a manner that might have begun as rage but now seemed more like euphoria, perhaps because they had control. Their mood clashed with the cool and bright still morning. Nor had I ever viewed Assembly from this angle, as Father typically would. Every foot of the amphitheater was filled. It was a human mass inside a larger mass of semicircular stone, now a singularity. In the Pit the herald was trapped, his hands above his head. He was not yelling for order; it would not have mattered if he were. Instead he swayed with the swaying of the crowd. The same was likely true of us: having gotten in, it was doubtful we could get out.

The spectacle of the crowd startled even the man who had brought me here; he seemed to have forgotten to enforce his grip. The guard stopped pressing forward too.

"Make them pay for the law that killed Teacher Scotes!" someone shouted from the seats.

"Make them pay!" others shouted.

On the stage the greatcoated representatives stood stiffly, like large black chess pieces mixed among the rest. Perhaps half of them were present.

"Make them raise their hands if they voted for the law!" someone shouted.

"Raise your hands!" others shouted. "Raise your hands!"

People poked at the representatives to get them to raise their hands.

"Hold them accountable!" someone shouted. "They can't do this to us!"

"I can't feed my family!" someone shouted.

"Never mind your family—think of what they did to Teacher Scotes!"

"Killers!" someone shouted, and others joined in generally. Calls of "Raise your hands!" and "Killers!" followed all around, and the representatives struggled to keep their balance. One or two had fallen and were being pulled back up. At any moment they could be lost to violence, were the crowd to tilt that way. Only the Army could have quelled them, but no one dared pit the Army against the people, and the soldiers would have taken the people's side. I wondered what was occurring elsewhere in the city. Events seemed to be careering.

Someone shouted, "They won't raise their hands! Cowards!"

Calls of "Cowards! Cowards!" rang out. A great laughter followed, prompted by words I could not make out.

"Where are the prosecutors?" someone shouted. "Where are the prosecutors of Teacher Scotes?" The calling of his name was beginning to make me angry.

"Bring us the prosecutors!" someone shouted.

"Killers!" someone else shouted.

Calls of "Bring us the prosecutors!" and "Killers" rang out.

"Where is Lycon?" "Where is Antonyn?" "Where is Alcidia?" As their names were called, there was increased jostling everywhere, as if the people were searching. Evidently the searches were in vain. "Where are they?" "They are not here!" "Keep searching!" "There are not here!" "Cowards! They have fled justice!"

"Don't forget that clown Mathias!" someone yelled.

"Bring us Mathias!"

"Imagine that! A clown prosecutor!" someone else yelled. A great roar of laughter went up.

"A clown poet!" someone shouted. A more dispersed laughter followed.

Someone yelled, "There once was a clown named Mathias, who prosecuted men with great bias!" A heartier laughter followed.

"I call for a trial!" someone shouted.

"Try them all!" someone else shouted.

"Trial . . . trial . . . trial" came the chant.

"Let's try them right now, in absentia!" someone shouted. "Let there be a vote!"

"Herald!" someone shouted. "Call the vote!" There was laughter.

"Vote! Vote! Vote!" came the chant.

The herald had waded toward the stage and was attempting to liberate himself from the dancing, shouting, and arm-waving that had turned the Pit into a writhing body.

"I vote guilty!" someone shouted.

Under our legislative rules, representatives could not be prosecuted for votes in Assembly. And no trials took place here; trials were the purview of the courts, which had rules. But this was not a day the people would abide by such procedures or by much of anything. As Father sometimes said, what a man would not do singly, he'll do in a crowd. I was experiencing something else Father had said: that within the wild emotions and inchoate impulses of the crowd, there is a latent sentiment, and whoever supplies the words for that sentiment leads.

Just in front of me, the big guard turned and yelled, "Palleias, sir, what are your instructions?" Again we were bumped from the left and right. Next to me the short man with the bushy sideburns still held my arm but seemed dazed. Right behind me his associates gaped. I saw the opportunity to extract myself and return to Teacher Scotes's house, secure it, and rescue Betsy. And escape witnessing any more of this madness.

I yelled to the guard, though he was feet away, "You have done me an honorable service, Sergeant. I am in your debt." My yelling must have aroused my captor from his reverie, because he turned. I yelled at him,

"We are not safe here." In response he did not speak, as if not registering my meaning, but his grip on my elbow tightened. With my free hand, I attempted to pry his off, but he pinched tighter. "Release your grip, sir!" I yelled. Someone from behind grabbed my shoulders.

The guard, witnessing this, yelled, "Palleias, sir."

"Palleias?" I heard my name called from the other side of the guard. "*Palleias?*" A man wriggled his way into our circle. To arrest his advance, the guard reached his hand across his chest. It was Dean Albright. From the seats beyond, a great roar went up. He tried to yell over it: "Palleias!" Then he swiped at the guard's arm. "*Unhand me, sir.*" The guard looked at me. I nodded, and the guard dropped his arm. "You should not be here," Dean Albright yelled at me. He was not wearing his greatcoat. Then he noticed that my arm was being held. "What is the meaning of this?"

"You should not be here either," I yelled back.

"I arrived to take the oath not a half hour ago," he yelled, then made a motion of his head as if to say, And you can see what has prevented it. "I am leaving myself. *Come with me.*" He again examined my captive arm and gathered that I was not at liberty to move, at which point, in the manner not at all like the gentle scholar he was, he threw himself forward and began wrestling to free me. The guard joined in, as did, in opposition, the rest of my captors from behind. No fewer than six or eight people pulled at one another. At least three had their hands on me.

"Do you know who this is?" Dean Albright yelled. "This is Palleias, son of Representative Antonyn. Unhand him or end up in your own restraints!"

"He is here at our request!" the man yelled back.

"Unhand him, you brute!"

"He is here at the request of the people!"

Dean Albright and the guard both continued to pry at him until his accomplices began pounding them with their fists, compelling them to defend themselves instead.

By now the crowd must have decided that none of the prosecutors was present, because someone shouted, from far across the amphitheater, "What about Palleias? He was there!"

"What about Palleias?" someone closer shouted.

The people just around us turned, having before heard my name. Shouts of my name flew away and into the crowd. "Palleias!" "Palleias is here!" People on the stage looked in our direction.

Dean Albright looked at me, white-eyed. The guard continued to wrestle. Some people pointed. "Over here! He's over here!"

"Flee!" Dean Albright yelled.

"*I* have Palleias!" the man holding me yelled. "I have brought Palleias!" He raised his free hand high.

Then several people began working their way toward us, their elbows at shoulder height, their hands ripping through, as if in chest-deep water. Someone yanked Dean Albright from behind; he fell into the crowd. Others pulled at the guard, who resisted briefly, before he, too, was swallowed.

I was surrounded in close quarters by ragged men, whose faces showed the strain of both rage and fear, as if their own anger frightened them. They hesitated.

"This is Palleias, son of Antonyn!" the man holding me yelled. He raised his chin and voice to those beyond our circle. "*I have delivered him on behalf of the people.*"

"Is he friend or foe?" barked a tall thin man who faced me.

"He has not answered."

In one lunge the tall man grabbed me and others joined. "Lift him," he yelled, and I was bouncing on a sea of hands, heading in the direction of the stage. Up and down as much as forward I went—floating, falling, and floating again. At the edge of the stage, outstretched arms awaited my arrival, grabbing then dragging me to the front, where a few dancers jumped off to make room.

And when at last I registered where I was, I felt myself in the funnel of a whirlpool, about to shoot to the bottom.

CHAPTER 44

There I stood at the center of the mass—thousands in the seats facing me, hundreds more to both sides and behind, and in front of and below me, a pack of bodies in the Pit. I was the bull's-eye, the target of their agitation. They had sought the representatives, they had sought the prosecutors, they had gotten me. Everything that had brought them there this morning, everything that had surged from them since hearing of Teacher Scotes's death, everything they had felt for years as their prospects lessened and nothing offered eased their pain—all this concentrated itself, and they yelled at me as if I were their release and I alone could relieve them. If they could only exhaust themselves on me, then they could feel that they had done something, taken some action, been in control for at least an instant—they who had no control and no understanding of what was happening to them but who still desired progress, still resisted suffering, even if all they knew to do right then was lash out at me verbally and perhaps worse. They had malformed themselves into raised arms, pointed fingers, open mouths, red faces. At their center, I could have been any person named Palleias who happened to have attended the trial, with any role whatever in the crime that had set them off.

From every direction came their stamps, their calls, their screams. I could hardly hear them any longer for the volume, could hardly see them for the spectacle, for they also moved rhythmically, like seaweed in the sea, and in their presence I felt myself do what I always did when facing

an incomprehensibility—retreat, stop seeing, stop hearing, as if sights and
sounds could not be processed anyway—but then I halted the retreat and
absorbed their reality, more so each moment I stood among them. Where
I was and why came into better focus—the people more individuated,
again calling for a trial, for answers, for names to add to mine, for the
herald to call for some vote, and I could see the herald looking up at me
and then away when he had to struggle for his balance. Those next to
him shouted in his face as those next to me shouted in mine, and then,
amid the repeated calls of my name and Teacher Scotes's, I heard someone
scream through a spitting kind of rage that *I* should drink the hemlock—
"Make him drink as Teacher Scotes drank!"—and I somehow thought
not of my own fate but of how yesterday he had been among us and of
our walks and visits and what I observed of him and heard him say and
what this year and last had been to me and again of the reality that he
was gone. From all around came calls for me to drink—"Bring the
cup!"—now with a mix of laughter, fear, and anger, though I saw no cup
anywhere in the stalks of arms, and I detected humor in the calls as well
as vengeance, and the shouting continued to the point at which the shock
of it wore off and something within me turned. As I was ever more aware
of standing in their presence, something dropped away, and they were
even less a blur and more as they might appear to the representatives, who
were accustomed to this setting, and I was calmer. Then, amid their
unrelenting calls, I burst into a scream. "Bring it, then, and I will drink!"

The wild rave of my first utterance seemed to stun them, and into the
lesser noise, I screamed again, "Who has the hemlock? Bring it! I'll drink
it now!"

Given that even a quiet voice in this acoustical place was normally
audible at the apex, my screams must have overtaken them. They quieted
further, or perhaps they did not anticipate in me a desperation like their
own, a desperation they would not recognize in the representatives, who
only listened and orated from where I stood. I was shaking. Faces all

around stared, as if assessing the nature of the creature they had captured. Murmurs then arose.

Someone from straight ahead and just beyond the Pit, in a row above the short stone wall that fronted the Pennsylvania section, pointed and called out, "This man is a friend. He was at the prison!" The murmuring intensified.

From higher up another shouted, "I saw them together on the road!" Then another. "They were together at our farm!"

Then someone from just behind me shouted past my ear, "Palleias was a friend of Teacher Scotes!" which was followed by further cries: "Palleias is a friend of the people! Huzzah!"

A great exhale left me, as if I hadn't breathed since waking. I had been given a reprieve, but this produced no happiness.

"We don't accuse you, Palleias!" someone shouted.

"We accuse only the accusers!" "The accusers!" others shouted. That quickly, they were back to those who minutes before they seemed to have forgotten. More calls followed about how I was friend not foe, how they sought justice only.

Then I heard, "Where is your father? It is he who must answer!" "Your father is the one, not you!" Then followed the cries, "Your father did this!" "Your father is the killer of Teacher Scotes!" "You are not your father!" "His guilt is not yours!" "Where is your father?" "You were a friend to Teacher Scotes!" "Your father, not you, is to blame!" "Your father!"

Their great singular motion resumed, and again I felt the sway, as the calls *for* me and against my father continued and became again that resounding chant that was its own voice, as if a thousand mouths were one. Once the cries had spent themselves, someone yelled, "Let him speak!"

Others followed. "Tell us where your father is!" "Speak! Help us, Palleias!" "Help us avenge Teacher Scotes!" "It was your father, not you!"

But I had no desire for them to see me as a friend. Into the opening they provided, I shouted, through the same pain as before, "It was *not* my father, it was *you*!"

Out came a kind of collective gasp and hush. I let the stillness sit.

"We never wanted this!" someone shouted.

I could never locate the speakers; when I turned toward any voice, the words had already gone.

"It is not us!" someone shouted.

"It is all of us!" I shouted. "It is not one man or three or ten. It is no one on this stage or in your seats." I thrust my hands high. "It is we the people!"

They regarded me as if assessing my sanity and not without expressions of bewilderment and concern.

"We do not pass the laws!" someone called out. "It was the law that killed him. The law!"

"Yes, the law killed him!" I called back.

"A law your father passed!" "Your father brought the charges."

"My father gave you what you wanted!"

"We did not want this!"

"My father gave you what you wanted. And for that you wish to murder him!"

Again this seemed to stop them, though only for a second.

"We did not want this!" someone shouted.

"You wanted everything he's given you." No one shouted back, so I continued. "Is this not true? Is it not true that you elect and reelect the reps precisely because they give you what you want? These men and women on this stage, do they not give you what you want?"

"We want food!" "We want shelter!" "We want clothing!" "We want work!"

"You want those things, and so do I. But *how* do you want them? What do you want the reps to do? Whatever you want them to do they do, in the name of getting those things. Whatever you want, right or wrong, good or bad, just or unjust. All in the name of what you want, what you think is right, what you think will work. What else do they do but give you what you want?" They held their tongues. "Yes, the laws we passed have killed him. But where did those laws come from?"

"From the reps!" someone shouted.

"From this system that we revere!" I shouted back.

Again the gasps returned.

If Teacher Scotes's case had illustrated anything it was that instead of culling violence from human interactions, we had made it central—that our laws did not defend against the threat but did the threatening. Under the law anyone could do anything to anyone if the representatives supported it. And if a law was passed on a group's behalf, others could retaliate, with forces wielded by representatives sympathetic to *them*. Life had become a legal battle, a never-ending push and pull of desire against desire, with no governing standard about what was right or wrong, other than who wanted or didn't want it, whose side represented the people's will. In this Teacher Scotes would have said we were as arbitrary as the monarchies of Europe, or perhaps more so, because there the monarchs were constrained by constitutions and by competing legislative powers. He would have said that civilization itself depends on constraining legislative power.

"Let him be," someone shouted. "He's mad!"

"I am mad! I am furious!"

"We are here to avenge Teacher Scotes!" someone shouted.

"And why is he gone?" I yelled. "Because what he was and what he believed were not what you are and what you believe. Because he was one and you are many and to you, the many is all. And because it is all, it is for your reps here too." I looked around. The few that caught my sight still looked terrified. "But for him," I yelled, "the *one* was all, and *that* idea you cannot abide. . . . I *was* present at his trial, and I was glad to have been there. I heard him speak. He spoke to me. He explained why he was there, what was happening. If any of you were there, you heard it also. But the rest of you did not because the newspapers are not free to print his words. And for those of you who have never heard him, you never will. What did he say? You'll never know."

"What did he say?" someone shouted.

"Tell us!" others shouted. "What did Teacher Scotes say?"

"Do you want to know?"

"Tell us, Palleias!" "Tell us what he said!"

"Do you want to know? Do you truly? I don't think you do!"

And there came frenzied calls for me to tell them what he said. He had been discoursing among them for fifty years, with never such interest before.

"He said that what you want is irrelevant and has no place in law. That voting is not a standard of right and wrong. That well-being is not the consequence of desire, individual or collective, and that to claim the right to violate others' rights only secures the loss of your own. All that and more he was brave enough to say. Are you pleased to hear it?"

Again came calls to tell them what he said, though this time less vehemently.

"*That*," I yelled, "was his distinction: might versus right. He had no might; he was one. This you have proved, and that only you, the many, possess it. But he did have right. And he knew that might, to be right, must serve the one; to be defensive, not aggressive; protecting, not control-ling. That is what he believed, and because he believed it, he was convicted and destroyed. For that and only that."

I looked behind me, where stood more representatives, intermingled with the others who had commandeered the stage. The representatives still stood in fright, but their captors I could not read, not even those who pressed in close. I did not understand them, and I do not think they understood me.

Yesterday they hated him. Today they were avenging him, ready to kill on his behalf. Now, with but a few words from me, their sentiment had shifted again. Still, for all that, I could not condemn them. They were not the problem. They were trapped in a system not of their making, using the levers available. We all were. Under a different system, we would be different. With our rights protected, we could respect each other's. To live your life, you need above all the freedom to live it.

"We deserve better!"

"You do deserve better," I called back. "You deserve to live unmolested by the desires of your neighbors or their agents."

"We did not want that law!"

Then someone shouted, "Palleias for representative!"

"Palleias for representative!" came another.

"Palleias!" "Palleias!" A great chant arose. It went on for some time.

Then someone else shouted, "He is not of age. He cannot be a rep!" There was a round of heavy booing. "But it is illegal!" the same voice shouted.

"We *are* the law!" someone called out, and there was laughter.

"We vote Palleias!" came the chant.

Which was the only answer they knew: replace one representative with another; no matter how wrong the people's existence, the problem was always who ruled them absolutely, not whether they should be ruled at all. What we truly needed none of us yet understood, myself included. We needed something radical—as Xephon said that day, a new constitution. Standing there, I felt for the first time what the representatives daily must have felt, what Father must have felt: that no matter what I thought or wanted, I necessarily was secondary to the people. I had already spent too many years guided by what others thought and subordinating myself accordingly.

Eventually the calls for me subsided and fell away, like the chimera they were, and calls again rose against the act that had taken Teacher Scotes, which became calls to repeal that act, which grew ever louder, till I thought the very stones that people stood on might give way. At this the herald jumped to the stage, as if sensing an opportunity to make productive a day that had looked only destructive, and he raised his hands and called above the din for whether anyone wished to speak, and when he heard only "Vote! Vote!" he called for it and turned and, comically, the hand of every representative on stage went up, above the heads of those who crowded them, mimicked by a few around and followed by a great "Huzzah!" and laughing and more earnest hugging and embracing of one's neighbors.

It was amid that joyous tumult that I wriggled off the stage and returned as I had come, and when I broke through the heavy mass outside the amphitheater, I could see that the road back to the river, though still spotted with stragglers racing this way, was otherwise open and I could descend the hill and cross the bridge without incident, the only person headed in that direction.

When I heard the next day that they had repealed not only the act that had taken Teacher Scotes but others like it in a sweeping new act that decreed writing and speaking to be free, I thought that remarkably something good may have come of that day, even if it could not last. But I had mostly been concerned with getting back to Betsy and the house, which I did soon after, having run all the way. Still Ansea and Sophia were not at home, and I took it upon myself to go out back and examine the rounded earth, and I found a shovel and as quickly as I could, scanning the fields for intruders with every gentle thrust, worked my way into the soil until I reached what was there.

Not feeling safe to examine it outside, I brought it in and unlatched the small chest, wondering whether I would conceal it here or bring it to the city for more secure protection. But when I saw its contents, I knew it had to be the city, because what it was was something far more precious than anything I had imagined.

CHAPTER 45

We have just finished a difficult winter. April cannot come too soon. The fever hit especially hard this year, not just here but also in many cities north. Those who could crossed the river and stayed away; the rest filled hospitals. Not in most people's memory have times pressured us so greatly.

But with the sun comes hope. It is a marvel that no matter what our troubles, the belief in something better never dies. It's as if we know that life itself is good and that our suffering is of our doing, from errors that are correctable. This year we mark our Jubilee—the fiftieth since the Treaty and our founding. This year I turn thirty. Teacher Scotes has been gone for nearly two.

Father returned safely last fall, did not resume his position in Assembly, and moved to Boston, where he could be closer to Mother. His role in Teacher Scotes's trial has been forgotten. I saw him briefly then; he did not look well but did seem happy in my presence. Our time together before he left for Boston was pleasurable to me, and I think to him too. He seemed to look at me differently—unburdened, in a way, as if what he carried all those years on my behalf he finally had put down.

Poet Mathias I never saw again, nor have I tried to know his whereabouts. Fleeing likely saved his life, because soon after that day in Assembly, when the crowd took over, he was tried in absentia and condemned. Father and Representative Lycon never were, in part because our procedures reasserted themselves in time and they were spared because of their official roles. Alcidia, however, was not. He was the only person not to flee, and he was found that very day of the riots, sipping quietly in a city tavern. They took him without incident to the prison, tried him in his cell, and sentenced him to drink, which he refused. All this was told to me. I went to see him. He told me that if they wished to kill him, they would have to do it by their own hands. So next day, under the law, they took him to the south wall of the prison grounds, tied his hands, and bayoneted him. Despite what he had done to Teacher Scotes, I cried, if only for what he could have been, for in him I saw the best that we can be, if only we can find our way. If Father had not come along and there had been more time, I wonder whether Teacher Scotes might not have changed Alcidia, but perhaps his long ambition was too ingrained. And in the end, the only person you can change is yourself.

That very week the city burned from the riots, and much was lost. Since then we have been rebuilding, though now atop an older foundation than we had before, as if history had taken a backward step and we were catching up. One day, after all had calmed and as I strolled down Market, I came upon Simon's, the shoemaking shop that Teacher Scotes used to frequent. Where once Simon sat behind his railing now were only cinders, and on the second floor, where he had lived, every book of recorded conversations with Teacher Scotes was ruined. I had hoped to use them, to make them available, to create a record of his life. Instead I have had to rely on my own notes and recollections. It is a project I have hardly begun.

But good has come from then too. They did repeal the act that took him, and for a time, we were liberated to read and write. I myself have read much more, have read that Socrates himself was prosecuted in remarkably similar circumstances to Teacher Scotes, and that even the fourth-century Athenians tried to constrain their own Assembly. And in a touch that likely would have amused Teacher Scotes, a statue did go up of him in place of General Pericles in the court: tall and white, bare feet and all. Now he stands for all to see who enter there, and perhaps he goads them still to think of good and justice and how they might apply. Our conversations in taverns, print, and street became freer, with the threats of legal punishment removed, but already I can see them changing back, as what people write and say again become blamed as a source of our misfortunes. Last year, to combat the rising prices and reduce the violence in our shops, the Bank restrained the demos and prices fell. But this sent even more people to the streets, upon the closing of their manufactories and farms. So now again the Bank expands our notes, in the hope of finding people work. It is a cycle we seem unable to break.

Xephon would not approve, at least I do not think so, from what he described back then of his book. I have yet to see him since. I imagine he still fears our laws, or perhaps he is too heartbroken. I wish he were around. I wonder if he is ever coming back. I began to doubt it right away, soon after it all happened, when I searched for Jailer Douglass and Keeper Daniels and discovered that both of them were gone too. I had hoped to thank them for their kindness and to offer friendship. I was told that each had taken up in different states, but I could never track them down. Nor did Ansea and Sophia ever reappear. No one knows the reason. Rumors were that, distraught, they had emigrated or gone to live far north or south. They left the house exactly as I found it. To understand what might have happened and do my duty by them, I sought Merchant Girard, who had been close at hand those last few days. But at his home were only family and some servants, who claimed that he was traveling for business. Even his two canary cages were vacant. I have not seen him since either, but I heard he may have passed away while visiting his homeland shortly after. His ship *Good Friends* has not returned.

Is it possible that they all escaped together—Teacher Scotes, Ansea, Sophia, Merchant Girard, Xephon, Jailer Douglass, and Keeper Daniels? I ask myself that every day. It is the same as asking, Who brought all this about? Surely it was Father's law and prosecution that set the wheels to turning, each enacted for reasons of his own. But did Teacher Scotes decide to use the threat somehow? He seemed almost to beckon his conviction, the way he spoke in his defense. Had he foreseen what his death would do to us—what it would make us question? He had suggested so at trial. I do not know. And I can't forget his comment to me in prison, that things are not always what they seem.

If he is alive, I wonder where he is. England, perhaps, though no one has reported seeing him and he is difficult to miss. If he did leave, he was right to keep his plans from me. Back then I was a boy who had proved himself to be the slave of others' direction and of impulse, one who could not yet be trusted, whatever my intentions. Nor could he risk the possibility that under pressure later, whether legal or otherwise, I might be forced to reveal his whereabouts. Again I can only speculate.

But he did see promise in me, I believe, as I see promise in myself. Every day I spend at my Academy, which I since established, for that is my profession now. My association with Teacher Scotes in the end became an asset in others' eyes as well, and I welcome students, young and old, to discuss the issues that make a life. I am forever learning. So long as the laws remain favorable, we will continue. I am even visited by Machinist Clark, who joins us when she can. These visits followed mine to her, when at her invitation I did go back and she allowed me to observe the work, as Teacher Scotes might have done, though I gathered she could tell that the work was not all I was observing. I return often. She is astonishing.

With respect to learning from events, Teacher Scotes once commented that if principle does not secure a lesson, perhaps calamity will. I better see his meaning now. He also said that with a vision of the future, you can find joy in almost any present. That fact, too, has helped me daily to create a vision of my own. I am freer within myself and share more freely with others what I think and feel, now that I have something to share.

What I have not yet shared is what I found that day at Teacher Scotes's house. Did he leave it for me to find? That, too, I do not know, but I have locked it in a safe in the cellar of my house. Our laws are still too fickle to reveal it and risk losing it forever; that must await a more receptive day.

But I use it nonetheless, in the questions I ask myself and others. In that chest was neither coin nor jewels but a single document, well-preserved and clean, with the date 1777 and a signature affixed at bottom—that of Lawyer Adams. It was a drafted constitution. I keep it like a beacon, and I try to understand its meaning. It is not like ours, but it is more like what I hope ours will someday be.

There is much we cannot control in life yet much we can: how we think, what we want, how we respond to what confronts us all around. My independence grows within, or at least I think it does, as hard as it has been in coming. Amid the turmoil of the past two years, I'm more at peace than ever. Perhaps it is a state that Teacher Scotes knew well. It certainly seemed so.

I hope he is alive and that I will see him again. If so, I will tell him what I think I've learned. I imagine he would like that. But if he is gone, or if he never wants to find me again, I still intend to share his story with the world.

It is the greatest story I know.

ACKNOWLEDGMENTS

A huge thank-you to my wife and first reader, Jessica Treadway; to friends and family, in-law and out, for all of their support; to Jean Williams of the Cary Memorial Library in Lexington, Massachusetts, whose informational GPS seems capable of finding anything; to Brandon Coward of APG, for guiding this project from manuscript to book; to August Henry, who is coming of age too; and to every independent thinker, past and present, in person and in prose, who has inspired me, including James Madison, who referenced Socrates twice in the *Federalist Papers* to argue why the new American constitution should be very different from the ancient, democratic, Athenian one. And especially to Socrates, whose story is the genesis of *Hemlock*. As a fictional retelling of his last days, set in a very different time and place, this novel takes as a principal source Plato's dialogues, especially his *Apology*. Readers familiar with that dialogue will notice nods to Plato's Socrates in some of the words spoken by my main character.